has worked on BBC radio since 1982. He is also the presenter of *Simon Mayo's Books of the Year* podcast. *Mad Blood Stirring* is his first adult novel.

'Well researched and full of action, Mayo brings a forgotten moment in history to life. ****' *Sun*

'Fascinating . . . it has genuine energy and drive.'
Sunday Times

'Wonderful – a story I never heard before, told with style, pace, character, texture, and tension . . . bliss.' Lee Child

'Bristling with energy, written with passion, *Mad Blood Stirring* is a joy to read.' John Boyne

'*Mad Blood Stirring* is an astonishing account of an explosive piece of neglected history. It's a rapid page-turner with dark humour, intellectual heft, and a gallery of deeply human characters that shake our spirits. This is a cracking novel.'
Sir Kenneth Branagh

'A spirited read inspired by true events.' *Woman & Home*

'If you like your historical thrillers dark and emotional, you'll absolutely love getting swept up in this one.' *Heat*

'Brilliantly described and sensitively explored.' *S Magazine*

www.penguin.co.uk

MAD BLOOD STIRRING

SIMON MAYO

Inspired by true events

BLACK SWAN

TRANSWORLD PUBLISHERS
61–63 Uxbridge Road, London W5 5SA
www.penguin.co.uk

Transworld is part of the Penguin Random House group of companies
whose addresses can be found at global.penguinrandomhouse.com

Penguin
Random House
UK

First published in Great Britain in 2018 by Doubleday
an imprint of Transworld Publishers
Black Swan edition published 2018

A CIP catalogue record for this book
is available from the British Library.

ISBN
9781784162962

Typeset in 10.5/13.5 pt Caslon 540 by Jouve (UK), Milton Keynes
Printed and bound in Great Britain by Clays Ltd, Elcograf S.p.A.

Penguin Random House is committed to a sustainable
future for our business, our readers and our planet. This book
is made from Forest Stewardship Council® certified paper.

1 3 5 7 9 10 8 6 4 2

Dedicated to the memory
of prisoner number 3154
and prisoner number 6520

Principal Players

The Americans

King Dick, sailor
Habakkuk (Habs) Snow, sailor
Sam Snow, sailor and cousin to Habs
Joe Hill, sailor
Will Roche, sailor
Ned Penny, sailor, lamplighter
Horace Cobb, sailor and leader of the Rough Allies
Edwin Lane, sailor, Rough Ally
Tommy Jackson, sailor, prison crier
Jon Lord, sailor
Robert Goffe, sailor
Alex Daniels, cabin boy
Jonathan Singer, cabin boy
John Haywood, sailor, lamplighter
Pastor Simon, reverend

The British

Captain Thomas Shortland, Agent, Governor of Dartmoor
    Prison
Elizabeth Shortland, Captain Shortland's wife, assistant to
    Dr Magrath
Dr George Magrath, physician at Dartmoor
Martha Slater, market trader
Betsy Wade, market trader
Alice Webb, seamstress

Historical Note

The novel is based on historical events . . .

Since 18 June 1812, America and Britain have been at war, fighting what some will call the Second War of American Independence. It has already cost the lives of twenty thousand men. Much of the fighting has been at sea and, by the end of the war, on Christmas Eve, 1814, seven thousand American sailors are incarcerated in Dartmoor Prison, recently built for French prisoners taken in the war against Napoleon. Isolated and forbidding, it is the most feared prison in the land.

'And if we meet we shall not 'scape a brawl,
For now, these hot days, is the mad blood stirring.'

Romeo and Juliet, Act 3, Scene 1,
William Shakespeare

'England being now at war with their own country . . . made them PRISONERS OF WAR, and close prisoners of war: shut them up in a close prison, on a bleak and naked down in Devonshire, called Dartmoor, in which prison we shall by-and-by see that some of them were *killed* on a charge of "MUTINY".'

William Cobbett, MP, radical journalist and
author, *History of the Regency and Reign of
King George the Fourth*, 1830–34

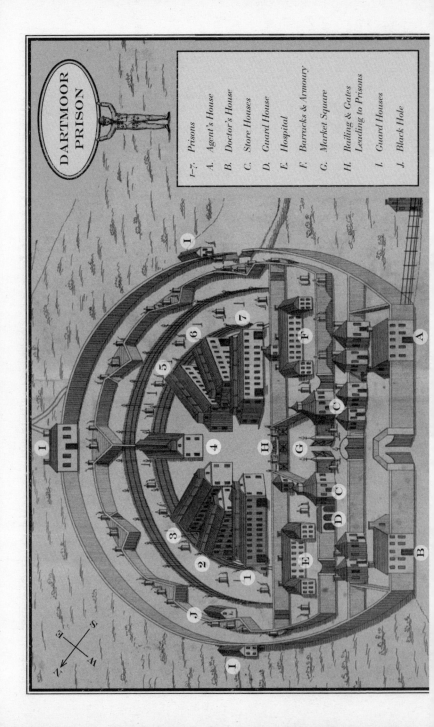

DARTMOOR PRISON

1-7. Prisons
A. Agent's House
B. Doctor's House
C. Store Houses
D. Guard House
E. Hospital
F. Barracks & Armoury
G. Market Square
H. Railing & Gates
     Leading to Prisons
I. Guard Houses
J. Black Hole

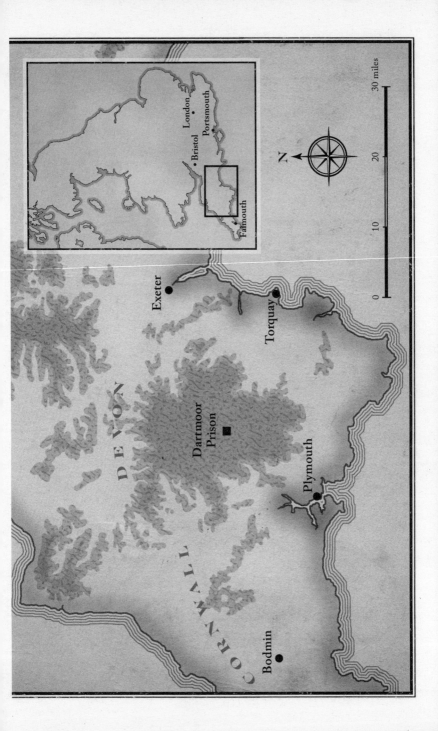

Prologue

April, 1815

THERE IS just one hymn left to practise. But already every member knows every note, every breath between, each rise and fall. Pastor Simon stands to conduct, but the choir is already singing. Most have their eyes closed; all of them are swaying.

> 'Farewell, dear friends, a long farewell,
> Since we shall meet no more,
> Till we shall rise with thee to dwell
> On heaven's blissful shore.
>
> We will meet you in the morning,
> Where the shadows pass away;
> We will meet, we will meet,
> Where all tears are wiped away.
>
> Our friend and brothers, lo! are dead,
> Their cold and lifeless clay
> Has made in dust its silent bed,
> And there it must decay.'

A giant of a man steps forward, his arms wrapped around himself for comfort, for support. He has been crying but, eyes screwed tightly shut, he is determined to lead the last verse.

'Farewell, dear friends, again farewell;
Soon we shall rise to thee,
On wings of love our stars will cross
Through all eternity.'

There is a moment's silence, a beat's pause as the final note dies. At first, no one moves. Then, as if emerging from a trance, the choir disperses, some of them still humming the melody as they clatter down the stone steps and wander out into the April rain.

ACT ONE

1.1

New Year's Eve, 1814
Dartmoor, England

THE TWELVE American sailors, starving, filthy, exhausted, who had been stumbling across the frozen moorlands since first light, regarded their well-fed and well-armed British captors, dressed smartly in bright red tunics, and concluded it was time for revenge.

They started to sing.

Full-throated and tuneless, the surviving men of the *Eagle* drove the guards of the Derbyshire militia crazy.

No one sang here, not ever.

'Will you ever shut up?' snapped one soldier, his unshaven face purple with rage and cold. He swung his rifle towards the prisoners, its bayonet missing one man only by inches.

'Let them sing!' called out another. 'When they see where they're heading, they'll be quiet soon enough.'

'And by the time they see the sun again,' called a third, 'the bloody pox will have taken their voices, anyway!'

The four soldiers laughed.

The small squadron trudged further up the hill, the narrowing track forcing the prisoners into six shuffling rows of two. The wildly uneven path, at best nothing more than trampled-down gorse littered with rocks, picked its way across featureless hills, the occasional dilapidated farmstead the only sign of human habitation. Many of the Americans had difficulty walking; arms had been linked and shoulders grasped. They were poorly dressed for the march and the

5

bone-chilling cold. A few had boots, but the rest slipped and fell in their canvas shoes. A variety of hats were on display, some barely more than a square of tarpaulin tied in place with rope, but one stood out. At the back of the parade, one prisoner sported a three-cornered felt hat, pulled low over his brow, a few inches of closely cropped blond hair showing beneath its brim. He looked no more than sixteen. A tat-tooed eagle, wings splayed, bill and talons slashing, was just visible above his collar, roughly inked at the base of his skull. He leaned towards his marching companion.

'Woman back at the dosshouse said it was fifteen miles,' he said. 'And seeing as that feels like at least thirty miles back, it can't be far now, Mr Roche.' He used both hands to steer the older man around a vast, rain-filled pothole.

'You sure that's what she said, Mr Hill?' said his companion. 'I didn't understand a goddamn word she said.'

Joe Hill snorted. 'Maybe you weren't listening, Mr Roche. It's Devonshire talk, that's all. Just Devonshire talk. She thought we were renegade English and that we'd lose the war for certain. That it was a right impertinence for America to fight England again. We deserved jail is what she said.'

Will Roche spat in the mud, strands of phlegm sticking in the whiskers of his straggly beard. 'She knows nothin' of our fine Yankee victories then,' he said. 'Renegade English? For shame.'

'Well, I reckon she'll find out soon enough,' said Joe. 'We have proper American news, Mr Roche. American news fit for Americans, and there's plenty where we're heading. Might even know some of 'em.'

Roche's voice dropped a little, flickers of tiredness and doubt licking at his words. 'And you're sure about this, Joe? You're sure 'bout what you heard? 'Cos if we're stayin' in Dartmoor, we might as well make a run for it now. I'd rather die in one of these frozen ditches than be tortured by some English ass-worm.'

6

Joe put both his hands on the older man's shoulders, his grip firmer than his narrow shoulders suggested. He spoke with all the assurance he could muster.

'I heard what I heard, Will,' he said. 'My ears might've taken a beating these last years, but those words I heard true and clear. So, yes, I'm sure. You're the father of the ship now. You should be sure, too.'

He hummed a few more bars and Roche nodded, momentarily reassured. Joe knew that Roche had always enjoyed hearing him sing, his shanties and songs of home always a welcome part of their life at sea. Since their capture, however, there had been silence. Joe had seen no reason to sing, no reason to dress their despondency with music, but now the tunes came again. Now, there was a purpose and a plan.

'We mustn't let them English think they've got us beat,' he said. 'They think this is their triumph, their victory. Well, they've got a surprise coming.'

Joe didn't smile – it wasn't his way – but any shipmates listening heard his excitement, sensed his buoyant mood. They knew his secret, and it helped to keep the gloom at bay.

The fog rolled away, blown by some unfelt zephyr. They had been climbing since first light, but this was no vantage point, just an endless, rotting-brown wasteland, a panorama as bereft and cheerless as a desert. Joe fought against the chills.

'If it wasn't for the hallelujah in our hearts, Mr Roche,' he observed, 'we might conclude this is the arse-end of England.'

'We might indeed,' said Roche. 'And looks like we're 'bout to climb right into it.'

Up ahead, the redcoats conferred, then steered their prisoners from the track towards a steep escarpment. As Joe scrambled past, two of them smirked at him. ''Ope you're not goin' to stop singin' now,' said the purple-faced one. 'Not now you're so nearly 'ome.' They laughed, then the purple one coughed and spat. The path they indicated was wider and less marshy, but the gradient was a tough one and the English knew it.

'What was wrong with the other track?' asked Joe.

'View's better this way,' said the purple soldier.

'Proper scenic it is,' sneered his colleague. 'Quite something, top of this 'ere hill. All the prisoners say so.'

The sailors' exhaustion was now bone-deep. Painful, bloodied feet began to slip from underneath tired bodies as they climbed, weary hands reaching out for balance. Leaden legs cramped then gave up altogether. Joe put both hands on the sodden, muddy hips of the barrel-shaped man in front of him, and pushed.

'Steady, Mr Goffe,' he said. 'You don't want to stay here, you'll miss the party. We're nearly there.'

There was a pained grunt from the man ahead. 'There'd better be a goddamn party,' he growled.

Joe recalled those miraculous harbour-side words he'd overheard just a few hours ago. The smiles. The back-slapping. The toast. Surely there could be no mistake.

'There'll be a party all right,' he muttered.

The summit was marked by a solitary, skeletal pine tree, and a militiaman sitting beneath it stood to greet them, his arms open wide. 'Welcome to Dartmoor,' he beamed. 'Why don't we rest your rotten Yankee bones here for two minutes, just so you can take it all in, like.'

Joe clambered his way over the top, pushing Goffe then pulling Roche as he went. Around him, the cursing told him everything he needed to know. This wasn't the casual profanity that was part of a sailor's life; this was fearful, terrified blasphemy.

'Sweet baby Jesus, would you look at that!'

'Christ alive!'

Across the fields – another half-mile of gorse and stones – a great prison city had been carved from the moor.

A huge encampment of enormous grey hulks, vast granite buildings with pointed roofs shunted hard together, seemed to grow from the earth. There were turrets, chimneys, fences and, surrounding the whole, two formidable encircling walls. All of it was grey. A deathly, exhausted, pain-filled grey. An unearthly silence seemed to spread across the fields, reaching out from the prison to envelop the sailors.

'What in God's name?' muttered Joe, dread settling deep in his stomach. 'It's a ghost town, a goddamn ghost town.'

'And we're the goddamn ghosts,' said Roche.

Joe was aware of Roche's hand gripping his arm.

'There ain't no windows,' said Roche.

'What?'

'No windows. None.' There was real fear in the old man's voice. 'Look at 'em, Joe, tell me I'm wrong.' Joe stared at the largest buildings; he counted seven in all. At first glance, they did appear to be solid, relentless walls of brick. But then his eyes adjusted and he picked out some detail that had been lost in his first, shocked sweep of the prison: rows of tiny squares ran like gun ports across the length of each wall.

'You're wrong, Will. There's windows, all right, just not so big as any light'll get in.' He felt Roche sag against him. 'What was it you used to tell me?' he continued. '"Tribulation worketh patience; and patience, experience; and experience, hope." That's what we need. Patience and hope, Will. Now more than ever.'

'I said that?' said Roche.

'You said that.'

'Must have been in my cups then. Sounds like a crock o' shit to me.'

'Really?' said Joe, surprised. 'Well, seeing as we're not going to be staying long . . .'

He began to whistle. He forced it to begin with, his mouth dry and his heart heavy, but its effect was instantaneous. The

9

melody of 'Yankee Doodle' worked a little magic of its own. Hunched backs straightened, shoulders squared, eyes lit up. It was musical insubordination. By the end of the first verse, twelve sailors were whistling in unison. By the end of the second, they had fallen into line and begun their own, voluntary march to the prison, the soldiers cursing and scrambling to keep up.

'It's hard to whistle and look unhappy at the same time, isn't it, Mr Roche?' said Joe.

'It is when you ain't got no teeth,' said Roche.

They marched and whistled towards a village; small, barely lit houses peppered the sides of the road. A newly built church stood closed and dark, piles of unused slate still propped up against its walls. A few curious souls looked up as they passed, most frowning. Prisoners, they had seen before; cheerful prisoners, they most certainly had not.

The road curved right and the ghost town they had seen from across the fields disappeared behind twenty-foot-high walls. The whistling faltered and a sudden cry of 'Sweet Christ!' told Joe they had arrived. It was impossible to see where the granite ended and the clouded, darkening sky began.

'What kind of an English Hell is this?' muttered one of the sailors.

'John Bull's finest dungeons for Uncle Sam's finest sailors, Mr Lord!' called Joe.

They approached the outer wall, its centrepiece a monstrous, angular arch. Huge slabs supported two heavy wooden gates, both reinforced with bolted metal bands. Sentries, oil lamps already lit, stood by them, watching their approach. Joe squinted at the two words that had been chiselled into the keystone at the arch's apex.

'*Parcere subjectis*,' he read.

'What's that, then?' asked Roche.

'It means "Spare the vanquished," I think.'

10

'Spare the vanquished,' repeated Roche. 'And how would you know that?'

'Oh, just more Devonshire talk, Mr Roche, that's all.'

'Is that right?' said Roche, persisting. 'An' how might they be sparin' us, then?'

'Who knows?' said Joe. 'Maybe it just means they ain't gonna kill us all. Not yet, anyway.'

The older man shrugged. 'If you say so. I don't find much comfort in them words myself,' he said.

'Maybe that's the point,' said Joe.

Two large houses had been built into the wall, one either side of the gateway. Faces flitted briefly in the window of one before rapidly disappearing again.

Will Roche cleared his throat, then called to his shipmates.

'Gentlemen of the *Eagle*, we have come a long way together. We are, as you see, about to take new, fashionable lodgings. And when we see the poor, miserable English faces of our captors, we might need to sing again. If anyone needs some good ol' American cheer, it's these poor wretches. If we can't put a sword through their chests, we should try to put a song in their hearts.'

The gates swung open and the Americans struck up their song again, the few hesitant, faltering voices drowned out by the wilfully defiant.

A wide courtyard sloped away before them. Plain slate buildings lined the far wall, larger ones standing hostile behind them. Once more, twitching curtains caught Joe's attention. A face at the window – a woman, Joe thought, this time – but she was gone in an instant. From somewhere within the echoing walls – it was impossible to judge where – wild yelling, cheers, howls: the unmistakeable sound of a brawl. The sailors exchanged nervous glances.

'Sounds more like a madhouse,' muttered Roche.

Six guards stood waiting for them. Their sergeant saluted

11

the nearest militiaman and they exchanged a few hasty words before cheerfully peeling away, clearly delighted to be free of their crazed American prisoners.

Now the sergeant took over the shouting.

'Enough! Enough!' he barked, a livid scar pulsing on his forehead. 'Can't you see where you are? Most Yankees shit in their breeches when they see where they're heading.' He rocked on his heels. 'And the French would have burst into tears, but they're gone now, thank Christ. It's just you Americans, all the way from Block One to Block Seven. This is Dartmoor. You might have heard of it. Word spreads. And it's all true.' He widened his stance, as if expecting a challenge. 'I'm Sergeant Cox. Most times, I'm called Ol' Fat Bastard, but you will call me Sergeant Cox or sir. In fact, you call anyone in a red coat sir and it'll go better for you. Treat us all as officers. Especially as all of yours are miles away, in their fancy billets. You, on the other hand, are all in Block Seven. It's full, of course, but if we keep capturing you Yankee buggers, we got to squeeze you in somewhere. So bloody move along there! You can howl your American songs at each other all night if you wish.'

A scrawny, leather-faced man, a gunner from Indianapolis called Jon Lord, raised a timid hand. 'What's goin' on, Sergeant Cox? Is that some kind o' fight you're takin' us to? 'Cos it sure sounds like one.'

The sergeant looked as though he might be thinking of smiling. 'Welcome to Dartmoor,' he said.

The prisoners were herded through another arch, this one topped with an alarm bell, towards more high walls and another pair of huge wooden, closed gates, these slotted shut with a thick iron bar. This was the inner wall they had glimpsed from across the fields.

'Well,' muttered Roche. 'Let's see what games they play here, then.'

Four sentries raised the bar and swung the gates open.

12

The square beyond was playing host to a fight, but not of the kind they had been expecting.

'Well, I'll be goddamned!' said Joe. 'It's a boxing match.'

The high-walled square rolled away downhill to more iron gates, this time open and draped with prisoners clamouring for a view. Behind them towered seven enormous, ghost-grey prison blocks. And in their shadow, a feverish crowd, many hundred strong, was watching two men spar.

The crew of the *Eagle* were marched unnoticed into the square, their guards halting to watch the fight. The boxers, one black, one white, were already exhausted, bruised and bloodied. They stalked or staggered in a makeshift ring as the crowd swarmed around the affray, ebbing and flowing, yelling encouragement, waving their pipes, exchanging money.

'The blackjacks have their man then,' said Roche, nodding at the far corner of the square. The crowd there was more tightly packed, black sailors shouting out their support, shaking their fists. Around them, white sailors jumped and hollered with equal fervour.

On the few occasions that the hubbub dropped, a single resonant voice could be heard issuing a steady stream of coaching advice.

'Push forward, push forward. Lean with your head, right foot first. Tie 'im up, push 'im back, push forward.' Joe and Roche exchanged glances; who was talking and who the words were intended for was impossible to tell.

'Who's the coach?' Joe chanced asking the nearest guard, but he just shrugged and continued watching.

'Careful,' warned Roche in a low voice, but Joe tried again.

'This happen much?' he asked, as casually as he dared.

'He might answer,' whispered Roche, 'or he might run you through . . .'

The guard peered at Joe, sizing him up, perhaps considering Roche's options. He shrugged again.

13

'Sailors like to fight,' he said. 'It's what they do.'

Joe persisted. 'Big crowd,' he said, but the soldier was done talking. Through the multitude, Joe could see that the black boxer had his opponent in a headlock, his free fist smashing relentlessly into the white man's face. And then the man went limp. Sensing imminent victory, the black man released his grip.

But the white boxer wasn't finished. From somewhere, he found a shaft of wood. To huge cheers from the white sailors, he flourished it like a rapier and the black boxer backed away. Joe couldn't see what happened next. The men of the *Eagle* heard the uproar, they saw the crowd surge, then they witnessed a black giant of a man climb into the ring, grab the black boxer with one hand and flatten the white boxer with the other. The snapping of bone and cartilage – presumably the white man's – crackled around the walls. Around the ring, scuffles broke out and the guards readied their rifles.

'By me!' called Roche, and the *Eagle* men inched closer. Joe noticed for the first time that there were guards stationed on top of the far wall – they, too, had their guns aimed at the melee.

'This is bedlam!' called Goffe. 'No one's goin' to listen to us here. No one will hear our news. How are we gonna tell 'em anythin'? They ain't listenin' to nobody or nothin'.'

Joe took a deep breath. 'We sing.'

'What?'

'We sing.'

'They'll crucify us.'

'Just do it.'

It was just Joe and Goffe to start with, but the crew caught on soon enough. Within moments, all the *Eagle* men were belting out 'Yankee Doodle'. By the second verse, heads were turning and, by the third, the fights in the crowd were breaking up.

'We must look ridiculous!' shouted Roche, mid-chorus.

14

'Yup,' agreed Joe. 'Keep going.'

'Do you think they can tell we're from out o' town?' Roche grimaced.

Joe glanced at the men in the crowd; their various shades of uniform-yellow were a big contrast to the bedraggled, sodden tatters worn by the *Eagle* crew.

'I guess they can,' he said. 'I guess they can.'

By verse six, they had everyone's attention. The crowd drew forward. Puzzled, curious faces mixed with the angry and the combative.

'What's with the noise?' called one man.

'Where you fellas from anyways?' called another.

Joe got the nudge. 'Go on, then,' said Roche, 'and pray God you got it all right.'

'But I don't speak for the ship,' hissed Joe.

'You do now,' insisted Roche. 'Tell 'em – before they fight us.'

A group of pale men, each with a long, forked beard, had forced its way to the front. They squinted hard at Joe.

'What in sweet Jesus's name is going on?' said one, his eyes perusing the members of the *Eagle* crew.

His bafflement, Joe realized, was only temporary. He'd want to hit someone soon enough. The man tugged at his beard as he spoke.

'We gotta fight on here, in case you hadn't noticed,' said one. 'You boys wanna join in, or you got somethin' to say?' He squirted tobacco juice from the corner of his mouth, then waited, arms folded. The challenge was clear.

'Sure,' said Joe, swallowing hard. He glanced briefly back at his crew, then to the sea of faces in front of him. High on the far walls, even the redcoats were watching. 'My name is Joe Hill, and these are my shipmates.'

'Can't hear!' floated a voice from the crowd. 'Louder!'

Joe swallowed again, and imagined he was shouting into a gale. 'We are what remains of the crew of the *Eagle*, out of

15

Boston. We were captured off Halifax, then held on a prison ship off Plymouth.'

He could hear his voice bouncing off the walls: everyone could hear him. On the never-ending march from the docks, it was the promise of this moment that had kept his feet moving.

'I've got some news you might appreciate. The captain of the prison ship was this morning being informed by his commander that a peace treaty has been signed between America and Britain and that, even now, ships are taking the papers to Congress.'

He stared out at his astonished, disbelieving audience. Even the bearded man in front of him had stopped chewing to process the information. Behind him, Roche muttered, 'Cannons all loaded, Joe. Fire at will.'

Joe nodded. 'Gentlemen, the war is over!'

1.2

The Market Square, Lower Gates

'IT'S A trick.'

'What?'

'It's a trick. A goddamn trick.'

'I know what you said, Ned, jus' not why you said it.' The two black sailors had to shout above the wild celebrations.

''Cos it's the truth, and you know it, Habs.' The taller of the two men – round-faced, bald-headed, liberally spattered with boxer's blood – spoke.

'What we just saw, that was a trick. The white boy appearin' from nowhere, jus' when we was winnin'. Them Rough Allies are at it again.'

'Winnin'?' said Habakkuk Snow, his hazel eyes wide with incredulity. 'Our boy jus' been hit by a piece o' wood the size of a damn frigate. Smashed his face in. That's mostly his blood on you, in case you ain't noticed.'

'I'da had him patched up, Habs. I got my tricks. John's a tough boxer. He'd've come back stronger . . .' Ned Penny pushed himself away from the huge retaining wall at the bottom of the square and stooped to pick up a large brass oil lamp.

'He was out cold, Ned!' Habs was speaking loudly now. 'He wasn't comin' back from nothin'.'

Four men danced between them, and Ned tried to swat them away with the lamp.

'And I say that if that white boy hadn't arrived from who

17

knows where, there'da been a riot here. The shame of it! We lost respect is what we did.'

'You lost money is what you mean.'

'That, too,' said Ned. 'The King got it all wrong.'

'The King got it right,' countered Habs, shaking his head in wonder, his black-and-ivory hoop earrings swaying as he did so. 'Probably saved that boy's life.'

The older man coughed doubtfully. 'S'all very convenient, if you ask me,' he said.

Habs shook his head and laughed, his corkscrew hair as animated as he was. 'But Ned, that ain't even the main news no more. It's true they stole the fight. 'Course they did – they steal everything. But look aroun' you. The war is over – we're goin' home!'

Around the square and the remains of the boxing ring, dancing and singing had taken hold. Fiddles, whistles and alcohol had appeared in an instant; even the soldiers were smiling. Ned shook his head, tugged at Habs's blue military-style jacket.

'Ain't you learned nothin'?' he said. 'You just gonna trust that white boy who you ain't never seen before, from a ship we ain't never heard of? Who don't even sound like no American neither? He tells us tales of peace 'n' joy, and you swallow it jus' like that? Man, everyone done lost their head today.'

Habs's shoulders drooped – he knew there might be something in what Ned was saying. Eighteen months in this godforsaken hole had taught him that betrayal was cheap and as common as bed lice. Instinctively, he looked for his old shipmates from the *Bentham*, but amid the mass of men in the square found only one. He saw his cousin approaching, a pipe clenched between his teeth and a bottle in his hand.

'Let's ask Sam,' he said. 'He was farther up the square. He mighta heard more . . .'

18

Ned laughed scornfully. 'O' course. Let's ask the *cook*. He'll know what's goin' on.' Lighter skinned and slighter than Habs but with the same electric hair, Sam Snow eased past a final line of singing prisoners, his arms spread wide.

'Hey, cuz! We goin' home!' he said. They embraced and Habs felt his cousin sag against him. 'Feels good to say them words and believe 'em.'

Habs wiped a tear from Sam's face. 'You goin' soft, old man?' he said.

'Uh-huh. Been here too long, Habs,' said Sam. He wiped the other tears away himself. 'Too many sick, too many dead.'

'Too many English,' added Ned. 'Always watchin', always aimin' their guns.'

'Amen to that,' said Habs. 'And you believe it, Sam? You believe that skinny white boy?'

Sam looked taken aback. 'Believe what? That the war is over?'

'Ned thinks it's a trick,' said Habs.

'Ned thinks everythin's a trick,' said Sam. 'When that cannonball took his ear, it took most part of his sense, too.' He nodded at Ned, who was pretending not to listen but rubbed what remained of his right ear anyway. 'For a lamp-lighter, Ned, you don't see too much.'

Ned shrugged.

'Who would you believe?' asked Habs. 'Who needs to tell you, Ned? President Madison? Their mad ol' king?' He picked some candle wax from his jacket, then checked all eight buttons were secure. 'If all this' – he swept his arms around the square – 'if all this is for nothin', this place would riot. Even the English ain't that stupid.'

'So you always say,' said Ned, examining the lamp's wick, 'but the English they send here are. We get the dumbest they have. It's insultin'.'

Habs laughed. 'You think everythin's an insult, Ned. Every day you survive without a brawl is a goddamn miracle.'

19

Ned shrugged. 'Uh-huh. Sometimes you jus' have to fight. You 'scape from the Red River plantations, 'sjus' what you do. You run north from Louisiana, 'sjus' what you do. Lord knows it. King Dick knows it.'

'And our boxer?' said Sam. 'Is the King sortin' him? 'Cos, war or no war, lot of us still mighty vexed 'bout the way that fight finished.'

Habs, realizing Ned was about to make another speech, cut across him. 'King Dick is sortin' John, and then he'll sort the bastards in Six. You know he will. He knows their fighter got that wood handed to 'im by one of the Allies, he saw 'em do it. We all saw it. Took it from the ring.'

'Tha's what I seen, too,' said Sam. 'And that blond white boy that made the speech? Him with the shaved head, tricorn hat?'

Habs nodded. 'What about him?'

'You seen what he's doin'?'

Habs hadn't seen, so he peered into the throng. The boxing crowd of several hundred had become an end-of-the-war, end-of-the-year party; the singing and cheering had summoned the entire prison population.

'Can't see nothin'. It's gettin' dark, Sam! Need your lamps, Ned!' he shouted back. He waited for the crowd to move, but there was no sign of the boy in the tricorn hat. He had disappeared. Habs thought he recognized some of his crew, but the tricorn was nowhere to be seen.

'Get closer!' called Sam. 'He's in there somewhere.'

'Why?'

'Just do it, cuz, you'll see.' Sam waved him away and Habs began to squeeze his way further into the square. As the last of the watery daylight faded, the lamplighters appeared, earning their extra sixpence. Their oil lamps swung high in the corners of the market square.

'Come and dance with us, Habs!' shouted a young black sailor wrapped in a roughly painted Stars and Stripes flag.

20

'You can't dance, Tommy!' Habs called back. 'And you're a lousy fiddle player, too.' He saluted the boy and pushed on. Close to where the boxing ring had been, Habs caught a glimpse of the tricorn boy. He'd drifted to the edge of his crew, crouched low on the ground, pulling bits of extravagantly painted wood from the smashed boxing ring. Oblivious to the scrum around him, he was examining the rough joints of a snapped timber. Habs watched his brow furrow, a single line appearing beneath the hat's brim, and he realized what had caught Sam's attention. Very slowly, Habs's face broke into the broadest of smiles.

1.3

The Market Square

IT WAS all Yankees now. The only redcoats visible were those patrolling the high walkway on the wall enclosing the blocks. A dozen guards paced along the perimeter, rifles held in readiness, bayonets fixed.

'Where we headin'?' asked Ned, as they inched past a row of accordion players. 'We should be movin' on. They gonna stop this party soon enough – I don't know why they not shootin' at us already.'

'That what you prefer, Ned?' said Habs, pushing him on.

'Like I said, jus' 'cos the singin' white boy say it's a peace, don't mean it is one. Tha'sall.'

Habs and Sam exchanged glances. 'Fair enough,' said Habs, 'but Sam here has an idea.'

''Course he does – ain't that always the way?' said Ned. 'Let's hear it.'

Sam nodded at the crowd that was pressing around the men of the *Eagle*.

'Well, that singin' white boy—'

'What? We still talkin' 'bout him?' Ned protested.

'. . . is takin' a interest in that ol' boxin' ring. Has somethin' under his arm, look.'

Ned looked again at the new arrivals, gave Joe an appraising stare. 'Maybe he jus' needs some firewood or somethin' so his lily-white bones don't freeze. Tha's what he wants that ring for. He don't look too well neither, all that mud 'n' shit all over him.'

22

'Enough, Ned,' said Habs. 'Tha's too many words. We looked like that back when we walked all the ways here from Plymouth Dock. You forget. And if you don't believe in the peace, don't believe what he's sayin', let's jus' ask him.'

The crowd around the *Eagle* crew was growing ever larger and more boisterous. The redcoats patrolling the walkway were beginning to look nervous. Each one of the twelve was engaged in vigorous, sometimes shouted conversation. Many ended with handshakes and backslapping.

'We'd be the first coloured folk tha's spoken to 'em,' said Sam.

'I noticed,' said Habs. 'Well, best to start at the top.'

He stared at the new arrivals, their haunted, half-starved faces briefly transformed by laughter and relief. At the end of the line, the boy in the tricorn hat stood slightly apart, the broken piece of the boxing ring acting as his prop.

Habs walked up and stuck out his right hand, revealing the letters F.A.S.T. tattooed across four fingers.

'Habakkuk Snow. Crew o' the *Bentham*, outta New York.'

Joe shook his hand, noticed the letters. 'Joe Hill,' he said. 'We're all from the *Eagle*, out o' Boston. "Fast"?' He glanced at Habs's fingers, still wrapped around his.

Habs laughed and held out his left hand. The letters H.O.L.D. were tattooed there, the O and the D partially obscured by rings. 'Hold fast. It was a joke a few years back, after I fell from the riggin' a couple times. Jus' a reminder.'

He withdrew his hands and stared again at the sunken-eyed, elfin-faced sailor in front of him. Joe had a delicate, almost emaciated appearance and there was mud plastered to his cheeks and forehead like warpaint.

'You fall or somethin'? Out there?' said Habs, pointing to the boy's face.

Joe stared blankly, then shrugged. 'S'pose I might've,' he said.

When it was clear no more explanation was forthcoming,

23

Habs waved Sam and Ned forward. 'My friend Mr Penny here needs a word.' He indicated to Ned to say his piece. Ned, arms folded, head to one side, just stared at Joe.

'Doesn't sound like he does,' said Joe, staring back.

The silence loomed loud in the noise of the crowd. Eventually, Ned spoke.

'Where you from, sailor?' The question sounded more like an accusation.

'Like I said, the *Eagle*. Out o' Boston.' His tone was neutral, matter of fact, but everyone knew that Joe Hill understood Ned's question perfectly well; he just hadn't answered it. A number of black sailors sharing a hatful of cold stew stopped to listen to the exchange.

'An' before the *Eagle*?' tried Ned, impatience etched into every word.

Joe sighed. 'Just so you know, I've had this conversation many times. What you mean is, I don't sound like an American. Correct, Mr Penny?'

Ned acknowledged the point. 'Correct, Mr Hill.' The smell of the glutinous mess of meat and potatoes hung between them.

Joe nodded. 'I'm from Norfolk County, Massachusetts. My parents were English, but I'm a naturalized American. I've been fighting the British, same as you. Catching tides, hauling sail and firing cannon, same as you.' The onlookers nodded, and Ned seemed to deflate.

Habs spoke for him. 'An' this news – the peace. How do we . . .' He broke off, unable to complete the sentence. Up close, this suffering sailor, gaunt and malodorous, was, Habs decided, telling the truth. Even to suggest otherwise would be an insult. But the damage was already done.

'How do you what?' asked Joe, incredulous. 'How do you know I'm telling the truth?' He closed his eyes and ran his hands over his face. 'I guess you don't. I can't prove anything. I might be lying – we all might be lying.' He pointed at his

24

Eagle crew mates. 'We might be . . . British agents. And if that's what you want to believe . . .' He broke off, exhausted. Habs thought he detected tears in his eyes. He wondered if Sam saw them, too.

'I believe you, Mr Hill,' he said, and Joe nodded his appreciation.

This wasn't the conversation Habs had intended to have.

'Joe Hill, this is my uglier cousin, Sam, and the bald, annoyin' one with half an ear missin' is lamplighter Ned Penny. He's from the *Bentham*, too. Tha's where the rest of his ear is.' Habs took the meat hat, offering some to Joe, who waved it away. There was a fire now behind his pale blue eyes.

'So, what do you think, Mr Snow, Mr Penny? Are we liars?' There was grit in his voice. ''Cos when you see the newspapers and you read of the peace, as you surely will one day, you may have cause to remember this conversation.' He stared pointedly at Habs first, then at Ned.

'That sounds like a goddamn threat,' said Ned.

Joe stayed silent.

'This here place is complicated, Mr Hill,' said Ned. He glanced over at the prison blocks that loomed over the lower wall. Lights had appeared in the odd window but, for the main part, the buildings remained dark and forbidding. 'Maybe less complicated for you than for us, but complicated all the same. You jus' arrived, you don't know nothin'. But you gonna find out soon enough. If you been cheated and lied to like we have, if you been treated lower than cockroach shit like we have, if you been winnin' a boxin' match then had it stole by a white man with timber in his hands, you might jus' end up suspicious as us.'

While Ned spoke, Habs tracked the movement of a number of white prisoners with long, straggly beards as they circled the square. Noticing Habs's scrutiny, two of them mimed the swiping action that had ended the boxing contest. Habs turned away.

25

'But I might warm to you, nevertheless,' Ned went on. 'So, tell me what you saw at the docks.'

Joe shook his head. 'It's the same story – the one you didn't believe,' he said.

'I wanna look you in the eye when you say it,' said Ned.

'*Do* you . . .' muttered Joe.

'I can judge a man—'

'*Can* you . . .'

'Try me.'

The crowd around them had grown still further, some white sailors now leaning in to catch their words. Joe removed his tricorn and rubbed a hand over the roughly cut stubble on his head, carefully avoiding several bloodied cuts on his scalp. He took a deep breath, his eyes flicking constantly between Habs and Ned.

'We were disembarking from the prison ship. Instead of counting us off like they should've, the crew were crowding round another man. Fattest man I ever saw. Amazes me they found a uniform wide enough. Must've been the captain's commanding officer. I heard him say a peace treaty's been signed between America and Britain. Words were clear enough. Then the prison boat captain shared his grog bottle with his crew. Right there.' Joe replaced his hat, pulling it low over his eyes. 'That's it. Believe what you want.' He pushed his way back to his shipmates and an old man offered him a bottle.

Habs watched him go then turned to Ned. 'Well, you said you wanted to look him in the eye,' he said. 'I saw a sailor with nothin' left to give who was tellin' the truth. What did you see?'

'I saw what you saw,' said Ned, his eyes still on Joe.

'So you believe him?' said Sam.

'Maybe I do,' said Ned. 'Maybe I do.'

Sam punched him on the arm. 'Well, maybe your war is over, too. And maybe you're findin' me a drink.' He pulled

Ned away then called back to his cousin. 'Try again,' he said. 'You might do better without us.'

Habs watched them go, Sam leaning on Ned as they found some mess mates with alcohol. 'Goddammit.' He watched as Joe settled into conversation with the toothless old-timer he'd arrived with, the plank of wood clutched protectively under his arm. 'Goddammit,' he said again, and walked over to them. Hovering over Joe's shoulder, the old man reacted first.

'There appears to be a Frenchman here, after all.' Roche scowled at Joe. 'And a Negro one, too. I didn't know they had any.'

Joe turned briefly. 'He's American,' said Joe. 'Just dresses like a French.'

'Why would he do that? Is that some kinda blackjack fashion?'

'No, it ain't.' Habs stepped forward. 'Won it fair and square,' he said, indicating his blue jacket. 'He was goin' home, like they all were, but still playin' Twenty-one. This was all he had left.' He stuck out his hand. 'I'm Habakkuk Snow.'

Roche declined to shake. 'You're the boy who don't believe us to be truthful.' He drank from a bottle then wiped his mouth and beard in one sweep. 'I known this one all his sixteen years, through peace and war. Now, apparently, peace again. And there ain't a more honest man on any ship in America. So 'scuse me if I find better company.' He turned rather unsteadily and was gone. Joe was about to follow when Habs held him back.

'I'm sorry 'bout that,' he said. 'Ned didn't mean nothin' bad or nothin'. Truth is, this prison . . .' Habs struggled for the words. 'This prison is a dark place. Everyone's dancin' and smilin' now, but we been here one year six months, and that's a lotta darkness to fight off. Ned, he said his piece. Sam an' I, we got other things to say. So I'm startin' again here. I'm Habs.' He held out his hand once more.

'Don't people have time for Habakkuk?' asked Joe, reaching out to shake the man's hand.

'Not on a ship they don't,' said Habs. 'You know how it is. You got to shout everyone's name like a cannonball is headin' straight for 'em. By the time anyone shout that at Habakkuk, he gonna be dead and blown to eternity. But Habs? He gonna be safe. Joe gonna be safe, too.' A throng of brawling inmates rolled their way towards them and they stepped aside, watching them pass.

'And are there lots of cannonballs flying round here?' said Joe.

'Uh-huh. English like to take potshots at us when they feelin' bad, which is pretty much all o' the time, or when the war ain't goin' great, which is only most o' the time.' Habs thought he detected the beginnings of a smile at the corners of Joe's mouth. 'I should apologize to your crew,' he continued. 'Who's the old-timer?'

'Will Roche,' said Joe, tracking him in the crowd. 'Father of the *Eagle*, on account of him not dying for longer than anyone else. Stole the gunpowder in Nassau back in '76. Fought the English back then, and every day since by my reckoning. He's a body full of injuries to show for it, too. Reckon if he finishes that bottle, he'll tell you it all and sing you some more for good measure.'

'He said he known you sixteen years?'

The single crease in Joe's forehead deepened. 'That's a lot of questions, Mr Snow.'

Habs couldn't see much beneath the brim of Joe's hat. 'There's a reason for that.'

'Why don't you get straight to it? You said you had other things to say.'

'I do. I was askin' about Mr Roche.'

Clouds of tobacco smoke drifted between them. There was a lengthy silence before Joe replied. 'He's a friend of my parents, from when we moved to Massachusetts. I was a cabin boy at twelve, then he got me a berth on the *Eagle*. He took it on himself to be my ship's counsel. Ship's parent. Ship's pastor. He might be just about everything I've got.'

'He don't strike me much as a pastor.' Habs was smiling, but Joe missed it.

'Not like he'd pray or sing hymns or anything,' he said, 'but when we lost men, if they got sick or killed, he would always say some words, you know? He always had words. Anyhow, why d'you want to know about him?'

Habs kept his tone neutral. 'He like theatre, too?' he asked.

'I'm not sure I follow . . .'

'Was it Mr Roche that got you into theatre?'

'No,' began Joe, 'but . . .'

Habs nodded down to Joe's arm, leaning heavily on the board he'd pulled from the boxing ring. 'From here, you look to be restin' on some clouds and sky,' said Habs.

Joe took the painted wood from under his arm. 'Oh, yes, I rescued it,' he said. He knocked his tricorn back and held up the wood to examine it more closely, trying to catch whatever light he could. 'It's a piece of scenery, isn't it? And quite a useful crutch, as it turns out.'

'Why the interest?' said Habs.

Joe seemed to have forgotten his reserve. 'My father made things like this back home. He took me to the Federal Street Theater, when he could.'

'What did you see?'

'Anything. Everything. Magic, ventriloquism, *The Beggar's Opera*, *The Taming of the Shrew*. Never seen anything so beautiful.'

Habs waited for the question he knew was coming. He watched Joe look back over to the hastily assembled boxing ring, watched him taking off his hat, rubbing his scalp. Then, finally, he said it. 'How did this get here, anyway? What are some flats, finely painted like that, doing in this shitty prison courtyard?'

''Cos you, sailor,' said Habs, 'done ended up in the only British jail with a theatre company.' Habs enjoyed the moment, laughing at Joe's astonishment.

'A theatre company?' he spluttered. 'Here? But Dartmoor's the most notorious English torture chamber in the world!'

'True,' said Habs. 'But it's a torture chamber with a theatre company. The Dartmoor Amateur Dramatic Company, we call it.'

Joe looked again at the scenery, as if he needed physical proof of this unlikely claim. 'The Dartmoor . . .'

'. . . Amateur Dramatic Company.'

'And you do shows?'

'Uh-huh.'

'Are you in it?' asked Joe.

''Course,' said Habs. 'We just did a pantomime.'

Joe leaned on his prop again, shaking his head. 'This has to be some kind of madness,' he said.

'Now you disbelievin' *me*,' said Habs.

Joe missed the sting. 'Who runs it?' he said.

'That'll be King Dick,' said Habs.

Joe almost smiled. 'You've got a King Dick?'

Habs kept a straight face until Joe realized what he'd said. 'Yes, but I'd advise you to get those lines right out of your head. Damn fast.'

'Can anyone join? Does this King Dick decide?'

Habs nodded slowly. 'He does. But you're Block Seven, Joe, and I'm Block Four.'

He offered no further explanation and, before Joe could ask for one, the redcoats returned.

30

1.4

The Physician's House

SHE HAD slept only briefly, she was sure – a few minutes, maybe. How lazy, how feeble, how *dangerous*. She scrambled from the bed, hauling a blanket from the covers to wrap around herself. It came to just above her knees, and she decided she was just decent enough. From the sheets, Dartmoor physician Dr George Magrath was stirring, too.

'Is that singing I can hear now?' he said, his eyes still closed, his mouth sticky with sleep. In a prison where routine meant order, anything unusual meant trouble.

'What is it, Elizabeth?'

'New arrivals,' she said, looking out.

'And they're singing?' He sounded incredulous.

'They are.'

'That's unusual. How many?'

'About a dozen. In a bad way, too.'

'But still singing.'

'"Yankee Doodle", I think.'

'You're wearing a blanket, Mrs Shortland.'

'You didn't appear to need it, Dr Magrath,' she replied, 'and you wouldn't want me standing by the window naked, now, would you?'

'Well, there's a thought to be considering,' he said, smiling. 'Are you quite sure you should be at those curtains at all?' Elizabeth didn't reply. Beyond the heavy velvet, her attention had been drawn to one of the new prisoners. Like many who arrived from the prison ships, there wasn't much to him; he was stooped with exhaustion and leaning on a comrade for support. But there was something about the way he held his head with that tricorn hat perched high, something about the way he conducted with one hand as he sang, that tugged at her heart. She found she was holding her breath as the new prisoners were marched away.

'At least the poor buggers won't be staying long,' said Magrath. 'They may be our last. Thomas is certain of the peace?'

She nodded, closing the gap in the curtains and dressing swiftly.

'He's telling his men now,' she said. 'He'll speak to the prisoners later, but it's the troops he's worried about. Peace with America means uncertainty. If there's no war, there'll be no need for them to be here.'

'Or us,' said Magrath.

'Another time, George,' Elizabeth said, repinning her hair with practised ease. 'Were we asleep long?' She watched him reach awkwardly for his clothes. Despite their intimacy, Magrath had always made it clear he loathed pity. Lame since childhood, he had learned to cope and to thrive. He wanted no charity.

'Mere minutes,' he said, pushing himself up with his black-and-silver cane.

'Still too long, George. I can't believe we fell asleep at all. What were we thinking?'

'You know the answer to that very well, Mrs Shortland.' He paused. 'And I'm not sure there was much thinking involved anyway.'

'You speak for yourself, George,' she said. By the time he was standing, she was ready to go; from petticoat to top coat, boots to hair, had been two minutes.

'Damn me, you're fast!' he said.

'I'll wait for you downstairs.' She collected her medical bag and stood waiting for him in the hallway. Their affair had made her happier than she had been in years. Magrath had once had to caution her to smile less on leaving his house. 'Everyone knows you are invaluable to me on the rounds, Elizabeth,' he had said. 'It would be best, I think, if they didn't know how invaluable you were to me . . . behind closed doors also.'

But the sailor she had spied from his bedroom had triggered a cascade of emotions: regret, longing, irretrievable loss. Elizabeth dug her nails into her palms. 'Pathetic,' she muttered to herself.

'What's that?' George shouted after her. He appeared at the top of the landing, buttoning his waistcoat. 'You said something . . .'

'It's nothing,' said Elizabeth. 'Talking to myself again.'

Magrath was down the stairs as swiftly as a man with a crippled leg can be. 'What's wrong?' he said. 'When you talk to yourself, it's never good.'

She offered him a sweet smile. 'Are all doctors like you?'

'Meaning?'

'Meaning,' she said, as she flattened his tangled, extravagant hair, 'your warm, wonderful heart seems to beat for mine also.' She kissed him softly. 'And the answer to your question is Willoughby.'

Magrath was instantly alert. 'Willoughby? Why, what's happened?' She had spoken often of her only son, a young officer in the Royal Navy. Now, he assumed the worst.

'Oh, no, George, it's not that,' she said quickly, sorry for the alarm she had caused. 'There was a sailor, one of the new prisoners. I saw him from the window. He . . .' She bit her lip hard. 'He just reminded me of Willoughby, that's all. I miss him so . . .'

Magrath reached for her and she folded into him. 'If he has his mother's instinct for survival, he'll be just fine,' he said.

'Is that what this is?' she said, from the folds of his high collar. She felt his smile.

33

'Among many other things.'

The extraordinary sound of wild, uninhibited cheering came from the direction of the market square and they broke apart.

'The peace,' she said. 'It must be the peace.' They moved to the back door. Magrath opened it slightly, the chilled air enveloping them in seconds. They listened to the swirl of shouts, applause and singing. 'Everything is about to change,' she whispered.

'You should go, Elizabeth,' said Magrath. 'Who knows what will happen now.'

Elizabeth Shortland pulled her coat tightly around her and slipped unnoticed from the physician's house. Keeping tight to the wall, she bustled past the prison entrance, locked and boarded, and under the shadow of its enormous arch, glided quietly into the darkness of her own home.

1.5

The Market Square

IT WASN'T an easy party to stop, even with rifles, bayonets and the onset of freezing rain. Fifty soldiers marched through the top gates into the square, urged on by the shouts of their sergeant and jeered by the prisoners.

'Go back to your blocks!' cried the officer.

'Kiss my arse!' came the reply.

The musicians were targeted first, their fiddles, accordions and drums snatched or smashed. Then the most obviously inebriated were dragged away. Any American protest that became too aggressive was silenced with a rifle butt.

Joe looked around, realized he'd lost his crew. He nodded once at Habs and was gone. When there was fighting to be done, most sailors wanted their ship's company alongside them, and Joe Hill was no exception. Around the square, there was a great reordering, a shifting of men as they moved towards their blocks, and Joe pushed his way through to where he thought he'd last seen the *Eagle* crew. He barged shoulders, dodged punches, ducked flying bottles. In front of him, three black sailors refused to make way for an intoxicated white sailor with teeth the colour of old pennies. After threatening Hell and damnation on them, the man fell face first on to the macadam. Tripped or unlucky, Joe couldn't tell.

He found Roche propped lopsidedly between other *Eagle* men and fell in behind them. Flat against the wall and halfway between the top and bottom gates, he observed the old ship's crews re-forming. With one noticeable difference.

35

'The Negroes are all separating out,' he said aloud. 'Why are they doing that?'

Roche shrugged. At the bottom of the square, the black sailors were gathering around the lower, more ornate gates.

'What are they down there for?' In front of him, some white crew turned round, their eyes narrowing as they took in the new arrivals. One sported the longest braided pigtail Joe had seen.

'You need to be told?' drawled the man with the queue. 'Does it look like we're still at sea?' There was a flash of red by the upper gates. Ten soldiers had appeared, led by a short, stiff-backed man in the uniform of a Royal Navy captain. He positioned himself on an improvised dais and waited, hands on hips. The rain swirled round him and briefly threatened to set him off balance.

'Well, we got the Agent out of his warm bed, then.' It was the man with the pigtail again. 'He'll not be wantin' to leave that wife o' his for long. I wouldn't be trustin' her alone in this place, that's for certain.' His crewmen laughed.

'Not with the likes of you around he won't.'

'Agent?' asked Joe, leaning forward. 'Who's the Agent?'

'The governor. He's called the Agent. God knows why. Arrogant cock of a man by the name of Captain Thomas Shortland. Or just call him Cock.'

Shortland raised his hands for silence. This triggered scuffles, a volley of jeers and abuse and another round of singing. Four men were roughly hauled away. The Agent waited a while, then reached inside his coat, produced a rolled piece of paper tied with a ribbon and held it aloft. It was instantly soaked, but succeeded where his upheld hands had failed.

'It's the peace!' cried a voice.

'It's the peace!' called a hundred more.

'Silence for the peace!'

'So we got it right,' muttered Joe to himself, as the square around him fell as close as it would ever get to silence.

On the dais, Shortland unrolled the document and took a deep breath.

'Men of Dartmoor!' he called, his clipped voice high and clear. 'I have in my possession a copy of a document signed on 24 December in the city of Ghent. It is a treaty of peace and amity between His Britannic Majesty and the United States of America.'

An almighty cheer erupted from the square and the dancing started again.

Joe grabbed Roche, holding his creased and scarred face between his hands. 'It's over, Will! It really is. The treaty is signed!'

Roche grinned back at him. 'Then, by rights, we should be able to walk straight out of here.'

By the high gates, Shortland had more to say. Realizing he had no chance of silencing an end-of-war party, he nodded at the militiaman next to him and pointed skywards. A single volley from the soldier's rifle silenced the crowd. The Agent had their attention now. He spoke quickly, knowing he might not have it for long.

'Our nations are desirous of terminating the war which has unhappily subsisted between us. Peace, friendship and good understanding are to be established again, so any mis-tempered weapons can be thrown to the ground. But, gentlemen, listen here, to Article Three.' He returned his attention to the scroll. '"All prisoners-of-war taken on either side, as well by land as by sea, shall be restored"' – and here Shortland laid a heavy emphasis – '"*as soon as practicable* after the ratifications of this treaty." His Majesty's Government ratified it yesterday in London but, until your Congress has ratified this treaty, then returned it to Parliament, nothing has changed. Return to your prison blocks. The turnkeys will be locking up. Anyone still outside in thirty minutes will be in the cachot.' He rolled up the treaty and placed it back inside his coat. 'Tomorrow is the Lord's day. No more brawls. No more drunkenness. All men, depart!'

It was only a matter of minutes before the militia squadron found the *Eagle* crew again. Same soldiers, same sergeant.

'Ah, our brave escort,' said Roche. 'And Ol' Fat Bastard too. You disappeared. Were you readin' the new peace? Are the terms good for you? Does the pride of Old England still float?'

'Peace, Will! Peace, for pity's sake,' said Joe, pleading. 'You need some yourself, I think.'

The sergeant moved so close that his bayonet tip pushed against Roche's shoulder. 'You don't have to be put in Block Seven, you know.' He had the air of a man who thought he should have been back in his barracks many hours ago. 'I could say you tried to escape, that you assaulted one of our brave militia, that you indulged in immoral acts. Or that you tried all three. That I had to put you in Four instead. That it was for your own good. So be careful, sailor. Now, march!'

They joined the throng staggering towards the square's exit, Joe once again steering Roche around obstacles. This time, most were unconscious sailors.

'What's wrong with Four?' asked Roche, once the sergeant had passed. Joe shook his head.

'No idea. That's Habakkuk's block. He says they've got a theatre company there, Will. Says they've just done a pantomime.'

Roche snorted. 'And he thought *we* were lyin',' he said.

They passed through the square's lower gates and, as they shuffled into a wide courtyard, the *Eagle* crew got their first real sight of the seven prison blocks. 'Dear God in heaven,' muttered Joe.

The black, rolling clouds had darkened the skies still further but, even in the dim light, the view of the blocks of Dartmoor Prison sucked out his breath. The seven buildings crowded in a rough semicircle, like massive ships at anchor around a courtyard harbour. Brick walls and iron palisades hemmed them in, surrounding and containing them, but it was the prison blocks, granite grey and running with water, that overwhelmed him. To his left, Blocks One, Two and Three were grouped together, hunkered against the storm. Straight ahead, Block Four stood apart, seemingly unprotected and adrift from the rest, narrow pathways leading either side into the darkness. Then, as far as Joe could see, Blocks Five, Six and Seven were close-hauled and line abreast, the mirror of the three blocks opposite. Behind him, the lower wall of the market square was revealed to be part of a large retaining wall, a radius separating the prisoners from the soldiers, the Americans from the British.

Joe had seen the USS *Constitution* once, back in '11. At three hundred feet from bowsprit to spanker and two hundred and twenty to the top of its main mast, she had filled Joe's vision, thrilled his heart, and he'd known her knots and guns would terrify her foes. Now, this unspeakable flotilla of jailhouses performed the same trick, striking black-hearted fear into the crew of the *Eagle*.

Each block had two rows of shuttered windows; a third row had been set into the middle of the gable-ended, slate-covered roof. The whole place was drenched in endless rain, as torrential now as any Joe could remember. Prisoners for Blocks One, Two and Three peeled off immediately, each returning sailor inspected by a uniformed man with a lantern. When each face had been seen, the man was nodded through large double doors. Joe suddenly stopped and a shipmate crashed into him.

'Don't stop like that, Mr Hill!'

'Sorry, Mr Lord,' said Joe, distracted.

'You seen a ghost or somethin'?' asked Roche.

'Look at the men waiting to get in, Will,' said Joe. 'That's what's different about Block Four. It's Negroes only.'

1.6

Block Seven

DESPITE THE hour, food was found for the new arrivals of Block Seven. Pickled fish, bread and water were served: 'The sweetest repast I have ever taken,' declared Roche. Each sailor had been issued with a hammock, a blanket, a pillow, rope yarns to sling the hammock, a piss pot, a wooden spoon and a three-gallon bucket. But that was the extent of the welcome. With the help of an old sailor, they walked the block in search of spaces. Lit only by the occasional candle, they passed row upon row of hammocks, sometimes slung in three tiers. Water dripped continuously from the ceiling.

'Such a smell men make,' murmured Joe. 'And there must be five hundred or more in here.'

'S'right,' croaked the old man, stepping around the puddles of rainwater which had pooled on the floor. "Nother five hundred souls upstairs, too. You'll get used to the stink, but you don't never get used to the cold 'n' damp. Nor the lice neither.'

When a meagre space was found, an *Eagle* sailor would peel off and sling his hammock. They had walked the floor twice, but four of them – Joe, Roche, Jon Lord and Robert Goffe – still needed a berth.

'How goes the war?' asked the old man, leading them up a stone stairway to the first floor.

'Didn't you hear?' Joe was astonished. 'The war is done. It's peace now. We'll be going home.'

The old man's weathered, deathly face showed no

40

emotion. Joe wondered if he'd heard. He tried again. 'They say it's peace. The treaty was signed in Belgium just last week.' Again, there was no reply.

They followed him to a wide landing lit with a solitary lantern, and through more doors. If anything, the stench was worse here; Lord and Goffe gagged as they breathed in the fetid air. This floor seemed warmer, thick with pipe smoke and ripe with sickness. Around them, the groans, howls and arguments seemed unrelenting.

'No folks'll be sleepin' here tonight,' muttered Roche. 'Bedlam, more like. If anyone ain't movin', they're most likely dead.'

'That sergeant seemed to think Block Seven was a cushy berth,' said Joe, holding his hat in front of his mouth.

'Maybe the others are worse,' said Roche.

'Hard to imagine,' said Joe, looking round. The four remaining members of the *Eagle* crew were on their own. 'Where's the old-timer gone?'

A brawl clattered past them. One of the men fighting was completely naked, the others carried bottles, whether as weapons or to sate their thirst was unclear.

'The stairs went on to another floor,' said Joe, as the tumult disappeared into darkness. 'Maybe he went up again?'

The landing lamp was weak, its flickering, feeble light reaching only as far as the first few steps, but as their eyes adjusted, they climbed further. With what felt like the last of their strength, the four sailors dragged their kit to the second floor. Another stone landing, more heavy wooden doors. Goffe and Lord eased them open. Silence. No fighting. No madness. The only smell was dampness.

'Here,' said Joe, dropping his hammock. 'Please, here.'

'But why is it empty?' whispered Goffe. 'There must be a reason. Why don't anyone come up here?'

Will Roche dropped his bucket and the resulting clang reverberated around the empty-sounding room. 'Whatever the reason, it can wait till the mornin'. We have marched, fought and drank. The war is finished, but the English still have us jailed. So now we sleep.'

No one disagreed. They walked a few paces, spread their hammocks on the wooden floor and were asleep in seconds.

Joe Hill slept like a dead man. He didn't notice daylight coming a scant six hours later or the small boy crouched by his side.

'Mister! Mister! Wake up! You shouldn't be here!' Slender hands shook Joe's shoulders. 'You have to move, sir. They won't like you sleeping like this.' He kept shaking and, when that failed, he kicked Joe sharply on his shins. That worked.

'Who are you?' Joe managed through sticky lips, looking up into bright blue eyes and a face full of freckles under a mop of red hair.

'Master Tommy Jackson, sir.' Great clouds of steam came from the boy's mouth as he spoke.

'How old are you?'

'Thirteen, sir. Fourteen this March 25th.'

'And why shouldn't we be here?'

The boy looked as though he might have a hundred answers, then decided on the best one he could think of. ''Cos you'll get stabbed with knives by Mr Cobb or Mr Lane if you stay,' he said. 'This is their space, you see.'

'Is that right?' said Joe, hauling himself up and wincing; every muscle was screaming. He had a pounding headache. He put his tricorn on his head and looked round the second-floor room they had collapsed into. It was vast: two hundred feet long, fifty wide and with a high ceiling. There were tables, chairs and piles of books.

The boy nudged him again. There was no doubting the urgency in his voice. He spoke in short, nervous bursts. 'Please, mister. You need to wake your friends.'

'All right, Master Jackson, I get it,' said Joe. 'I'll see what I can do.'

'And quietly,' urged the boy.

'Quietly,' agreed Joe, smiling. As he tried to rouse his shipmates, the boy stood lookout by the door.

Joe gave Roche, Goffe and Lord a gentle nudge with his boot. 'Downstairs. Clear for action.'

Sailors wake fast. Even exhausted, crapulous sailors can be fully alert in seconds if the order demands it. Their departure wasn't as silent as young Tommy Jackson would have liked – he winced at every clank of the buckets on the stone steps – but as they stumbled on to the ground floor he seemed to relax a little. The main prison doors were open, but he steered them into the living quarters. Wooden shutters had been opened on small, glassless windows, but what light there was seemed weak and ineffectual.

'Are we safe now?' asked Joe.

Tommy wasn't sure. His words still tumbled from him. 'You can sleep here or on the first floor. But not in the cockloft.'

'But it's empty,' said Roche, wiping sleep from his eyes. 'Who says we can't sleep there?'

The boy looked anxiously between the four new arrivals. 'It's orders is all.'

'What was your ship, Master Jackson?' asked Joe.

'HMS *Orontes*,' said Tommy, relieved to be on surer ground. 'There were five of us Yankees on board who'd been pressed to fight for the English. We gave ourselves up when the war started. Never wanted to fight our own country.' The boy's eyes darted between the *Eagle* crew. 'Only four of us left now. Joe Addis got the bloody flux. Buried in the graveyard outside the wall he is. With two hundred and twelve other good Americans. Maybe two hundred and thirteen soon – Mr Bloom was taken sick last week.'

'Sorry to hear that,' said Roche. 'So is he in the hospital?'

Tommy shook his head. 'It's full, so he's here. Block Seven, floor one.'

'So that's why it smelled like death last night,' said Joe. 'It *was* death. We need to find a berth down here. Do the English care where we sleep, Master Jackson?'

Tommy shrugged. 'You go where you're told.'

'Which block are you in?' asked Lord.

'I'm in Three. Been there since June 13th last year.'

'So how come you were in Seven?' asked Roche. 'Do you go on patrol, lookin' for sleepers who are out o' bounds?'

'No, sir. I'm the crier,' he said, his obvious pride making Roche's frown melt a little. 'Mr Snow caught me in the square, asked me to check on you. And he also said you might want to come to church. I can show you, if you like.'

The four men from the *Eagle* laughed.

'Church?' exclaimed Roche. 'They have us in English chains as it is. I'll not listen to any more Englishmen than I must.'

'And you can barely understand what they're saying, anyway, can you, Mr Roche?' said Joe.

'Ain't my fault they can't speak properly,' said Roche. 'I'm stayin' here, where all these happy Americans live and talk clearly. But you go, Joe, you have your cross to bear. Give me your things. I'll find us a nice room with flowers.' He took Joe's hammock, ropes and buckets and dragged them off, muttering, 'And down with the English!' into the gloom, Lord and Goffe following behind.

'It ain't no English church,' said Tommy, watching them go. 'I should've told 'em.'

'Church is church,' said Joe. 'Unless you have dancing girls, Mr Roche will not be attending. But I'll come to your church, Master Jackson, if I'm not too late.' He paused. 'It was getting dark when we arrived, and I confess I didn't see a church . . .'

'Oh no, sir, there's no building. Church is in Four. The cockloft of Block Four.'

Halfway down the steps to the main entrance, the sound of heavy boots interrupted Joe's reply. Five heavily bearded men armed with cudgels and knives appeared in the doorway then took the steps four at a time. They glanced briefly at Joe and Tommy as they went past.

'Let me guess,' said Joe. 'That's who you came to warn us about?' Tommy nodded. 'Who are they?' asked Joe.

'It's them Rough Allies,' said Tommy in a whisper. No further information was forthcoming.

'And who are the Rough Allies?' Joe persisted.

Tommy, hands deep in his jacket pockets, frowned. 'They get things done,' he said flatly.

'I bet they do,' said Joe, as they walked quickly out of the block.

Freezing rain assailed them and they found shelter at the back of a crowd taking warmth from a blazing coffee stove. Joe squinted into the gale. There was no view to speak of. Low, rolling cloud blanketed whatever there might be to see. The seven prison blocks looked, if anything, even more forbidding than they had the day before.

'How old?' asked Joe. 'How old are these monsters?'

Tommy shrugged. 'They were built for the French. So six years? Maybe seven.'

'They look ancient,' said Joe. 'A thousand years old at least.' He edged round the coffee crowd to the narrow, buffeted alley that ran between Six and Seven and gaped at the monstrous edifices.

Tommy read his face well. 'You get used to it,' he said.

The storm had only served to enhance the prison's unmistakeable air of menace. The blocks, it seemed to Joe, had been built to avenge a nation's wounded pride at the loss of their America. He had survived British ships, their cannonfire,

45

rifles and pistols, but now he wondered if it would be their buildings that would be the end of him.

'I'll take your word on that,' he said, and he and Tommy made their way to Block Four.

'Them cuts on your head,' said Tommy, looking up at Joe.

'What about them?' said Joe, staring at the ground.

'Where'd they come from, then?'

But the memories were too raw, too recent. 'They come from bad times,' Joe said eventually.

'Worse than these times?' asked Tommy, and Joe heard again the voices of the savages he had been chained to on the prison ship.

'Worse than these times,' he agreed.

'Well, that's somethin', ain't it?' said Tommy.

'Yes, I suppose.' Joe smiled one of his almost-smiles. 'I like you, Crier, I think we'll be good friends.'

'Really?' Tommy's face radiated pleasure. He looked, momentarily, like the thirteen-year-old boy he was. 'Thanks, Mr Hill.'

'Joe is fine.'

'Thanks, Joe,' said Tommy, sounding pleased with his morning's work.

'These Rough Allies,' continued Joe, wiping rain from his face, 'was one of them boxing last night?'

Tommy nodded.

'Of course. The one with the wood. And you said if we didn't move from the cockloft in Seven that a Mr Cobb and a Mr Lane would stab us.'

Another nod. 'S'their space, so they say. In Six *and* Seven. They say they don't like intruders.'

'I'm sure,' said Joe. 'And was that Mr Cobb and Mr Lane we just saw? Do they have many men working for them?'

More nodding.

'There are thugs and bullies on every ship, so it'll be the same here. They run the place?'

'When the Brits ain't looking,' said Tommy.

'Which is when?'

'Most o' the time.'

They had walked past Block Six, which was set slightly further back than its neighbours, then a busy Block Five. Sailors, indifferent to the weather, huddled around fires, eating bubbling stew or smoking pipes. Tommy strode on, but Joe called him back.

'Block Four is a Negro prison?'

'Yessir.'

'The Rough Allies run that, too?'

Tommy laughed. 'No, sir.'

'But we can go in?'

'Yessir.'

'How is that possible?'

The crier smiled. A proper, uninhibited, face-splitting smile. 'It is possible, Mr Hill, 'cos King Dick says it is possible.'

1.7

Block Four, Cockloft

JOE AND Tommy climbed the steps to the cockloft of Block
Four. In physical appearance, the block appeared to be
identical to all the rest: the same wide doors, the same stone
steps, the same air of pervading darkness.

'You see much church, Mr Hill?' said Tommy, as they
climbed.

'Sure,' said Joe, surprised by the question. 'I was bap-
tized back in Suffolk, England. And when we came to
America we attended the local chapel at least twice a week.
Baptist, I think it was. At sea, there were services aplenty.
Reckon I seen enough church.' He realized his new compan-
ion was smiling again.

'You say your prayers, Mr Hill?'

Joe, amused at all these questions, raised an eyebrow.
'Sure,' he said. 'All sailors do. I've been praying for a full
stomach, for us to go home, for America to win this damned
war, and for my sweet mother and sister to stay well. Maybe
I'll say them again today if . . .' He broke off as a sound like
a low rumble came from above them. He glanced upwards.
'Church?'

Tommy nodded.

'And you're sure Mr Snow invited me?'

'He did, sir, yes.'

They had reached the top landing, and Joe paused, listening at the door. He frowned at the stomping and shouting they
could hear within. 'Sounds more like fighting than praying.'

Tommy shrugged.

'How many in Block Four?'

'Nine hundred and ninety-five, sir.'

'And are they all in here?'

'King Dick likes everyone to be there, but 'bout twenty-three don't come no more. Black Simon throws some folk out sometimes. He's the pastor.'

'And are you coming in?' Joe couldn't believe he was seeking the support of a thirteen-year-old boy to attend a church meeting.

'Sure.'

'Then lead the way.' Joe removed his hat and stepped aside as Tommy pushed at the doors.

They opened just enough for the boy to squeeze through. He disappeared inside. For a moment, Joe thought he had been deserted, then the doors were wrenched wide and he, too, stepped in. He couldn't see Tommy, but then, apart from the backs of heads, he couldn't see much at all. At five feet nine, Joe was taller than most sailors he'd met, but he still couldn't see what was causing such a clamour. He tried pushing in further, but the men were too tightly packed. From the looks cast in his direction, he wasn't sure they would let him in, anyway.

Straining as high as he could on his tiptoes, Joe finally made out what he guessed was a choir, lined up in three rows. The men stood on a stage littered with instruments: tambourines, clarinets, violins and flageolets. On the back wall, painted battlements gave the room a theatrical flourish. 'The Dartmoor Amateur Dramatic Society,' he said. 'Of course.'

Distracted, Joe hadn't noticed that the room had gone quiet. Or that the best part of a thousand people had turned to look at him. Now, he did. And every face black, he thought. He suddenly felt profoundly alone. A trespasser, an intruder – an imposter.

'My apologies,' he mumbled, and had turned to leave when a massive voice filled the room.

'I spy a stranger!'

Joe froze, then turned back slowly. Now, he could see the far end of the cockloft. Habs and Tommy Jackson stood next to a bear of a man who was sitting on a wooden chest. He beckoned Joe over with one huge hand and, miraculously, a path cleared through the multitude.

As he stepped over arms and legs, a distant memory of a Baptist sermon back home on the parting of the Red Sea came to him, but this new miracle was happening right now. I am being summoned, he thought. This must be King Dick.

The man wore a bearskin hat high on his head, and a battered club swung in one hand. An image from Sunday School came to Joe: the hat was a crown, the club a sceptre. Courtiers sat scattered at this giant's feet. There was no doubt in Joe's mind who this man thought he was and who his subjects considered him to be. He found himself staring into a solemn, serious face – monumental, a broad nose, a powerful forehead overshadowing intense, burning eyes. Deep scarring was clearly visible on both cheeks and ivory-and-pearl earrings hung from his ears. He was magnificent. Joe held his breath.

The King pulled the bearskin low on his head then rearranged the embroidered cape that was wrapped around him. Underneath, a sash with four gold stars. Joe wondered briefly whether he should bow.

Habs stepped forward. 'King Dick, this is Joe Hill from the crew of the *Eagle*. Arrived last night. Put in Seven. He brought the news of the peace—'

'I know who he is,' said the King, his words rumbling deep like a storm on the horizon. Gathering his cape, he rose from the chest and Joe looked up, dumbstruck.

King Dick was, without doubt, the tallest, broadest man he had ever seen. Six feet seven, maybe six feet eight, he seemed to go on for ever. On his feet he wore polished military boots. His thick woollen trousers were held up with a wide belt, and an ornate silver clasp kept his cape in place.

'Mr Hill.' The King was looking at Joe, but his voice reached everyone. 'Our stranger.' He raised a steaming cup of something. 'You look . . . un-com-for-tab-le.'

Joe dropped his head, twisted his cap. 'I guess I am, sir.'

'Welcome to Block Four,' said the King, waving his club expansively in front of him. The weapon – for that is what it undoubtedly was – looked as though it might originally have been some sort of bat, but it was now painted black and the square edges had been rounded off. Its many dents and scratches revealed it to be a working cudgel.

'So, Mr Hill, have you read Thomas Hobbes? He was English, like you.'

Joe's brow creased. Was this some kind of test, a trap he'd walked into?

'No, I have not. And I am a naturalized American. My family moved from England when I was a small child.'

'But you read, Mr Hill?'

'Yes, whenever I can.'

'Where is your home, Mr Hill? Please tell us.' The King sat back down, being careful not to spill his drink. In sharp contrast to everyone else Joe had seen in Dartmoor, King Dick's hands were clean, his nails neatly trimmed.

Joe cleared his throat. 'Boston, sir. Dedham, Norfolk County, to be precise.'

'And who do you have waitin' for you?'

'My mother and sister, God willing. Not seen them these two years past.'

The King nodded. 'We don't have no Fours from Norfolk County, I don't believe. Though we come from all over.' He turned his head to Habs. 'Where's home for you, Mr Habakkuk Snow? Remind me.'

'Philadelphia, sir!'

'Uh-huh. You, too, Mr Samuel Snow?'

'Yes, sir!'

'Where else is home?' The King picked up his club again, pointing it at random.

'New York!' shouted one man.

Many others nodded and called out, 'That's where I'm goin'!'

Then came a flurry of shouts from around the room.

'Massachusetts!'

'Virginia!'

'I'm goin' back to Delaware!'

'Rhode Island.'

'Mississippi, King Dick! Come an' visit!'

'Connecticut!'

'South Carolina.'

After each had spoken, the King said, 'Going home, going home . . .'

And other voices sounded out.

A thin-faced, white-haired man raised a hand. 'I am going home. I am from the Tupi people. My home is Brazil. I am the last one here.'

Another stood, then another. 'We are Bakongo. From Kongo. That is our home,' one of the men said, before wrapping himself in what appeared to be a tarpaulin and sitting down again.

Hundreds were calling out to name their state or city, as if, by saying it publicly, reaching their destination became more real. Joe assumed this show was for him, though perhaps they performed this roll call every week.

'Goin' back to Georgia!'

'Washington, DC.'

'Vermont.'

'I am a Jivaroan from Peru.'

'New Hampshire.'

'My home is in Bengal.'

'North Carolina.'

King Dick pointed, acknowledged, moved on. Then it was his turn.

'And from Maryland?' he asked. The loudest shout so far. The King beamed. They had all waited, knowing he would give them pride of place. He called out the towns in Maryland and they hollered them back.

'From Annapolis!'

'From Baltimore!'

'From Frederick!'

Eventually, the names fell away, and the King stood again, an elaborate unfurling.

'King Dick is from many places,' he announced. 'The seas and oceans first, o' course, then Salem, Boston and Baltimore. Also Haiti. And also Guinea. Before it all, was Guinea. My grandfather, he was taken.' He paused. 'Snatched!' A longer pause. 'Stolen from Africa!'

A few voices echoed: 'Stolen from Africa!'

The King nodded. 'He was always told, his brothers and him, never trust the men with the mahogany skin. The men who move like ghosts, who smile like beasts. That if you let them, they swallow you whole, they take you, take your soul, they take your ev-er-y-thin'.'

The King emphasized each syllable of this last word, the shiver in his voice triggering shivers in his audience. Joe assumed everyone in the room had heard this story before, maybe many times, but they were as captivated as he was; it wasn't just the story's rhythm, cadence and tragedy that gave it power, it was its familiarity. The King was pacing now.

'But they came for him. They came from the coast, they came when he was playin' by the river, he and his brother. Twenty of the ghosts, with fearsome knives, stabbin' an' pokin' till my grandpa and his poor brother were in sacks a hundred miles away, 'fore they knew what was happenin'. One day he wakes from a beatin' and he find he been sold to

53

the Europeans. His brother gone – never to see him again. When he gets out of that sack, he thinks he will truly be eaten by these men with red skin, their women's hair an' disgustin' faces.'

'An' they no prettier now!' Ned called out.

Joe shuffled his feet uncomfortably, eyes to the floor. The King waited for the laughter to die away, then refocused on Joe.

'You feel like I'm pickin' on you, Mr Hill?' Joe nodded before he realized what he was doing. 'You want to look at me, Mr Hill?'

Joe whipped his head up. The black eyes were waiting for him.

'We are jus' tellin' you things you need to hear. Tellin' you things maybe you missed back in Norfolk County.'

Joe nodded again. 'Thank you, King Dick.'

Satisfied, the King waved his club in front of him to clear some space. 'Leave room for Mr Daniels and Mr Singer,' he said. 'They will come soon, bringin' sustenance.'

Some of his entourage shuffled away from the throne.

'We need sustenance 'cos Pastor Simon likes his words and, when he runs out, he tries out some new words. Things get . . . exhaustin'.' When he smiled, the King's enormous eyes glittered; they were glittering now. 'And when he asks, we will pretend we understand them.' He turned again to Joe. 'Why did you come here?' he said.

Joe was caught off guard, unsure. 'Well, I . . .' He glanced at the crier. 'Master Jackson there said I'd been invited. Me and the *Eagle* crew.'

'Uh-huh,' said the King. 'But why d'you come and the others stay behind?'

Joe was again unsure how to respond, not wishing to incriminate his shipmates.

'Maybe,' the King prodded, 'they weren't feelin' too spiritual, havin' jus' woken up in this particular Hell?'

'Yes. Maybe,' mumbled Joe.

The cockloft door swung open and two white boys, maybe twelve years old, appeared, walking slowly, concentrating hard on balancing the cups and plates they carried.

'Ah. At last!' boomed the King, his basso profundo cutting through the chatter. 'With speed now, m'boys. Let's see what you have.'

They tried a faster step but succeeded only in spilling hot, steaming liquid on the ground.

'Steady, then!' called the King. 'Make way for the bearers of coffee and plum gudgeons.'

The crowd parted to allow the diminutive figures to pass, their faces a study in concentration. King Dick took a cup from one and a plate from the other, swapping it for his club. He slurped coffee, then spooned fish and potatoes until both were gone. The smells, sharp and familiar, reminded Joe how hungry he was and he wondered how long it would be before he ate.

The King thanked the boys, then from his cape produced two coins and gave one to each. 'Mr Daniels, you did well. Mr Singer, thank you. I declare I have forgotten what real coffee tastes like. When we go home – how sweet that sounds, when we go home! – I declare I will brew my own coffee like this, made only from English peas.'

The King swallowed the rest of his coffee. 'I'll keep the next one for when the pastor here tells us about Hell. I can see he's itchin' to start his service.' He pointed his empty cup at Pastor Simon, who had edged himself into King Dick's eyeline. 'He will talk about "good news", I expect. Am I right, Reverend?'

Joe swivelled to see the pastor, dressed in yellow prison clothes but with a voluminous black cloak pulled over the top, raise a hand in acknowledgement.

'You're right, King Dick. Praise God!'

'You see?' said the King. 'But it is you that brought us

the good news, Mr Hill. And today is Sunday. It is the first day of the new year. Some of our people were not in the market square last night. So, as you have come to us, please, let us hear it from you. You spoke well in the square, a fine performance, but we demand an encore.' He beckoned Joe forward. He took a few hesitant steps, but the King waved him closer. 'A word . . .' he said, and Joe lowered his head. He smelled soap and fish. 'You can put the hat on,' the King went on, his words slow and hushed. 'This ain't church. Not yet.'

Joe stepped back, sliding the tricorn gratefully into position. He stared at the King. He knew. Somehow, he knew.

With a flick of King Dick's fingers, Joe was waved back into position.

'And speak loud!' called the King. 'There are many who are still cannon-deaf.'

Joe turned to face the sailors of Block Four. When Tommy Jackson had invited him to church, Joe had, to the extent that he had thought about it at all, assumed it would be familiar. Maybe even comforting. But familiarity and comfort seemed remote right now. A wall of black faces stared back at him; he didn't see individuals, he saw merely colour. He saw the dirty yellow of the Transport Office uniforms, he saw cream tarpaulin, grey blankets, the greens and browns of the theatre scenery, but mainly he saw his two pink hands in front of a thousand black faces. His throat felt tight and dry.

'Are you all right, Mr Hill?' asked the King.

'Yes,' said Joe, 'just feeling a bit . . .'

'A bit white?' suggested the King, and a wave of laughter rippled out across the room.

Joe nodded. 'Just a bit,' he said.

'Well, you feel a bit white to us, too.' More laughter. 'And we not used to be bein' addressed by white folk on our own deck. But today is different, don't you think?'

Many cries of 'Yes, King Dick!'

56

Joe felt a tug at his sleeve. One of the King's boys was handing him a cup.

'Have a little Dartmoor coffee to start you off,' said the King. Joe took the cup and sipped tentatively. It was thin and bitter, but better than the stickiness in his mouth. 'It's just a speech,' said the King, 'and this is your cue.' Joe handed back the empty cup, nodded his thanks.

He tried again. 'Good morning. My name is Joe Hill. I'm from Boston.' Better. He could see a few hands raised and heads nodding. 'I was part of the crew of the *Eagle*, but we were taken off Halifax. We lost plenty of good men to the Yankee cause, many more in the ship bringing us here.' He saw movement: the men were nodding in understanding. 'We arrived in Plymouth Dock three days ago, held there for reasons we couldn't fathom. But we heard the captain tell his crew that there was peace. That America and Britain had signed a treaty.' The nods had become smiles. Joe added, 'That no one else need fight, and that no one else need die.'

The smiles became shouts and the shouts became singing. King Dick shouted, 'Pastor Simon? *Now* it's your turn!' and within seconds the choir was in full voice.

1.8

Block Four, Cockloft

HABS CAME over, blue jacket buttoned. Joe tugged the tricorn a little lower.

'You see!' shouted Habs above the hymns. 'An audience that needed a speech.'

'I thought I was coming to church,' said Joe. 'Had no idea.'

They stood with their backs to the cockloft wall. At the far end, the band and the choir were taking it in turns to fill the room with the loudest church music Joe had ever heard; for a moment, he thought he recognized the hymn they were playing but then the tambourines started and he was lost again.

Habs was laughing. 'You lookin' like you maybe confused.'

'It isn't exactly the way of things at our Baptist hall.'

'That may be true,' said Habs. 'So let me guess. The coloured folk worship somewhere different?'

'I suppose they do.'

'You know where?' asked Habs.

'Can't say I do.' Joe stared at the floor, aware he was floundering.

'And why is that?'

Joe noticed Habs's full, arching eyebrows for the first time – both were raised in expectation. He knew his answers mattered. He struggled on.

'There's not a lot of . . . mixing goes on back home, if

58

you know what I mean,' he said, and instantly knew that wasn't going to be good enough. If Habs's eyebrows indicated a challenge, he'd failed it. The truth was, he'd never been questioned like this before, never felt he had to justify himself, and Habs knew it.

'Not a lot o' mixin' goes on here either,' said Habs. 'So you'll get on fine. It'll be jus' like home.'

Joe frowned. 'You know I didn't mean that.'

'You ever been the only white man before today, Joe?' said Habs. 'The only white man in a big room like this?'

'You know I haven't,' said Joe, irritated. 'But I was invited. You invited me. That's why I came. Did you invite any others?'

'No. Jus' the crew o' the *Eagle*.'

Joe shook his head. 'But this is England. My parents came from here. They never said the whites and the coloureds were kept separate. They never told me it was like this.'

'It ain't,' said Habs. 'This is new. This here's an American idea. Last year, some o' the white sailors went to the Agent and told him they couldn't stand the "thievin' o' the Negroes" no more. That we didn't "wash like white folk", that our hygiene was so bad we had to be separated.'

Joe whistled slowly. 'And did you know these white sailors?'

Habs's voice hardened. 'Did I know them?' he said. 'They were my crew.'

'The *Bentham*?' said Joe, astonished. 'The men of the *Bentham* asked for this?'

Habs nodded. 'Some o' them. Enough o' them.'

'But we all share the same ships,' said Joe. 'We had lots of Negro sailors on the *Eagle* before the fighting started . . .'

'Uh-huh. There's no room to be separate on a ship,' said Habs. 'But soon's there's space, it seems the white sailor wants it all to himself. So the Agent agreed and put anyone who wasn't as white as him in here.'

'Where's the rest of your crew?'

'In Six. You'll have seen some around – they like to be noticed. Long beards, most of 'em.'

Joe pushed himself off the wall. 'The Rough Allies? Two of them tried to get to us this morning. Mean-looking bastards.'

'Well, that's the truth,' said Habs. 'And pathetic, mostly. But Lane and Cobb – they're the ones you have to watch out for.'

Joe grabbed Habs's arm. 'Lane was there this morning.'

'Had the *Bentham* hammock three along from me,' said Habs. 'Always hated us, but was only when he got here he was able to do anythin' 'bout it. Cleaned us all out, then put us all together. Tha's why you bein' in Block Four now is a big deal.'

There was movement in front of them. Ned and Sam had brought plates of plum gudgeon with them, and Joe eyed them keenly.

'No breakfast?' laughed Sam. 'It's cold, but it only costs a penny.'

'Oh, I have no money,' said Joe. 'We arrived with nothing, not even a King's penny.'

'You'll get your wages soon enough,' said Ned. 'Eat what you will. I got it from Mr Daniels and Mr Singer. Seemed to have more than two small lads could need.'

Joe gulped down the thick paste of fish and potatoes. It was tasteless and stuck to his mouth like molasses, but he didn't care. He had weeks of hunger to assuage. 'Who are those boys?' he said, his mouth still full. 'I saw them next to King Dick.'

'They, well, we call them his secretaries,' said Habs.

'Secretaries?' said Joe. 'They can write and organize a ledger?'

Sam put his hand on Joe's elbow. 'We call them secretaries, and then we don't have to call them anythin' else.'

'I see,' said Joe, surprised by his candour. 'And they stay in Four?'

'Yeah, Alex an' Jonathan are here,' said Sam. 'An' a few other sailors who ain't fit in where they been put. Or they got themselves into trouble, needed to be somewhere else. If King Dick allow it, they stay here. He picks up strays. That's what he does.'

'An' when Sam says, "ain't fit in",' said Ned, 'what he means is freaks. And when he says, "got themselves into trouble", he means criminals. Welcome to Big Dick's Circus, Mr Hill.'

At the front of the cockloft, the hymn died away and Pastor Simon climbed on to a makeshift pulpit made of two card tables. Every man present immediately seemed to realize they had something better to do; conversations sprang up, packs of cards appeared, and dice rolled. The pastor tried to speak above the hubbub.

'The preacher is popular, then,' said Joe.

'He has only a few things to say,' said Habs. 'We're in prison with him – we heard 'em before.'

'Church and gambling at the same time? The folks at the Baptist Union back home would rather be struck down by Satan Himself,' said Joe.

'Well, Pastor Simon runs the church and King Dick runs the gamblin',' said Habs. 'Though, if he wanted, I think the King could have the church, too.'

As if he'd heard their talk, King Dick had climbed on to the pulpit. His head now nearly touching the ceiling, he stood with his eyes and arms wide. He was clearly waiting for silence, and he had it within seconds. The talking died down, the cards and the dice were pocketed. All eyes were on the stage.

The King held out his club then swept it in an arc. 'How poor are they that have not patience!' he called, staring around his audience.

Joe's eyes narrowed. 'What wound did ever heal but by degrees?' he whispered.

Then, as if an echo from the stage, the King thundered, 'What wound did ever heal but by degrees?'

Joe dropped his head, sliding down the wall. Habs followed him to the floor.

'But this is Shakespeare,' Joe said.

'The Dartmoor Amateur Dramatic Society,' said Habs. 'They're the King's shows. He runs everything anyways, but the theatre? That's what he really loves.'

'That line,' said Joe. 'That line was Iago's. From *Othello*.'

'It was,' said Habs, 'and it was my line.'

'You put on a production of *Othello* here?' Joe failed to keep the disbelief out of his voice. 'You played Iago?'

Habs looked intently at his new friend, then jumped up, offering Joe his hand, the one with H.O.L.D tattooed on the fingers.

'Come,' said Habs. 'Close haul.'

Joe followed Habs as he fought his way through the crowd. Finding gaps to get through took time but, when they saw who was doing the pushing, most made way.

'In a hurry, Habs?' asked one voice.

'Look alive there!' hissed Habs, turning sideways to squeeze between two scrawny sailors who were sharing a large bottle.

'Habs, what are we doing?'

Joe received no reply.

As they reached the front, the King appeared as if a giant, his club still swaying dangerously close to the heads of the sailors. As it passed, many ducked or leaned out of its path. He flourished it again then brought it to rest on his shoulder. The King was wrapping up.

'Do we have Pitch and Toss? Yes, gentlemen, we do.' Cheers from many in the crowd. 'Do we have Twenty-one? O' course.' The cheers were louder now and came with applause. The King nodded, acknowledging the approval. 'And we have Rat Race – o' course – but . . . in time. Keep your coins for the moment. Patience, m'boys.'

Habs, still with Joe in his wake, stuck up his hand. 'My noble Lord . . .'

King Dick saw Habs and laughed, his temporary pulpit rocking. He stuck his hands on his hips, his cloak parting to expose the large buckled belt around his waist. He edged his feet apart, his stance strong.

'What dost thou say, Iago?' said the King, and applause rolled around the room.

Habs called back, 'Did Michael Cassio, when you wooed my lady, know of your love?'

From somewhere behind them a voice shouted, 'Do the play! Do the whole play!'

King Dick called to Habs. 'He did, from first to last. Why dost thou ask?'

Habs leaned close to Joe.

'So here's your answer. Yes, we put on *Othello*.'

Habs leapt on to the stage, followed by Ned Penny and two others. Joe saw Pastor Simon shrug and usher the choir away. Dick jumped from the pulpit and, to a backdrop of cheers and clapping, they performed lines and scenes from *Othello*, seemingly at random. Joe looked on in wonder as a stooped, grey-haired man miraculously became Desdemona, one of the drunks he'd squeezed past became Michael Cassio and Ned recited the lines of Roderigo.

When the players were spent, the applause and stomping went on, Joe clapping long and hard, too.

When Habs finally jumped from the stage, King Dick wasn't far behind. 'So, Mr Hill from Boston,' said the King, sweat running from under his hat, 'what say you?'

'I know the play, King Dick,' said Joe, smiling, 'and . . . I am speechless.'

King Dick nodded appreciatively.

'How many players do you have?' asked Joe.

'We manage with eleven,' said the King. 'We lost our clown to the pox and Montano to jail fever, but everyone came to see it anyway.'

'And did you have white men play any parts, King Dick?' asked Joe.

The King's eyes narrowed slightly and he adjusted his hat. 'Do we need white men, Mr Hill?'

Joe realized that many of the nearby conversations had quietened or stopped altogether. 'Well, no, I suppose—' began Joe.

'Shakespeare was black, Mr Hill. We all know that,' interrupted the King. 'So why would we need any white men?' It was a question, but it still sounded like a threat.

To Joe's puzzled expression, Habs slowly, subtly, shook his head.

Joe swallowed his question and pointed instead at the stage and the scenery. 'Oh, you don't . . . I was just hoping,' he said, 'to maybe offer my services . . .'

'That so?' said the King, his face solemn again. 'And what would we do with a young sailor so fair of face?'

Joe stood rooted to the spot, unsure of his reply. 'I . . . I don't know, sir,' he stammered.

'Ha!' King Dick shouted, and everyone jumped. 'Mr Snow here does. Tell 'im, Mr Snow, and be done with it.' The King gathered his cape around himself and walked off, young Alex and Jonathan running to catch up.

'Shakespeare was black?'

Habs waited for the crowd to drift away to the gambling tables. 'You wanna argue with him?'

'Not really,' said Joe. 'And what is it you know? What was he talking about?'

Habs placed a hand on Joe's shoulder. 'Before the French left, the King was thinkin' of puttin' on a play with 'em. They had their own theatre company, made some fine

64

scenery. Then Napoleon went an' lost and they all went home. We took some of their flats, and the rest made that boxing ring you were leanin' on last night.'

Joe nodded. 'Neat painting, too. But they were white French?'

'White French,' confirmed Habs. 'They were in Seven, too. They never knew about the King's idea. Coulda refused. But it would've been perfect. A play with two families living in a lawless town. It was a good fit.'

It was then that Joe got it. '*Romeo and Juliet*,' he said. 'Of course. So, when the King says you have plans for me . . .' Joe raised an eyebrow. 'Let me guess. You will play Romeo?'

Habs nodded solemnly.

'And . . . you want me for Juliet?' Joe asked. 'Have you lost your senses in here?' His head was spinning – he needed some air. 'Maybe you have the jail fever that took your Montano,' he said. 'I need to see my crew. We need to find our berths in Seven. We need food and money. And then? Well, then, God willing, we'll be sailing home.'

1.9

The Agent's Study

SHORTLAND (*standing, awkward*): Mr Crafus, you seem to have made quite an impact. Please sit.

King Dick also standing, at ease, his bearskin hat under his arm, looks around Shortland's study, taking in the pictures and portraits; is silent.

SHORTLAND: The men in your block respect your . . . strength and your control.

King Dick continues to study the paintings; is silent.

SHORTLAND (*puzzled*): This isn't a game, Crafus. I am the Agent, I am your governor, your commanding officer. I ask questions, you answer them. I respect the discipline you have instilled in your men. I appreciate the order in Four, but I need that order in all things. And that includes prisoners answering questions when asked.

KING DICK (*still not looking at Shortland*): You ain't asked me any questions. You jus' been talkin' at me, tellin' me things.

SHORTLAND (*smiles, impatient*): Quite so. Very well, then. How are your men in Block Four?

KING DICK (*looks at Shortland at last*): They are sick, as you well know. We lost four to the pox this month. Sick and hungry and wantin' for home. If you want peace in your camp, if you want order in your prison, you gotta do somethin' 'bout that. 'Bout all o' that.

SHORTLAND: You are a prisoner-of-war. It is a Dartmoor winter. Conditions here are no worse than in all prison camps;

indeed, considerably better than some. There is fresh water, the courtyards are swept and clean, you have ample food and supplies. If there is a shortage of money, that is a problem with your government (*checking himself*). However, I will raise the matter of sickness with Dr Magrath . . .

KING DICK (*sharply*): You will 'raise these matters', but my men will still die, Captain Shortland. You are in charge, but you choose to be weak. Your men, your soldiers, are stupid, and you permit the Rough Allies to disrupt your prison . . .

SHORTLAND (*annoyed*): Enough! I did not ask you here to deliver one of your speeches . . .

KING DICK: And from a Negro, too . . .

SHORTLAND: From a prisoner! It's a miracle you Yankees have any ships sailing at all, with this insubordination.

KING DICK: It's a miracle you Brits are still in the war . . .

SHORTLAND: And a war you declared for what? Washington at least fought for 'liberty' – you have been fighting for shadows (*controls himself*). What I wanted to say was simply this. I admire the way you have taken control of Four and made it your own.

KING DICK: I am an unaccountable sovereign.

SHORTLAND (*puzzled*): I'm sorry, I didn't catch that . . .

KING DICK: An unaccountable sovereign. He keeps chaos at bay, keeps the state of nature in check. We have order in Four, Captain. This is *Othello*, this is *Leviathan*.

There is a silence between the men.

KING DICK: Shakespeare and Hobbes. These are your great Englishmen.

SHORTLAND: Indeed. Though I confess it's been many years since I read either. But I can be clear on this: I only wish the other blocks were as, well, efficient and, er, organized as Four.

KING DICK (*laughing*): I served in some of your ships that were 'efficient' and 'organized'. Royal Navy words for 'brutal', I believe.

SHORTLAND (*ignoring him*): It seems amazing to me what you can achieve without those damned prisoner committees. The other prisons seem to like them. A lot of voting goes on, I believe – and constitutional talk, I hear (*pronounces 'voting' and 'constitutional' with a sneer in his voice*). You've not been . . . tempted?

KING DICK (*angry*): And how do you think that constitution has been doin' in lookin' after people like me, Captain? What d'you think we make of it over in Four? When we are back home, all that votin' don't seem to be helpin' us much. We are not 'tempted', 'cos it's a sham, a trick to let those in charge feel better 'bout themselves. Everyone's jus' fine with the way it is in Four. I am in charge, or it is the war of all against all. And when the Rough Allies are allowed to go 'bout attackin' whoever they fancy, someone needs to do somethin'. I am the someone, Captain.

SHORTLAND (*smiling*): You are indeed the someone, Mr Crafus. I assure you I will speak to Dr Magrath shortly. And I will order the guard to be more watchful of the Rough Allies. (*As if an afterthought*): What do you hear of the other prisons, Mr Crafus? Are they restless?

KING DICK: Restless? You think prisoners desperate for home after a war that has ended might be restless? You got that right. But I won't be your spy, Captain Shortland. You have enough men here – they can tell you. And case you hadn't noticed, the white blocks are quite happy keeping themselves 'part from the likes of me. You allowed the separation. You put us in Four—

SHORTLAND: For order! If I had refused, we would have had riots. You weren't here, but the committees were very clear that they wished to have their own with their own—

KING DICK: The natural order of things—

SHORTLAND: Something like that, I believe, yes.

KING DICK: Only atheists and Jacobins would say anythin' else . . .

SHORTLAND (*uncomfortable and unnerved*): Those issues were raised.

KING DICK: So you listened to 'em. And you said yes.

SHORTLAND: This is an American problem, Mr Crafus.

KING DICK: And a British solution.

SHORTLAND: Tell me you're not happier in Four. Tell me you'd rather I broke it all up and mixed you all again.

KING DICK (*pauses, runs a hand over his hair. An uncomfortable time passes, then he straightens as if he has decided*): We'd be happier at home, we'd be happier if we wasn't fightin' and we'd be happier if we wasn't treated like we was lower than dogs. In Massachusetts, y'know, they promise all men are born free and equal. We'd be happier like that. But right now, we need each other. Right now, the men of Four need each other and need me to fight for 'em. Don't know 'bout the other prisons, but the men of Four would want to stay men of Four.

ACT TWO

2.1

Monday, 2 January 1815
Block Four

BY DARTMOOR's standards, the overnight snow had been thin and watery, settling no deeper than a few inches. The strong southwesterly carried the freezing air across the moor and deep into the prison blocks; the shutters had kept the flakes out, but little else. By dawn, the temperature inside was barely different to that outside.

Two slight, shivering boys flittered around King Dick's bed, then settled, one on each side of his mattress. They nodded to each other then folded the bedding back. In a single fluid movement, the King rolled over once, opened his eyes and sat bolt upright. He wiped his face with his hands.

'All quiet, Mr Daniels?' he said, his voice thick with sleep and rum.

'All quiet, King Dick,' said the boy.

'All well, Mr Singer?'

'All well, King Dick.'

'Very well, then.' The King stood, the blankets falling from him. He had slept in stockings, vest, jacket and trousers, worn for warmth but in truth barely fitting his huge frame. He loosened the trousers and held out his hand; Jonathan Singer handed him a favoured black woollen pair. He tugged each leg on then threw his yellow prison jacket to the ground. Alex Daniels handed him two white muslin shirts, one inside the other, and he pulled both on together. Alex stepped on to the mattress to button both up to their high collars.

'Sleep well, Mr Daniels?' said the King.

'Yes, sir, thank you, sir,' he replied, pressing home the last button. The King pushed both shirts into his trousers and Jonathan handed him a wide grey stitched leather belt with battered pewter buckle and he strapped it to his waist.

'Sash next,' he said, and Alex handed him a silver band with four gold stars sewn into the fabric. 'Made where, boys?'

'Haiti,' they parroted together.

'Which is?'

The boys glanced at each other to coordinate their words.

'An independent nation of free peoples,' they said, their words memorized but said with emphasis and vigour. King Dick nodded solemnly then adjusted the sash across his chest. He closed his eyes and inhaled slowly, untroubled by the malodorous air. 'I was born a slave,' he intoned, 'but nature gave me the soul of a free man.'

'Toussaint L'Ouverture, 1743 to 1803,' chanted Alex and Jonathan.

'Of course,' said the King. 'Good, good.' He opened his eyes. The lesson was over.

'So. Are we the first, Mr Singer?'

'Yes, King Dick. And Mr Snow, Mr Snow and Mr Penny are waiting for the keys.'

The King grunted appreciatively, his eyes quickly surveying the rows of hammocks and mattresses; if anyone else was stirring, they knew to keep their distance and their silence. He stepped off the mattress. Alex passed him a pair of black leather boots with brown leather trim at the top and front; square-headed nails on the bottom formed an ornate pattern around the edges. King Dick grunted again.

'Everyone admires my boots, don't they?'

'Yes, King Dick.'

74

'I admire them myself. And they fit only me. So . . .' He eased each foot past the bootstraps. 'Amazin' what that cobbler could manage, don't you think?'

'Yes, King Dick,' said Alex and Jonathan together. Their snatched glance and brief smile at each other anticipated the King's next comment. 'Though I seem to remember he needed a little . . . encouragement.'

'That he did, sir,' said Alex, smiling openly now. Next came a heavy brown leather jacket and a military greatcoat, but the King waved the coat away. 'Just some blankets for now, Alex. I can hear the turnkeys at the door. My hat 'n' bat, and we can go.'

One floor down, opposite Four's heavy double doors, Ned, Sam and Habs, dressed in as many layers of clothing as they could muster, sat shivering together on the cold stairs. Sam's first pipe of the day was freshly lit, enveloping them in a cloud of yellow smoke.

'That gotta be the piss of a fox you're smoking, cuz,' coughed Habs. 'Some swindlin' sailor sold you some bad flakes there and that's the truth.'

Sam looked aggrieved. 'Threepence for four ounces,' he said. 'I like it. Man in Two said it's called Virginian River.'

'Where foxes go to piss,' said Ned.

'Guaranteed,' said Habs, standing up. 'I swear my ass'll be ice before they open these goddamn doors.'

Across the yard, the turnkeys were about their work, two to each block. Habs could hear their handiwork. The cries of 'Tumble up and turn out! Tumble up and turn out!' were met always by the anger of woken men, as vicious as they were predictable.

'Son of a bitch!'

'Go back to yer English whore!'

'Kiss my arse, duck-fucker!'

In Blocks One, Two, Three, Five, Six and Seven, the

75

turnkeys would bark their morning greeting around the floors, occasionally loosening the hammock yarns of the most virulent and most drunk. The louder the crash of bodies, the more the English laughed. But they didn't enter Four. It was always different in Four.

The sound of heavy, booted steps approaching brought Habs, Sam and Ned to their feet in an instant. Two keys inserted and turned, two opened doors, two swathed turnkeys. It was a tiny moment, but Habs found the unlocking a daily emboldening, an unintended encouragement; even when conditions outside were worse than inside, their night was through and their incarceration, for a moment at least, lifted.

'Good mornin', Mr Turnkey One and Mr Turnkey Two,' said Habs. 'Whoever you are under those mufflers.'

'King Dick knows what time it is,' said Ned. 'He's already hard at it. He don't need . . .'

One of the turnkeys pulled down his scarf. 'We know. He don't need the English to tell him when the day starts. You tell us every day, but we're tellin' you, anyway. Please inform His Darkest Majesty that he needs to tumble up and turn out, along with the rest of his poor, unfortunate subjects.' They turned and were gone, and so missed Ned's dropped-trousers salute.

'My naked weapon is out!' he called.

'And it'll snap like a tiny icicle if you don't get decent,' said Sam, lighting some more Virginian River. 'C'mon. We'll find King Dick is this way.'

The ground floor was stirring and thick with tobacco smoke. Some had heard the exchange with the turnkeys, others needed the piss tub or their first pipe, but everyone awake knew King Dick was on his way. Men slid from their hammocks then lashed them away; they woke neighbours and called warnings. A man holding tightly to his wooden crutch hopped past them with a coffee pot in his free hand.

'When your fire is lit, we'll be your first customers,' called Sam.

'Penny each,' came the reply, followed by a series of racking wet coughs and noisy hawking.

Ned, Sam and Habs looked at each other.

'Maybe someone else can be his first customer,' muttered Ned.

Behind them, they heard deliberate footsteps.

'Good mornin', Mr Penny and both Mr Snows,' called King Dick, as he descended the stairs.

Habs felt the voice reverberate in his chest as he heard it with his ears, rich, full and deep. Once more, the King wore the bearskin hat high on his head; the rest of his torso was draped in blankets of contrasting colours. The diminutive forms of Alex Daniels and Jonathan Singer peered from behind him.

He returned the greeting. 'Mornin', King Dick,' he said, and, glancing at the boys, touched the knuckle of his index finger to his forehead. The King swung his club absentmindedly, its handle now tied to his wrist with a leather thong.

'Show me,' he said, and strode away, a ship's captain inspecting the decks.

A few of the shutters had been flung open but, for the most part, they were still closed against the cold. A thin, milky light barely illuminated the King's path but was just sufficient for him to follow the forest of upright wooden stanchions that lined the floor. Eighteen inches apart, they gave each man a space of nine inches for his hammock. As King Dick walked the aisles, some men nodded; others saluted as they squeezed past. He called to some by name, and embraced others.

'Damn but you're good at this,' Habs muttered.

Not everyone was awake. The King stopped at a stanchion tied with three clearly occupied hammocks. In the lowest, a fully clothed sailor lay spreadeagled across the stretch of hemp, two empty bottles wedged under his neck.

Above him, a blanket covered all but a sleeper's booted foot, and on the top hammock, barely six inches above the King's head, a single upturned hand protruded over the side. The King looked ominously from berth to berth, the club spinning loose on its thong as it dangled from his wrist.

'Thoughts, Mr Snow?' he said.

Habs stepped forward and considered the spreadeagled man. 'That's Mr Kale, so the others'll be Dean and Boyce. I think a turnout might be quite somethin', King Dick.'

The King flicked his wrist, caught the club. 'I think so, too,' he said, and, reaching up, pulled hard on the top hammock. The hemp cloth spun on its clews, depositing the still-sleeping sailor on top of the man below. They cracked heads, woke with a roar and toppled on to the splayed Kale beneath them. His hammock split in two and all three men lay stunned and groaning on the granite floor. From the wrecked beds, a collection of dice, cards and coins scattered around them.

'Mr Penny,' said the King, his voice barely more than a growl, 'will you collect those, please? Mr Singer, Mr Daniels, perhaps you could assist?' Ned and the boys scrabbled to retrieve the fallen evidence, then offered it to the King in fistfuls. He waved them away.

'On your feet, sailors,' King Dick ordered. Still stunned, the three fallen men struggled to stand. The King, slowly, meticulously, wrapped just enough of the thong around his wrist to place the club's ribbed handle neatly in his palm. Running his fingers along its shaft, he appeared to find a blemish a few inches from its tip. He picked at it with his fingernails, fussing, then seemingly content, polished the club on his trousers. The three tottering prisoners urinated where they stood.

King Dick stepped forward.

'Asleep past turnout; too much grog and gamin'.' The King prowled around them. 'You know the rules, and you know that gamin' happens upstairs or outside. If it happens inside, in the dark, under blankets . . . well, then, what am I to conclude?' Kale, Dean and Boyce were now very awake and very scared. They inched closer together, trembling. Dean and Boyce both had blood in their hair. Kale wrapped his arms around his ribs.

'Sorry, King Dick,' began Dean, his head bowed, his speech slow. 'We ain't tryin' to take your money or nothin', really we ain't. It was the peace, we forgot . . .'

Not good enough, thought Habs.

'Oh!' the King breathed, as he walked behind the men. 'After your celebration, you was goin' to declare your winnings?' His words had slowed to a drawl; everyone knew what was coming next.

Habs held his breath. Two small hands found their way into his and he held them fast.

The King paused. One of the men, Kale, frantically turned his head to see where he had gone. He found the club six inches from his eyes.

'You wanna watch?' said King Dick, and pushed the tip hard against Kale's forehead. The King twisted his wrist one way, then the other, grinding the club into Kale's skin.

'N–no, King Dick,' he whimpered. The King held him there, as he squirmed like a worm on a fishhook. Habs counted the seconds. He got to eleven.

'Too late,' said the King. Kale didn't see his wrist snap, just felt the club momentarily lift from his forehead then slam into him with the force of a battering ram. As he staggered then collapsed, the King, both hands to the handle, swung the club into Dean's ribs, then, reversing the action, into Boyce's. Both men dropped to the floor and Boyce took an extra blow to the head. King Dick knelt by the fallen men, gently touching each one with his club. 'I want two shillings by tomorrow. Each. Now, go see the physician.'

Rising to his feet, he strode off, Habs and the rest of the entourage running to catch up.

'I seen worse,' breathed Habs, relieved.

'Don't they know nothin'?' whispered Ned, glancing back at the injured men. 'You can wake up here with most anything you might fancy, but dice? Why, tha's terrible. Cards? An abomination!'

Sam shook his head. 'They say gamblin' the French disease. Well, before they left, we all got infected.'

Ahead of King Dick, the room had emptied. Now, the ground floor had its shutters open, its hammocks stowed and its mess tables put out for breakfast. The stench of sweat, smoke and urine was slowly being blown away by the winds from the moor and replaced by the smell of breakfast cooking in the kitchens. As they reached the final stanchions, Habs noticed two men still in their hammocks, one curled into a tight ball, the other sat hugging his knees. He steered the King in their direction.

'And what is this?' called King Dick. Both men looked up. Their movements were slow and painful. 'What ails you, then? Are you sick?'

Sam went closer. 'They're bruised, King Dick. And cut, too.'

The King stepped closer. They both sported deep burgundy bruises around the eyes, and the knee-hugging man had a deep cut on his arm running from shoulder to elbow. Torn sheets had formed impromptu bandages; they were all soaked in blood.

'Speak,' said the King. 'Explain.'

Behind him, the sound of hundreds of sailors clattering down the stairs filled the room. The two injured men glanced quickly at each other but said nothing.

The King nodded. 'Very well. I seen that look before. I seen the fear. I'll make some guesses. You were last to bed. Found yourselves outnumbered.'

An almost imperceptible nod from the knee-hugger.

'Rough Allies.'

80

Another nod and then, finally, some words. King Dick leaned in close to hear.

'Didn't have no chance,' the man whispered through swollen lips. 'Now, me and Daniel there can't get up soon of a mornin' no more.'

'You shoulda come to me,' said the King. 'Why didn't you come to me straight 'way?' The two men looked down, unwilling to meet King Dick's eye.

He sighed. 'If you won't speak, we'll do the list. You were buggerin' each other?'

Both men shook their heads.

'Tradin' bad liquor?'

More denials.

'So gamblin', then. Gamblin' without the King's approval.'

Neither man moved, both frozen in fear.

The King turned to Habs, exasperated. 'Is every man here trying to swindle the King? Do they not know we spend all that money on the shows?'

'I'm sure they do, King Dick,' said Habs. 'And these seem to have been punished already.'

This time, the King's club cracked a stanchion. 'If there's punishment to be had, by God Almighty, King Dick will do it, not some cocksuckers from Six!' His explosion of rage terrified everyone who heard it. 'Goddamn those Allies to Hell, I will not have this. Get some breakfast for these men.' He handed coins to Alex and Jonathan, and they scampered for the door. 'We'll send for the physician. We'll not let this stand.'

2.2

Dartmoor Hospital

THE MEN of the *Eagle* lingered as long as they could. The room was stark and high-ceilinged but its roaring fire was the first proper heat they had felt in weeks. They stood as close as they dared, relishing every flame.

'Will, I do declare you're cooking nicely,' said Joe.

Roche was the closest, and his woollen coat, still soaked with rain, condensation and snow from the day before, was steaming.

'Smellin' like a laundry is better'n smellin' like a latrine,' he said, arms spread wide to absorb as much heat as he could. 'And if I burn, why, this is the place to be. There'll be nurses and their lotions right at hand.'

Joe scoffed. 'So when they've stopped dealing with smallpox and jail fever, they can attend to your scalds and blisters?'

Roche smiled, his eyes shut. 'That's 'bout it, Mr Hill. That is jus' 'bout it.

The sailors formed a ramshackle queue. Three plump men sat at desks, glancing between their records and their new arrivals. A weighing machine and a pile of prison uniforms stood behind them, an empty chair before them, and the largest of the men gestured with his dip-pen, waving the sailors forward, his voice shrill and impatient.

'Come. Let's get this done.'

None of the *Eagle* men moved. 'Go bugger yer eyes,' muttered Lord. 'I ain't leavin' this fire.'

'Really?' piped the clerk. He was standing now.

'Makin' Englishmen mad seems to be somethin' we do with ease,' said Roche, still staring into the fire. 'We can have sport with this one. He's puffed up and red-faced already. Let's make him yearn for the feeble-minded French.'

There was just one guard left in the room, a lumpy, pock-faced youth who was easing dirt from his fingernails with a small knife. It took him a while to realize that the irate clerk was shouting at him.

'We need order here, sir!'

The guard looked startled, pulled the rifle from his shoulder and walked towards the men of the *Eagle*. Before he'd had a chance to be threatening, the Americans took him by surprise.

'Make way for this fine soldier!' called Roche. 'Give him space by the fire, please.' He added, 'Are you cold, sir? You look as though a few minutes by this fine fire would stand you well on a day like today. We Americans shouldn't have all the heat, now should we?'

The guard looked bemused. 'S'pose not,' he said.

'English heat for English bones!' called Joe. 'Can't say fairer than that, can we?'

The guard edged closer. 'No, I don't think you can.'

Joe held out his hand. 'I'm Joe Hill and these are my shipmates from the *Eagle*. What's your name, soldier?' The militiaman was about to tell him when an eruption of right-eous fury shut his mouth.

'You damnable fool! Soldier, please approach the bench. This instant!' Now, the other two clerks had pulled them-selves to their feet and were waving their ledgers. As the guard shuffled away from the fire, the men of the *Eagle* laughed heartily.

'When you've faced an English broadside of forty can-non or more,' called Roche to the clerks, 'you'll not be scared by men flappin' their books!'

'But as an act of goodwill,' added Joe, 'as the war is over and we are at peace, we will agree to be signed up to your register. Just as soon as we're warm, eh, boys?'

The militiaman returned, his face flushed and rifle cocked. 'You line up by Mr Nellist now or he says you'll be in the cachot.' Then he added quietly, 'And I'll be there, too, I reckon.'

'What did he say?' Roche asked Joe.

'He said we sign their book or we get thrown in the pit.'

'And d'you believe there's a warm fire in that pit, Joe?'

'That I do not.'

'So . . .' Roche saluted the guard and led the way to the clerks' desk, pulling Joe behind him. He sat down and bowed to the clerks. 'I'm Will Roche from the *Eagle*, and this man with me is Joe Hill – he's my translator, case I can't understan' you.' The laughs behind him only served to agitate Nellist further.

The sound of a heavy door opening made everyone turn and suddenly the three clerks were on their feet, Nellist smoothing his shirt as he spoke. 'Mrs Shortland. Dr Magrath. We were just about to start. Please . . .'

Nellist pulled out two chairs as the newcomers approached the tables. Mrs Shortland wore her high-waisted Empire-style dress neatly; her hair was pulled back in a chignon. Behind her, a drawn-looking man with unkempt grey hair and a cane limped as he tried to keep up with her. Having reached the table, the woman paused and smiled at the prisoners.

The physician held her chair for her as she sat. A low, square décolleté was softened by a chemisette worn underneath; every sailor present was transfixed.

'Gentlemen, good morning,' she said. 'My name is Elizabeth Shortland, and my husband is Captain Shortland, the Agent here. This is Dr George Magrath. I assist him in the hospital and, together, we are responsible for your health. We will do what we can for you while you are here. Which, God and your Congress willing, will not be too long.' Her voice was powerful; there was no doubt where the authority in the room lay. 'Dr Magrath?'

The physician rose awkwardly to his feet, sweeping his hair from his forehead as he did so.

'Yes, hello. I'm Dr Magrath. You'll be seeing me most days, I fear. My hospital is just down the corridor here. It is full today, as ever; Dartmoor is no place to be sick, gentlemen. But we strive, Mrs Shortland, my staff and I, to do our best. I can't stop the pneumonia or the measles, but I am in the process of inoculating everyone against smallpox. You know the signs. If you see anyone with the rash . . .'

Roche turned his head to Joe. 'Where's he from? That accent is familiar . . .'

Joe leaned down. 'Ireland, I reckon,' he said. 'You understand him then?'

'What I understan',' whispered Roche, 'is that the good doctor is certainly injectin' the good lady whenever he can. Look at 'em watchin' each other.'

Joe reprimanded Roche with a punch on the shoulder. Joe was still smiling as the physician finished his speech.

'Also, if I may,' he said, looking around the men in front of him, seemingly engaging each one in turn. 'Your allowance, when you get it, is tuppence ha'penny a day. That, I know, can get you five chews of tobacco or a pot of beer, but I've seen men go hungry here for their thirst and need to expectorate. A few pounds of potatoes from the market will serve you better.' He nodded to Mrs Shortland to indicate he had finished, and she rose to her feet again.

'Once you are weighed, you will be given fresh clothes. We have uniforms in most sizes. You are to take a woollen cap, one cloth jacket, two cotton shirts, two stockings, one pair of trousers, one vest. They are supposed to last eighteen months, but it looks like you won't need them for that long.

Mr Nellist here will need to take records. Please help him, and this shouldn't take long.'

'We ain't in no hurry, miss,' called Goffe. 'We can stay for tea if you like.' The men laughed; all except Nellist, who pointed his pen at Roche.

'You first. Name?'

'And good mornin' to you, sir,' Roche replied. 'How is Mrs Nellist today?' He sat, grinning at the reddening clerk.

'Do you have a name?' Nellist said curtly, his lips barely moving.

Roche leaned forward and, mimicking his tone, he said, 'Yes, thank you, sir, I do.'

'And what is it?'

'What is what?'

Nellist had had enough. Calling the guard over, he put his elbows on the desk, folding his fingers together. With the militiaman standing behind him, he tried again.

'I don't know if you have seen the cachot yet, sailor. Essentially, it's a bricked-up shit-pit. You boil to death in summer, you freeze to death in winter and it is where you are heading if you cannot answer the next three questions. Understood?'

'I think it's your accent,' said Joe, stepping forward. 'Try again.'

Nellist threw a disbelieving glance at Joe. With the other clerks poised with their pens, and Elizabeth Shortland and Dr Magrath listening, he sighed deeply.

'What is your name?' he asked.

'He wants your name,' said Joe.

'Oh. Will Roche of the *Eagle*. You should've said . . .'

'What type of ship is the *Eagle*?'

'He wants to know . . .'

'It's one of America's finest brigs,' Roche continued, understanding perfectly. 'Sixteen guns and many prizes.'

Nellist's eyes narrowed. 'Not a Navy vessel, then. You

are a privateer.' He scowled. 'Little more than a chartered pirate.'

'A proud privateer, to be precise,' corrected Roche. 'We are savin' our country and more than a match for your fat-assed admirals.'

Nellist glowered. 'Where are you from?' he managed.

'Boston, Massachusetts. And I'll be back there before—'

'Age?' said Nellist, cutting across him.

'Fifty-two.'

'Complexion,' said Nellist, now staring at Roche's face and dictating to his clerks, 'sallow. Scars on nose and forehead. Now' – he gestured to the scales behind him – 'you need to be weighed and measured. Then be gone with you, Roche.'

'Actually,' said Joe, 'that's *Mr* Roche.' And before Nellist could complain he continued, 'Joe Hill, also from Boston, Massachusetts. I'm sixteen, complexion poor after being in your prison-ship hells for weeks on end but normally radiant. I'll go and get measured.'

'Sit down,' said Nellist. 'You'll go when I tell you to.'

Elizabeth Shortland appeared at his shoulder, smiling at Joe. 'Mr Hill, good morning. Your accent is different, I believe. You sound a little English at times, if you don't mind me saying.'

Joe was taken aback; he couldn't remember the last time a woman had addressed him directly.

'Oh. Well. Good morning to you.' He found himself bowing slightly. 'Yes. I was born here. In Suffolk. We – my parents and I – left when I was two. I'm told I sound like my father, which might explain the accent. But I am a naturalized American now. I have my papers about me still.' Joe reached into his pocket, but Nellist banged the desk with his palm.

'Scoundrel!' he shouted. 'Your "naturalization" papers will not serve you here. You were born English yet you fight for our enemy? You'll be hanged for a rebel and no mistake!'

Elizabeth Shortland sighed. 'Oh, Mr Nellist, haven't

87

you heard? The war is over. Let's not keep stoking those fires. Come, Mr Hill, let's get you weighed before Mr Nellist finds his noose.' Joe stood gratefully from the chair, saluted the now purple-faced clerk and walked over to the scales. Another clerk adjusted a calibrated shaft with a brass pointer then balanced some weights on a dish.

'Those are nasty cuts on your head.' Elizabeth Short-land had followed him round. 'Are they healing? Would you like me or Dr Magrath to examine them?'

Joe, embarrassed, avoided her gaze. 'No, thank you,' he said. 'They're healing just fine.'

She looked unconvinced. 'If you change your mind . . .'

Joe nodded his thanks.

'Do you still have family in Suffolk?' she asked then.

'Oh yes, ma'am,' said Joe, relieved at the switch of con-versation. 'I believe my grandparents are still alive there. In a place called Dunwich, but I have been at sea for so long I've had no news for many a year.'

Her face clouded. 'You poor boy,' she said, and for a moment Joe was sure she was going to reach out to comfort him.

'It's no matter,' said Joe. 'We'll be going home soon enough.' Am I reassuring her now? he thought. 'You have seen the peace? Your husband read it out . . .'

'Yes, I have seen it,' she said. 'Though I am not sure what will change.' She paused, and Joe wondered if he was about to discuss the terms of the peace with the Agent's wife, but then she emerged from whatever reverie had settled over her and looked at him brightly. 'Well, good day to you, Mr Hill,' she said, and, clasping a small, round box between her fingers, was gone.

Joe breathed deeply. 'Lavender and rosewater,' he said to the weighing clerk. 'In case you were wondering what her scent is.'

The man shrugged. 'Certainly makes a change from piss and shit,' he muttered. 'Get the uniform and be gone.'

Upstairs in Ward B, which echoed with the cries of the sick, Elizabeth Shortland pulled the bedsheets tight then brushed them smooth. She glanced again at her patient before moving on.

The fifty-bed ward was, as usual, full; there were the newly injured from a recent brawl on three mattresses laid out along the aisle. Dr Magrath, a wooden splint in his hand, was crouched over one man, whose howls of pain had been tormenting the ward. He was quieter now, Magrath's words and medicine finally taking their effect. She would be alongside George in eight beds' time. She knew they would speak. Her time on the wards was usually a frenzy of poultices, bandages and ligatures, but where there was an opportunity for innocent interaction, they always took it.

Elizabeth's next patient, an exhausted sailor from Two with a severe coffee scald over most of his face, was wide awake. She found some words of comfort for him as she adjusted the gauze and he managed a murmur of thanks in return. All the sick men wanted was a word, a smile, some encouragement; she had become very good at that. A 'gift' is how George had put it. She had been surprised how natural it had felt, this tending the sick.

Now she poured a linctus on to a spoon and held it out for a recovering sailor. He swallowed, grimaced, then nodded his thanks before falling back to his pillow. As she turned to move on, he was there.

'And how are your patients, Elizabeth?'

He meant one thing only: is anyone showing any smallpox symptoms? Broken bones, burns, stab wounds, influenza and syphilis he could handle, but any smallpox and the prison would cease to function.

'All is well. They are recovering slowly, George. Lingering even, in some cases. No rashes.'

'We need more vaccine,' he said. 'I'm afraid my supplies are too old to be properly effective. I am promised more by the end of the week, but I am impatient, Elizabeth.'

'I know you are, George.'

Then he added, more softly, 'I imagine that was your Willoughby downstairs.'

The briefest of smiles. 'Was it that obvious?'

'Only to me. Who is he?'

'He's Joe Hill from Boston. From an English family. They moved to America when he was two.'

'One for the recruiters?'

The question pulled her up short. Time was, she would without a second thought have marked Joe Hill for the Royal Navy. Her nation's battle was her battle, her husband's battle hers, too. But now she shivered.

'I'll not do their work again. This war is done.' She fidgeted with an untucked blanket.

'Well, if the war is done,' said Magrath, 'then that is good news for Willoughby, no?'

She nodded. 'Of course. But . . . if the prison empties of prisoners, we'll be moved on, too.'

He moved behind her, bent to inspect the patient. 'Come,' he murmured. 'We need supplies.'

There was a small store cupboard for medical supplies between the two wards. With both doors open, they effectively disappeared from the view of anyone in wards A and B, orderlies and patients alike.

'Elizabeth,' he began, his manner earnest but his eyes smiling. Leaning against the shelves meant he didn't need his cane. She felt his hands pull her close.

'George,' she said.

'I am devoted to my patients. Devoted to getting as many of these men home as I can.' His words were softly spoken but, as usual, steely with intent. 'But you know I am devoted to you, too. So, as long as you and the Transport Office want me here, this is where I'll be.'

She wrapped her arms around him. 'Well, I have a feeling the Transport Office will need you here for the foreseeable future.' She pulled her head back, looked straight at him. 'I can't go back, George, not to how it used to be. I couldn't bear that listless existence again.'

His forehead wrinkled in sympathy.

'Do you remember that first influenza outbreak?' she said, her voice barely more than a whisper. 'When Thomas suggested I help you?'

'My God, I was exhausted,' said Magrath, shuddering at the memory. 'I could hardly stand. You were a godsend.'

She sighed again. 'And I had forgotten – somehow completely forgotten – how much I loved it as a girl. The medicines, the potions, the healing, the – the sheer magic of it all. My father used to let me itemize the contents of his medical bag. Over and over, I'd lay out his instruments, the bandages and the mysterious brown bottles. Then one day – I must have been about six – I told him I, too, wanted to be a doctor.'

'Oh,' said Magrath, frowning. 'I can guess what happened next.'

'He laughed,' said Elizabeth, the resentment and embarrassment flooding back. 'He actually laughed.'

'Well, if I may,' said Magrath, 'he was a fool.'

'Sometimes, yes. I see that now. But I don't remember mentioning it again,' she said.

Elizabeth was silent now, her head resting on his shoulder. She cherished these stolen moments, their secret dance while the hospital and the prison carried on without them.

'When I married Thomas I had these grand ideas of foreign travel, Thomas's swift promotion, an ambassadorial posting with me by his side. Exotic society. And I ended up here. How stupid I was. I wonder sometimes if I hate this place every bit as much as the prisoners do.'

'Well, I am grateful you did come here,' he whispered. 'Looking back, I can see that I was lost.'

'No, you were a brilliant physician with the respect of your patients. As you are now.'

'And yet I was lost. You had to practically throw yourself at me before I realized what was happening.'

'George, I did throw myself at you.'

He laughed at the memory. 'I couldn't for the life of me think why I had to put down my books.'

'I think I explained well enough.'

'You did indeed, Elizabeth. As I recall – and I do quite often – it was an excellent analysis.'

2.3

The Market Square

THE GUARD with the still-dirty fingernails had slammed the gate behind them, and the freshly uniformed men of the *Eagle*, having pushed their way through a densely packed crowd of unruly prisoners, were marvelling at the sensual splendour that the market had brought to Dartmoor. It was the same square, dominated by the same blocks, surrounded by the same two walls, but, for the moment, everything had changed.

First, the colours – reds, greens, yellows, purples, pinks and blues; then the smells – fish, fresh meat, milk, beer. The drabness, the soul-destroying drabness of prison life, had temporarily lifted. Monday through Saturday between nine and midday, some sort of external normality descended. It was the lifeblood of the sailors' lives.

'I think I can smell turnips,' said Joe, sounding shocked. 'I didn't know they even had a smell.'

'And . . .' began Goffe dreamily, 'other people.'

'You mean women,' said Roche, staring at the traders.

'Yes, I mean women. I had forgotten how beautiful they are.'

'Mrs Shortland sure looked like a woman to me,' said Roche.

'But these' – Goffe pointed at the market-stall holders – 'these're women like us. These're women who might take a fancy to us . . .'

'Not when we're dressed in yellow,' said Joe, 'and with the Transport Office's mark stamped all over us.'

93

'But these're women who wish to sell their wares,' said Roche.

'To anyone who has money,' cried Joe, 'and we have none.'

'Well, we'll jus' stare, then,' said Goffe, staring.

Joe walked around the rows of traders' stalls; covered crates, trestle tables and slabs of granite had been pressed into service. He stopped at a display of small cakes and pastries, drooling, his mouth flooding with saliva. He groaned with longing. The man behind the table, swathed in scarves, appraised this new customer with old clothes over his arm.

'New uniform, new arrival,' he said. 'Another poor Yankee bastard. I got queen cakes, currant cakes and carrot cakes. And pumpkin bread. Threepence each.'

Joe shrugged. 'I have no money,' he said. 'Not yet, anyways.'

'I could trade for your hat,' said the man. 'I like a tricorn I do. Any two cakes you fancy.'

Joe tugged it firmly to his head. 'It's not for sale.'

The man's eyes narrowed. 'You *are* new,' he said. 'You'll soon find everything's for sale in here.'

'Maybe,' said Joe, 'but not the hat.'

'Well, bugger off, then,' said the trader, waving him aside.

Reluctantly, Joe peeled himself away. He forced his way down the aisles, past mounds of coats, old boots, vegetables and fish. Behind each one stood a man or woman hailing prisoners as they passed, calling their names and shouting out prices. In front of the top gates, a large number of the long-bearded Rough Allies had gathered around beer tables.

Then came a voice Joe recognized.

'Well, the grey-eyed mornin' smiles indeed!' called Habs, from behind a baker's tray. 'I thought the sun come out but it was just the burnin' bright yellow men of the *Eagle*, now weighed, measured and recorded, I bet.'

Joe twisted and squeezed his way over. 'Grey is right,' he said, 'but those clouds are thinning, the barometer rising.'

'And how do you like your new outfit?'

Joe grimaced. 'They're the first clean clothes I've worn for three months. They've been warmed by the fire. And I hate them with all my heart.'

Habs laughed, head tilted skywards and hoop earrings swinging against his neck. ''Course you do. Everyone does. But we can trade, swap, borrow. You'd be amazed what comes your way.'

'I had no idea,' said Joe. 'Really. It seems like the whole of Dartmoor is here.'

'It's the peace,' said Habs. 'Everyone is spendin' like they'll be home in the mornin'. The beer will be soon sold and then we should all look out. Too much wild talk, too many sore heads.' He tailed off and Joe followed his eyeline.

'What is it?' he asked.

Habs nodded at two black sailors twenty yards away, leaning casually against the market square's lower wall. 'When's the last time you saw your piece of French scenery?'

'Can't recall,' said Joe. 'I just left it behind, I think. Why?'

'Well, somehow,' said Habs, 'it's now in the care of two of our young boxers.'

Joe looked again. The pale blue and white of the painted wood showed clearly behind one of the men. 'Friends of the poor bugger who lost the fight on Saturday?'

'Friends of the poor bugger who got felled by a piece of wood, yes,' said Habs. 'They musta smuggled it out and back in again.'

'So they know what they're doing.'

The two boxers had eyes everywhere and were speaking constantly.

'You wanna reclaim your wood?' asked Habs.

'No, I think it's yours,' said Joe.

'Too late,' said Habs. 'Look who's comin' past.'

95

A Rough Ally tottered in front of Joe, hands holding a tarp hat firmly to his head. The boxers had seen him too, guessed his trajectory, knew he was within range.

'If he manages to walk straight,' said Habs, 'he'll walk right into 'em.'

'And take it in the face,' said Joe.

'Just like Saturday night, then.'

Both boxers were off the wall, the wood held lightly between them, eyes darting between the gates and the staggering Ally. Briefly, his balance went and he stepped away from the trap, only to veer straight back again. He didn't look up, didn't see the swinging timber.

Most in the square heard the crack of wood on skull; very few saw what happened. The boxers had timed their attack well; as the Rough Ally hit the ground, both men were already through the gates.

'They'll be inside Four in seconds,' said Habs. 'Safe.'

'Until they come out again,' muttered Joe, but didn't force the point.

The Allies swarmed to their man, pushing and yelling as they went. A few ran from the square, only to return, shaking their heads. The square buzzed, then, slowly, the trade resumed.

'A grand morning so far,' said Habs. 'The *Eagle* crew are dressed and a bastard with a beard has had a beatin'. Let's get some food. You're lookin' hungry again.'

'Hungry and poor,' said Joe. 'None of us has a cent.'

'Well, let me introduce you to Betsy Wade, watcher of the square and one of Tavistock's most beautiful bakers.'

Joe hadn't noticed that Habs was standing next to a woman. Enveloped in a brown shawl with a dark green bonnet that tied under her chin, she smiled, then curtsied.

'Actually,' she said, 'Tavistock's only beautiful baker. How do you do, Mr Hill.' She offered her hand and Joe shook it clumsily.

96

'Joe. Please call me Joe.'

'If you're hungry, Joe, we're always here, same spot. High in the top-right corner by the storehouse – best position. We see all the fights. And this is my friend, Martha Slater. She helps me with the ovens.' Another muffled-up woman appeared, long strands of red hair framing a face that was even younger than Betsy's. Another curtsey.

'Betsy. Martha,' said Joe. 'How far is Tavistock?' He was talking to Betsy, but he was looking at the tray of loaves in front of her.

Habs laughed and tossed a coin to him. 'Here. Till tomorrow. You'll get your allowance then, but eat now.'

Joe's eyes sparkled. 'Really?' He passed the penny to the baker.

'Help yourself,' said Betsy, and Joe snatched the nearest loaf, tearing it roughly as he forced handfuls into his mouth.

Betsy and Habs laughed. 'No breakfast in Seven today?' he asked.

Joe took it in turns to shake then nod his head, unable to speak.

'What's your bread ration again, Habs?' asked Martha, her voice a gentle, even whispery Devonian burr.

'Most days it's one and a half loaves,' said Habs, still watching Joe devour his penny's worth. 'And it's gone by noon.'

'So how can he be this hungry?' wondered Martha. 'Most folk round here could feed a family for three days on that. Is that all you get?'

Betsy folded her arms tightly across her chest. 'No, they're just getting started,' she said. 'Then there's a pound of beef, half a pound of cabbage, turnips and onions.'

Martha whistled her amazement. 'A day? If most men round here heard that, there'd be a queue outside wanting to stay here.'

'Maybe there would,' said Habs, 'and while they're

enjoyin' the King's food, they can catch his smallpox, measles, rubella and pneumonia, and die in his graveyard, too.'

'Sorry, Habs,' she whispered.

At last, Joe swallowed. 'Prison bread is like eating tar and sawdust. This' – he waved what remained of his loaf – 'this is heaven itself.'

Betsy kissed Joe's cheek. 'That,' she said, 'is what happens when you say lovely things about my bread.'

Joe offered a chunk to Habs, but he wasn't looking or listening.

'Habs?'

'It's Lane,' he said, his voice changed in an instant, all levity gone. 'Comin' this way. Cobb, too. I knew that fight would bring 'em out.'

Through the square's lower gates, two Rough Allies were approaching. They both wore extravagant, forked beards elaborately worked; small black ribbons and string had been deployed to separate and shape each half. The taller man had the more fulsome beard, each prong twisted into a spiral. The shorter sported a battered black stovepipe hat and clenched a cigarillo between his teeth. Their advance was all poise and swagger, and heads turned as they passed then stayed turned to see what the two were doing.

'I recognize them,' said Joe. 'They obviously believe themselves to be some kind of pirate.'

'A pirate'd have more honour,' said Habs.

'Which one is which?' asked Joe.

'Cobb's in the hat, he's in charge. We got no officers here, we got Horace Cobb instead. Spent his time back home counterfeitin' and swindlin', so they say. He don't normally come out to the market. Lane's the madman with the curly beard. The gaps are on account of the burnt face he got when a pistol blew up. Guaranteed he'll have a weapon on him,' said Habs. 'And a shillin' says it's you they'll be talkin' to.'

'Haven't got a shilling,' said Joe.

'They'd steal it from you if you did, anyways,' said Habs. 'They just a band o' thieves, Joe, that's all. It's like their church. It's the one thing they all believe in – helpin' themselves to everythin'. Clear your stalls, Betsy.'

From behind him came the sounds of scores of loaves being swept into a basket. Cobb and Lane strode to within a few yards of Joe and Habs, as though they were about to march straight through them, then stopped abruptly. The dozen Rough Allies who had appeared in their wake fanned out, protecting their leaders. Lane looked as if he was about to speak but deferred, with difficulty, to Cobb. As Habs predicted, it was Joe they were after.

'Joe Hill, is it?' said Cobb, ash from his cigarillo dropping into his beard as he spoke. He sounded as if he'd been smoking since dawn.

'It is,' said Joe. He felt his tattooed skin tighten.

'Nice speech you gave yesterday,' said Cobb.

Joe didn't respond.

'D'you see what happened just now? One of our men was assaulted. Viciously.'

Joe shook his head. 'I'm sorry, no, we were just eating our bread here. We missed whatever it was.'

Cobb nodded. 'Of course. How is it in Seven?' His words were clipped, he sounded foreign somehow, but Joe couldn't place his accent.

Joe shrugged. 'Same as in Six?' Then, thinking that maybe he'd sounded too curt, he added, 'It's a shit-hole, but I've seen worse.'

Cobb nodded again and it was Lane's turn.

'Mr Hill,' he said, his voice strangely high-pitched. 'We wanted to warn you. We're concerned with the company you keep.'

Joe's flesh crawled again.

'And what business is that rightly of yours?' he said.

The attendant Allies bristled. Lane cocked his head to

one side, apparently surprised. 'Mr Hill,' he said, 'you're new here. You may not know how things work.' His beard twitched and jumped with every word. 'I am Edwin Lane, this is Horace Cobb, and we lead the Rough Allies.'

'I know who you are.'

Lane seemed pleased with that. 'Good, well, you'll find us good friends to have on your side. *If* you want to work with us.'

'You want to work with us, Joe Hill?' asked Cobb, exhaling a cloud of smoke in Habs's direction.

'Seems unlikely,' said Joe, his hands deep in his pockets and balled into fists.

One of the Allies spat.

Lane frowned. His voice crept higher. 'You a nigger-lover, Mr Hill? Is that what you are?'

Joe felt every cut on his scalp throb. His voice came out louder than he intended. 'I know Mr Snow here, if that's what you mean.'

'We are . . . *separate* here, Mr Hill. To avoid . . . contamination. You are Seven. *They* are Four. It's for our mutual benefit.'

'I have heard that said.'

''Course you have,' acknowledged Lane. 'The Negro always tends to violence and lawlessness. They can't help it, it's just their manner. The way they are. Best if we . . . keep out of their way. That's the way the good Lord intended it to be, and that's the way it should stay.'

'I . . .'

'Leave it, Joe,' said Habs, 'leave it. Don't take no notice of 'em. They won't be wantin' trouble here when they got trouble with their own.' He pointed to the lower gates.

The market had a surprise visitor.

2.4

The Market Square

UNLIKE EVERYONE else, King Dick wasn't shopping. He stood momentarily by the lower gates, surveying the square in front of him. Head high, club loosely resting in the crook of his neck, like a shouldered rifle, his eyes darting from stall to stall. Predator, thought Joe, the word flashing across his mind as the King spotted his prey. He moved with deadly purpose and precision, his eyes locked on his target. Where they saw him coming, the crowd moved aside. Where they didn't, he used his club. Cobb and Lane disappeared.

Men were pushed into stalls in his wake. Betsy hastily scooped the remaining loaves to her chest. Joe and Martha threw what they could into a basket, seconds before three men fell on to her table, splitting the wood in two places.

Joe watched the King move, then looked at Habs. 'This is what he does, isn't it?'

'This is what he does, and this is how he does it,' agreed Habs. 'It's why he's the King.'

'Where did Cobb and Lane go?'

'Who cares? C'mon. You gotta see this.'

Habs and Joe pushed their way towards the melee, reaching the beer tables just after King Dick. The crowd here were slower to respond and the King cut a swathe through the revellers, Habs and Joe stepping gingerly over the bruised and battered. The King forced his way to where three heavily bearded men stood laughing and toasting each other with large jugs of ale. One spotted his arrival and fled, the others were too slow and too late.

'That's Parker and Tupper from Six,' said Habs, speaking quickly in Joe's ear. 'And that was Wilson who ran away. Last night, they set upon two of our men from Four.'

'So it's nothing to do with the boxers?'

'Nothin' at all.'

'An eye for an eye, then.'

'Goddamn right. They're villains and thugs. And they got away with it till King Dick came,' said Habs.

The clouds had thinned, the light in the square now brighter than it had been all day; it gave each man present a sharply defined shadow. For a few moments, the King stood motionless, hands on hips, club swinging on its strap, his eyes fixed on the startled, trembling men in front of him. Parker was hunched and round-faced, his friend shorter and heavier. They both looked as though they were trying to speak, but no words came from their mouths. No one moved; no one made a sound. Habs and Joe held their breath, waiting for the show to begin. Habs counted the silence. He reached fifteen. Then, in a swift lunge, King Dick stooped down and grabbed the smaller of the two men by his ankles. As he rose up, the man fell, his head cracking against the granite. He howled and the King adjusted his grip; one hand now on the drinker's leg, the other on the man's belt. The King had a new club. He was called Tupper.

'The men of Four are, by providence, my men!' he bellowed at Parker, who still stood, despite his trembling. The King began to brandish his new club. The club started to howl.

Those who found themselves nearest his swinging arc stepped back a few paces.

'So when you Christian white savages attack my men, you attack me. I am the men of Four!' he cried, and swung the club.

102

The Rough Ally Parker was still holding his beer when his friend's head crashed into his ribs. As he tottered backwards, the King swung again and two heads cracked. Like a rifle shot, the sound bounced around the walled square, and the King dropped one unconscious man on top of the other. Tupper on Parker, legs splayed, heads bloodied. The King surveyed the damage, straightened his hat, brushed down his coat and strode away.

Habs applauded solemnly, Joe was astonished. 'I have never, in two years of war, seen anything like that,' said Joe. 'He turned that man into a battering ram.'

'I heard that he done that before. Never seen it, though,' said Habs, still clapping.

The King acknowledged him as he left. 'Blood, blood, blood,' he said and walked from the square. Joe watched him go, certain he was the only man in Dartmoor without a stoop.

Around them, excited conversations. The men from Four beamed, re-enacting some of the King's moves; the Rough Allies, outraged all over again, hurried to their fallen. Joe and Habs pushed their way back up the square.

'Do the Brits just let that happen?' asked Joe. 'Don't they try to stop him?'

'They like the King,' answered Habs. 'Like the way he do things. And they'll be talkin' 'bout that one for a while.'

Betsy and Martha were laying out their stall again, making what they could of their broken table.

'And what was the blood he mentioned?' said Joe. 'I've seen a lot worse.'

'Oh, that's *Othello*. It's always *Othello*.' They stopped to pick up some displaced loaves, placing them on the now-sloping stall.

'I'd've liked to see your play.'

'You've heard a lot of it already, and by Sunday next, you'll pretty much've heard it all.'

'And where did you get to know such things? I never met anyone talk theatre talk like you.'

Habs threw Joe a glance. 'What with me bein' all Negro an' everythin'?' he said.

Joe considered his answer, studied Habs's face. 'Truth to tell, Habakkuk Snow, I hardly know you, so I don't rightly know what to say to that. But I will say yes, you being Negro is some of it, but you knowing so much is the most of it. I've been at sea a while and I've never found anyone else who talks about plays like you do. Not one.'

'Well, that'll be books, Joe Hill,' said Habs. 'Jus' books.' He made a neat pile of five loaves while Joe worked on the small rolls. 'My ma sent me to Quaker teachers, back in Philadelphia, when I was seven. Taught me everythin' in two years. Once I started, I couldn't stop. We had a little company right there in class. We did ol' legends and Bible stories, but then our teacher tried us out with some *Twelfth Night*. Got me to read the part of Malvolio, and he said I was good. And he was right 'bout that. Looked like nothin' on the page, but when it came out of my mouth it was different. Sounded . . . normal. Like the way it was meant to sound, almost. Does that make any sense?'

Betsy snatched a roll from Joe's hands and sold it to a drunk from Three who devoured it whole. Joe barely noticed.

'Well, what I heard up in your block yesterday?' he said. 'Sure sounded like you knew what you was doing, like it was natural. I give you that, Mr Snow.' He looked down the square, then along the semicircle of prison blocks, and shook his head. 'This is quite something. It really is. Here I am, in the biggest cesspit in the world, and I'm talking Shakespeare.'

'And with a coloured man, too!' said Habs.

'And with a coloured man,' agreed Joe. 'Though, for the record, whatever King Dick says, William Shakespeare was as white as I am.'

104

'Joe, no one is as white as you,' said Habs.

'Maybe. And going whiter by the day, no doubt.' Joe licked some flour from his hands. 'Did you stay with those teachers for long?'

Habs shook his head. 'My pa died a couple years later and I took up sailcraft. Still loved the books, though, and they let me back when I wanted. Read all them plays in the end. We should try one, Joe.'

'Let me guess,' said Joe. *Romeo and Juliet*?'

'Why not?' said Habs. 'The pretty bakers of Tavistock here can assist in matters of deportment and kissin'.'

Martha was holding a wooden tray with three small loaves on it. She shot Habs a look. 'We've sold nearly everything,' she said. 'Everyone seemed as hungry as you, Joe Hill.'

'It's the peace you're profiting from,' he replied. 'We'll be home soon enough, but there was much celebrating last night. Some have sore heads – your bread can work miracles.'

'And did we win the war,' asked Martha, 'or did you Yankees win? I'm not sure I could say.'

'Not sure I could say either,' said Joe. 'That's about the measure of it. You should know better than us.'

'The *Flying Post* doesn't concern itself with such matters,' she said, 'but if you're all going home, I'll need some new customers.' She sounded glum.

'I'm hoping to persuade Mr Hill here that we could produce one more play before we go,' said Habs. 'Let's at least read it through, Joe, there can be no harm in that.'

Joe shrugged. 'Agreed,' he said. 'I can see no harm in that either.'

'And Ned and Sam'll read their parts, too.' Habs was getting busy. 'All we need are the manuscripts.'

Joe waited for an explanation of where they would appear from, but none came. 'You don't have them?'

Habs shook his head.

'So where are they?'

'Where did you wake up, Mr Hill?'

'Block Seven,' Joe said, surprised, 'but you know that.'

'Where in Block Seven?'

'In the cockloft.'

'And what did you see there when you woke up?'

Joe thought awhile. 'Apart from the crier's face? I saw . . . of course! Books, I think. Rows and rows of books. Is that right?'

Habs nodded. 'Old sailor in Seven by the name of Morris came into some prize money a while back and bought a library. Charges for it, but I know he has some *Romeo and Juliet*s.'

'That's a library?'

A shrill voice cut through the market hubbub. 'Noon bell! Noon bell! Afternoon watch!'

Tommy Jackson's crier duties included timekeeping the daily market. Running into the square, woollen cap perched high on the back of his head, he tapped every stall with a stick before moving on to the next. 'Noon bell! Noon bell! Afternoon watch!'

As soon as they had been tapped, each stall-holder began packing away their produce.

The militia barely seemed to notice fights or drunkenness, but the market was different; the Agent's rules said it shut at noon. So it shut at noon.

'I swear that boy is getting louder,' said Betsy, and she thrust a bundled cloth at Habs. 'We need to be away. A few crumbs and crusts for when your friend here needs a taste of Tavistock.'

'He's certainly had that,' said Habs.

Tommy approached and smacked his hand on one of the trays. 'You've been tapped, Miss Elizabeth,' he said, grinning as he flew past.

'Hey, Tommy!' called Habs, and the boy glanced over his shoulder. 'Cockloft in an hour.'

'Yes, sir!' he called back.

'He's a player, too?' asked Joe.

'Uh-huh,' said Habs, as they watched the crier shutting down the market. 'He plays a fine Paris. The play says he's a young count and there's none younger than him here.'

'Only King Dick's secretaries,' suggested Joe.

The briefest pause. 'Yes, Mr Hill, only the secretaries. Who are busy bein' secretaries.'

2.5

Block Seven, Cockloft

JOE AND Will were back where Tommy Jackson had woken them with such urgency the day before. They knew this was their room; as residents of Block Seven, albeit new ones, they were entitled to use it whenever they chose. But they appeared to be trespassers, intruders who had stumbled into a forbidden land.

'So this is where they ran to,' muttered Joe, looking at the gathering before him.

Around forty men were arranged around card tables, another dozen sprawled on the floor. The air was thick with stale ale, pipe smoke and molasses. Discarded plates of food were scattered on the floor. Horace Cobb and Edwin Lane stood to greet them.

'What've they done with their beards?' asked Roche.

'Don't stare, for pity's sake,' hissed Joe. 'If you're in the Rough Allies, you have a forked beard, that's all.'

'Tied with rope? What kind o' sailor does that?'

'The ones as rough as untamed bears. It's what they do.'

'And they just ran from that King Dick?'

'After calling me a nigger-lover, yes.'

'Well, we are all free Americans,' said Roche. 'Even if we might be in prison.' He stepped forward a few paces, then checked back. 'I faced the tars of HMS *Glasgow* back in '76,' he said to Joe. 'Now, *they* were scary.'

With Joe a few paces behind, Roche walked towards the Allies.

'Prodigious fine day!' he said, hailing them like officers on the bridge. 'My friend and me are jus' borrowin' a book or two. We've settled with Mr Morris below. We'll jus' find what we need – you . . . carry on.'

Roche and Joe turned and walked a few paces to the book tables.

'They can "carry on", can they?' whispered Joe. 'And in their own cockloft?'

'It's our cockloft. Theirs is in Six . . .'

Lane's weasel voice stopped them in their tracks. His words were laced with threat. 'Mr Roche, ain't it?' he said.

Roche nodded.

Cobb shrugged. Ash tumbled on to his beard. 'You been associating with the wrong kind, Mr Roche, like your friend here?'

'You mean King Dick?'

Cobb leaned forward, the burnt-out stub of the cigarillo now stuck to his upper lip.

'His name is Richard Crafus and he's just another sailor from Maryland. He's no king to us, though it serves the English well to treat him like one. You'll not call him king in this block. He's a thief, a cockroach. A leech that has attached itself to all of us.' He sat back, staring at Roche. 'And as we just saw, a wild man, a thug who threatens us all. You'll be needing to guide this boy. Help him get used to things . . .'

'I don't need any guidance,' said Joe.

'Oh, but that's where you're wrong,' said Lane.

'We jus' wanted some books,' said Roche.

'So you said,' said Lane. 'And that's strange, when we're all s'posed to be goin' home, Mr Hill. Why the need for books when the peace is about to be ratified?' He used both hands to smooth and separate the two forks of his beard.

'For readin',' said Roche. 'A useful distraction, don't you find? C'mon, Mr Hill.'

They turned and carried on towards the shelves.

'Quick as you can,' whispered Roche, his eyes flicking along the rows of books.

'Found them,' hissed Joe, and pulled two volumes down. He turned for the door.

'Mr Hill, if you please.' Lane was pointing at the books.

Roche steered Joe around. 'Oh, I see. You're the librarians!' he said. 'I thought we'd fallen upon a gang of cut-throats and pirates. Then we really would be in danger. But if you jus' want to see the books . . .'

All the Allies now jumped to their feet, chairs flying. An assortment of knives had appeared on the tables, but Lane's was already in his hand. Joe and Roche halted mid-stride, Joe holding out the books as if a peace offering.

Cobb squinted at the title then sat down again, the other Allies following suit.

'You both need copies?' said Cobb. 'You putting on a play or something?'

'We're jus' readin', Mr Cobb,' said Roche, getting irritated. 'C'mon, Joe, we got to be goin'.'

Lane hawked noisily. 'Is Habakkuk Snow in your play, too?'

Joe could now see the evidence of the gun that had exploded in Lane's face. His beard had grown around a burn which had charred his skin to the colour of tobacco. His eyes narrowed but the thickened skin around them barely moved.

'It's not my play . . .' he began.

'Precisely,' said Lane. 'Then leave it to 'em. The Negroes like a pantomime. I seen one of them . . . it was most entertainin'.'

'You saw a show in Four?' said Joe, surprised. 'With all those coloured men around you? Must have been like the old days on the *Bentham*.'

Lane held up his knife, pointed it at Joe's chest. 'I've cut men for less,' he spat. 'Take your books and run away, boy.'

110

Joe and Roche had got to the door when Cobb called after them. 'Either of you two sailors been in prison before?'

They shook their heads.

'Getting out and going home,' said Cobb. 'They're thoughts that can do strange things to a man. It can be a dangerous time. We all lose our inhibitions. Act a little crazy, do things we shouldn't. You should be watching yourself, my young friend.'

'What was that?' said Joe, as they hurried down the steps. 'Was he warning us or threatening us?'

'Both, I reckon,' said Roche. 'And he's right, too. We saw it in the market square: if you've got money, you spend it; if you've got liquor, you drink it. And if you've got a score to settle, you might feel you need to make haste.' By the front door, he held Joe back. 'You happy playin' in Four, Joe? If you spend too much time in the Negro prison, that might look like you don't want to be with your own mess. Word'll spread quickly here.'

Joe looked disgusted. 'Will, you sound like the Allies.'

Roche shook his head. 'This is nothin' to do with 'em. This is 'bout us.'

'Really?' said Joe, unconvinced. 'Well, where do you suggest we meet, given that the Negroes aren't allowed in the other blocks?'

Roche heard the edge in Joe's voice and shrugged. 'Jus' lookin' out for you.'

2.6

Block Four

J OE KEPT his eyes on the frozen path round to Four. It helped him to avoid the assault course of prisoners-turned-hawkers who stood in his way but, if he was honest, he did it because it meant he could avert his gaze from the overwhelming presence of the prison blocks. Tommy had said he would get used to them. 'I hope to God that's not true,' he murmured.

Habs met Joe on the steps of Four and ushered him inside. 'In a hundred yards,' Joe said, 'I've been offered more coffee than I could ever drink, something looking like a stew made with mice, and a small model of the USS *Constitution* in a tiny bottle. Norfolk County boys like me are not used to this.'

'Coffee made o' peas ain't coffee,' said Habs, as they climbed the stairs. 'There's some brewers outside o' Two make better. And the best stews just have molasses in the oats. Trust me.'

He pushed the doors open and Joe marvelled at the cockloft's transformation. The stage where King Dick had performed his impromptu *Othello* was now a boxing ring; two bloodied men in prison-issue stockings and trousers were grappling with each other as scores of onlookers yelled encouragement. It took Joe a few seconds to recognize them as the boxers who had run from the square. Two men at ringside tables exchanged money and scribbled in ledgers.

'They're mighty impressive,' called Joe. 'They run fast and box hard.'

112

'Pugilism is all the rage in these parts!' shouted Habs. 'And if you can bet on it, we like it all the more. They just started, but there'll be more fights, till the money runs out.'

They stepped over four men propped up against a fifth, his eyes glazed and a bottle in each hand, then weaved their way between the card tables. 'They'll find me a mean contributor,' said Joe.

'Oh, you don't need money. Your clothes'll do just fine. You could trade that stylish hat of yours for many a round of Pitch and Toss. Over there.' Habs pointed at a section of the wall where men were lined up, pitching coins. 'Or you could trade provisions. Save your herring and potatoes, swap 'em for some games of Twenty-one.'

All round them, dealers and gamblers hedged and shuffled, triumphed and failed.

'It's the Palais Royale of Dartmoor,' said Habs, his voice dropping to a murmur. 'This man here with the beaded queues' – he indicated a man with a hand full of cards and an elaborately tied ponytail – 'he has debts o' twenty pounds or more. There's talk that anyone with debts won't be let home. He's gettin' desperate.'

'Cobb warned us it could turn dangerous,' said Joe.

'Ha! Well, if it does, he'll be the instigator of most of it. C'mon.'

At the back wall, Ned and Sam sat at a table, clay pipes in hand. They took their time with the loading, lighting and kindling but, as Habs and Joe approached, great clouds of grey smoke billowed around them. Habs coughed theatrically.

'I swear the cannons of the *Bentham* blasted less smoke than your goddamn pipes, Ned Penny. And you, too, Sam Snow. We ain't gonna be able to read for the fumes.'

Ned blew more smoke. 'It's a pitiful pipe and rank tobacco, too, but it's better'n Sam's fox piss. Besides, you rather stink o' Craven pipe tobacco or unwashed sailors? Filthy bastards, all of 'em.' He drew deeply on the lip and the bowl glowed red, the strands of tobacco catching and crackling.

'And when I'm home,' said Sam, pointing the long stem of his pipe for emphasis, 'I'm gonna find me my father's wood and metal pipes, some sweet smoke from Mount Vernon, and lie in my bed till three. And there'll be no turnkeys, no British and nobody to tell me I can't.'

'Well, till that sweet day,' said Habs, 'here's some readin'.'

He placed the books on the table and Ned grabbed the one nearest him. 'Are there enough?'

'If we double up,' said Sam, 'we can perform most of it.'

Joe placed his tricorn on the floor. 'So you know the roles you're playing? Is it always the same?'

Ned laughed then coughed, small wisps of smoke shooting from his mouth. 'Well, now, I read for Mercutio, Sam for Benvolio and Habs is Romeo, but kinda overdramatic.'

'Enthusiastic and passionate's what you mean, but I take your guidance, fair Mercutio.' Habs bowed his head and Ned returned the gesture.

'Have you read Juliet's words before, Joe?' asked Sam.

'I read the whole play on my first ship.'

There was a sudden flurry of feet, shouting and movement; Tommy the crier had arrived at speed. 'King Dick is on the way!' he managed, before a huge cheer rolled down from the far end of the cockloft. 'Or should I say,' he corrected himself, 'King Dick is already here.'

They all rose to watch.

Standing by the boxing ring, the King was distracting the fighters so much they stopped moving altogether. The applause rolled around the cockloft, eventually picking up even the most incapacitated sailor.

Joe, clapping heartily, leaned in close to Habs. 'Looks like the men o' Four liked what they saw this morning.'

As the rest of the block heard the tumult, many more

came rushing through the doors to join the applause. King Dick pushed the bearskin hat off his forehead, held his hands wide and turned his face to the ceiling.

'Is he praying?' asked Joe.

'No, he's actin',' was Ned's whispered answer. 'But it's the same kinda thing.'

After the ovation faded, it was the gamblers who picked up first, followed by the boxers. The King stayed to watch, calling out corrections and suggestions.

'Will he want to join us?' said Joe. 'Was he a part of the *Romeo and Juliet* you were planning before?'

'Was he a part of it?' asked Sam, incredulous. 'He's a part of everythin' round here. He's a part of that boxin' match, he's a part of that card game. And the traders outside Four? He expects to be a part of their takin's, too.'

'He was playin' the Count of Verona *and* Friar Lawrence *and* the Apothecary.'

'All right.' Joe nodded slowly.

'Jus' assume he's the captain o' every ship round here,' said Ned. 'New ship, ol' ship, same captain.'

'I get the picture.'

Habs sat back at the table. 'So. Let us begin.' He handed one book to Joe, who sat opposite, and opened his own. 'King Dick, he can join in when he gets to us. Tommy, sit with me. You can be Paris again.' The crier sat and grinned across at Joe.

'I learned to read here, Mr Hill,' he said. 'In Block One, they had advertisements for classes. There was writin'. Readin'. Maths. Navigation. It cost a whole shillin' a month, but King Dick paid. Said I should do all of 'em. Now I'm the crier *and* in a play.' This speech produced a round of applause of its own.

'And what would your folks at home make of that?' asked Joe, still applauding.

Tommy's face clouded in an instant.

115

Joe realized his mistake. 'Tommy, I'm sorry . . .' he began, but the boy shook his head, wiping his eyes.

'It's all right, Mr Hill, really it is. I got no folks back home no more. That's that. Can we do the play?'

'Uh-huh,' said Habs. 'Tommy, maybe you start?'

The crier leaned over Habs's book and was smiling again.

'The Most Excellent and Lamentable Tragedy of Romeo and Juliet,' he read.

2.7

The Agent's House

9 p.m.

ELIZABETH SHORTLAND hadn't changed for dinner, just removed her chemisette. She had known her husband wouldn't notice and known, too, that Dr Magrath would think of nothing else. She spun an ornate wooden box between her fingers as she waited for her husband to stop speaking. Fuelled by fine food and brandy, he seemed just as upset by the peace as he had been by the war. Head in hands, he squeezed his hair high above his forehead.

She fiddled with her place setting, flattening the lace cloth where it had ruffled over the mahogany table. She should engage in their conversation, of course – it was the hour for discourse and her participation had been hard won – but, tonight, she longed for her bed and her books. She stared at her husband, puffy-faced now and with a distinct list to starboard, and wondered what had happened to her dashing lieutenant. The man who, the month before they married, had captured an armed French brig from under the batteries of the Bay of Corréjou. She reached for her snuff.

'I tell you this, George,' spluttered the captain. 'We have gained nothing. We have finished nothing. The treaty merely restores the status quo *ante bellum*. And for what, I ask you? We have lost countless ships, many thousands of men. For what, I say?'

George Magrath paused before offering a measured reply.

'Canada is secure, sir. All the invasions of her border were defeated. And the blockades worked, did they not?'

Thomas Shortland poured himself another brandy then offered the bottle to his wife. She declined, and the Agent frowned.

'You always say no these days, Elizabeth. You used to enjoy a Duret – will you not take a small one?'

'I'm fine, Thomas, really. It gives me headaches,' she said. 'Has done for a while now.'

Shortland swiftly returned to his war arguments and Elizabeth marvelled again at his blindness. Her losing interest in alcohol had coincided precisely with the start of her affair, and the affair had coincided precisely with her and Magrath working together. But her husband saw nothing, understood nothing. As the men talked of Castlereagh's troop levels, she unscrewed the top of her box and tapped out a small portion of snuff.

The action was enough to cause both men to look up. The Agent moved the conversation back to include his wife.

'I hear there is an English boy in the new arrivals, Elizabeth,' he said. 'Might he fight for us if we get him out of here?'

'I would think not,' she said. 'He's an American now, Thomas. Besides, the war is done and they all think they will be home soon.' She pinched the ground tobacco on the back of her hand. 'Dr Magrath and I met the crew of the *Eagle* this morning. Spirits were high – they believe their war to be over. None of them will want to fight any more. Except perhaps against us, here.' She raised her hand to her nose and in two well-practised, sharp inhalations, the snuff was gone.

'So' – she snapped the box shut, immediately dabbing at her nose with a lilac handkerchief – 'will Congress ratify the treaty, Thomas? Do they not want to be rid of this war, too?'

'I have my doubts, Elizabeth, I really do.'

Shortland's hair was now higher than ever. 'What is stitched into all the flags in all the prisons here? What do you see written on the walls when you do your rounds, Dr Magrath?'

'"Free trade and sailors' rights" is the usual one,' said the physician.

'Precisely!' cried Shortland. 'They'll get their trade, but there is nothing in Ghent about sailors' rights, no mention of impressment. The first reason President Madison gave for the war was the Navy snatching Americans, forcing them to work on our ships. On this singular issue, the peace treaty is silent. I fear Congress may not ratify.'

There was silence in the dining room. The men lit pipes and Elizabeth took to spinning her wooden box between her fingers.

'In which case, Thomas, I fear for the future,' she said. 'There is an easier humour in the blocks since the announcement. In spite of the cold and the sickness, you can hear them sing most days. They dance, too, sometimes. They seem to have hope once more.'

'Piffle,' said Shortland. 'They dance and sing because they are drunk. That is the end of it.'

Dr Magrath eased his chair back and, clasping his stick, pushed his body upright.

'If I may, Captain Shortland, I believe you are both correct. The gaiety is fuelled by alcohol, of course, but it may, in time, also fuel anger. And it will be us who are on the receiving end of that anger. Your militias may well come under extreme provocation. They need to be ready.'

Shortland gripped his pipe between his teeth, inhaled deeply then blew smoke at the chandelier. His lips pursed.

'I have lost Major Joliffe to the palsy, as you know. I have two guard commanders who are doing their best. We are all doing our best. Your advice on military matters is always . . . an education.' He got to his feet and marched from the room.

Magrath and Elizabeth stood and faced each other across the table. She smiled briefly then held up her hand for

119

quiet. In the silence, they listened to him walk to his office and slam the door. She walked around the table and, as she drew alongside a bewildered Magrath, kissed him full on the mouth. He recoiled, pulling away and glancing at the open dining-room door.

'Are you mad?' he spluttered.

She waited for the shock to subside. 'He'll be some time,' she whispered. 'At least half a bottle's worth.'

Magrath exhaled slowly. 'My heartbeat is out of control, Elizabeth.' He reached for his chair, needing its support. 'How can you be so . . . so . . . daring?' She put a finger to her lips, placed her legs either side of his and kissed him again. This time, she held him in place until they were both breathless.

2.8

Block Four

9 p.m.

Habs finished tying his hammock, pulling the ropes, testing the knots. His was the lowest bunk and had been since he'd arrived; he preferred it that way. 'Too many falls,' he'd say. Three feet up the stanchions, Ned was already splayed across his hammock and humming, loudly.

Habs winced. 'That ain't like no tune I ever heard.'

'It's a harmony, Habs,' said Ned.

'Tha's what you think?'

'Tha's what I think,' said Ned. 'And my one and a half ears still better'n your two.'

Habs laughed, slid into his hammock and pushed his feet against the sagging shape above him. 'But I have two good legs here sayin' it's time to hush, old man,' he said. 'King Dick can't be far away.'

They both lay still and listened.

The turnkeys had called the roll then shut and bolted the doors. This was the daily cue for nine hundred and ninety-five hammocks to be slung, but in Mess 190 they were still waiting for the King. Habs peered from his lowly vantage point. King Dick's mess was at the back of the first floor, two mattresses and a heap of blankets marking his sleeping quarters. Above him, two hammocks held the already sleeping forms of Alex Daniels and Jonathan Singer; one pale arm dangled from the lower, a mop of brown hair from the upper. In the other berths, the King's favourites: the sailors he could rely on. Some acted with him, some made him laugh, others ran the gaming. All would fight for him.

Outside, it was snowing again, a few flakes making their way through the prison's shutters and melting into small puddles. Inside, the temperature had been pushed above freezing only by the sheer number of men clustered together and their flickering pipes. As usual, a cloud of grey smoke rose from Sam's hammock.

'Good night, King Dick!' and 'God bless you, King Dick!' came from all around and, instinctively, Habs rolled back out of his hammock.

'You gonna blow his candle out for him or some such?' said Ned, peering from under his thin blanket. ''Cos I'm sure he can do that by himself, y'know.'

'Shut up, Ned,' said Habs. 'He's here now.'

Lamp in one hand, club in the other, the King strode up to the mess. 'Mr Hobbs, Mr Watson, Mr Palmer.' He raised the flame to each in greeting, and three voices shot back, 'Good evening, King Dick!' He walked to his bed, nodding at Habs as he passed, gently placed Alex's arm inside the hammock, then slumped to the floor. The hammocks trembled and Habs fancied that everyone in Four always knew the exact moment King Dick had reached his bed. And maybe in Five and Seven, too.

'Mr Habakkuk Snow, Mr Sam Snow and Mr Ned Penny,' said the King. 'I enjoyed that readin' today. And your new friend, Mr Joe Hill, is quite somethin' as Juliet. Providence has been good to us, don't you think?'

'I say so, too,' said Habs, 'and by the end we had quite a crowd, didn't we? They was sorry to see us go.'

King Dick propped himself up against the wall, blankets behind him, blankets on top of him. Swapping his club for a bottle of rum, he poured a large portion into a cup then swallowed half in one deep draught. 'For never was a story of more woe,' he intoned, his voice easily projecting through the prison din, 'than this of Juliet and her Romeo. I love that line,' said the King. 'Ever since I first read it. No wonder they applauded – I wanted to applaud, too.'

'Poor Master Jackson shed a tear,' said Sam.

'Which,' said Ned, 'as he was playin' the recently slain Paris, was mighty clever.'

A voice from a nearby mess. 'Will there be time for a show, King Dick?' Then another: 'Will we be home soon, King Dick?'

'Who is that callin'?' said the King, peering past his candles.

'Fountain, sir,' came the reply. 'Fountain MacFall, freeman from New York.'

'And before New York, Mr MacFall? Where did your family call home?'

'Charleston, South Carolina, sir. Place called Rocky Point.'

'And before that?' said the King. 'Do you know your history, Mr MacFall?'

'My folks said we come from a country called Senegal, but I never been there and I know nothin' 'bout it. Like I said, home is New York. Place called Fresh Water Pond, but there's no fresh water there, King Dick, case you come callin'.'

The King laughed and raised his cup towards Fountain's hammock. 'Well, I might just do that, Mr MacFall from Fresh Water Pond and Senegal. My ol' family musta been your neighbours, jus' down the coast.'

Ned, his mouth up close to Habs's hammock, whispered, 'Penny on the kidnap story again.'

Habs reached out to shake Ned's hand.

The King finished his rum in two mouthfuls. He had seen the transaction.

'You got some business goin' on there, Mr Penny, Mr Snow? Somethin' I should know about?'

Habs jumped in, thinking fast. 'No, sir. I was jus' offerin' Mr Penny here one penny to tell *his* story, if you need him. You know how reluctant he is . . .'

A voice from the hammocks. 'Yeah, you got that 'scapin' story, Mr Penny, tell us that one.' A chorus of agreement around the messes.

'Say your piece, Mr Penny,' said the King, 'then Mr Snow can pay you.' He wafted his free hand. The stage was Ned's.

'If you sure, King Dick,' protested Ned. 'I reckon pretty much everyone knows . . .'

He was silenced by the King's theatrical coughing.

'I have a question for Mr Penny,' he said, after loudly clearing his throat. 'You a free man, Mr Penny?'

Ned was now sitting upright on his hammock. Sam handed him a pipe, Habs a bottle. 'Uh-huh. In my head, yes. In my soul, yes. Always.'

Applause and shouts of 'Amen!' greeted that.

'But legally speakin' and in truth, I am property. I am 'scaped from the Pointe plantation, state of Louisiana.'

Applause rolled around the room.

'Had an overseer on that land, name of McDonnall. I still shiver to say his name. Meanest fucker I ever saw. We cut his stalks, did his grindin', did his boilin', workin' sixteen hours a day, an' if we dropped dead then he'd jus' buy another one of us. When them census takers came callin', they was jus' chased off the land, on account of McDonnall not wantin' anyone to know who's alive and who ain't. So when he died – I forget how that happened exactly – many of us jus' took to the road. We knew we was headin' north, knew Massachusetts was the only state, so we was told, with no slaves. And we said that over and over. We said that all the time, it was like a magic spell to us. No slaves! Who'd heard o' such a thing?' He took a swig of beer and inhaled deeply from the pipe. 'This story takes two years, by the way – you want it all?'

There was laughter and some encouraging cheers, but Ned batted them away.

'You know what happens. We moved at night, a few miles where we could, find friends where we could. Lot of us didn't make it. Bounty-hunters, slave-catchers, white devils of all kinds, traitors, too, they all come after us.' Ned's voice tailed away. He closed his eyes and shuddered, the remembrance too easy, too familiar. There was an almost-silence, the closest to quiet Habs could recall for many years.

'You want me to finish it for you, Ned?' he whispered.

'No, I'm not an imbecile jus' yet,' Ned replied. 'We was in North Carolina, hidin' in some woods outside o' Wilmington, I think it was, when we got news of a ship would take us north. There's only three of us by now. Me an' two boys, names of Otis an' John. They don't trust no boat captains but I persuade 'em to stow away, as we ain't fit for walkin' an' hidin' no more. The captain, he put us in crates, an' I arrived in Boston June 18th 1809, sharing a box with some printin' press machinery stuck in my face.'

'That explains why you so ugly, then!' called Habs.

'Oh, I was pretty back then, real pretty,' Ned said over laughter. 'Everyone said so. S'jus' the war and that cannon-ball gone an' done for me.'

From a distant mess: 'An' what happened to the boys? Otis an' John?'

Ned dropped his head, his shoulders sliding forward. 'You know what happened,' he said. Ned lay back on his hammock as the word 'slavecatcher' was muttered around the block.

'A penny for Mr Penny,' growled the King.

2.9

Block Seven

9 p.m.

'AND NOW we need the house to order! I said, this house to order!' The straining voice was at least a mess away and Joe turned in his hammock to see what was happening. A tired-looking man in a long brown coat was pacing the aisle, shouting through a rolled-up newspaper in the hope it would provide some means of amplification. 'House to order! Please, gentlemen, bring this house to order!'

Above Joe, Roche's head appeared over the edge of his bed. 'This house is playin' backgammon, scratchin' them bugs away, drinkin' ale an' sleepin'. It does not want to come to order.'

The men of the *Eagle* had been scattered around the two floors of Seven, Joe and Will eventually finding berths with some privateers from Maine, most of whom had passed out.

'But he's the President,' said Joe. 'I think we're supposed to take notice.'

'President?' Roche's inverted face had appeared again. Even upside down, he looked baffled. 'What kinda nonsense is this?'

'We vote, Will,' said Joe. 'That's how they do it here. We vote on who'll be President for the week, who'll be the judges, who'll be the committeemen . . .'

'And who, pray, is our President, then?' said Roche,

peering at the increasingly irate man in the coat. 'He's no Madison, and that's the truth.'

Across the aisle, a voice from under a tarpaulin. 'His name is Rose, and I wouldn't trouble yourselves with anythin' he tells you.'

Joe and Roche exchanged a surprised glance.

'So why is he President?' asked Joe.

''Cos he wanted to be,' came the reply. 'But mark my words, he's an imbecile.' The top of the tarp flipped down. 'Joseph Toker Johnson. How d'you do?'

Joe just got sight of a pile of ginger hair before the tarp flipped up again. He was about to introduce himself when 'President' Rose returned, now armed with a frying pan. 'And here come the ship's bells!' said Joe.

This time, the 'House to order!' was accompanied by a vigorous, clanging assault on one of the metal stanchions.

It worked. Everywhere, the buzz and jaw died, the games halted, the sleepers awoke. Looking rather startled, 'President' Rose jumped into the silence, speaking fast.

'Men, we need a tub inspector, a master-at-arms, a sailor-lawyer and three committeemen for next week. Do I have any names to take forward?'

Close to two hundred voices all bellowed their suggestions at once, and the hapless Rose scribbled what names he could pick up out of the babble.

Roche's face again. 'Did I jus' hear Uncle Sam and Dolley Madison's names bein' called out? 'Cos if the President's wife is in charge of the beatin's, I might just sign up for a few stripes myself!'

Joe addressed the man under the tarp. 'Mr Johnson, do the committeemen decide the punishments here? Or is it the British?'

The tarp was pulled away and Toker Johnson swung himself over the side of his hammock. He pulled a tall, slightly conical hat over his red, unkempt hair and folded his arms tightly across his chest. His eyes narrowed as he stared at Joe.

'We don't need them British to tell us how to run our lives. We punish them that needs punishin', no matter if he's one of ours. There's an order of things. Sailors in Two last month had to give a thief fifty stripes, but he fell after fifteen. So he was handed to the British, who put him in the cachot. That's the way of it. And one of the cooks here – man by the name of Wilston – he was caught skimming coppers. Them cooks are always at it, but this rogue was caught doin' it. Eighteen lashes tomorrow after turn-out.'

Joe was about to argue with Toker Johnson when a judicious cough from the hammock above alerted him to his imminent folly. He slumped back, his eyes closed. The sea was his life and sailors his family, but their brutality always angered him.

Once Toker Johnson had disappeared again beneath the tarpaulin, Joe whispered through the hemp.

'So we hate the British for their brutality, then, just to make sure they know how superior we are, we're even more brutal? Can that be right?'

Roche's upside-down head appeared above him again. 'Joe Hill. Have you learned nothing? We don't hate the British 'cos they're brutal – we kind of admire 'em for that. Didn't you read how we behaved in York? No, we hate the British 'cos they're British. And they all have faces you want to punch. Those two things together. And that's quite enough.'

2.10

Block Six

9 p.m.

THREE NEW flags had been hung. A thin rope had been tied between two stanchions and the unfurling was the cause of much merriment. Roughly cut from sheets and painted with black and red ink, they formed rough and ready American flags: fifteen horizontal stripes, and the blue square with fifteen white stars. But there were additions. New, eye-catching additions.

The first flag had crude images of the King, the Agent, Elizabeth Shortland and farm animals in each of the stars; the second depicted black men hanging from gibbets; the third had a new verse for 'Yankee Doodle' written in the longer white lines.

'I'm enjoyin' your handiwork tonight, Mr Cobb,' said Lane, gazing up at the colours. 'I knew you could paint pretty much most things, but these are somethin' else.' He laughed as he read the words; it was a shrill, discomforting sound.

> 'Ol' Miss Shortland, she's a witch,
> Of that we can be certain.
> She casts her spell, goes straight to Hell,
> Goes home and fucks the surgeon.'

He laughed again then clapped himself. 'Bravo!' he said.

'We must sing that out loud when we see the Agent next. You wrote the words, too?'

Cobb, spreadeagled on his hammock, an empty bottle on his chest, nodded. 'Wrote the words, drew the pictures.' He pulled his stovepipe over his eyes. 'They're not as useful as the dollars I used to print. But so much more fun.'

As each sailor read the rhyme, they toasted Cobb. Their spirits were raised; they weren't ready to sleep.

'Tell us the trial story, Mr Cobb,' called one.

'Too tired, too drunk. And you've heard it before. Know every word,' Cobb replied.

'The crew of *Imperious* only came in last month. They ain't heard one word. Not a single word. They know nothin'. Tell 'em.'

Horace Cobb lay still for a moment, then peered from under his hat to check the status of his drink. Finding it empty, he offered it to Lane, who swiftly found a full bottle to replace it. Cobb leaned towards an oil lamp that was hanging on a stanchion, touching the tobacco to the flame. He inhaled sharply as the leaves caught then blew a cloud of smoke into the thick, swirling curtain that fell from just beneath the ceiling.

'All right, so this is the old days. We'd been operating out of Queens for three years. Had a good business there, just the three of us. My two brothers and me. We did documents and we did 'em all day and all night. There wasn't nothing we couldn't do. Certificates, divorce papers, travel documents – we could make 'em all. If you wanted some paperwork to prove you were a magician from Paris, we could do it. If you wanted to be a lawyer from Pennsylvania, that was no problem at all. What you did with them papers once you got 'em was your lookout. But there was this one customer, name of Smith, got himself a new set of papers to show he owned this piece of land. Well, he got himself into a fight with some Irish and was about to explain to them nice gentlemen where he got his documents when he found he had his throat cut from here to here.' Cobb drew the bottle across his neck to cheers from his audience. 'And then, just to make sure . . .' He reversed the action, to even louder cheers.

'What happened next, Mr Cobb? Come on, tell us.'

Those who were near a stanchion began a slow tapping like a drumroll, others banged pipes against lamps.

'Me and my brothers stood trial, o' course we did.'

The noise and speed of the drumming increased.

'But it turned out – and praise be to Almighty God for His ways are mysterious! – that the judge's recent divorce was less than entirely legitimate. Some of his documents weren't so very legal.'

The percussion was reaching a crescendo now.

Cobb sat bolt upright, waving the cigarillo in one hand, the bottle in the other. 'And so, gentlemen!'

The drumming stopped abruptly. Cobb looked around at the keen, expectant faces, nodding at them all. 'And so His Honour declared me not guilty!' Wild cheering greeted this news and, in the neighbouring mess, two fiddles began a reel.

Edwin Lane, lying across the aisle from Cobb, raised his bottle in salute.

'It's a good story,' he said.

Cobb smiled. 'It is, isn't it?' he said, and relit his cigarillo.

Lane leaned forward, then nodded towards the second flag. 'You're showin' what we need to do, I think.'

'The hanging pictures?' Cobb looked surprised. 'You think we should go hang the men of Four?' He laughed, a staccato burst that dropped ash on to his pillow. 'You been drinkin' too long, Mr Lane. They're just cartoons.'

'Maybe,' said Lane, acknowledging the rebuke. 'But I got me some money to pay my favourite turnkey. I got a trip planned. The blackjacks are jumpin' too high for my likin'.'

Cobb was intrigued. 'You think they need . . . cutting down a little?'

'Somethin' like that, Mr Cobb,' said Lane. 'Somethin' like that.'

2.11

The Agent's Study

King Dick has been shown in by two members of the guard who wait, fidgeting nervously, for the Agent. The King walks the book-shelves, stopping every now and then to read a title and run his hand down its spine.

SHORTLAND (*arrives, bustling, late; takes off his greatcoat*): Mr Crafus! You are an educated man, I see. Tell me, what has caught your eye?

KING DICK: It all catches my eye, Captain, every single one. We have some books in Seven. But the choice is poor and I believe I have read everythin' that takes my fancy. These, on the other hand . . .

SHORTLAND: Well, select one, then. I can trust you, I believe. They are underused, I'm afraid. I inherited most of them from my father. They are mainly military history, the classics, that kind of thing. I don't get a lot of visitors who browse the shelves.

KING DICK (*still looking at the books*): Perhaps that's because most of your men can't read, Captain. When they deal with us, they seem . . . slow-witted. Maybe it's them you need to lend your books to.

SHORTLAND: My men are the best I can find, Mr Crafus. While there are wars to be fought, I fear Dartmoor will never receive the finest the British Army has to offer. Added to that, my major is sick and unlikely to be replaced anytime soon. Now, about that book . . .

KING DICK: I'll play along with your game, Captain. (*He pulls a small book from the shelves, leafs through its pages, selecting one; looks at Shortland.*) You have some poetry on your shelves, Captain Shortland.

SHORTLAND: I do?

KING DICK: William Wordsworth. His poem to Toussaint L'Ouverture, the leader of the Haiti slave revolt.

SHORTLAND: (*astonished*) Really? I never knew . . .

KING DICK: You should know your people better, Captain. It concludes (*he reads*):

> There's not a breathing of the common wind
> That will forget thee; thou hast great allies;
> Thy friends are exultations, agonies,
> And love, and Man's unconquerable mind.

SHORTLAND: I'm not quite sure what to make of that, I'm afraid. (*He takes the book and reads.*) He calls him 'O miserable chieftain'. Is that you, Crafus? Is that what you're telling me? I hope not, because I know where I am with you and with Four. I can speak directly to you, and I know you can speak directly to your men. (*He throws the book on the desk.*)

KING DICK: And so?

SHORTLAND: So do your men understand that, though the war is over, for them, nothing can change until the ratified treaty arrives back in England?

KING DICK: But it has changed already, Captain, you gotta feel that. You can wave papers at us, but we know we should be goin' home. And when Congress has ratified, you'd better be gettin' us out swiftly or you'll have a riot so big you'll need a whole army to deal with us.

SHORTLAND: Are you threatening me, Mr Crafus?

KING DICK: I'm jus' tellin' you how it is. Once there ain't no war, we can't be prisoners-of-war. Many of us will likely wanna jus' walk outta those gates.

SHORTLAND: Then you will be shot.

KING DICK: Then you will have a riot.

SHORTLAND (*exasperated*): If there is a breakout, your men will end up arrested, impressed back into the Royal Navy or dead. If you stay here, at least you will be safe until your ships come. You have to make them see that!

KING DICK: Safe here? Where so many of us have died? Have you visited the graveyard recently, Captain?

SHORTLAND: I regret every death, Mr Crafus. Dartmoor is an unforgiving place and, when disease takes hold, I know the results can be devastating. British prisoners-of-war face similar conditions in American jails, you know that? And usually chained up with common thieves and murderers too. The food, allowance and medical treatment you have been given are the best available – but out there? That's an awfully unforgiving part of the country, Mr Crafus, it's one hell of a walk to civilization once you're out those gates. How many of your men would actually make it home?

KING DICK: We fought you and your country to be free. Your guns, locks 'n' keys tell us we are still not free. Did you know, your Navy offered freedom to the slaves of Mathews County, Virginia, if they came on over to your ships? Did you know that?

SHORTLAND: I had heard, yes . . .

KING DICK: Well, the war is over, Captain, the war is done. So we ain't goin' to 'come on over', but you can offer us hope. If you choose to. You better be ready for ratification, Captain. That's all I'm sayin'. (*He reclaims the book from Shortland's desk and waves it at him.*) The poem says it is possible for a powerful white man to be on the side of righteousness. If he chooses to be.

ACT THREE

3.1

Friday, 6 January
The Blocks

THE TURNKEYS' message was different this morning. After the usual dreaded 'Tumble up and turn out!' they added an extra cry. 'Snow-clearing at Russets, Rounders and Hexworthy. First two hundred.' The response in all blocks was instantaneous.

The hammocks spun.

'Sixpenny crash!' yelled Habs and a hundred others, as the more sober, able-bodied and awake inmates tipped out of their beds. The deliberate painful self-tipping ensured that the more robust inmates snatched an extra few seconds in the dash for the courtyard. Habs and Sam almost fell over each other in their eagerness to volunteer. 'Crashing' promised an extra sixpence in wages and, tantalizingly, a chance to leave the prison.

'How much snow?' called Sam, pulling gloves from his makeshift pillow.

'Enough,' said Habs. 'Enough to warrant that extra sixpence. Where are my damn boots?'

They snatched what bread they had saved and threw coins at an early riser who had fired up an illegal stove for some coffee.

Still buttoning, tying and wrapping, sailors from each of the seven prisons swarmed to the courtyard gates. The few inches of snow that had fallen overnight ensured that those with poor boots had a precarious sprint. Everywhere, men were sliding and falling. Habs and Sam were amongst the first out of Four, merging quickly with the fastest of Three and Five. They could see the gates to the square were open, the lines of militia poised, waiting to slam them shut again once they had the number they wanted.

Habs took an elbow in the face, Sam a fist to the stomach. Arms and legs tangled; clothes were pulled and ripped as they closed on the gates. Sam was fastest through, then applauded Habs, who made it as the gates started to move.

'Slowin' down, boy,' he laughed. 'Too much liquor and tobacco.'

Joe, red-faced, tricorn pulled low, forced his way through the crowd.

'Thought you'd slept in. What kept you?'

'Block Four is farthest from the gates,' said Habs, 'so not surprisin' you Sevens got here so easy.' Habs offered Joe some bread from his pocket, Joe produced some rolled-up meat from his and they swapped some breakfast.

'Thanks for the advice,' Joe said. 'If you hadn't warned me about the crash, I'd never have been ready.'

'Ol' man Roche not here, I see,' said Habs through a mouthful of food.

'Said he was cold and in pain anyway,' said Joe. 'Didn't see the point in getting more of both.'

The throng of inmates were surrounded by redcoats, guns held at the ready. Six officers were shouting and waving their arms, succeeding eventually in dividing the men into working parties. Habs, Sam and Joe were herded into a group with three other messes from Four then joined by a noisy gang from One. The latter made their displeasure felt immediately.

'We don't do the same work as fuckin' Negroes,' spat one man from the swathe of wool wrapped around his face. Clouds of steam billowed around him.

'You do if you want the money,' replied the nearest sergeant. 'If you want to go back inside, Yankee boy, there's plenty who'll take your place.'

140

Their march through the recently swept courtyard and gates was straightforward. But as they filed under the arch, their progress slowed. Overnight, the Dartmoor hills had been covered by a foot of snow and the track that led from the prison to neighbouring Princetown had vanished. In the half-light of the early morning, each sailor turned his head to the dark, grey, overcast sky, judging wind and temperature; it was clear there would be more snow soon.

The men were split into left and right, and half the troop was directed left, towards Princetown, while Joe, Habs, Sam and a hundred others were forced to the right.

'What's this way?' called Joe.

'A whole load o' nothin',' said Sam. 'I did this last year – the moor goes on for miles. Grass, piles o' rocks, bogs, grass, piles o' rocks an' bogs. For ever. But somewhere there'll be some poor English farmer with his poor English cows and pigs that need rescuin'.'

'How far away are these farms?' Joe had his hat pulled low, his hands deep in the pockets of an old coat he had traded for in the market. He walked in the footsteps of the men in front but still trod gingerly, their progress painfully slow.

'Hexworthy's an hour off,' said Habs, holding on to Sam's shoulder, 'more like two in this snow. That'll be where the others have gone. Russets is closer, and Rounders before that.'

'Well, let's pray we're Rounders and the snow waits awhile,' said Joe, shivering hard.

'Amen to that!' said Sam. 'And that the farmer has beautiful daughters who're bored o' their usual grass-combers and dreamin' of meetin' an American sailor.'

'. . . who smells like shit,' added Habs.

'It's a farm, Habs,' said Joe. 'Everything will smell like shit.'

Two men in front of them turned their heads. 'We were there last snowfall,' said one, his eyes and nose watery with

141

the cold. 'The ol' boy there's not so bad, even tried to offer us liquor, but the guards wouldn't let 'im. Though they took plenty, mind.'

''Course they did,' said Joe. 'You from One?'

'Yup.'

'You're all better now? Sounded like you had a real bad attack of the fever in there some days back.'

'Back on our feet now, but it was bad, and no mistake. Headaches, sickness, and shit everywhere. Couldn't wait to get out.' He stuck a hand towards Joe. 'Bill Gramm and Jonathan Tilson. Sailed with the *Plainsman* outta New York. You from the *Eagle*?'

'Yeah, Joe Hill from Seven.' They shook with gloved hands. The men from One glanced at Habs, Sam and the rest of the Fours and nodded. There was, apparently, no need to ask where they were from.

'And we're from Four,' Habs said pointedly. 'Sam and Habs Snow.' The men turned again, nodded again.

'We know who you are. You were fast!' said Gramm to Sam. 'Saw you run. Not many from Four made it.'

'One's as close to the gates as Seven is,' said Sam. 'You have it easy round there.'

Tilson snorted. He spoke over his shoulder. 'Sure don't feel that way. Some in the mess still sick with the flu or some such. Lotta groanin' goin' on most nights.'

The troop of snow-clearers and militia trudged on for an hour. Starlings screeched around a clump of battered pine trees, then swooped suddenly into its branches. The track to the farm was marked out with large granite stones every quarter-mile, ditches, hedges and spoil heaps from old tin mines taking it in turns to run alongside the route. The men saw no one. The excited chatter that had marked the first mile faded as the cold began to bite and the damp to seep. Aside from the cursing, coughing and sneezing, they walked in silence.

142

A sharp right turn produced a change in vista: fields with moss-covered, dry granite walls dipped away from the track. Farm buildings, most no more than tumbledown shacks, appeared, scattered ploughs and broken wheels propped against the drystone walls.

'Rounders Farm,' said Habs.

'This it?' asked Joe.

Habs shook his head. 'Just the edge of it, but not far now.'

Bill Gramm turned again, checked for redcoats. 'Ever thought of escapin'?' he said, his voice only as loud as it needed to be. His question hung between them.

'You suggestin' we make a run for it?' whispered Sam, incredulous. 'Here? In the snow? With footprints 'n' all?'

'No. Just wonderin' if you ever think them thoughts.'

'Uh-huh. Don't everyone who ever lived here?'

'I been watchin' these redcoats,' said Habs. 'They know nothin' and see nothin'. We could fall in a ditch an' they wouldn't notice.'

'So we could escape,' said Joe, 'and with peace not yet ratified, we'd be caught by the press gangs and sent to fight for the British.'

'Or shot on sight,' said Habs. 'Less painful, maybe.'

They shuffled, slid and fell towards Rounders farmhouse. A florid sergeant handed out sticks, shovels, forks and slates and a militia colleague counted their charges. Satisfied, he set them to clear the snow that had drifted five feet deep against the farmer's stables and cow sheds, imprisoning the horses and cattle. Around the farmer's yard, the small army of inmates made short work of his animals' predicament. Joe, Habs and Sam toiled alongside their new acquaintances from One. The work was welcome, their faces now red with exertion as well as cold.

'These stables are better than our prisons,' commented Joe, catching his breath.

'Even if there's no sign of the farmer's daughters yet!' said Bill, wiping his brow with his sodden sleeve.

'You've got something on your forehead.' Joe frowned at him.

Bill wiped again but the mark remained.

'Maybe it's the straw?' Joe asked.

'Yeah, I guess so, I get these rashes all the time here. Goddamn this country, and God bless America. Please ratify that peace and take us home soon.'

'Amen!' said anyone who'd heard him.

As the sailors cleared the courtyard of snow, the grateful farmer tried to shake every one by the hand, but few wanted his thanks. Within two hours of their arrival at Rounders, the inmates from One and Four were being marched back out again. Snaking up the hill before turning back to Dartmoor, their pace was slow, the men exhausted, their mood sombre. The sky, too, was against them, showing ominous layers of grey, cream and blue-black.

The soldiers talked and smoked among themselves, checking on their prisoners only with reluctance. Joe watched two redcoats amble along their line; they looked almost as cold and miserable as their prisoners. When the redcoats were no more than four strides away, they stopped alongside Gramm and Tilson. For a few seconds, the soldiers fell into step alongside the men from One, then they fell away.

'What?' said Habs to Joe. 'What's goin' on?'

The prisoners at the back of the line had stopped marching, spilling off the track to see what was happening. More shouted orders, and the men at the front stopped, too. Joe and Habs circled round to try to see what the redcoats had seen.

'Jesus Christ Almighty,' muttered Joe, his hands covering his mouth. They stared at poor Gramm and Tilson, who were now on their own in the middle of the track, their friends and comrades retreating in an ever-widening circle. Terrified, they looked at each other and started to weep.

The guards, now at some distance, called to them. 'Show us your hands! Remove your gloves!'

Both men pulled gently at the cotton fabric which they had wrapped around their hands.

The material fell to the ground. 'Hands up! Hands where we can see them!'

Both men raised their hands as if in surrender.

All eyes, both of prisoners and guards, switched from their hands to the faces of the two men. Then from face to hands. From the deep red marks on their foreheads to the ferocious red spots on their palms.

They didn't need a physician. Every man had seen it before. One word came from a hundred mouths.

'Smallpox.'

3.2

Dartmoor

JOE HAD known fear all his life. He had seen it in his mother's face when his father was dying. He had felt his whole body shake when an *Eagle* crewman had spotted the first Union flags on the horizon and quiet despair when he realized their bloody battle was lost. He remembered the trickle of sweat that had run down his back as he descended the decks of the prison ship. He felt that same terror now.

'I shook his hand,' he said. It was a hoarse, harsh whisper.

'You both had gloves on,' said Sam, then added, 'Of a kind . . .'

'His were more like bandages,' said Joe, unconvinced. 'And anyway, they'd be full of the pox.' He held his arms away from his body, as though that might keep infection at bay. In front of him stretched out a long, chaotic, single file of men. No one walked near anyone else. He could just see Gramm and Tilson out in front: stumbling, wretched, hysterical. They moved only at gunpoint, four guards with scarves over their faces stalking them like wild animals. Joe made out multiple, overlapping, panicky orders as they were hurled forward. 'What they sayin'?' asked Sam.

'They're saying they'll shoot them if they come any closer,' answered Joe.

Next came the One inmates, panicking, fearful and constantly, relentlessly, checking their own hands for any sign of a rash. A gap of fifty yards, then the men of Four, and behind them, in self-imposed isolation, Habs, Joe and Sam.

'We was all too close. We was too close!' said Sam. 'We was walkin' in their shadows. Oh, my dear God.'

'How close is too close?' asked Habs. 'Anyone know?'

They trudged on a few steps, the last of the troops, bayonets drawn, dictating their pace.

'We had an outbreak back in '09,' said Joe. He wanted to talk. It drowned some of the groaning. 'That's what my folks told me. A village near us lost nearly everyone – three farms, I think it was. A few houses. Ma said it was the most terrible thing she ever saw. They used to leave food in baskets at the village boundary, then retreat. They watched from a distance. Men and women covered in bloody sheets came to get it. She knew everyone in that village – called out to them – but they just took the food and went away.'

'So living in the same house is too close?' Habs looked at Joe, who nodded.

'Well, tha's everyone in Block One,' said Sam. 'Tha's a thousand men.'

'And what about us?' asked Habs. 'Did we march too close? Work too close?' He stared at Joe, then at Sam.

Joe, head down, said nothing. He was too busy fighting the voice in his head. Its message was clear: 'You know you were too close.'

By the time they got to Dartmoor, the hospital was already overwhelmed. The first cases had been confirmed shortly after the work party had left, and Magrath had ordered Block One to be quarantined. Soldiers stood at its closed door with orders to shoot anyone who tried to break out.

In Shortland's office, Magrath, his hand shaking on his stick, was brisk.

'It will be a miracle if we keep the outbreak confined to Block One but, at the moment, all sixty confirmed cases come from there. Two were on the work party with inmates from Block Four. They're being watched, but that's all I can do. Three hundred and seven have early signs of the rash. Nearly all my extra staff have deserted, so we need help from Plymouth, from London, from anywhere we can find it. There will be deaths, of course. Many deaths, I fear. They will need to be taken away for burial. Your men must do this. I will inoculate all of them, naturally, but I can't say it will be popular work.'

Shortland, his face grey, regarded his surgeon. 'I will ask for volunteers,' he said.

'And then you might need to order them,' said Magrath. 'I need all the resources you can find me.'

'I will make sure you have them, George, but I think, too, of your safety. Without you, we are lost. I should have had the vaccination back on the *Canopus* in '02. I will rectify that error right away.'

'I am safe from the disease,' said Magrath. 'I caught cow-pox a few years back, and it has made me immune. But I suggest I vaccinate you and Elizabeth immediately. I would inject you with a tiny amount. It is the only way to stop it. We can bandage, we can soothe, but we'll only stop it with the needle.'

Shortland swallowed. 'Very well.'

'And Elizabeth?'

'If you recommend it, I'm sure she will oblige.'

'Thank you,' said Magrath, 'and I would like it done in public. In the courtyard. So the men – the prisoners *and* the soldiers – see your example.' As Shortland made to protest, Magrath pressed. 'If this breaks out of One, the whole prison will sink. I'm sure of it. If the men take the vaccine, you have a chance of holding the prison till they go home. There is no time, Thomas, none at all. As your surgeon, I must insist.'

Shortland looked up from rearranging his books, blotter and pen and rose from his desk.

'As you wish, George,' he said wearily. 'As you wish.'

*

Thomas and Elizabeth Shortland, escorted by a guard commander and six of the Derbyshire militia, walked the short distance from their house, across the market square and through the gates into the prison courtyard. With every step, they could hear and see more of the gathering crowd before, finally, an improvised stage came into view, King Dick standing tall at the front of it. A clearly uncomfortable Dr Magrath was standing high on a dozen crates that had been dragged from the barracks, two medical bags at his feet.

'This feels more like an execution than an injection,' said the Agent.

'Agreed,' said Elizabeth, their pace brisk. 'But it was the right decision, Thomas.'

'Thank you.'

She interpreted his swiftest of glances as surprise at a rare moment of agreement.

As the gates were unlocked, Elizabeth's eyes swept the courtyard. 'I've never seen it this full,' she said. 'Maybe they're hoping for an execution, too.'

'Never heard them so quiet either,' said Shortland.

'They're scared, George. We all are.'

Redcoats stood at each corner of the stage, rifles held in anticipation of an imminent attack. One of them produced some crates to make steps and the Shortlands climbed up. Elizabeth surveyed the sea of faces for another sight of her newcomer before remembering he was one of the quarantined.

King Dick and Magrath were talking head to head for the first time.

'Physician, my men from the work party have been isolated in the cockloft. How long must they stay there?'

'A week,' said Magrath. 'Preferably longer. Ten days. You'll know by then.'

'Uh-huh. You doin' the needles?'

'Actually, no needles. It's a skin stab with a fork. Many

will not allow it, I know that. The Agent and Mrs Shortland have agreed, as you can see.'

'You come to Four,' said the King. 'When you're done with them, you bring your science to us.' He turned and pushed his way back towards his block. Magrath was nodding his thanks as he was summonsed by Shortland.

'Get this done, then, Magrath,' he said, removing his jacket and rolling up his sleeve. He glanced at the physician's brown glass bottle. 'That it?'

'That is it, yes.'

'What is it, exactly?'

'It's actually material from lesions in the udder of a cow with cowpox,' said Magrath. 'Local man called Jesty injected his whole family with it back in '74. Made them immune. It'll do the same for you.' The Agent nodded, then looked away.

The crowd surged forward, straining for a view. Elizabeth saw her husband's jaw lock and his fists clench. The procedure didn't concern her overly but she knew he would rather lead a frigate into battle than face the vaccination. Magrath uncorked the bottle then dipped in a long silver two-pronged fork. The size of it brought an audible gasp from the watching inmates, followed by a shout of 'Stick it in the bastard's eye!'

Shortland blanched.

'Don't mind them,' said Magrath, 'they're just being tars. Ours'd be no different.' He wiped Shortland's arm when he was done and pulled his sleeve down.

Next, Elizabeth sat down, her sleeve already rolled high and her eyes flashing Magrath a warning. When the Agent had turned to talk to one of the soldiers, she leaned in close. 'Someone will shout about us. I'm sure of it.'

Magrath nodded, his face taut with concentration. Again, he dipped the fork in the bottle; again, he checked he had taken enough vaccine. With one hand, he held Elizabeth's

150

arm; with the other, he stabbed her skin in two short, jerking motions. She winced, and a voice, clear and unchallenged, rang through the courtyard.

'Prickin' 'er, like most nights, then!'

As the laughter rolled, Elizabeth jumped up and took her husband by the arm, escorting him from the stage.

'It was the right and the brave thing to do, Thomas, even if we did get abuse. I'm proud of you.'

The colour had returned to the Agent's cheeks but he was silent as they returned to the house.

3.3

Wednesday, 11 January
Block Four

Habs, Sam and eighteen other Block Four inmates from the work party had been put in the rapidly cleared cockloft. Joe had to be admitted, too. There hadn't been any discussion about it, just an acknowledgement of the obvious: you couldn't quarantine the whole of Seven's cockloft just for one man. Joe sat cross-legged against the stage, his hands on his knees, palms up.

'Suddenly, we're equal,' said Habs, slumping against the stage. 'Sick white men allowed. Healthy white men: keep out.'

They were just twenty-one sailors, after all, terrified of dying. Four oil lamps on the stage drew each man in turn to examine their hands, each blister-free verdict greeted with a grim nod or relieved sigh. Food, grog, tobacco and pipes were left at the doors; the yarning took a predictable turn.

'We was docked in Madrid few years back,' said one, clouds billowing from his freshly lit pipe. 'On the *Matchmaker* outta Boston. Soon as we got ashore, we all smelled somethin' like rotten flesh, and this crazy woman come runnin' at us, half naked, covered in red spots and the like. She was screamin' somethin' we didn't recognize, but we turned right round and ran back to the ship. Whatever it was killed thousands, and we shouldn'ta even been in the harbour. We unloaded and got the hell outta there. We got lucky.'

A few of the men whistled their agreement.

'Damn right!' called a man shrouded in a tarp. 'I survived

152

the influenza two winters ago, off Nova Scotia. It took some o' the younger boys, mind, worst fevers I ever saw.'

There was some silence then, followed by a hawking cough and an extravagant spit.

'I got syphilis in Lisbon back in '10,' said the coughing man.

'Uh-huh. Me, too,' said another voice. 'Mine was in San Domingo. We all got the pox in San Domingo.'

'That pox don't count,' said Habs. 'You have to go lookin' for that one. This pox finds you where you are. And maybe it'll find us here still.'

In between the yarning, they heard the suffering. Magrath had ordered all the illegal stoves in all the blocks to be extinguished and the windows unblocked, decreeing that the uncirculated air was in large part to blame for the spread of the disease. As a result, the hundred yards between Block One and Block Four melted away and the agonies of their neighbours cut through the thoughts of the men in Four and animated their fear.

'Ev'ry time I hear that sound,' said Sam, pointing through the window towards One, 'that caterwaulin', I look around here. I look at all o' you. And none o' you is sick. Not like that sailor – may God have mercy on his soul – is sick. So maybe we'll survive, after all.'

'Sometimes,' said a white-haired sailor, shivering in the new draughts that had been encouraged into all the buildings, 'sometimes, it sounds like the whole o' One is dyin'. If I end up at the gates o' Hell, it ain't gonna sound no worse than that.'

Another inmate stepped up to a window and leaned out. 'We hear you!' he shouted. 'God bless you all!'

Within seconds, others took up the cry and from every prison block came shouts of sympathy and encouragement.

'Any singers here?' asked Joe, looking around. 'Anyone in your choir?' The man who'd told the influenza story, a round-faced man with a thin covering of grey hair, raised his hand.

'Me,' he said. 'Just me. Joshua.'

'Do you know any songs for the sick, Joshua?'

'Sure I do. We all do. They might not be in the choir, but they all know the songs.'

'Of course,' said Joe. 'Pardon my ignorance. Can you sing loud?'

Joshua laughed. 'You kiddin' me?'

Joe nodded. 'Loud enough to reach One?'

Joshua slowly got to his feet. 'Well, now,' he said, 'seein' as we ain't too sick ourselves, let's see if we can administer to the needy and sufferin'.' He stood by the first window. 'Wind's a nor'easter. Blow the song straight to 'em.'

Joshua started a marching beat, both feet stomping the floor in turn. All the men scrambled for the windows, clapping and stomping as they went. Joshua, leaning through the window, turned his head to the rooftops.

'Ain't gonna let nobody turn me around,' he sang, his full baritone loud enough to fill the cockloft and bounce off the roof of Block Three.

'Turn me around,' sang the men.

'Ain't gonna let nobody,' led Joshua.

'Turn me around, turn me around,' repeated the men. Habs nodded at Joe, who was learning fast. He'd never heard the song before, but he understood a work song when he heard it.

Joshua was finding his range now. Still stomping, he coughed and cleared his throat. From somewhere, he found more volume.

'I say I'm gonna hold out,' he sang.

'Hold out, hold out,' repeated his chorus.

'I say I'm gonna hold out.'

Then they sang together: 'Until my change comes.'

They carried on stamping their feet, but before the

154

third verse the crunching sound of boots on timber grew. Puzzlement was replaced by wonder. The extra feet were from downstairs. Suddenly, there were hundreds of boots hitting the floor – the noise was astonishing.

Habs and Joe leaned out of a window, only to see faces staring right back up at them.

'Joshua! They're waiting for you. You lead!' shouted Joe, still clapping.

Joshua nodded and leaned out further.

'I promise the Lord that I would . . .'

And what sounded like the whole of Four sang. A broadside of benediction.

Later that night, with most of the cockloft asleep, Habs and Joe lay on a mattress, listening again to the sounds of men in torment.

'D'you think they heard the singin'?' whispered Habs.

'Must have,' said Joe. 'Couldn't have missed it. And the clapping after. Went on and on.'

'Reckon the whole damn place was joinin' in,' said Habs.

They lay silent again.

'But they're still dying,' said Joe.

'Sure sounds like it. You feel all right?'

Joe propped himself up with an elbow. 'I ask myself that every second,' he said. 'I inspect my hands every second. We look at each other's faces every second. All the time. I know every inch of your forehead – everyone's forehead – mapped every spot that we don't need to be scared about. Worst thing about the night is that we can't see what's happening.'

'Or not happenin'.'

'Agreed.'

'You inspectin' me now, Mr Hill?'

In the near-darkness, Joe studied his friend. Rough blankets pulled high, only his head exposed to the frosty night air, Habs's eyes were closed and deep lines were etched into his forehead. Maybe he was frowning, maybe he had just aged. Joe couldn't tell. He counted the days since they had met. It was just twelve. Not even two weeks had passed since he'd marched under that hideous arch and announced the end of the war. What cheer remained in him came, still, from that proclamation and, he realized, the man lying next to him.

'I said, you inspectin' me?'

Joe leaned closer.

'Not officially,' he said.

'Do I pass?'

Joe lay back down alongside his friend, their wrapped bodies close enough to feel each other's warmth.

'You'll probably do,' he said.

3.4

Tuesday, 17 January
Block One

ELIZABETH SHORTLAND stood alongside a hammock, her hands resting on the canvas and rocking it gently. When her patient closed his eyes – he had said his name was Gramm – she covered her mouth with her arm to mask her nausea. She had soothing ointments and bandages but nothing that could stop his rash spreading. The pustules had become as hard as a thousand beads in his skin. When they leaked, crusted and flaked, she had nothing for that either.

The outbreak had unfolded in a series of waves, eventually claiming most of Block One.

There were protestations, but Magrath had reordered the block his own way. The dead and dying were put on the ground floor, the sick on the first and the few healthy remaining in the cockloft. Elizabeth was in what had once been, according to a nailed-on sign, Mess Nine on the ground floor. She blocked out the hellish noises of the diseased, their crying and their prayers, choosing instead the creaking hammock and the shouted commands of the newly inoculated soldier-orderlies. There were already five bodies by the door, wrapped in sheets and stacked like flour bags; they would be gone to the Dead House soon enough. Gramm, she knew, would join them before the day was out. Until a month ago, she had seen only two dead bodies – her grandmother when she collapsed at home, and a prison suicide the previous summer – now, she expected at least twelve a day.

'Mr Gramm, I have water if you're thirsty,' she said. She might have added, 'It's all I have and I'm sorry I can do no more.' He swallowed and winced, trying to speak. She leaned in close.

'Pray for me,' he breathed. 'Pray for me.'

She nodded. 'I will remember you in my prayers.'

A slight shake of his head. 'No, you must pray for me now.'

Elizabeth thought she understood; he hadn't the time to wait.

Magrath had given her a count of five hundred and fifty-three smallpox cases in One, with another two hundred in the hospital. It was an epidemic. Even now, she could see a score of patients awaiting her, but she rested a hand on Gramm's shoulder. She would pray for him, she would pray for all of them. In spite of her doubts, her feelings of inadequacy, the words came easily. They were the words of her upbringing.

'Remember not, Lord, our iniquities,' she said, 'nor the iniquities of our forefathers: Spare us, good Lord, spare thy people, whom thou hast redeemed with thy most precious blood, and be not angry with us for ever.' Gramm's lips cracked an amen. She found she had more. They were, she knew, words for a priest, but, from her lips at that moment, they seemed to have power.

'Unto God's gracious mercy and protection we commit thee,' she said. 'The Lord bless thee, and keep thee. The Lord make his face to shine upon thee, and be gracious unto thee. The Lord lift up his countenance upon thee, and give thee peace, both now and evermore. Amen.' Gramm was still now and Elizabeth stepped away. 'Amen,' she said for him, and moved on to the next hammock.

Tilson was raging. Bound with rope, he convulsed and kicked against his restraints, the hammock swaying precariously. Magrath stepped away, Elizabeth appearing at his side. 'He has a fire inside him,' she said. Magrath nodded. 'And we cannot put it out, Elizabeth, cannot get close.'

Tilson's face seemed to have disappeared, his skin now host to a hundred sharply raised orbs. His hands and feet, too, looked fit to burst.

'But we have to get close,' she said, and stepped towards the hammock. 'What's his name?'

'Tilson,' called Magrath.

Elizabeth grabbed one side of the hemp with both hands, and the wild rocking ceased. The crazed shouting calmed to a babble of unrecognizable words. She steeled herself, then looked directly into his bloodied, contorted eyes and smiled.

'Mr Tilson,' she said, her words fighting his delirium, 'I'm Elizabeth Shortland, and Dr Magrath is here, too. You are not forgotten, and we are doing all we can for you.'

Magrath handed her the jug of water and she dribbled some over Tilson's swollen, contorted lips. He swallowed some, coughed some up, then spoke again. This time, she recognized the words, but they came fast.

'My Sarah is here somewhere,' he said, his voice thin and rasping. 'She needs me . . . she needs all of us . . . we must go to her . . . do you know her?'

'Mr Tilson . . .' began Elizabeth, but Tilson wasn't to be stopped.

'You must take me to her, she has gold, she has everything, have you seen her? Take me to her.' The rocking was starting again, and Magrath stepped up to steady the hammock.

'Hallucinations,' said Magrath softly. 'A wandering of the mind. Come, there are others who need us. Many hundreds . . .'

'Can he hear me?' she asked, holding on to Magrath's sleeve.

'I couldn't say, Elizabeth, but let us assume that he can.'

Under the ropes, Tilson was beginning to twist and writhe again, his clothes tearing, his skin splitting.

'I want Sarah!' he screamed. 'I need her now!' Elizabeth had seen enough. She turned to Magrath.

'I am vaccinated, yes?' She saw his startled look.

'Yes, of course.'

'I am safe?'

'Yes, Elizabeth, but . . .'

'What's his first name?'

'I don't know.'

A voice from a nearby bunk. 'It's Jonathan. Jonathan Tilson.'

She reached out and laid her hand on Tilson's forehead, the beads of his disease hard against her gentle touch.

'I'm here, Jon,' she said. 'It's Sarah. I'm here. You're going to be all right. Everything will be all right.'

The writhing slowed, the hammock calmed, and the storm passed.

'You sleep now,' she said. Tilson closed his eyes.

And Elizabeth found she was saying her prayers again.

By the end of January, when new staff and supplies arrived, the epidemic appeared to have peaked. As more inmates took the vaccine, the death count started to fall. From a peak of thirty in one day, it tailed away to five, to one, and then, finally, a whole day, 7 February, passed without a fatality. By the end of the epidemic, they had buried two hundred and two American sailors.

'When is it over, George?' whispered Elizabeth in their cupboard office between wards A and B. 'When can we say we are done with it all?' They had both sunk to the floor, exhausted, barely able to speak, move or think.

'When the last scab is gone,' he replied quietly. 'But we will not be truly free of it. Many who have survived will lose their sight; some are blind already. So it will always be here, Elizabeth.' In the silence that followed, she heard him sigh so heavily she thought he might be expiring.

'Containing it to one block was astonishing,' she said. 'It was a miracle it never spread.'

'It was science, Elizabeth. It was medicine. If more had taken the vaccine early, or we'd had more supplies, who knows how many we'd have saved?'

She reached for his hand. 'When this is all over, George,' she whispered. 'When this bloody disease is gone and the whole bloody war is over, then everyone will leave. But if you go, if you are posted somewhere else, the thought of . . .'

Magrath had never seen Elizabeth cry before, but now she sobbed with such fury, such intensity, he feared they might be discovered. He buried her head on his shoulder as her whole body convulsed with grief. She wept for the dead, the blind, the scarred. She wept for her marriage, her son and for her own limitless incarceration.

3.5

Saturday, 11 February
Block Four

'WE GETTIN' the bread, that's what's happenin'.' Sam's words registered slowly, and Habs felt his hammock pushed harder. 'It's our watch.'

'I can't get up if the ship is rollin',' he murmured.

'I reckon you can,' said Sam. 'We all gettin' bread. No reason you gettin' off, cuz.' He rocked the hammock again, then tried rousing Ned.

'You, too, Mr Penny. I ain't gettin' it all on my own.' The lamplighter wrapped himself in the folds of a thin blanket.

'You know, I can't never hear you, on account o' my ear goin' missin',' mumbled Ned. 'Anyways, I can see it's still dark. And man has no use or purpose until there is light to guide his path . . .'

'He does if there's bread to be fetched and it's his turn to fetch it,' said Sam. 'Mess rules, and you know it.' Habs could hear the exasperation in his cousin's voice and opened his eyes. First, he checked his hands, front and back, a habit he guessed would now be with him for ever. Tattooed fingers, four rings and no smallpox blisters. He looked up. Sam was leaning on a stanchion, already working his clay pipe hard, clouds of grey smoke billowing into the thick, fetid air. He caught Habs looking.

'Can't be last, cuz,' he said, shaking his head. 'If we come back with nothin' but ship's biscuits, King Dick'll go crazy.'

Each morning, the bread rations were available from the two storehouses that stood in the top corners of the market square. Each mess sent out enough men to collect the rations; one and a half pounds of bread per person was one white loaf each and, with twenty or more men in each mess, it was a job for three. The local contractor usually delivered enough for the whole prison, but occasionally there would be a shortfall and the stragglers, the last messes in the queue, were left with the hated ship's biscuits, the hardtack that had cost so many sailors their teeth.

Habs slid from the hammock, pulled on his boots and jacket then dragged Ned from his slumbers. By the time the turnkeys arrived, Habs, Sam and Ned were among the first at the doors. The icy winds took their breath.

'Guide me, Habs,' said Ned, clasping his shoulder. 'My eyes has to stay shut till the storehouse.'

'But you'll miss the beauty of a Dartmoor sunrise.' Habs shivered as they joined the shuffling groups of men now tumbling from all seven blocks and heading for the square.

'Let me guess,' said Ned, his eyes squeezed shut. 'The sky is grey, the clouds are grey, all the prisons are grey, the English are grey, the coffee'll be grey and even the bread will be goddamn grey. How'd I do?' He opened his eyes, looked around, nodded and shut them again. 'Perfect score,' he said.

Habs and Sam laughed. 'You left out the grey fields,' said Habs. 'The miles and miles of grey desert.'

'Uh-huh. My mistake. You're right there. The only thing that ain't grey here is your new friend, Mr Hill. He's the shiniest, whitest white boy I ever seen.'

'Give him time, Ned, give him time,' said Sam. 'The deathly Dartmoor grey will get him in the end.'

'Musta seemed strange,' said Ned, 'having a white boy up in the cockloft like that.'

'In the end, it got strange,' conceded Habs. 'To begin

with, it was like bein' back on the ships. We was all scared. Like there was an enemy out there and it could take us all. We could hear it killin' every night. Then, when we all got to thinkin' we would survive, Joe was suddenly the visitor, the stranger again.'

'So we did some actin',' said Sam, 'put on some scenes we all knew. Any lines we didn't know, we jus' made 'em up.'

'This is you, Habs and Joe?' asked Ned.

'Uh-huh,' said Sam. 'We even got applause sometimes.'

They passed through the gates into the market square, streams of men now choosing which storehouse queue to join. Habs pulled them left and counted fifty-seven men ahead of them before they reached the small counter in the storehouse. He sensed he had heard a tone of censure in the words of his friend. He frowned at Ned, whose eyes were closed again.

'Are you disapprovin' of Joe Hill, Ned Penny?' he said.

His friend opened his eyes. 'Is there anythin' to disapprove of?'

'I've sailed with you, an' been jailed with you, for two years or more,' said Habs. 'There's a long list of things you disapprove of.'

Ned closed his eyes again. 'Some more'n others.'

'What Ned is sayin',' said Sam, 'is you stand out. Folk notice you and Joe around . . .'

'Chrissakes,' said Habs, annoyed. 'You want us to send letters? That way, we wouldn't be seen together so much. That better for you?'

'No, I jus' . . .'

'Enough, Ned, you've said your piece,' said Sam. 'It's too early for this.'

Lines of men, laden with loaves, were streaming past them now, some of them finishing their ration before they had left the square.

'All I'm sayin',' said Ned, 'is you have *us*. You know us, is all . . .' He left the sentence hanging.

164

They collected their bread from the hatch of the store-house, four pasty-faced soldiers shovelling loaves into their hands. One raised an eyebrow, and Sam slipped him four coins. The bread stacked under-arm in columns of threes and fours, they tottered back down the square.

'Carryin' goddamn cannonballs was easier,' muttered Sam. 'What do they put in this bread, anyhow?'

'A seditious rag, I'm hopin' for,' said Ned, peering closely at his loaves.

'Jus' wait till we're inside,' said Sam.

Habs was still frowning. 'If we do the play, do *you* want to play Juliet, Ned? Is that it? You jealous of Joe?'

Ned coughed up his laughter.

'Of his ears, yeah! I'd like 'em like they was before the cannon took one. He has fine ears, I'll say that. But of the rest of him . . . Maybe you seen more, what'd you recommend?'

'I'd recommend,' said Habs, 'that you keep them eyes open and that mouth closed. At least till after breakfast.'

The mess table was up, the loaves were dropped. Ned found the paper first, gently prising its pages from the dough. 'How much do we pay that grey weasel for this?' he said, assembling the paper in a loose order. 'It says one shillin' on the front. I'm guessin' he ain't cuttin' the price 'cos it's a week old.'

'You guess right,' said Sam. 'Two shillings and sixpence we pay, but at least it ain't a traitorous Federalist rag.'

'Though, truth told, you can wipe your ass with them,' said Ned. '*The Times* is most absorbent in that regard.'

Breakfast arrived, four mess men delivering the kitchen's herring and potatoes in large pans, and they waited for the King.

Habs bent over the front page. 'Is the news good? We had any more victories?' Each of the men around the mess table eyed the food and the newspaper with hungry eyes. The coalition of subscribers needed for such an expensive publication had been hard won, and they waited eagerly for their allocated pages.

'Sometimes I see them papers the Agent lets us see,' said Sam, 'the ones they want us to read. Ain't nothin' but British lies.'

'But they're free lies,' said Ned, 'and if I'm outta credit, I find I can make do with England's lies for a while.'

The heavy tread, the tapping club, and the King was there, steaming coffee in hand. He'd been listening.

'And when even England's papers write about our victory in New Orleans,' he growled, 'you know it musta been a hu-mi-li-a-tion.' The King stretched the last word, emphasizing each syllable. He spooned a pile of food into his bowl, the fish now indistinguishable from the potatoes, and stared at the paper. He swallowed half his breakfast down, then distributed the pages. 'Call out the news when you see it. Don't imagine there be too many more battles – news o' the peace'll reach America soon.'

Breakfast was gone in seconds, chunks of the bread used to mop up the last dregs.

Habs licked his bowl then took his sheet and scanned the densely printed script. It didn't take him long to find the words he was looking for. 'Ha!' he shouted, 'I got it.' He put down the bowl, grabbing the sheet with both hands. The other mess readers lowered their pages to listen. '"On 8 January 1815, ten to twelve thousand British troops sent from France, an army furnished with all the means of destruction, were attacked by the American General Jackson."'

Applause punctuated Habs's reading; other messes were now listening intently. He enjoyed the moment. He had a speech. He read on. '"With as much coolness as if he had been aiming at harmless birds, Jackson opened fire upon them and swept them down like grass before the scythe of the mower."'

More applause, but Habs urged them to stop.

'Wait, wait. Hear this. "He sallied in pursuit, marching over blood and brains and mangled carcasses, and finally drove the survivors to their ships and bade them carry to England the proof that the soil of freedom was not to be invaded with impunity."'

The metal plates were banged loudly, spoons rattled against the stanchions. King Dick conspicuously folded his arms, his expression grave. The clamour subsided as each man realized he was out of step with the King.

'Like I was sayin',' he said, 'a hu-mi-li-a-tion. So then, then comes the re-tal-i-a-tion. If we was in Louisiana or Mississippi, it would feel good. Real good. But we ain't. We in England and, if the English are humiliated, then our guards are humiliated. The militia on these walls is humiliated. And we all know what kinda men they are. They'll have friends and brothers in that expedition. The blood and brains you read about, Mr Snow, is the blood and brains o' them. We should expect some score-settlin' sometime soon.' He threw his bowl on to the table. 'Now, find me some other news. Preferably containin' the word "ra-ti-fic-a-tion".'

3.6

The Blocks

TOMMY JACKSON, crier, left the clerks' house and sprinted past the weary militia (who barely saw him coming), took a hard left at the alarm gates and was in the market square within seconds. Soon, it would be full of troops on parade but for now it was empty, save for the sweepers finishing their work after the bread handout. One of them raised his broom in salute, but Tommy had already gone, under the military walk and away.

The seven prison blocks had already turned out, and everywhere the fires of the coffee-makers and meat-boilers filled the yards with smoke, steam and fumes. Some of the recently extinguished indoor stoves were in evidence, too, most of them adapted to fry the bread, beef and cabbage that made up the bulk of the rations. Trails of grey smoke drifted across the courtyard before disappearing into the granite.

Tommy fought his way left into the reopened Block One, stood at the bottom of its stairs and bellowed, 'All hands! All hands! News this day! I have news!'

Instantly, a crowd had formed around him. The stairs filled with the half dressed and the barely dressed and those who had been outside now scrambled to get inside. All the men had livid, corroded, pockmarked faces and arms, the scars of their recent nightmare; some were now blind. They stared at Tommy, but he had trained himself not to stare back.

The men heaved forward and all but enveloped him. An old sailor with a model ship for a hat hauled him from the scrum and stood him on the first step. Tommy took a breath. The prison flooded with hope.

'Is it the peace?' 'Have we ratified?' were the first shouts. Then: 'The English must have given up?' 'Has the King died?' 'Let the boy speak!' Since they had heard of the American victory against the British in New Orleans, any news was greeted with wild enthusiasm. Tommy had to wait a full minute before reading out what he had to say. Clasping both sides of the paper, he read slowly, and with a furious concentration.

'The Agent of the Depot for Prisoners of War at Dartmoor, Captain Thomas G. Shortland, wishes it to be known that at 08.30 hours, there will be a proclamation read to all prison blocks. An unarmed senior officer will attend in each case.'

When Tommy had finished, there was a brief silence as the men waited to see if he was going to say anything else. But when he folded the piece of paper and they realized he was finished, the bedlam was greater than ever.

Tommy pushed his way outside – half the prison seemed to be camped out in One's courtyard. He had been ordered by the clerk to 'make great haste' in distributing this bulletin, but he couldn't even see Block Two, never mind reach it. 'Read it again!' came the cry. Tommy looked at the wall of sailors facing him and understood that, even though it was most irregular, repeating the dispatch outside was the only way he was going to be allowed to leave. So, framed in Block One's wide doorway, he read his script once more.

They were already waiting for him at Two, where he delivered his news, again. A swarm of men then followed him to his own in Three.

At Four, Tommy leapt inside to find King Dick reclining over three steps, Habs, Sam and Ned all sitting on the stairs beneath, waiting for him.

'We saw you comin'!' called Ned.

'We heard you comin'!' said Sam.

'So now let the crier do his cryin',' declaimed King Dick.

Tommy read aloud from the piece of paper once more.

'So you are preparin' the way, Mr Jackson,' said the King when he was finished. 'Like John the Baptist, there is another comin' after you. Well, we shall wait here till he comes but, first, whisper to me.' From the folds of a purple blanket, he beckoned Tommy closer.

The boy edged forward in small, reluctant steps.

'Come, come!' urged the King impatiently, until Tommy stood at the foot of the stairs. King Dick inclined his massive head, the bearskin hat hovering inches above the crier's head. A fog of sweat, tobacco and pine enveloped him as the King whispered, 'Will it be the peace, boy? Do you know?'

Tommy stood rigidly to attention. All he could see was the side of the King's head – the old scars, a pierced but empty lobe, the wisps of black hair protruding from under the bearskin's brim.

'I . . . I don't know, sir. I haven't heard, King Dick, sir. I'm sorry. And I got to go.' He bowed, just to be on the safe side, then turned and ran.

The throng had moved to Five. Tommy ran through the men who lined the route and now packed in to the entrance. 'It's the same news! It hasn't changed!' he shouted in exasperation as he fought his way inside. He had to get to Seven before the Agent sent his men in, or he would lose his job, for certain. One reading of the papers did for Five, and then for Six. By the time he reached Seven, his cry was a breathless one.

'All hands! I got news!' They all knew what was coming but they listened anyway, and when Tommy was done he was relieved to see Joe beckoning him outside.

'I don't know any more, Mr Hill, honest I don't,' he called.

Joe offered him some coffee. 'It's cold and tastes of rotting wood, but I found I got used to it after the first pint.'

Tommy took a small sip then grimaced and spat. A sudden silence fell over the prisoners, and Joe and Tommy glanced towards the market square. A voice carried from one of the blocks: 'Here we are, boys. Look alive there!'

Across the courtyard, a small platoon had appeared by the gate. Red coats, green epaulets. 'The Derbyshire militia,' said Roche. 'Our favourite.'

To Tommy's puzzled look, Joe replied, 'They marched us here. We sang at them all the way. They hated us.'

'And we hated 'em back,' said Roche. 'Ugly sons of bitches, ain't they?'

From their ranks, seven men now marched, fanning out, one heading for each block. The clapping and the shouting started in Seven, but it quickly spread across the blocks. The sailors around Joe had no doubt what was coming.

'Here we go, m'boys! America is calling!'

'Lady Liberty wants us home!'

'Send the ships, we're ready!'

Approaching the crescent of prisons, the British officers for One and Seven arrived first, rapidly followed by those for Two and Six. The soldier who had stopped just a few yards from Joe stood rooted to attention, staring straight ahead, apparently seeing nothing of his audience. Many of them had dropped their trousers and were calling, 'Here's to your mad old King!' As the officer waited for his colleagues to reach Three, Four and Five, he was subjected to the full range of insults that the sailors had perfected in the course of their incarceration. The recently gleaned news of America's overwhelming victory in New Orleans was fresh in every sailor's mind.

'Hang your head, John Bull! England is routed!'

'Our victory is certain!'

'The Mississippi runs red with British blood!'

The officer glanced left. One colleague had just reached Four, and Joe thought he saw a flicker of a smile pass across the officer's face.

'This might not be what we think it is,' he murmured, but no one was listening.

'Here we go!'

'Send us home!'

The officer produced a sheet of paper.

'There it is! It's from Uncle Sam!'

The officer in front of Four raised his hand then lowered it. All seven proclamations were read together, the voices overlapping with each other around the square.

'From the Agent at Dartmoor to all prisoners. Following the signing of the Treaty of Ghent, which provided for peace between our nations, many among you hoped for a speedy release. His Majesty's government was also desirous of a swift return of our soldiers and sailors held in American jails. I have to report to you that your Congress has still not ratified the peace. Until such time, there can be no prisoner release or exchange.'

There were other words, but they were lost in barrage of groans, catcalls and abuse. Despair turned to fury in a flash. Breakfasts suddenly became weapons; all seven officers were hit by a rain of fish, pastries and scalding coffee. In front of Seven, to huge cheers, a plate of hot plum gudgeon arced over the sailors' heads then splashed on to the officer's tunic.

'Thank the Lord he's unarmed,' said Joe.

'Sure, but them others ain't,' said Roche. 'Look.' Behind the officers, many of the platoon had instinctively raised their rifles, aiming straight at the prisoners. On the military walk, each of the patrolling soldiers had men in their sights. A swift, bellowed command from their sergeant and they were reluctantly lowered again. The humiliated, food-splattered officers performed a swift about-turn, then made a swift retreat.

'Runnin' away like your brothers in New Orleans!' shouted Roche, joining some of the other sailors shaking their fists at the departing British. 'Cowards! We want our freedom.'

A group of them advanced towards the militia, arms wide, taunting.

'Will!' Joe shouted. 'You'll get us all shot. Why fight them when we have nothing to fight with?'

''Cos this,' said Roche, stabbing his finger where the troops had been, 'ain't about Congress. It's 'bout the British gettin' whipped in Louisiana. And losin' two thousand men. And losin' their general. That's what this is 'bout, and this is their revenge. This is a provocation.'

Tommy, next to Joe, looked close to tears.

'This is bad, Mr Hill, ain't it?' he said. 'You should've seen all them faces. In all them prisons. They thought they was going home. Smokin' their last pipes, you know? Things gonna be bitterer now, and no mistake.'

Joe knew the crier was right. And Will, too. The war was over, but they couldn't go home.

'Yes, Tommy. Just when we thought we might be gone. Then their silken thread plucks us back again.'

Tommy slid an arm through Joe's.

'That you speakin' or Juliet?' he asked.

'Both of us, Tommy,' said Joe. 'That's both of us speaking.'

3.7

HABS AND Joe walked fast. Their circuit took them round the back of all seven prison blocks – a vast semicircular track that ran alongside the twelve-foot-high iron palisade that ringed the prisons. If they walked tight against the fence, they were for long stretches invisible to the watching, twitchy British who peered down from the military walk. The late-morning air carried a welcome tang of salt and the sun cut the sharpest shadows of the year so far.

'And you're sure this is King Dick's idea?' asked Joe.

'Would I make that up?'

Joe was frowning, persistent; he needed this to be clear. 'But was it his suggestion?'

Habs's response was measured. 'He said somethin', jus' to see what I thought.'

'And what did you think?'

'That it sounded 'bout right.'

Everywhere, groups of men huddled to discuss the morning's events. Habs and Joe paused their conversation each time they negotiated a knot of prisoners.

'And this is because of what happened in the courtyard?' asked Joe.

'King Dick woulda said somethin' anyhow,' said Habs. 'And you spent those days with us in the cockloft. But yes, he thought you might change your mind 'bout the play now. If we're not goin' home, well, then . . .'

'What were the English thinking?' Joe was distracted for a moment. 'If they were trying to start another revolution, that was a goddamn fine effort.'

'When it comes to provokin' Yankees,' commented Habs, 'they 'bout the best there is.'

Round the back of Five, a small huddle of sailors looked up to see who was approaching, then resumed their conversation. With a glance to the guards beyond the palisades, Habs leaned in close. 'I heard talk of an escape this mornin'. Never heard that before. Not in Four.'

'How d'you escape from Dartmoor?' asked Joe, surprised. 'Is it possible?'

'If it's just you, you bribe a guard. You need someone to get you out. If there's more than you, it's the tunnel.'

Joe stopped in his tracks. 'There's a tunnel?' He realized he'd spoken too loud, checked for eavesdroppers, then glanced up at the military walk.

Habs tugged at his coatsleeve to get him walking, then spoke softly. 'Used to be three. First one was in Two, longest was in Five, and the French built one in Four. But Two and Five got discovered. So that leaves Four.'

'Have you seen it?' Joe asked. 'How far does it go?'

Habs shook his head. 'I ain't, but Ned says he seen it once. Heads north from the cookhouse, he said. But tha's a lot of diggin' 'fore you reach the outer wall, and King Dick stopped all that kinda talk soon as he heard it. Said the press gangs always out there lookin' for more victims and, anyways, there was enough dead Yankees here and he sure wasn't goin' to help 'em kill any more.'

Four Rough Allies appeared from the back of Three. Joe thought he recognized the shortest of them from the library, but the forked beards made it hard to tell them apart. Their uneven walk suggested they'd made an early start on the ale. Their eyes flicked from Joe to Habs and back again.

The short Ally hitched up his trousers and squirted tobacco juice from the corner of his mouth. 'Still workin' on your nigger play, then?' he breathed as they passed.

Neither of them said anything, just kept walking. A whole block later, Habs sighed deeply. 'Hadn't thought 'bout this,' he said. 'Not properly.'

'What do you mean?'

'I'm invitin' ... we're invitin' you to move to Four. Makes sense to us, but not to them.' Habs gestured back at the Allies. 'In here, if you get recruited and go fight for the British, you're branded a traitor 'fore you go. I mean, really burned. Like with irons. Well, if you move in with "the niggers" to perform in some "nigger play", many here'll be thinkin' 'bout you the same way. Even some o' your own crew. Maybe it ain't such a good idea.'

Joe pulled Habs's arm back until he stopped walking. They had reached a sheltered space between Blocks One and Two where the sun had reached and melted some of the snow.

'But there's a berth near you that's free?' Joe fixed his eyes keenly on Habs.

'It'll be free, yes.'

'So it isn't free now?'

'Listen, Joe,' said Habs, his normally restless eyes settling on Joe's. 'You know that if King Dick asks, King Dick gets. He wants you to join us in Four. You'll be 'cross the aisle from me, Ned and Sam.'

'And the King.'

'And the King, yes. He likes you, Joe, else he wouldn't be offerin'. He don't do this very often.'

'You mean, he doesn't invite whites very often?'

'I do mean that, yes.'

'But I would be leaving my mess,' said Joe, turning away. 'It's not the Rough Allies worrying me. I haven't been firing cannon and rifle at sea these last two years only to become a coward as soon as I get to England. No, it isn't them. But if my ship think I am deserting them . . . well, I can't come. We survive in groups, Habs. I'm not sure I can change just like that. I need to know which group I'm in, where I belong.'

Habs twisted a button on his coat. 'You're right. 'Course you right. And you've only been here a few weeks – King Dick'll understand when you explain it like that. But in the long days before home, we can still put on a show.'

'We can,' said Joe, leaning back against the wall. 'Hard to believe – Shakespeare in a jail. *Romeo and Juliet* in Dartmoor. It's quite something.'

Habs stood next to him, their shoulders touching, heads turned skywards. 'The show most certainly will be somethin',' he said, 'once all the rehearsin's done. And we need to make this memorable. The last show of the Dartmoor Amateur Dramatic Company.'

The cockloft's wall of tobacco smoke and beer fumes hit them hard; here, everyone had a pipe, everyone a jug. Most of Block Four had forced their way inside. There was no music, not even any gambling; but arguments, loud and impassioned, had taken over. It started at the door: Habs and Joe found themselves squeezed between four men who were yelling at each other.

'They done that on purpose.'

'D'you expect them to jus' let us go?'

'You lost your thinkin' in here!'

'Show me the tunnel! I'll dig us home myself.'

They ducked and weaved around the shouting, Habs leading the way. A man with hollow eyes and intricately braided queues grabbed hold of Joe, but Habs pushed him away. 'Later, Eli. We're seein' King Dick.'

'Far corner,' said the man, as though he were passing on a great wisdom.

As he walked through the crowds, Joe couldn't help but take in the glances, the nods, the squints of displeasure.

'They don't like me here, Habs,' he called, a sense of foreboding in his voice.

'Don't matter!' was the shouted reply. 'King Dick's pleasure's all you need.'

And the King's pleasure seemed to be what they had. He saw them approach and summoned them closer. They waited while he finished a detailed discourse on British naval tactics. When he had, he waved his audience away. The slight figures of Alex and Jonathan lurked behind his throne.

'Mr Snow! Mr Hill!' he boomed. 'Join me here, these men are just leavin'.'

Joe removed his hat, his damaged scalp now invisible beneath a new growth of soft blond hair.

'So, I assume the reason you're here is that you two've been talkin' 'bout these matters.'

The King glanced from Habs to Joe then back again. Habs nodded and turned to Joe.

The King's black eyes narrowed, his voice dropping to a murmur. 'I want you to understand this. We don't *need* you, Mr Hill, you know that?' He let his words hang for a moment. 'We don't *need* you in Four. We don't *need* you in our theatre company.'

A small white hand appeared, offering the King coffee. Eyes still on Joe, he took the cup and sipped slowly. Habs shifted his weight awkwardly. Joe kept quiet.

The King held out the now-empty cup and the white hand appeared again. 'Thank you, Mr Daniels,' he muttered.

'Yes, sir,' said Alex from behind him.

King Dick picked up his club, striking it against the floor as he spoke. 'We are sufficient,' he said. 'We are complete. We *need* nothin' from you.' He rose now and peered

178

down at Joe, one hand tucked inside his starred sash. 'Have you read your Thomas Hobbes yet, Mr Hill? There's a copy in Seven, I'm sure of it.'

Joe, bewildered and unprepared for this course of conversation, shook his head. 'No, King Dick, I—'

The King waved the club. 'Don't matter. I'll tell you what you need to know. Out there . . .' He stabbed his club six times, one for each block. 'Out there, you have to save your skin by whatever means you deem fit. In here, in Four, there is order. *I* save your skin; *you* follow me.'

'I see—' began Joe.

'So, we don't *need* you,' repeated the King, 'but we *invite* you.' Now he smiled, suddenly welcoming. 'We *invite* you to join our company – but you follow the rules. You might like it. You might not. But before you give me an answer, you know that your crew, your mess mates, your block . . . they will not understand.'

Joe waited a few seconds then took a deep breath. 'And that is why I cannot accept your invitation, King Dick. On the *Eagle*, we fought together, we nursed together, we buried so many of our friends together . . .' He held the King's stare, the black eyes impossible to read. 'We saved each other's skin. I should stay with them, I think. But your play, your *Romeo and Juliet* – that, I could do. That, I would very much like to do. If I can join that company, I should like that very much.'

King Dick hadn't moved. No one had. After a long moment he removed his bearskin, wiped a hand over his neatly trimmed hair then placed the hat back on his head.

'Are you negotiatin' with me, Mr Hill?' he asked, his tone neutral.

'Why, no, sir,' replied Joe swiftly, nervously.

'Yes, you are,' said the King, 'but you gettin' me wrong: I *like* negotiatin'. *I'm* negotiatin'. I'm a businessman, and I accept your terms. If you play Juliet for me, you can sleep where you want, even with the pigs on Dartmoor if you wish. Or maybe with the Agent – but the pigs got more style.'

The men around the King roared with laughter, fuelled more by relief than comedy.

'I admire your loyalty,' he went on, 'but the offer will remain open.' King Dick banged his club on the floor like a gavel. He was moving on. 'We shall perform *Romeo and Juliet* in one month. It will be the last performance of the Dartmoor Amateur Dramatic Company and men will talk about it for ages to come. We rehearse today. Mr Snow, call everyone together.'

3.8

Block Four, Cockloft

THEY REHEARSED for the remainder of the day. As soon as Pastor Simon had finished his service, the choir their last song and the gamblers had started rolling dice, Ned and Sam tabled off a corner of the room. The two copies of *Romeo and Juliet* were set on two wooden barrels and the players stood or sat, depending on who was speaking. If anyone dared to watch, one glance from the King sent them away.

Habs had a problem. 'So I'm a Montague. I am a coloured man. My father is played by King Dick; Benvolio and Mercutio are my relatives, played by Sam and Ned. We are all coloured men. Not the same colour, it's true – why Sam is lighter skinned than the rest of us, we'll never know.'

Everyone laughed and Sam took a bow. 'But Joe here is a Capulet,' continued Habs. 'And he is a white man, a rival, an ofay. There are many Capulets in the play – his parents, for example – so they got to be white, too. But Tommy here is the only other white-skinned actor we got.' The crier flushed slightly at being called an actor but all eyes were still on Habs. 'Now the French have gone, don't we need to find us some new Capulets?'

Instinctively, everyone waited for the King to pronounce on this. Hunched on his box, hat folded across his lap, he chewed on the unlit pipe between his teeth.

'We don't have to do the full play, Mr Snow. You know how everyone gets . . . restless after a certain amount of time has passed. We gotta keep this one fast. So all them servants, fiddlers and musicians, they can go. Also, as I explained to Mr Hill here, we don't *need* anyone. We can do this play with these players here right now.' He stood and pointed the pipe stem at each of them in turn. 'If Mr Hill can be playin' a fourteen-year-old girl, you can all sure as hell play some white folks. It's actin', Mr Snow.' The King was starting to uncoil now, expanding as he spoke, each word inflating him further. 'But you do have a point so, yes, a couple o' new actors might help tell our story. Mr Jackson, you know all the blocks better'n most. What d'you say?'

Tommy had only just stopped blushing after being referred to as an actor; now, being asked his opinion by King Dick sent his cheeks reddening furiously again.

'Well. There was a – erm . . .' He swallowed before continuing. 'There was another theatre company in Five for a while but no one really went to their shows.'

Ned snorted. 'They tried to charge a shillin' for lettin' folk in,' he said. 'That was their problem – well, one o' many, if truth be told. *The Heiress at Law* they put on last, and it was so goddamn feeble. Every scene had goddamn sugar bowls and goddamn speeches like they all shitted soap. And I know for certain some of those players was intoxicated before they started. Two of 'em was sick all on each other, jus' 'fore the interval. Biggest applause o' the whole goddamn night. Soon after, their main man – Wells, I think it was – he caught the flu and died. Best thing for him, too. They ain't done a goddamn show since.'

The King looked around and, catching Alex Daniels's eye, summoned him over. 'We need coffee an' black fritters. Some freco stew, too. Here.' He produced a handful of coins and slapped them into Alex's outstretched hand. 'Mr Mason outside o' Two usually has the best, try him first. Tell him who it's for.'

'Yes, King Dick.'

As he and Jonathan scampered away, the King turned to Joe.

'Mr Hill, did you bring any players in with you from the crew o' the *Eagle*? It's jus' that, what no one has said jus' yet, is that many here in this fine prison don't wanna act with Negroes. They'll shoot cannon with us, sink ships with us, but bein' on a stage with us?' The King feigned a shiver. 'It's not *natural*, you see.'

Joe considered the question. 'No players that I could rightly say, King Dick,' he answered. 'There were no shows on the *Eagle*; we never had time to do much else than fight. We had five coloured sailors in all, but we never talked about . . . such matters. They all passed bravely when we lost the ship. I could ask Mr Goffe and Mr Lord if they'd be interested. They're good men, sir.'

The King nodded slowly. 'Ask 'em tonight. If they agree, bring 'em tomorrow; we have enough here for now. Sam, Habs: Act One. Benvolio and Romeo are talkin' 'bout love and Benvolio is unimpressed with his cousin.'

'Uh-huh, tha's about right,' said Sam.

They traded lines for thirty minutes more before Alex and Jonathan returned with food and drink. They all ate where they sat, the conversation, between mouthfuls, only of the theatre. 'On my first ship,' said the King, 'there were two stewards. Both men outta Washington, both blacker than me and both had travelled to England many times. They seen so many plays, gone to so many theatres, it was all they spoke about. So they put on shows, right there on the ship. They shortened the plays, added a whole lot of singin' and dancin' to some Shakespeare, and I was hooked. Like a whale on a harpoon line. I'd never heard such words before, but it seemed to me, this boy outta Guinea, that this William Shakespeare, whoever he was, he knew 'bout my life. Knew 'bout my sadness, 'bout my trials, 'bout my joys.

And that is why, Mr Hill, despite what some paintin's might show, I know this man was coloured like me. I'll hear no other view.'

Joe, with a mouthful of stew, mumbled quickly, 'And I'll not offer one.' When his mouth was clear, he had a question. 'What scenes might you cut, King Dick? The chorus at the start of the show says it'll last two hours. How much shorter will it be?'

The King narrowed his eyes and Joe wasn't sure if he was being squinted at or appraised further. 'We need to lose some o' the longer speechifyin', for certain. Keep it movin', Mr Hill, keep it fast. Your Juliet has a speech – Act Three, if I recall: "Gallop apace, you fiery-footed steeds . . ."'

Joe picked it up: '". . . Towards Phoebus' lodging . . ."'

The King raised an eyebrow. 'Uh-huh. That's fast, Mr Hill, you're ahead of me. Well, I sure hope you didn't spend too long learnin' that speech. It has thirty-one lines. Thirty-one! The audience'd rather hear Pastor Simon preach once more on sin and damnation than hear Juliet speak so long. No one dies, no one fights, no one does nothin' – jus' you and your speech for thirty-one lines. So I cut it to four.' To Joe's shocked expression, he responded, 'Ain't no time for poetry here, Mr Hill. You'll thank me once you're on that stage and your audience has taken to yellin'. You see if you don't.' The King swallowed the last of his coffee. 'But here's one scene we play in full. Act One, Scene Five. It all starts here. Romeo meets Juliet, they fall in love, they kiss . . .'

'Everything so soon?' asked Tommy, incredulous. The King laughed.

'Everything so soon indeed, Master Crier. They meet, fall in love, kiss, marry, shake the sheets and die, all in four days.'

Tommy blushed once more and looked to the ground.

'So, page fifteen,' said the King. 'Tybalt has jus' left.'

'So we need a Tybalt,' said Habs.

'Patience, Mr Snow,' said the King, annoyed. 'We are attendin' to that. Your speech, I think.' Habs moved to one barrel, Joe to the other. Habs looked across, smiling, but Joe had his head in the script. Habs drained some cold coffee and began.

> 'If I profane with my unworthiest hand
> This holy shrine, the gentle sin is this:
> My lips, two blushing pilgrims, ready stand
> To smooth that rough touch with a tender kiss.'

Joe, following the script, mouthed Romeo's words. Now it was Juliet's turn.

> 'Good pilgrim, you do wrong your hand too much,
> Which mannerly devotion shows in this—'

The King interrupted.

'Can't hear you, Mr Hill. Louder. Assume we're all drunk, we're growin' bored and wanna go home.'

Joe snatched a nervous glance at the King, then at Habs, and was back to the book.

> 'For saints have hands that pilgrims' hands do touch
> [He was louder this time.]

'And palm to palm is holy palmers' kiss.'

Tommy looked puzzled but said nothing. Sam asked the question for him.

'What's that mean?' he said, looking in turn at the King, Joe and Habs.

'We should be holdin' hands,' said Habs, 'and Juliet's sayin' that when a pilgrim holds a statue's hand, it's somethin' like a kiss, I guess.'

Sam looked unimpressed. 'You both sound mighty

annoyin' to my way of thinkin'. I know this was a long time ago, but ain't that a strange way o' courtin'?'

King Dick ignored the exchange. 'So Romeo says, "Then move not while my prayer's effect I take" and kisses Juliet.' He looked at Habs then Joe. 'Well, then?'

Now it was Joe's turn to blush. 'You mean here? We probably shouldn't.'

'Because . . .?' probed the King quietly.

Now Joe looked directly at him. 'With respect, King Dick, you know very well why.'

'Tell me . . .' Even quieter.

'Because,' said Joe, a hint of steel in his voice, 'a coloured boy kissing a white boy would be considered an abomination. And if that happens on a stage, well, we'd most likely be locked up. And if it's that stage there' – he pointed to the other end of the cockloft – 'we'll all be in the cachot. For ever.'

King Dick found his bearskin hat and placed it on his head. He was seven feet tall again. 'Let me guess, Mr Hill. You gotta small little Baptist church round the corner from your mamma's house? 'Cos that sounded mighty like somethin' you'd hear in a sermon, and not from the lips of a smart boy like you. This here is a play. A fiction. Romeo can't marry Juliet if they don't kiss. This isn't pully-hauly, it's jus' a kiss.'

Ned and Sam were mute, Tommy reddened again, while Habs twirled some hair between his fingers, eyes to the floor.

'Maybe you an' I should work somethin' out, Joe,' he said. 'Maybe when there's no one else lookin' at us and watchin' everythin' we do.'

'Yeah, maybe,' said Joe. 'Is there anywhere in this prison where no one else is watching you?'

'Few places,' said Habs.

The King picked up his club and rose from his box.

186

When he stretched, the club hit the ceiling. 'So, we rehearse again tomorrow. Mr Hill, please talk to your shipmates, to see if we can find us some white players. Then see if you can work out a way of kissin' Mr Snow here without it bein' some kinda a-bom-in-a-tion.' He swept out of the cockloft, Alex and Jonathan darting in his wake.

3.9

Block Seven

I T SEEMED as though, all Joe's life, he had consulted Will
Roche. More than anyone else, it was Will who had been
there when Joe had needed advice or counsel. It hadn't, as it
turned out, always been wise advice or timely counsel. But
old habits die hard, so Joe found himself back at his mess
and talking to the bunk below.

'Do you even know the story, Will?' Joe realized he
sounded exasperated.

'Only what you told me. Never had much time for
books, myself. Got to kinda relyin' on you to tell me things
if I really need to know 'em.'

'Well, you need to know this. I'm playing Juliet, and in
Act One, Scene Five she gets kissed by Romeo.'

'I assumed. You did say it's 'bout love an' all.'

'And you don't have a problem with that?'

'What's to have a problem with?'

'Habs Snow is playing Romeo, Will. I'd be kissing a coloured man. On stage.'

Roche was out of his bunk in seconds. He appeared
inches from Joe's face, shock written into every feature, surrounded by a cloud of liquor and tobacco fug.

'Have you lost your mind, sailor? Taken leave of your
senses?'

'It's the play, Will. It's just acting,' said Joe, realizing he
was already parroting King Dick's arguments.

'Well, you'll have to act your way out of a lynchin' then, and I won't be able to do nothin' to stop it.'

Joe had known what Roche would say but was annoyed to hear him say it all the same. 'Won't be able or won't want to?' he asked, and saw that his words had stung.

'You gotta know where to draw the line,' Roche snapped, dropping his voice to an urgent whisper, 'and kissin' Negroes on a stage is way, way across that line. By God's truth. That's what your mother would say if she were here beside me now, and you know it.'

Stung to sudden anger, Joe swung himself to the edge of the hammock.

'You've no idea what my mother would say. You're just mentioning her because you think it might make me do what you say. Hell, Will Roche, that was unfair, and *you* know it. I'm telling you 'cos I always tell you, but maybe I just need to decide everything for myself now.'

Roche stepped back, pained by the force of Joe's reply.

Joe took a deep breath. 'It's a play, Will,' he said. 'I don't live in Verona, I'm not a fourteen-year-old girl and I'm not getting married. And after that, I'm not going to die. Happy so far?'

Roche nodded.

'The man who falls in love with Juliet is called Romeo – Habs Snow's playing him, like I said. He isn't a sixteen-year-old Italian, Will, he's a dumbass sailor just like me, pretending to be something he's not.'

'But when you kiss,' said Roche, his finger raised, 'that ain't pretendin', is it? That's goin' to be happenin' right in front of everyone.'

Joe felt his skin prickle. 'But we're telling a story . . .'

Roche had hung his head then retreated to his berth. Joe jumped down and balanced himself on the end of his

189

hammock. Roche lay with his hands behind his head, eyes fixed on a spot somewhere above him.

'I hear what you're sayin', Joe Hill, I really do. I understand it ain't real, but I also understand men. These men.' He pointed around at the other occupants of the prison. 'And whether you like it or not, most of 'em will not have it. Maybe all of 'em, for all I know. They're not gonna pay sixpence to see a fine young white man like you kissin' the likes o' him. And if you think they'll just sit there and take it, well, you're not as smart as I took you for. This ain't somethin' you need to think about, this is jus' somethin' you *know*.'

Neither of them moved for a long time. Roche was on his back, looking at the hammock canvas above him; Joe was perched on the edge, his feet on the floor and his head in his hands. He knew that, whatever happened next, things wouldn't be the same again. He was no clearer about the kiss, only that the person he wanted to talk to was Habs. Not Roche.

Joe felt a tap on his shoulder and looked up to see the ginger-haired tarp-man Toker Johnson, looking agitated. 'Hurry, boy, you gotta hurry!' he said. 'Or we'll be late and that'll be noted.' He moved on to Roche, who got a shaking. 'C'mon, old man, stir yourself.' He scurried off to round up a few more stragglers.

'Well, I wouldn't want to be "noted", would I?' said Joe. He'd said it to himself more than anything, but it seemed to galvanize Roche. The old sailor hauled himself from the hammock, then pulled Joe to his feet. 'C'mon. You should see this,' he said.

They joined a stream of men walking up the stairs, most chatting or calling out to shipmates, but Joe and Roche walked in silence. Joe's head was so full of the argument, the play and the kiss, he gave no thought to where he was heading or what he was doing. He was just following Roche because he had asked him to. As he had so many times in the past. As he might not do again in the future.

What would his mother say, anyway? Their last conversation seemed so long ago he wasn't even sure he could summon her voice, never mind what words she would say. Then, unbidden, his father came to mind. Joe hadn't thought of him for an age but now the force of the memory left him reeling. He might not know what his mother would say but, even after all these years, he felt certain he understood his father. The thought of him in the theatre, his delight in watching the dubious Polly hiding her highwayman husband in *The Beggar's Opera*, how he had applauded the courting of Bianca in *The Taming of the Shrew*.

When Joe came out of his reverie, he was in the cockloft. On a makeshift stage at the far end, a man was about to be flogged. Stripped to the waist and hands tied to two metal rings that had been knocked into the ceiling, he was already in distress. Whether he was sobbing or merely trembling, Joe couldn't tell.

'What the . . .'

He turned to go but Roche held him back. 'You should see this – this is what happens.'

'Really?' Joe's eyes blazed. 'We didn't witness enough floggings at sea? You think I've forgotten mine? The scars haven't just gone away, Will, and you think I need to see this again?'

'It's Larson,' said Roche, nodding in the direction of the stage. 'He was buggerin' one of the New York crew. Caught him in Seven. Fifty lashes. The Brits'd hang 'im.'

As he spoke, the flogging began. The prison's master-at-arms, also stripped to the waist, let fly with his adapted hammock rope. The knotted cords whistled through the air, followed swiftly by the rip of tearing flesh. Joe winced at the memory, but he still hadn't taken his eyes off Roche. Larson screamed as the master lined up again. When the thongs hit him a second time, the sound changed: a duller, wetter sound. This master knew his art; by hitting Larson in the

191

same place the pain would be deeper, the wounds more terrible.

Joe forced himself to speak. 'Fifty will kill him,' he muttered.

Roche nodded silently.

'Are you . . . enjoying this?' Joe asked him. 'Is this good for you?'

'This,' said Roche, 'is good for *them*.' He indicated the crowd around them. 'It's their justice. Not British justice, not officers' justice, but their justice. Our justice.'

Amidst the infernal noise around them, Joe took Roche's head between his hands and waited until the old man could do nothing but stare at him. 'Well, I'm telling you,' he breathed, 'as Christ is my witness, it sure as hell isn't my justice.'

Joe made it to Block Four just as the turnkeys arrived.

3.10

Outside Block Six

10.30 p.m.

BLOCKS Two and Six were slightly set back in the arc of buildings that made up Dartmoor Prison. They had been late additions, hurriedly built, and appeared to have forced their way in; the crescent of buildings was now somewhat jagged and irregular. As a result, there was a small patch of ground, no more than a few yards square on either side, where it was possible to hide. Edwin Lane and two other Rough Allies were taking full advantage. Crouched in the shadows between Five and Six, he pointed a gloved hand at the thirteen flaming lamps that lit the path from Four all the way up to the market square.

'Top six got to go out,' he said, his high nasal twang travelling easily to his colleagues. 'The ones nearest the square. They're yours, James. I'll snuff out the ones on the block. And the six on the palisades behind are yours, Hitch. The darker we make it, the better.' He gripped both men's arms, silently pulling them back against the wall while a British patrol passed along the military walk above their heads. 'We got about a minute before more of them cursed Brits come back the other way.' The Allies watched as the redcoats ambled beyond the roof tiles of Four. 'Let's go.'

Armed with a thick glove and a wet cloth, they each set about their work. James sprinted, crouching low, across the patch of open ground. Reaching the path's first oil lamp, he flung open the glass and smothered the wick in a fluid motion. As he moved on to his second, Lane had just reached the corner of Four. Each block had six lamps – one on each corner, one halfway down each side – and he extinguished the first. As Lane's lights started to go out, Hitch began his work on the iron palisades. These were by some measure the highest of the lamps, and Lane had been glad to persuade the six-foot Hitch to join him in the task. As Lane ran around Four, he glanced in through the cracks in the block's stuffed-up windows: through one he saw a game of cards, through another men reading. 'Nigger games, nigger books,' he said. 'Ain't nothin' good gonna come from that.' He ran to the next lamp.

By the time Lane had put out his fourth he knew the minute was up and he'd have to leave the rest lit. He ran for the no-man's-land behind Five, the two shadows of James and Hitch closing in from left and right. They dived into darkness just as the next patrol swung into view. Lying low and breathless, they surveyed their work.

'Put out seven on the path.'

'Four out on the palisades. Sorry, boss. There weren't no time.'

'Still enough,' said Lane. 'I only got four o' the six. Now we wait for them dopey Brits to realize they need the lamp-lighters out again.'

3.11

Block Four, Cockloft

10.30 p.m.

THE SCENERY on the cockloft stage comprised a large, roughly painted backdrop with two side flats at each end. From the front they formed a good setting for any play but, at the back, the construction provided a small, concealed space. Unless there was a search, anyone hidden backstage would go unnoticed. As soon as a distressed Joe had appeared, Habs had brought him here.

'We got punishments, too, y'know. King Dick can be brutal to his own as well,' said Habs. They were both sitting on the floor, backs to the backdrop. 'You seen a bastinado?'

Joe shook his head. 'No, but I've heard of it. Used for foot-whipping.'

'Or ass-whipping. Tha's what we use it for. One poor bastard got twelve last week. 'Nother chef who was stealin' the food and sellin' it round. The King didn't like it. And that was it.'

They sat in the dark, the only light coming from the lamp on the landing and some moonlight through the tiny windows high on the wall. The silence of the cockloft contrasted sharply with the noise coming from the two floors below them.

'A thousand men not sleepin',' said Habs. 'Tha's a lotta noise.'

They sat a while listening to the sounds of the block, both suddenly aware of every breath.

'I've changed my mind about moving to Four.' Joe's voice was barely a whisper, but Habs detected a new determination. 'If you think the King's offer is still open, I'd like to say yes. I know my crew are in Seven, but I don't want to stay there any more.'

Habs stayed silent. These weren't questions, they were statements, and he sensed Joe had more to say. The pine box beneath them creaked as Joe shifted his weight.

'The first captain of the *Eagle* was a savage.' Joe's voice was the smallest Habs had heard it and he held his breath to make sure he didn't miss a word. 'Jenson was his name.' Joe paused. 'He was a monster. Always whipping someone, sometimes every day if the mood took him. He would get to us all in turn. For whatever reason took his fancy – insolence, laziness, drunkenness. I took three beatings.'

'You had the lash three times?' Habs was incredulous. 'What was the count?'

'Three the first time – wasn't so bad. Six the second,' Joe wrapped his arms around his knees. 'Then it was supposed to be twelve . . .'

'Twelve? Jesus Christ.'

'But I fainted after nine, and the master-at-arms took pity on me, so . . .'

'How old were you?'

'Just turned fourteen.'

'Why'd it stop? How'd it stop?' He felt Joe shift against him and squinted into the dark. 'Joe, what you doin'?' In the dark and shadows, Joe was taking his clothes off. 'Joe?'

'Something to show you.'

Last to go was the prison vest.

'Sweet Mother of God.' Habs's whisper was brittle with shock. Even in the backstage quarter-light he could make out the huge tattooed cross that covered the breadth of Joe's back.

'What have you done?' Habs's fingers slowly traced the outlines of the cross on Joe's shoulders and down his spine.

He felt the scar tissue like raised stripes across Joe's skin and held his palm flat against them, like a preacher with a healing touch.

Joe shivered. 'It was all I could think of,' he whispered. 'Jenson was a religious man. Someone had told me a cross would ward off a flogging, that even Jenson wouldn't dare abuse a cross. It would be like whipping Christ himself. So after that third beating had healed, I got this.'

'And did it work?' Habs sounded breathless.

'In a manner of speaking.' Joe pulled his shirt and jacket back on. 'Jenson dropped dead a week later.'

Habs snorted with laughter, then started to cough as he tried to control himself. 'Tha's 'bout the funniest, nastiest story I ever heard. And you ended up with the best damn tattoo I ever saw. Maybe I'm gonna find one of them tattoo boys here and get me a cross done, too.'

'Don't,' said Joe, now back on the floor. 'They're drunk most of the time, they'd mess you up for certain.'

'Like your eagle? Back o' your neck?' said Habs. 'Not the neatest I seen.'

Joe was silent for a moment. Then: 'I suppose not,' he muttered.

'In truth, I barely knew it *was* an eagle,' said Habs. 'Could be an albatross.'

'I guess.'

'Or a penguin.'

'I did it myself,' said Joe. 'That's why it's shit.'

Habs was lost for words. 'But why . . . how d'you . . .'

'I wanted to make myself ugly,' said Joe. He swallowed hard. 'No: I needed to make myself ugly.'

'When was this?' Habs's question was barely more than a whisper.

'On the prison ship. Before Plymouth, couple of months back. There were some men, they . . . thought I'd be their fancy boy.'

197

'Oh, Christ,' groaned Habs.

Joe kept his voice flat and emotionless. He had steeled himself for this moment and he didn't want to stop now. 'They kept telling me they loved my hair. How I looked "unspoilt". Then they told me all the ways they wanted to "spoil" me.' He paused and breathed deeply.

'And did they?' In the near-dark Habs caught the smallest, briefest of nods. He felt his stomach turn. 'Oh my Lord,' he said from behind his hands.

'So I bribed my way to the sharpest knife on the ship,' said Joe, 'which wasn't very sharp at all. And instead of cutting their cocks off, which I should've done, I cut my hair off. Then, after about a hogshead of rum, I cut myself an eagle, too.'

'Those gashes on your head!' exclaimed Habs. ''Course.'

'As you saw, I didn't make a very good job of it. But that was kind of the point.'

Habs rubbed a hand over Joe's scalp, tousled the new growth. 'Growin' it again now?'

'Growing it again now. Got a play coming up, you know. Longer is better.'

Habs jumped to his feet. 'I jus' thought o' somethin'. Stay here.'

'Right now I haven't got anywhere to go,' said Joe, 'so I'm not planning to leave any time soon.'

Habs climbed over the flat and Joe was alone. He listened to the sound of his friend disappearing, footsteps on wood, on stone, a swinging door, then nothing. He pulled his knees up to his chest and closed his eyes. He didn't dare move in case it all changed, the spell broke and everything went back to normal.

For six weeks, he hadn't talked about the scars, hadn't needed to. Everyone on his ship knew the story, everyone on his ship had one of their own. But he had told Habs and it had felt good; he wondered why it had taken so long.

198

3.12

Block Four, Steps and Courtyard

NED PENNY stood with Four's other lamplighter, the beanpole John Haywood, and wondered what the hell had happened. The lamps had been lit at 5 p.m., as usual. His duties included all the lights of Four as well as the thirteen along the long, straight path up to the gates of the market square. Haywood, a veteran from Virginia, had lit the twelve along the iron palisades that ran behind their block. The job was simple: when the oil needed lighting, you lit it; when the oil ran out, you replaced it; and if the weather blew out your flame, you came out and relit it. Sixpence a week said it was worth doing. But from the steps they could see that most of their lamps were out, while, as far as they could see, all the prison's other lights were still lit.

'Could be a mighty wind,' said Pastor Simon, walking outside with the King next to him. 'It's blowin' across the moor then funnellin' straight through the middle o' the camp.'

'You reckon?' said King Dick. 'That kinda religious wind only happens in the Old Testament. And ain't too usual in Devon. More likely they just ran outta oil. You check the lamps tonight?' he called to Penny and Haywood. They both nodded.

'Sure we did, King Dick.'

'Well, looks like you need to go and light 'em again 'fore the British come round. Take some more oil jus' in case.' King Dick turned and went back inside.

Penny and Haywood trudged out, a lit taper and a jug of oil at the ready. They looped Four then walked along the palisade, lighting and cursing as they went.

'All these lamps are full o' goddamn oil,' said Ned. 'Ain't nothin' wrong with my wicks neither. Folk call me King Wick. You know that, John?'

Haywood laughed. 'All hail, King Wick!'

Ned saluted Haywood as they cut back past Four, heading for the still-gloomy path to the market square. They walked passed the lit lamps, each one flaming healthily. 'Ain't nothin' wrong with these,' said Ned, 'so what happened up here?'

The first extinguished lamp told them everything they needed to know. Its protective glass cover had been left open and the wick was wet. They looked down the line of lamps. They all looked the same.

'This was done deliberate,' said Haywood. 'No doubt about it. No way did we leave all them lamps jus' flappin' like this. We got to tell King Dick.'

'Let's get 'em lit back up again,' said Ned. 'Then we tell him.' One by one, they got each wick burning and carefully covered them with the glass.

'That closed, Lamplighter Ned?'

'That surely closed, Lamplighter John.'

They were at the penultimate lamp when John's shoes slipped on something.

Ned lowered the taper to see what it was. 'You know anyone in Four chews tobacco, John?'

John considered for a minute. 'Mostly it's the Allies, ain't it? They prefer it to pipes.'

Instinctively, Ned glanced across to Six. 'Well, tha's what you slipped on, John. I'll light this one and we can get back.' Ned held the taper to the wick until it was dry enough to light.

'I don't like this, Ned. Somethin's wrong here. Don't take so damn long,' said John, his voice urgent and low. 'So what if we miss one goddamn lamp.'

Ned's hand was cupping the taper. 'Jus' a few more seconds.'

3.13

Block Four, Cockloft

Joe started as something enormous was thrown over the scenery, landing softly in front of him, closely followed by Habs himself.

'Brought us a mattress and some liquor,' he breathed. 'Felt like it might be a long night. And the longer you can be away from everyone else, the better.'

The mattress filled the floor space under them and they returned to their sitting positions against the backdrop. Habs uncorked the bottle and passed it to Joe, who sipped and swallowed. 'Do you think King Dick knows . . .?' he began.

'King Dick knows everythin',' said Habs, taking his turn with the bottle.

'You told him?' Joe was alarmed. 'I should've done that.'

'You should. Tomorrow. I said we had a visitor, tha's all.'

'A visitor?'

'It was enough,' said Habs. 'He guessed. He was kinda busy, sendin' Ned out to relight some of the lamps, but yeah, he guessed.'

'How do you know?'

'Cos he called me over and whispered to me.'

'Habs, just tell me what he said!'

Habs swigged again. 'He said, "Act One, Scene Five".'

Joe allowed himself a small, rueful laugh. 'Of course he did. I don't think Will is ever going to accept me doing this play,' he said. 'And any mention of this kiss is going to drive him crazy.'

'And Lord knows there's a lotta men like Will here. How d'we play it, Joe?'

There was a silence, then Joe reached for the liquor. 'You should know that I stink,' he said.

Habs drank some more then wiped his lips on his coat sleeve. 'Me, too.'

Joe cleared his throat. 'What's my line?'

'Saints do not move . . .'

'Oh, yes,' said Joe. Habs felt him shift against their wooden rest. When he spoke again, it was a tremulous whisper. 'Saints do not move, though grant for prayers' sake.'

'Then move not while my prayer's effect I take,' said Habs, and he leaned over and kissed Joe. It was brief, chaste, their lips barely touching.

'You really do stink,' said Joe, and they both snorted with laughter.

'You need a shave,' said Habs.

'No, that's not your line. You say, "Thus from my lips, by thine, my sin is purged."'

'Quite right,' said Habs. Then added, 'D'you think this is a sin?'

'Habs, it's a play.'

'But what if it wasn't?'

'You mean . . .'

'What if . . . I was kissin' you . . . 'cos I wanted to kiss you?' The cockloft was silent. Habs's heart was leaping in his chest.

'It would be an abomination,' Joe said.

Habs exhaled slowly. 'That what you really think?'

There was another long pause as Joe shifted uncomfortably. 'Then have my lips the sin that they have took,' he said eventually.

'Give me my sin again.'

'No, you missed a line, Habs, it's—'

'Give me my sin again,' insisted Habs, and he waited.

Joe's mind was a tumult, his heart a convulsion. Shocked by his own desire, terrified of the consequences, he dug his nails into his hands and froze, becalmed by confusion and conflict.

Somewhere out in the courtyard, he registered a commotion: raised voices and a brief cry. Habs caught it, too, his head turning briefly to the window.

Joe called him back. 'Can this just be a rehearsal?' he whispered. 'Please?'

Habs hesitated. Joe's gaze was intent, watching, he thought, for disappointment or annoyance. He hid them both. 'It can be a rehearsal, yes,' he said. ''Course it can.'

Outside, again the sound of running footsteps. A whistle. The alarm bell.

''Nother time,' said Habs.

3.14

Block Four, Courtyard

HABS AND Joe may have been the last to emerge from Four but they knew Ned had been killed before they reached the first landing. Most of the rumours in Dartmoor turned out to be false, but these – the ones that flew up the stairs of Block Four – had the speed and force of truth about them. The two gave up fighting through the melee and moved outside at the crowd's pace. Sam was waiting, and he flung himself at Habs, the words tumbling out.

'They beat him, Habs, then they used a blade. Haywood's pretty bad, too. King Dick was callin' for you.' The three of them pushed their way into the throng. The now-lit lamps around Four showed thirty militiamen penning in seven or eight hundred angry prisoners. The crowds made way for Sam, and they made way for Habs. Joe tucked in just behind. When the throng resisted, Habs, tear-filled eyes fixed on the black bearskin hat at the centre of the pandemonium, shouted, 'Crew o' the *Bentham* coming through!' Joe glanced up. All around them a scattering of lights flickered from the other blocks' unshuttered windows, illuminating the curious, all straining for a better view.

When the three broke through the cordon, a tableau of tragedy confronted them. A few yards from the last of the path's lamps, Elizabeth Shortland knelt at John Haywood's side, a blood-drenched cloth held to a wound in his stomach. Dr Magrath was holding a cup of water to his pale lips. King Dick and Agent Shortland were arguing. And just beyond them all, Pastor Simon knelt over the stricken, sackcloth-covered body of Ned Penny. Habs ran the final few yards then collapsed at his friend's feet.

'Dear Mother of God, what'd they do to you?' he whispered. He lifted the sheet and answered his own question. Two stab wounds to the heart. Many fists to the face. Sam knelt beside him and, when they had replaced the sacking together, joined in another one of Pastor Simon's prayers.

'They was trapped, Habs,' said Sam. 'Tricked. Someone put the lamps out then waited for the lighters to come. When Ned and John got to the end here, they was set upon.'

'Rough Allies,' said King Dick, appearing next to them. 'Only the Allies'd do this.' A new detachment of guards ran to form a line in front of Block Six. 'And tha's what Shortland thinks, too.' A few of the prisoners started to run towards the guards.

'If the Rough Allies break out now, there'll be a bloodbath,' said Habs. 'You gotta say somethin', King Dick. Right now.'

They exchanged the briefest of glances, and then the King roared. It was the loudest, most commanding order anyone there had ever heard. Everyone present in the courtyard had fought at sea, all had followed orders as cannon and musket fired around them; they knew how to distinguish order in the chaos, knew when to stop their own thinking and take notice of someone else's.

'Men of Four!'

The first shout grabbed their attention, the second demanded their action. 'Men of Four! We kneel together now. There will be time for anger, but now we grieve. We kneel together for our fallen brothers.' The King removed his bearskin and stood with his arms outstretched, head turned up. 'We kneel!' he shouted again, and around him, hundreds of men got on the ground. They knelt in waves all the way back to the steps of Four. Elizabeth Shortland and Dr Magrath

206

were already kneeling at the side of John Haywood, but what the crowd saw was a white man and a white woman following King Dick's instruction. And they marvelled.

'We been here before,' he said, his words now edged with anger and grief. 'All o' us been here before. We know this. We see our brother lyin' on the cold ground and our hearts break. We seen it all before.'

Shouts of agreement from the sailors of Four.

The King's whole body shuddered. ''Cos he is not jus' one!' he cried. 'This is not jus' Ned Penny from Philadelphia. He is many. He is hundreds. Thousands. And sometimes it seem as though we have seen 'em all. Every one. And the truth is, we're still countin'.' The King's black eyes swung to Shortland and fixed him with a ferocious stare, the bearskin stabbing into the space between them. 'So now the Agent will do his work. The Agent will bring us justice. And, for today, for tomorrow, we will wait for him.'

The two men held each other's gaze. It was Shortland who looked away first.

The King waved Pastor Simon forward. The preacher prayed over Ned then over John Haywood, before Magrath and some of his orderlies carried the injured man away, Elizabeth Shortland still holding a compress to his side.

By the time the prayers had finished, heavy rain had started falling. Many prisoners were too cold and too wet to stay outside any longer. For now, the situation was under control.

Shortland stood in the downpour with his troops, watching the prisoners of Four withdraw, until he was sure the danger had passed, then he nodded briefly at King Dick and marched away.

'He owes you more'n that,' said Sam bitterly. There was desperation in his eyes. 'But what do we do, King Dick? Ned is gone and there's a murderer right there, in those walls.' Rain and tears streamed down his face.

'Do, Mr Snow?' echoed the King. 'What do we do? We survive. Tha's what we do. Tha's what we always do. And we wait. If the British find who killed our friend, he will hang. If they don't, we'll have our own justice.' Sam nodded, pacified for the moment. 'We need our justice, Mr Snow, I know, but we also need to get home alive. All of us. The Rough Allies want a fight. If they can't fight the British, they'll fight us, but we gotta deny them that pleasure, whatever it takes. Then maybe they'll fight each other. Mr Hill. You have somethin' to say?'

Joe, in shock, stumbled over his words.

The King cut him off, anyway. 'You have somethin' to say 'bout why you're here?'

Joe blanched, glancing at Habs, who gave the tiniest of reassuring nods.

'Well, if the offer is still open . . .' began Joe.

'It is,' said the King. 'Move in soon as you can.'

3.15

The Hospital

Midnight

C WARD WAS full – every ward was full – but Elizabeth Shortland had carved a space out for John Haywood. A mattress and three tea chests had been pushed between the hammocks. There were shouts from every side – the sick had heard the tumult and were desperate for news. The arrival of a wounded and stricken inmate confirmed their fears.

'Who's that come in?'

'Is he stabbed, Doc?'

'That some kinda riot out there?'

Magrath and Elizabeth ignored them all.

The four wards of Dartmoor hospital were an improvement on the prison blocks: the windows had glass in them, the floor was washed daily and there was, usually, no fighting. There was also no segregation. When Block Four had been designated 'for non-whites', Magrath had refused to follow suit. He had told the Agent that he could accommodate and allocate the sick only according to their illness. 'The pox can turn a man's skin as black as night,' he had told Shortland. 'What then? Should we change his ward because he's no longer white?'

Under some hastily assembled oil lamps, Dr Magrath examined Haywood more closely. Two stab wounds, one shallow, across his right hip, the other deeper, much deeper, under his rib cage. Magrath bent close, a bloodied gauze in his hand, catching the rivulets of Haywood's blood as they rolled down his side.

'The wounds are clean now, as far as I can see. He might have a chance if he avoids infection. This second cut troubles me; he was bleeding heavily out there. The knife, or whatever it was, may just have missed the kidney. He might be lucky. Strap him tight, Elizabeth.' He stepped away as she produced fresh bandages.

'I don't think "lucky" is quite the word,' she said quietly, her hands making quick work of the dressing.

'Of course,' he said, accepting the correction. 'Then let's hope the fates are kind to him now.' Haywood groaned then gasped as his bandages were tied off.

'Mr Haywood, you're in the hospital,' called Magrath. 'You have stab wounds and we are attending to them.' He studied the green-and-blue bruising around Haywood's eyes. 'Do you remember what happened?' said Magrath. 'Who attacked you?'

A pained whimper was the only reply, Haywood's eyes staying squeezed shut.

One of the nearby patients spoke up. 'Is he gonna die, Doc? Looks like they cut him bad.'

Magrath turned to the man, another resident of Four, who was peering across from his bed. 'I don't know, Mr Miller, to be honest with you. You might say some prayers for him, maybe.'

'That bad, then,' said Miller, and turned away.

'Prayer and morphine,' said Magrath.

Elizabeth Shortland took his arm. 'He'll need more than that, George.'

'All I have is my supplies, Elizabeth.' He reached for his bag. 'This batch came up from Plymouth yesterday . . .'

She shook her head and pulled him away from the beds. They walked in silence to the small corridor that linked C and D wards, ignoring the shouts and questions from the beds. When they were out of sight, she pulled Magrath as close as she dared.

'He can't stay here,' she whispered. He tried to pull back, but her hands were on his jacket lapels, holding him in position.

'Whyever not?' he whispered. 'Where else can he go?'

'Think about it, George. He probably witnessed a murder tonight. If it was the Rough Allies and they find out he's still alive, they'll be back.'

'But that's preposterous,' Magrath insisted. 'This is the hospital! There are guards outside and a brick wall between us and them.'

'What if they don't need to break in?' she said. 'What if there's someone already here? Two hundred beds, and at least a hundred and fifty have white sailors in them. At least seven Allies that I can recall. You can't possibly . . .' She let go of his jacket, brushing down the lapels as she did so. 'Can we really take that risk?'

He walked a few paces across the corridor, then turned back. 'Would Thomas put guards in the wards?'

She shrugged. 'He's always complaining about being short-staffed,' she said, 'but he might do. For a while.'

Magrath squinted at her. 'I know that look, Elizabeth. Just tell me what you're thinking.'

She stared back at him. It was quite possible, she realized, that he was the only man who had ever considered her opinions at all, and here he seemed to have learned more of her in a matter of months than her husband had in eighteen years.

'If he can, he needs to recover in Four. There's a thousand men in there, George. You can visit him, too, but they can protect him. We can say he's been taken to the hospital in Plymouth.'

He glanced back at the ward. 'This makes me nervous, Elizabeth.'

'Of course it does,' she said, 'because you care. But we don't have time for nerves. Is he stable?'

Magrath looked aghast. 'You want to move him now?'

'He's in danger *now*. Right now. And every minute he stays in here.' Elizabeth strode to the ward doors, peered inside then nodded. 'Maybe we have a few hours before the full story gets round, but that's all. If Thomas agrees, we can have the turnkeys rouse King Dick within the hour.'

There were shouts from the ward. Elizabeth and Magrath exchanged panicked glances then crashed through the doors. Haywood's new neighbour, Miller, was out of bed and squaring up to a white sailor wrapped in sheets and peering down at John Haywood.

'Step away!' thundered Magrath, making up in volume what he lacked in speed. Mrs Shortland did the running, pulling the man in sheets away from the yelling Miller.

'You got no right!' he shouted. 'You got no right. What you want, anyways?' He aimed a boot at the man in sheets, who had now scuttled back into a bed on the other side of the ward and was curled up and muttering incomprehensibly. When the boot hit him on the head, he fell silent.

But now the whole ward was awake and troubled. Elizabeth thought at least half the patients were getting out of bed, when Magrath let rip.

'If anyone is out of their bed, it will be taken as a sign that they are completely well and ready for an immediate transfer back to their block.' He glowered at the two rows of beds. 'One step – that's all it'll take. I will call the guard in and you will be gone in seconds. Is that clear?' he demanded, flushed with the effort.

It appeared as though it was. Everyone stayed where they were. In the momentary silence, a voice called, 'Who's the new Negro? Anyone know?'

Miller answered. 'The man's name is John Haywood and he's from Virginia. Lamplighter. He's a good man.'

212

'What happened to him?'

'Stabbed. Looked like it, anyways.'

'Must be the Allies. S'always the Allies.'

'One less nigger can't be bad, though, can it?'

A few in the ward laughed, and Magrath had heard enough. He pulled a chair to where Haywood was lying.

'You're right,' he said to Elizabeth, settling himself down. 'Go and see Thomas, this is intolerable. I'll stay here till it's done.'

3.16

Monday, 13 February
Dr Magrath's Study

3 a.m.

KING DICK arrived with an escort, four militiamen coming with him to Magrath's study door. The ground-floor corridor rang to the sound of boots on stone. Elizabeth found herself standing.

Magrath answered the brisk knocking, his eyes meeting the King's.

'Mr Crafus, come in. I'm sorry to get you from your bed and sorry, too, for what happened tonight.'

The King removed his bearskin, then stooped as he entered Magrath's tiny study. Once inside, he unfurled himself again, seeming to fill the entire room. One desk and two plain chairs were the only furnishings; books, jars and bottles occupied the rest. The King nodded at Elizabeth, surprised to see the Agent's wife in attendance.

'Mrs Shortland. I was 'spectin' your husband, but no matter. You have news o' the killer?'

'Alas, no . . .' she began.

'So this is all 'cos John Haywood has passed?' He aimed his question at Magrath, but it was Elizabeth who answered.

'No, it's because he hasn't. He is alive, but in grave danger, even if he survives his wounds. He's in C ward upstairs, but he needs to be under guard. Earlier, there was an incident with another patient.'

'You can't control the prison? Even here, in the hospital?'

'Not at the moment' were the words that formed in Elizabeth's mind, but she said nothing.

Magrath came to her aid. 'The Agent has declared the matter a medical emergency, so the responsibility has passed directly to me. John Haywood has two knife wounds to the gut, severe bruising about the eyes and, for the moment, he isn't speaking. Given the non-segregated wards, tonight's murder of Mr Penny and the current demands on troop levels, we think Haywood should be transferred immediately, for his own protection, to Block Four. He would have to be hidden, away from view, away from the turnkeys, away from everyone. You have nearly a thousand men, Mr Crafus. Can you hide him, guard him and guarantee that your men won't talk about him? Can they keep this secret? Without that, he's a dead man.'

The King looked from Magrath to Elizabeth and then back, unsure who to address. 'Do we pretend he died?' The King sounded unconvinced.

'No, we say he's been taken to Plymouth Hospital for treatment,' said Elizabeth. 'It happens from time to time.'

The King fidgeted. He had nowhere to pace, barely any room to move. He wants his club, Elizabeth thought, he wants to hit something.

'Do you realize what a disgrace this prison is?' he said, his voice loud in the enclosed space, the anger barely controlled. 'The war's done, the fightin' between our countries is over. New Orleans is over, Lake Erie is over, Chesapeake Bay is over. Everywhere is over 'part from here. In Dartmoor, the dyin' continues.' He shook his head in despair.

'Mr Crafus . . .' began Elizabeth. She waited until he was looking at her. 'I understand your anger, but the fighting here is between Americans and other Americans. Mr Penny was killed by Americans, the threat to Mr Haywood is from Americans—'

215

'We nothin' but rats in a sack,' interrupted the King. 'You know that. O' course we fight.'

She continued, 'Before the sun rises, we need to know if you will take Mr Haywood to Four. It will be difficult to manage in secret, but we'll think of something.'

'We don't never give up on one of our own,' said the King. 'O' course we'll watch over him. And I'll give you your reason, your "somethin", so you don't need to trouble yourselves no more. Mr Joe Hill in Seven wants to transfer to Four. Bring him here now, and we can cover up Mr Haywood's arrival with his.'

Magrath and Elizabeth looked relieved.

'Good,' said Magrath, 'I know the man to help us out here. Thank you, Mr Crafus.'

The King had been dismissed, but he didn't move. He had something else to say and the room waited impatiently for him. His sigh when it came was the deepest exhalation; anger, exhaustion and fear seemed to fill the room.

'Mrs Shortland. I need to say this, and I've earned the right.' There was a sudden tiredness in his voice which he made no attempt to hide. 'You seem to be losin' control of this hospital, and I believe your husband is in danger of losin' control of this whole prison.' Elizabeth started to protest, but he raised his hand and pressed on. 'You ain't seen nothin', you ain't understandin' nothin'. You see things from the quarter deck. I see things from the gun deck. For us down there, for us in Four, we are surrounded, twice over. Surrounded by white prisoners who want us locked away, surrounded by white soldiers jus' itchin' to open fire at any damn Yankee they see. We have to be 'fraid of both. We have to be 'fraid of everybody. All it would take is for Captain Shortland to be away on one of them fancy trips, one of his dumbass guards to have a twitchy trigger-finger, and you'll be buildin' a bigger graveyard.'

He'd said what he needed to say, stinging Elizabeth and

Magrath into silence. King Dick replaced his bearskin; it touched the ceiling as he turned to the door. 'When you bring Mr Haywood, we'll be ready.'

Joe was put in Four at just after 4 a.m., deposited by two baffled guards and an early-rising turnkey. As they turned to leave, Dr Magrath, with the King and an ensign named Crouch, bustled in with what appeared to be provisions carried between them. Crouch ordered the turnkey to wait for him outside and then they gently unpacked John Haywood from under the boxes and blankets that had been placed on his stretcher. Within fifteen minutes he'd been put on the mattress nearest the kitchens; within thirty, and with most of the floor still asleep, the King had arranged men to stand watch for what remained of the night.

'I've left some spare dressings,' said Magrath to the King on his way out, his voice thick with exhaustion. 'I'll make sure I visit tomorrow, or today, whenever it is.' He leaned heavily on his stick then. 'Look, Crafus, about what you said earlier. I agree this' – he gestured around him to indicate the whole prison – 'this could all blow at any time. I'll talk to the Agent. But anything you can do to keep it calm in here . . . With your men, with your block . . . you make quite a difference, you know.'

'And anythin' you can do to get us all out o' here,' said the King, 'that would make a difference, too. Now, if you'll 'scuse me, I have a funeral to prepare.'

3.17

Block Four, Cockloft

12.05 p.m.

EVEN THOUGH they buried Ned that morning, King Dick called a rehearsal in the afternoon. On the way back into Four, the King steered Joe, Habs and Sam through to the kitchens. 'Come an' see,' he said.

They found a pale and dazed-looking John Haywood propped up on a small mattress that had been squeezed into a deep storeroom, a guard of three vigilant inmates armed with sticks standing among the displaced potatoes, cabbages and turnips. He was staring unblinkingly at the roof.

'I don't rightly know where John is,' said the King, 'but he sure as hell ain't here, with us. The physician says this happen sometimes. He seen it before. John can't remember nothin'. He might get better, might not. He might talk to us, might not.'

They stood at Haywood's bedside.

'What happened out there, Mr Haywood?' called Habs, his voice bouncing loud in the small brick-lined room. 'Can you hear me?'

'Why you shoutin'?' said Haywood, his voice thick and groggy. ''Course I can hear you. Jus' can't remember shit, tha's all.'

'Do you remember goin' out to light the lamps?' said Habs.

'I do not.'

218

'Do you remember Ned sayin' anythin' . . .'

Haywood closed his eyes. 'That's precisely the kinda shit I'm talkin' 'bout.'

'We'll be back to sit with you later,' said Joe.

Before they climbed to the cockloft, the King spoke to the inmate guards.

'No one gets in here, you know that. You see anyone who isn't Four, you arrest 'em, tie 'em up, cosh 'em – whatever you have to do. Then you come get me. Yes?'

'Yes, King Dick,' came the three voices in unison.

'We doin' it in watches,' said Sam as they climbed to the cockloft. 'First watch is eight till midnight, middle watch till four, mornin' till eight, and so on. Reckon pretty much everyone in the block knows now.'

By the time they reached the top of Four, the gambling tables were out, though most were empty. Joe, Habs, Sam and the crier had been joined by Pastor Simon and a rather awkward-looking Robert Goffe, with Jon Lord at his side. Alex and Jonathan sat apart but watched intently. The theatre company had their tabled-off section of the cockloft again, each of them standing mute, painfully aware of the absence of Ned Penny.

'Everythin' the same, even when it ain't,' said the King. 'Everythin' the same. The play goes on, the market goes on, the gamin' goes on. If it don't, well then, we get to sittin' round talkin' 'bout tunnels, escape and all o' that. We keep our tragedy on the stage, gentlemen, but we jus' sell tickets to Four this time. We can't be doin' with the others, not with Mr Haywood in his predicament.'

Murmurs of agreement floated between them. 'We don't need to tell no one 'bout that, we jus' keeping the play to ourselves,' continued the King. 'I'll play Mercutio, 'cos there ain't nobody else to play him now. Mr Snow, we still need to recruit some more players. Welcome, anyways, to Pastor Simon, Mr Goffe and Mr Lord. We need your help.'

He nodded a salute to the newly enlisted, ignoring their obvious discomfort.

'So. I believe we had got to Act One, Scene Five.'

Habs and Joe shifted nervously. They hadn't spoken of the night before. Their rehearsal kiss seemed a lifetime ago.

'Mr Snow, did you sort out the matter?' said the King.

Habs looked briefly at Joe. 'Well, we did start to rehearse, King Dick, but . . . we was interrupted.' He gestured impotently around him. 'Never sorted it out, really.'

The King tapped his club on the floor impatiently. 'Never sorted it out, really,' he repeated. 'Well, let's do a little sortin'. Mr Hill, your line, please.'

Joe had no more wanted to rehearse than anyone else present; in the hours after the burial most had just wanted to talk and drink. But the King had been insistent – there was an urgency now to everything he was doing, as though to delay would be to surrender. Joe stood awkwardly and closed his eyes.

'Saints do not move though grant for prayers' sake,' he said flatly. Everyone looked to Habs.

'Then move not while my prayer's effect I take,' he said, equally stilted. Then, without looking up, Habs bent over to Joe and kissed him on the cheek. There was the briefest of silences before Goffe snorted with laughter. Once the King started to smile, the laughing spread fast.

'That was pathetic,' said Joe.

'Well, what else could I do?' Habs protested earnestly. 'What kinda kiss would you have preferred?'

King Dick summoned one of the gamblers he knew, a thin, stooped sailor out of Maryland called Palmer. The whispered instructions elicited the beginnings of a protest, but a handful of coins from the King's pocket quickly silenced it.

'What's happenin' there?' asked Habs watching the man leave. 'Never seen Palmer walk so fast. He took a bullet back in '13, says he can't move fast no more.'

220

'Anyone ever offer him money?' asked Sam.

'Can't say they have.'

'Maybe tha's the reason right there.'

They waited for ten minutes before the newly nimble Palmer hurried back in. He gave the King a confident nod and sat himself near the cockloft door.

'So, gentlemen, the matter of this troublesome kiss,' said the King. He stood, stretched, then wheeled his club with one arm and then the other.

'Christ, he's going to flatten us,' muttered Joe.

'We all saw what Mr Snow was capable of earlier,' the King continued. 'A kiss that wouldn't win a spinster's heart, never mind that of the fair Juliet.' He was enjoying himself. 'This prison done its best to provide an education for the needy, as Tommy here will agree.' The crier nodded sagely. 'So King Dick has decided to help Mr Snow and Mr Hill, if he can.' He waved at Palmer and waited.

'This is going to be terrible,' Joe whispered. 'I just know it.' They both stared at the cockloft doors, Joe holding his breath. The whistles and applause began as soon as Betsy Wade and Martha Slater appeared in the cockloft.

'The beautiful bakers of Tavistock,' he said in wonder and relief. 'At least, I assume it's them ...' Sporting Derby high hats and hidden under enormous overcoats, the market women were bustled into the room.

'O' course,' exhaled Habs.

The two bewildered women cast glances to all corners as they were ushered down the aisle of the cockloft by the less-than-stooped Palmer. When they saw Habs and Joe, they smirked, and Betsy curtseyed.

She pulled her hat from her head, tying a pile of black hair back with a strip of cloth from her wrist. 'Hey, boys!' she called.

'Hey, Betsy,' said Habs.

'We were just packing up,' said Martha. 'Your man here

221

caught us just in time.' She looked around. 'This your theatre, then?'

'And church, and concert hall,' said Joe.

King Dick bowed extravagantly. 'Ladies, you are most welcome, but ain't got much time. You are not allowed in the blocks, as you know, but I hope Mr Palmer has paid you for your time? Your disguises seem to be relyin' on the redcoats not lookin' too hard.'

Martha waved the hat she'd been given. 'Aye, sir,' she said, 'and we can keep the hats, too, he says.'

The King waved them forward. 'We need your help. We're rehearsin' the magnificent tragedy of *Romeo and Juliet*. Mr Snow here is Romeo, and Mr Hill here is Juliet.' Both women whistled and curtseyed again. 'But our Romeo is unsure how to kiss our Juliet. He tried it earlier and, well . . .' Goffe and Lord started to laugh again. 'Let's just say it was none too impressive. Would one of you ladies show him how it can be done?'

Betsy beckoned Martha forward. 'It beats selling bread, girl,' she said.

Martha, hands on her hips, stared at the King. 'All that money is to come here and just kiss Joe? That beautiful boy? Well, Your Majesty, or whatever it is I should call you, you're a very generous employer. I'll come and work for you anytime.'

'Oh, help,' muttered Joe, as the women strode towards him.

'We'll need a chair,' said Betsy.

One from a gaming table was passed over, and Joe, blushing scarlet, sat on it, hands clutching both sides.

'You watchin' this, Mr Snow? You got a good view?' called the King. Habs, amused, walked to within a few paces of the chair.

'I can see jus' fine, thank you, King Dick.'

Martha then, without pausing, without hesitating, hoisted

222

her skirts and sat astride Joe. He squirmed as she settled herself into position and tucked some loose strands of her red hair behind her ears, then did the same to Joe, his growing hair just staying back off his face.

'Ready?' she whispered. He nodded, and Martha lifted his face to hers. She slowly leaned forward till their lips were barely touching. Her hand reached for his, then placed it firmly on her right breast. 'Why are you holding your breath?' she whispered.

As Joe went to apologize, Martha's lips were on his and her tongue was in his mouth, warm and probing. Then it was over. Joe heard the wild applause and cheering, flicked a glance at Habs, who was clapping, too.

'That's how you do it,' she said, and without pausing for breath, swooped again. The chair rocked back and Joe, pinned under Martha, lost his balance. He fell hard on to the ground, the wooden chair slamming hard into his spine, Martha hard into his chest. She raised her head briefly as they landed, then kissed him again. Winded, Joe could only accept the kisses, until Martha stopped and sat up. Gasping for air, Joe rolled on to his side, aware the applause had become laughter.

'Something like that?' she said to the King, brushing her skirts back down.

'Somethin' like that,' he replied.

'So, Habs. Reckon you can try it now?'

'That's supposed to be their first kiss?' Habs was incredulous. 'You want Romeo and Juliet to kiss like that?'

'Maybe don't break the chair,' said the King.

'And don't break his ribs neither!' called Sam.

Martha stepped back. 'All yours,' she said to Habs.

On their 'stage' and in the cockloft, the mood had become surprisingly light. In contrast to their grief-filled morning, the disastrous kiss, then Martha's tuition, had filled the company with laughter. But Habs was nervous now. He fidgeted with his hair, rotated the miniature beads on his

223

earrings, adjusted the straps on his boots. He had been ready to kiss Joe in the silence and the darkness of the night before, and he thought Joe had been ready, too, but here? With an audience watching? Now, he wasn't so sure.

Joe was standing, studying the script. Or, Habs thought, more likely, he was merely staring at the script. Habs walked over to Joe and leaned in close.

'Still a rehearsal,' he whispered.

Joe tried a smile, relief in his eyes. 'Still a rehearsal,' he echoed.

'Give us the line, then, Romeo!' called the King. 'Let's see what you learned from Martha here.'

Habs and Joe took deep breaths at the same time. Joe noticed Goffe and Lord whispering to each other and held up his hand to halt Habs. 'Mr Goffe and Mr Lord!' he shouted. 'If you don't like this one, you two can perform the next.'

The ice broken, the tension gone, Habs said, 'Then move not while my prayer's effect I take.' He reached out to tuck a loose strand of blond hair behind Joe's ear as Martha had, and leaned forward slowly until their lips just touched. It was more a caress than a kiss, but Habs pulled back.

'Thus from my lips, by thine, my sin is purged.' There was a silence.

Joe gulped some air. 'Then have my lips the sin that they have took.'

Habs was barely an inch away. 'Sin from my lips? O trespass sweetly urged! Give me my sin again.'

Joe felt Habs's fingertips on the back of his head, then their delicate push as their heads were gently pulled closer. This time, the kiss was longer.

Then King Dick was speaking. It took Joe a few seconds to realize he'd missed his cue.

'You kiss by the book,' said the King, prompting Joe, clearly for the second or maybe the third time.

'You kiss by the book,' muttered Joe, his head spinning.

3.18

Tuesday, 14 February
The Market Square

Just before the noon bell

KING DICK strode around the square, club trailing from his hand. He chatted easily with stall-holders, took payments from some, gave advice to others. He handed coins to sailors for errands he needed and some that he didn't. Everything appeared normal, but many sailors, well used to spotting the smallest of changes in weather, ship or crew, suspected otherwise. When the King was on his own, and especially when Alex and Jonathan weren't with him, violence was usually never far away. They passed on the information to the stall-holders, who surreptitiously began to pack up their stalls.

When Horace Cobb and Edwin Lane appeared at the market square entrance, everyone else packed up, too. A few minutes away from the noon bell, staying open wasn't worth the risk. Since Ned's murder, tension in the prison was knife-edge sharp. Shortland's men had snatched the first Rough Ally they'd found and thrown him in the cachot. Block Six had been told he would only be released if they surrendered the real culprit. Until that happened, they would assume they had the right man and hang him if they had to. Six and the other white blocks accused the British of bullying, but the Ally stayed, chained and howling, in the cachot.

Cobb had requested to see the King, and this was their chosen meeting place. It was a good venue, King Dick had conceded; it was neutral territory, a public space and one viewable, albeit from their distant platforms behind Blocks One and Seven, by the militia patrolling on the military walk.

Cobb and Lane waited, arms folded. Cobb relit his cigarillo, Lane smoked his clay pipe, the stall-holders rapidly put their goods away. A hundred yards away, the King stood in the middle of the square, next to a clothing stall, his free hand playing with a tartan blanket. The market trader, an emaciated retired Scottish sailor who had done a lot of business with the King, fidgeted nervously.

'Might there be something you'd like, sir, King Dick, sir?' said the man, his eyes darting from his stall to the Rough Allies at the gates.

'There is somethin',' growled the King.

'Happy to help, sir.'

The King was taking his time; he knew Cobb would prefer to wait until all the stalls had been taken down.

'What can I do for you?' urged the stall-holder, now the only one still trading.

The King pointed his club at Cobb and Lane. 'Never grow a beard like them,' he said.

'Oh. Right you are, sir,' he replied, trying not to sound too surprised.

'Not unless you want to be seen as a criminal or a rogue or a murderin' bully.'

'No, I don't want any of those things, sir. Will that be all?'

'Yes,' said the King, 'and I'll take this blanket.' He handed over some coins and the stall-holder swapped them for the tartan. He was packed and gone within a minute.

King Dick looked up as the noon bell rang. Tommy Jackson appeared, glanced over at him, the Allies and the emptying market square and obviously concluded he wasn't needed. The King wrapped his new blanket around himself and waited. As the blanket-seller left the square, Cobb

226

and Lane sauntered over. They both wore long coats and had ensured that their beards were freshly decorated and on view.

Cobb and Lane stopped a dozen yards away. The King was used to this; any closer and they'd feel like dwarves, any further away and they'd all be shouting.

'Mr Cobb, Mr Lane,' said the King. 'Good day to you both.'

'Good day,' said Cobb, adjusting his stovepipe hat, pushing it back from his forehead.

He inhaled deeply on his cigarillo, seemingly intent on finishing it before proceeding further. The King's patience was draining fast, but still he waited. Faces now at the windows of the prisons were rapidly joined by others as the word spread.

Eventually, King Dick had seen enough. 'If you gentlemen jus' needed some smokin' time, you shoulda said. I coulda brought you some new tobacco I found from Virginia, has a special flavour. You want me to fix you some?'

Cobb spat out the cigarillo and ground it into a paving slab. 'You know we don't trade with you, Crafus,' he said, his voice tight, the words more clipped than ever. 'You know what we think of your business activities.'

'My "business activities"?' said the King. 'I was merely passin' time till you gentlemen get to the point.'

'The point' – Cobb's voice dropped – 'is escape. We hear you've got your tunnel going. That true?'

'Well, now,' said the King, 'the point as I see it is Rough Allies killin' and attackin' black men jus' when they fancy.' The King addressed everything to Cobb. Cobb was the power in Six, his control over their committees almost total.

'That was . . . unfortunate.'

'That ain't quite the right word, now, is it, Mr Cobb?' the King snapped back. 'How 'bout "shameful"? Or maybe "disgustin'"? Maybe we could try "scandalizin'" and "horrifyin'".

And how 'bout "murderous" while we're at it? How do those words sound to you, Mr Cobb?'

Cobb ran his hands over his beard, separating the two strands, then looked up. 'I grant you,' he said, 'Mr Penny's death *was* shameful. The attack on Mr Haywood was shameful, too.'

The King, surprised, sensed a sudden nervousness from Lane. Maybe he had been surprised, too. 'The man in the cachot,' he asked. 'Is he the murderer?'

'Might be.'

'Are there others?'

'Might be.'

'And what will you do if there are others?'

But Cobb was done with the revelations. 'I don't answer to the likes of you, Crafus. None of us do.'

'"The likes of me"? Now, what does that mean, I wonder?'

'You know.'

'Oh, you meanin' slaves – you shoulda said. It would avoid any misunderstandin'. "Those who think themselves the master of others are indeed greater slaves than they." D'you know who said that? Mr Cobb? Mr Lane?'

Lane looked annoyed. Cobb sighed. 'These foolish games of yours, Crafus. It's tiresome is what it is.'

'Now, I might be wrong 'bout this,' said the King, 'but I think you might just be pretendin' to be stupid. I'm *sure* you've read your Rousseau; I have some in my mess if you'd like a reminder. He has a lot to say on the matter.' He raised an eyebrow. 'You wanna talk tunnels, first you talk Ned Penny. You know exactly what happened and who was involved. If you want some kind o' peace deal, some kind o' 'scape plan, justice comes first.'

In the prison blocks, every window was occupied. Cobb made up his mind. 'The man in the cachot wasn't involved in killing your precious Ned Penny or sending John Haywood crying to Plymouth. It was two others.'

228

'Who?'

'I'll tell the British.' The briefest of glances from Lane at Cobb.

'You might wanna tell your deputy, too,' said the King. 'He's lookin' . . . un-com-for-ta-ble there.'

'We know there's a tunnel in Four,' said Cobb, ignoring the barb. 'It's the only one that was never found. We know that much.'

The King acknowledged both points. 'Yeah, there was a tunnel. And yeah, it's the only Dartmoor tunnel the Brits never found. That is true.'

'And we think,' said Cobb, 'that your little play, your little *Romeo and Juliet*, is just a cover. No one needs another one of your Dick shows now, not when the only thing anyone is interested in is gettin' home.'

The King covered his surprise with a rearrangement of his new blanket.

'We need an escape plan, Crafus. The war is over, but we ain't ever getting out. I do believe that. My men are desperate – they'll fight their way out if they got to. We wanna use that tunnel.'

'But it's a nigger tunnel, Mr Cobb! You surely would prefer a separate one, a less con-ta-min-at-ed one? There were tunnels in the white blocks, y'know – surely a white tunnel'd suit you better? I'm sure with a little diggin' you could get it all goin' again.'

The challenge was plain, but it went unanswered. Cobb said nothing. Lane was twitching.

After a while the King shook his head. 'There ain't no 'scape plan, Cobb, the play's a play. We've been waitin' all this time for home – why get yourself shot when it's this close?'

'We don't believe you,' said Cobb, stepping closer.

The King pointed his club at Cobb's chest. 'No nearer,' he growled.

'I've told you 'bout your colleague's murder,' continued

229

Cobb. 'Now you tell me what you're really doing with your Shakespeare.'

The King was disgusted. 'You tradin' with me now? You kill an innocent man, try to kill another – *my* men, Mr Cobb – then think you can fix some kinda deal?'

They stared at each other.

'You do deals,' said Cobb. 'I do deals. It's what we do.'

The King took a deep breath and turned to Edwin Lane. 'I seen you come to our shows, Mr Lane. Ain't that right? Saw you at *Othello*, at some of our musical evenings and at the pantomime, too. I am correct in that, I think? We don't have too many of the Allies watchin', so you kinda stand out.'

Lane nodded. 'You are correct in that,' he said, his tone wary.

'Well, then, may I invite you to join us in rehearsals? Come 'n' watch. Look for yourself. Then you see all you need to see.'

Cobb and Lane appeared caught off guard. 'We'll consider that,' said Cobb, 'but hear me now. We reckon you do have your 'scape plan and we reckon your play ain't nothin' but a fake. If we're wrong and you're jus' dressing up for another sixpence, you're a bigger fool than everyone says. We are free-born Americans, Crafus, and, as God is my witness, the British won't hold us much longer.'

'So, let me be clear as the sun in this sky,' said the King. 'You plan all you want. I'll not be a part of nothin' that puts more Americans in that graveyard.'

'Ain't none of us going anywhere near that graveyard,' said Cobb.

'The redcoats'll probably be disappointed we ain't started beatin' and stabbin' each other,' said the King.

Cobb turned to walk away. 'Oh, there'll be time enough for that.'

3.19

The Agent's Study

SHORTLAND: Good morning to you, Mr Crafus.

KING DICK: My name is King Dick.

SHORTLAND: Not in this room. I have only one king, King George.

KING DICK: 'In England a king has little more to do than to make war and give away places.' (*Shortland looks puzzled.*) It's Thomas Paine, Captain. We all read him back home.

SHORTLAND: But I thought you like crowned ruffians. You're a crowned ruffian. Isn't King George one of your 'unaccountable sovereigns'?

KING DICK: Not if he's mad, he ain't. And you'd choose a crazy fool of a king over me? No wonder this war gone so badly for you.

SHORTLAND: This war has gone badly for both of us. Thousands dead, so many ships sunk, your White House burned to the ground and the peace treaty says, 'No change.' It says, 'As you were.' But it is done, and the treaty is ratified by your Congress at last. Here. (*He hands King Dick a document.*) It says here that the Senate voted unanimously for ratification.

KING DICK (*reads, then reads aloud*): 'The Senate do advise and consent to the ratification of the treaty of peace and amity between the United States of America and his Britannic Majesty.' Well, that is good of them, and good news o' course. We can all go home.

231

SHORTLAND: Once the treaty has been returned to London, the measures for your return will be put in place. You must tell your men. They will have to be patient, I'm afraid. (*Sighs deeply.*) Can I offer you tea? I might have a pipe of tobacco here . . .

KING DICK: There somethin' else you wanted with me, Captain? Only I warned you 'bout the mood here and you didn't take no notice or nothin', so I don't exactly see the point. Mr Ned Penny, murdered in your prison, Captain, and on your watch. Mr John Haywood, hidin' in Four and 'fraid for his life.

SHORTLAND (*stops rummaging and fussing*): I take counsel and then I make my decision, Mr Crafus. This is not a committee. I have expressed my regret at the circumstances of Mr Penny's death; a suspect is in the cachot, awaiting trial. Mr Haywood's relocation was vital for his safety, and that is that, Mr Crafus. I am grateful for your cooperation.

KING DICK: You got the wrong man in that hole, jus' so you know. There's two Rough Allies gettin' away with murder.

SHORTLAND: He will do. For now. (*The words trigger a memory.*) The words you used in your eulogy for Mr Penny, I believe. You said you supported me 'for now'.

KING DICK: I was bein' generous. There was many there that night woulda taken up arms if they'd had the means. You know that. I will bring the killers to you. You'd be wise to arrest 'em.

SHORTLAND: You forget your place. (*King Dick remains impassive; Shortland becomes more awkward.*) Now, on other matters. (*He shuffles some papers.*) You're in charge of this play? The *Romeo and Juliet* I've been hearing about?

KING DICK (*not surprised*): You heard 'bout that?

SHORTLAND: Of course. A fine play, I know it well, but your production is a problem.

KING DICK (*knowing what the problem is, playing with him*): Too long? Some folks like it better shorter.

SHORTLAND: That is not the issue, as you are well aware. Your Romeo is coloured, yes? (*Dick nods.*) And your Juliet is white? (*Dick nods again.*) And they kiss? (*A third nod.*)

KING DICK: It's in the play. They kiss, they get married, they die. Jus' like in life. But shorter. Thought you said you knew the story?

SHORTLAND (*sighing again*): They have kissed in rehearsals?

KING DICK: 'Course they have. We've rehearsed the play. The dyin', too, if you wanna discuss that.

SHORTLAND: We have talked, you and I, about the tensions between your block and the others. What will they make, I wonder, of that kiss? When your audience roll in, flagon in hand and already rowdy with drink, will they admire the acting? Or will they riot, Crafus? That's what I fear. The prison will not have it. The department will not have it.

KING DICK: You're a Navy man, Captain. You never seen a white man kissin' a coloured man before?

SHORTLAND (*ignoring him*): This is the stage, Crafus! It speaks powerfully to us. It speaks of who we are. The mood in the prison is febrile, dangerous – you keep telling me so yourself. There are attacks every day. My men are nervous. We are sitting on a powder keg here, all of us, and your play is a burning fuse. If you insist on the kiss, I will be forced to forbid the production.

KING DICK: So to get this straight: Romeo and Juliet can marry and spend the night together . . .

SHORTLAND (*standing, angry*): Don't play games with me, Crafus. You know very well the power of that kiss. And you know very well that it can be faked. It can be skipped. I don't care. But it is your choice. It is very simple. I will ban your play. I will shut the cockloft, if I have to. If your men need protecting, as you claim they do, then protect them. Do not invite a riot into Four. Lose the kiss or lose the play.

ACT FOUR

4.1

Friday, 17 March
Block Four

11 a.m.

THE SOUND of marching boots filtered in through the open windows and every sailor rose instinctively to his feet. Recent searches in Six and Seven for Ned Penny's murderer had caused widespread fury, but it was only ever a matter of time before the British tried again.

'Sounds close,' said Habs, jumping from his hammock.

''Cos it is!' called a sailor from a nearby mess.

Peering through the sacking which had been stuffed into the opening, Habs counted the arriving troops. 'Reckon that's at least twelve redcoats approachin'. And they're stoppin' here.'

'Maybe they lookin' for Napoleon!' called one.

'I'd hide him for sure!' called another.

Habs looked around. 'Why'd they come here?'

'Someone find King Dick!' cried a voice.

'He's already there!' called another. 'They talkin' to him.'

Habs and Joe stood together.

'Could be the tunnel?' suggested Habs. 'But I can't remember this happenin' before.'

They waited for an update from the troop-watchers crowded at intervals along the wall.

'When's the next rehearsal again?' asked Joe, although he knew the answer. He'd had the routine in his head for days: a read-through in the cockloft today at midday, full dress rehearsal at seven, then the play itself the next night. 'Saturday, 18 March at 6 p.m.' was what it said on the hand-bills. 'Admission 6d, Rear 4d' is what it said. Seeing it written down, even in the scrappy version Sam had pinned up in Four, had been a thrilling moment.

'Still midday,' said Habs, amused.

'You nervous?'

'Right now, I'm nervous 'bout these soldiers. When they're gone, then I'll get nervous about the play.'

There was movement at the windows.

'King Dick's comin' back in!' called a voice. 'Redcoats goin' nowhere.'

They heard the King climbing the stairs and everyone fell silent. Habs and Joe stood by their hammocks, Sam sliding in next to them. 'I'm tryin' to think how this might be good news,' he muttered.

'And how you gettin' on with that?' asked Habs.

'Not so very well.'

The King appeared in the doorway and made straight for his mess. Every head turned to follow him: where he was going, what he was doing, who he would speak to. From about thirty hammocks out, Joe and Habs had no doubt he was heading for them. From ten hammocks, it was obviously Joe. Bearskin under his arm, the King pointed his club.

'Mr Hill. A word, if you please.'

Joe shrugged and looked around. 'Sure,' he said. 'What is it?' He looked up at the King, trying to read his face.

'You're wanted at the Agent's house,' said the King.

Whatever Joe had been expecting to hear, it most certainly wasn't that. 'I'm what?'

'The troop outside is to take you to the Agent's house. The sergeant says he can only return with you and he has no knowledge of what it's concernin'. Told me you'll be back in an hour. C'mon.'

238

As the King walked with Joe, it was clear that word had spread across the floor.

'Tell the Agent he's a dog's ass!' called one.

'We need more bread. Tell him that!' cried another.

As they walked down the stairs, King Dick put a hand on Joe's shoulder. 'Might be a trick, Mr Hill. Might be a recruitin' sergeant from the Royal Navy. They'll have noticed the way you talk, might think you'll still fight for ol' England. Might offer to get you outta here.'

Joe nodded dumbly. If that was the explanation, if there was going to be some admiral offering him a ticket to a British ship, he'd be wasting his time. Joe had spent the last two years trying to capture or sink British ships. He had no intention of joining one.

He was placed in the middle of the redcoats. Joe hadn't marched anywhere since their arrival in Dartmoor but now he matched the stride of the guards as they trooped their way across the courtyard, towards the market square. A thin, milky sky provided the brightest light they'd seen in days and, from every block, sailors spilled out to see what appeared to be the arrest of Joe Hill, the white sailor from Seven who'd chosen to live with the coloureds in Four. The prisoner who was playing Juliet. The man who'd had to be told he couldn't kiss a coloured man. If they hadn't known who he was by then, they did now.

Joe heard the jeers, assumed many of them came from Seven and hoped his old shipmates weren't participants. He wondered what Will Roche would say, then realized he didn't really want to know after all.

The soldiers' heavy tread echoed off the walls as they marched through the square. It *must* be the play, thought Joe. It looked as though he was being arrested, it certainly felt like he was being arrested, so maybe he *was* being arrested. The rumours around the blocks had been rife; news of the rehearsed kiss had spread rapidly and predictable conclusions reached. A shiver ran through him as he remembered the yarning of an *Eagle* shipmate, a witness to the hanging of a British lieutenant for buggery. Appalled, Joe looked at his guards. Is that what they think I've done? Will Habs get arrested, too? At the King's direction, they had agreed to drop the kiss and proceed with a vaguer 'embrace', but maybe the damage had been done. Maybe it was already too late. Maybe – and the thought caught his breath – he wouldn't see Habs again.

Through the alarm bell gates, and they were marching towards the Agent's house. Joe remembered this courtyard from when they had marched under the Dartmoor arch for the first time. *Parcere subjectis*. 'Spare the vanquished'. He had used the inscription's translation to reassure Will, but now it was he who needed reassurance; Joe was shaking as he was led into the house. He removed his hat and held it tightly in both hands, inhaling deeply.

Lavender and rosewater. His first reaction to the Agent's house was the remembered perfume of Elizabeth Shortland. In the small sitting room, her scent was everywhere. It was a bright front room with armchairs, a small baize-covered card table and a writing desk in the window. Flowers had been arranged on a small stand near the door; a polished upright piano was positioned against a cream-painted wall. Her room, Joe thought, and took some comfort in it. Although two soldiers were still guarding him, if he was being accused of 'the unnatural act', surely he wouldn't be in Mrs Shortland's private office? He fidgeted, shuffled, agitated, then the door swung open.

'You may leave us,' said Elizabeth Shortland to the soldiers as she strode in. 'Wait by the door, please.' She wore the same high-waisted dress Joe remembered from their first meeting, with the addition of a simple pearl necklace. Her chestnut, curled hair was piled high, little ringlets allowed loose about her ears. She stood waiting for the door to close, then turned to Joe.

'Mr Hill, good morning. I hope I haven't alarmed you too much. I needed a private conversation with you, and this seemed to be the only way.'

For a moment, Joe was speechless. It was as though he had stepped into another world, a world of courtesy, delicacy and manners. When he realized she was waiting for some kind of response, he managed a spluttered, 'Oh, I'm, fine thank you,' then cursed himself for sounding so tentative.

'Will you sit,' she said. It wasn't a question.

Joe stepped awkwardly towards a small upright chair, its red velvet upholstery contrasting with an elaborately embroidered cushion. 'Are you sure, ma'am?' He looked down at the heavy woven trousers he was wearing. Thick with dust and mud and streaked with spilt stew, they seemed incongruous with such finery, but she waved him on.

'Oh, nonsense,' she said, balancing on a mahogany couch. 'Don't worry about that. Please.' She gestured towards the chair, and he lowered himself on to its padded seat. 'How is your production?' she asked. 'Your *Romeo and Juliet*?'

Joe's heart sank. So it was about the play. He looked around the room, avoiding her gaze as he fought for an answer. 'It's tomorrow,' he said eventually, 'and I think I know all my lines.' She smiled at him, kindly, he thought.

'Well, it is certainly the first time my husband has become involved in any drama,' she said. 'Have the issues been resolved?'

'Yes, ma'am, I think they have.' Joe had no idea what she wanted to hear. 'You don't need to worry,' he added, and hoped he'd said enough.

There was a knock at the door and one of the redcoats who had escorted Joe brought in a tray, which he placed on the stand, next to the flowers. 'I assumed you might like some tea,' said Mrs Shortland, and suddenly Joe felt like laughing. It had taken barely two minutes to walk from the grime of the prisons to the elegance of the Shortlands' house; enough time,

241

he had discovered, to become terrified at the thought of being arrested, charged, tried and hanged. Now he was being offered tea from a china pot. 'You're smiling,' she said. 'I don't believe I have seen you smile before.'

Joe couldn't help himself. 'There aren't many reasons to smile in your husband's prison, Mrs Shortland. The war is over, but we are still held like cattle.' He felt himself wringing his hat between his hands. 'So, if I was smiling, it was because I'll be back in my pen shortly. I'll not take the tea, thank you all the same.' Joe gulped, knowing he had spoken too sharply. It wasn't this woman's fault that the prison was still full and the gates remained locked.

'. . . Ma'am,' he added, and stared at his boots.

She nodded. 'I am sorry, that was careless of me. I hope, too, that you may be able to go home very soon. Your Congress ratified the peace; we are waiting for the signed treaty and then ships to take you home.' She sipped some tea. 'And that is really why I asked you here.' She waited until Joe was looking straight at her. 'Mr Hill, you have a visitor.'

'Oh. Oh, I get it,' said Joe, annoyed again. 'King Dick said you'd try this. Well, I'm not meeting no admiral, no British sea lord or anyone.' He stood and brushed some dried mud on to the carpet. 'I think I should go.'

'Joe, sit down.'

'I'll not join your Navy—'

'Mr Hill, sit down. Please. It is true our Navy would take you and, that way, you could leave Dartmoor immediately. With Bonaparte escaped, the French war needs to be won again, but that is not why you're here. This isn't what you think.' She smiled nervously. 'Your . . . your grandmother is here.'

It took a while before Joe had his bearings again. He'd been lost just once, when fog had rolled in fast off the Grand Banks, enveloping the *Eagle* with such speed that no one on board knew quite where they were or which direction they were heading in. He was enveloped again in that Newfound-land fog now. Joe sat down. When he spoke, his words were whispery and thin.

'My grandmother?'

'Alice Webb. You mentioned your grandparents were in Suffolk. I'm afraid your grandfather passed away three years back, but I wrote to Alice. She's come to see you.'

Joe hadn't moved. 'My grandmother? She's ... she's here?'

'She's next door. Having some food from the kitchen. She's had a long journey.'

'But no one has visitors,' he mumbled, still in the fog. How could this be right? He had held on to the hope that, please God, he still had a mother and a sister back at home, that somehow they might still be there when this damnable peace treaty was ratified. Two family: that was it, that was all he had. He had no memories of his old life in England, just a few fragments, scraps from a tapestry of pictures he had formed in his mind from tales his parents had told him.

'My grandmother . . .' he said out loud, trying the word out for size. His mother had spoken sometimes of the parents she had left behind, but would usually become upset, so he or his father would change the subject. He thought his grandfather may have been a fisherman – a church elder, possibly – but when he tried to recall anything about his grandmother, Joe found nothing.

And with the visibility still clearing, there was a knock on the door and he stood, suddenly nervous. 'Would you like to open it, Joe?' Elizabeth Shortland's invitation surprised him.

'No, not really,' he blurted. If it was his grandmother, would he even recognize her? And what should he call her? How should he greet her? He was still listing the questions in his head when Mrs Shortland spoke.

'Come in,' she said, and Joe held his breath.

The door was opened by a member of the guard, on his left arm a hunched old woman who straightened as she peered deep into the study. Joe stared back, transfixed. White hair, green shawl, long fingernails, black bonnet, a heavily grooved, perplexed forehead, a dragging left leg and pale, curious, familiar eyes – the images tumbled into Joe's mind. While he stood, unmoving, the old woman freed herself from her escort and stepped into the room.

'Well,' the woman said, 'let me see you.' An English accent. A Suffolk accent. His mother's accent. Two more shuffled steps and her hands were in front of her mouth. 'Joe-boy?' The sound she made was little more than the driest of whispers, but there was no denying the wonder in her voice. 'They said it were you. They told me over and over. And I didn't really think it could be but . . . look at yer.' She reached for him: frail fingers, parchment skin and a lopsided smile. Joe found himself laughing.

'You smile like Mother,' he said. 'Exactly like her. It's been such a long time, I'd forgotten.' He took her hands and they embraced. 'Hello, Grandmother,' he managed.

'You look so much like yer mother,' she whispered. 'Hello, Joe-boy.' They stood together without speaking; there was so much to say, they said nothing.

After a while, Mrs Shortland cleared her throat. 'I'm afraid you can only have a few minutes together. I'm sorry, but there it is.'

'Why?' asked Alice, still holding on to Joe's shoulders. 'Why just a few minutes?'

'He's a prisoner-of-war, Mrs Webb,' said Mrs Shortland. 'Strictly speaking, you shouldn't be meeting at all.' The words were still kind but were now laced with a certain brusqueness. 'You may have privacy, if you wish, but just for five minutes. I can step outside.' She produced her snuffbox and headed for the door.

'But you arranged it all, Mrs Shortland, didn't you?' said

Alice, calling her back. She wiped her eyes with a small handkerchief that had appeared at her fingers. 'You sent for me. Yer man – that guard you sent – he persuaded me to make the journey, then you served me some of yer food, ordered yer chef, no doubt, to cook me some of that liver. Seems to me yer in charge. If you want to give us longer, who will say no to you?' Before Elizabeth could answer, Joe found his voice.

'And why, Mrs Shortland? Why did you get my grandmother to travel here? What do you want with her?'

Elizabeth Shortland spun the wooden box in her fingers, glancing from grandmother to grandson.

'No one else here, as far as I know, has such close English family,' she said. 'It' – she paused, as though the next words were difficult to say – 'it seemed the right thing to do. Five minutes.' And with that she left the room. As the door closed, Alice slumped on to one of the chairs.

'I'll not be told what to do by the likes of her. So, quickly, then, Joe-boy. What of your mother – is she well?' There was a lightness in her tone that couldn't disguise her sudden, quiet desperation.

Joe felt helpless. 'I have been at sea for more than two years and so . . .'

Alice placed her hand on his arm as he tailed off.

'I haven't seen her for fourteen years,' she said, then smiled the crooked Webb smile. 'Anything that's happened since then will be news to me.'

Joe sat opposite her, pulling up a chair. He took a deep breath. 'Father died seven years ago. The flu, Mother says.' Alice held a hand in front of her mouth; the other stayed on Joe's arm. 'She took it hard, of course – we all did – but when I last saw her she was strong. The Webb women are tough, it seems.'

Alice cleared her throat. 'Who is "we"?'

'Pardon me?'

'I'm so sorry to hear about yer father, Joe, he was such a

245

kindly man. But you said, "We all took it hard" when he died.'

'Oh, yes!' said Joe, realizing his omission. 'I have a sister. She's Alice, too.' A small gasp, and Alice closed her eyes for a moment; for the first time, tears rolled down her weathered face. 'Oh, Mary,' she whispered. 'Oh, Alice.'

There was silence in the study as he watched his grandmother process this new addition to her family. He couldn't think what other 'news' he had. Aware that their time would be gone soon, he forced the pace.

'The war is over,' he said quietly. 'All the men hope to be going home soon. What should I tell Mother of you?'

Now Alice clasped both his hands in hers. 'That her father passed. That never a day went by without us talking about her. And now, never a day passes without me praying for her. And you, Joe-boy. And now I shall pray for Alice, too.' She closed her eyes again, and Joe wondered if she was praying for them already.

'Help me up, I want to get a better look at you.' Joe gave her both his hands. 'Your mistress is tough but, Lord knows, I shall hurt the same after three minutes as after thirty. If you ever feel like you need to see yer old house, there'll be a welcome for you and a bed made up. There's always a bed made up, in case.' She reached up and took his head in her hands. They trembled slightly but her voice was firm. 'You keep this head high, Joe-boy.'

The door burst open and Alice jumped. The guard who had escorted her tumbled in.

'The *Favorite* has docked . . .' he began, then stopped as he scanned the room, surprised to find only a prisoner and an old woman present.

'The *Favorite*?' asked Joe.

The guard nodded. 'Arrived from America. It brought the Treaty of Ghent, signed by your President Madison himself.' The soldier shrugged his shoulders. 'So that's it.'

246

4.2

Block Four

BY THE time a prisoner escort had been gathered to take Joe back to Four, news of the *Favorite*'s arrival had spread across all the prison blocks. As he was marched across the market square, Joe was aware of the sound of the celebrations, but it was all submerged, overwhelmed by a torrent of emotions. One of the guard unlocked the gate to the courtyards but then had to push him through before locking up again. The image of his grandmother's smile came to him again, so like his own mother's it hurt.

At sea, at war, there was no time for reflection or regret, but in prison it could be all you did. Some inmates were so lost in their longing for home they had become ghosts in the present. Joe had avoided that fate but now he felt its power, felt once more the need to be with his family. Might American ships finally come to Plymouth and carry them home? He hoped so, with all his heart, and he set about committing everything about Alice Webb to memory: her hair, her clothes, her smell, her voice; what they spoke of, how she had embraced him and her final sad wave as she left the study. For his mother's sake alone, he needed to remember everything about her.

Joe detoured around a circle of dancing sailors. He felt sadness at the death of his grandfather, a man he had never known and, until an hour ago, had never thought about. That his grandmother prayed for him every day moved him profoundly. And the offer of the permanently made-up bed. So,

247

the *Favorite* had made it back and the treaty was signed. There was no war, so there could be no prisoners-of-war. He squeezed his way past a nine-man brawl, stepped over a sailor sprawled on the ground and into an almost-deserted Block Four. The stairs echoed to his trudging steps as he climbed to the first floor.

And the kiss, he thought, as he collapsed into his hammock. Sweet Jesus. King Dick had cut it from the play, and most of Joe was relieved. He knew what everyone had said, what he himself had thought. It was for the best, he was sure of it. The prisons had been fevered enough without the added tension of that kiss. But, in truth, he had thought of little else since their last rehearsal. He remembered his heart rate, remembered the sweat that had run down his back, remembered the way he had trembled afterwards. The total shock of it. He recalled an old sailor yarning once about how his ship had been hit by lightning and how the bolt had scorched down the mast and blown his cannon apart. He had claimed that his whole body had prickled and twitched for days afterwards. Joe hadn't believed it possible at the time, but he believed it now.

He still had his eyes closed when Habs found him.

'Ha! So here you are. I saw you cross the yard an' I tried to follow, but the crowd was too crazy. Looked like you were in some kinda stupor. What happened over there? You all right?' Joe swung his legs round so Habs could sit on the hammock, too. The ropes creaked as they took the weight.

'I'm all right,' he said. 'Hit by lightning, but all right.' He looked at Habs, who, for once, was staring straight back, puzzled.

'Not sure I follow . . .' he said slowly.

'It was my grandmother,' he said.

''Scuse me? It was who?'

Joe told him the whole story, wishing with every word that they were back in their hidden space in the cockloft.

248

'When you were marched off,' Habs said, his face serious, 'King Dick said it would be fine, but I wasn't so sure. Thought you'd be in the cachot or the Royal Navy by now.'

'I thought so, too.' Joe faltered briefly, then added, 'I thought there was a chance I might not see you again.' The ropes squeaked as Habs edged closer.

'And you'd miss me?'

Joe knew they were always watched, knew that from somewhere on the floor there'd be eyes on them. Waiting for them to do something wrong. So he just nodded.

'I'd miss the play,' he said, 'so I turned them both down.'

Habs smiled then. 'Six o'clock tomorrow,' he mused. 'If we're still here. Mightn't they jus' open the gates now the treaty is back? Some o' the men got their things with them – they're all ready to go.'

'But go where, Habs? Till there are ships to take us home, all we'd do is wander around the lanes of Devon and end up pressed into the King's Navy.'

'You could go to your grandmother. Wait there for news of the ships.'

'You serious?'

'Why not?'

'Because it's the wrong side of the country, Habs, that's why. By the time I heard the ships were in, they'd have sailed, and no mistake.'

Habs laughed. 'Fair 'nough. So we jus' wait here for the ships.'

'Depending on their destination. What if the first few ships are all heading south?'

'Then they sail without me. Better to stay in your Suffolk than travel to our Carolina. Ain't nobody from Four gonna take a ride back to a slave state, even if that's where their folks are.'

Outside, there was a shift in the sounds coming from

249

the yards. Habs and Joe noticed and reacted together, turning to the nearest window. A wind change.

Urgent voices and running footsteps reached them from below; some ran to their ground-floor beds; others were heading up. Habs and Joe exchanged glances as a crew from the *Boston* flew past them and dived into their hammocks. 'What's happenin' out there?' demanded Habs, clambering to his feet.

'Headin' to bloodshed is what's happenin',' came the reply.

'What?' cried Joe. 'That was a party when I walked through it.' He and Habs walked over to the *Boston* crew. One of them, a one-armed seaman name of Joshua, looked panic-stricken.

'We was just teasin' the redcoats – y'know, sayin' things 'bout Bony escapin' and how they was goin' to be fightin' long after we was safe at home with our women and family . . .'

'I can imagine that went well,' said Joe.

'Well, you imagine wrong,' said Joshua, missing the sarcasm. 'This soldier then says how our money would stop, seein' as the war was over. And that seem to be the truth of it. There's no more money comin' to us.'

After a stunned silence, Habs said, 'That ain't true, jus' can't be.'

'We checked it with another man, ol' sailor outta Five, and he said the same. No war, no money.'

By the time Joe and Habs had run from Four, all the men were out in the courtyard. Most had headed for the market square gates, and an angry crowd thirty or forty deep were yelling at the militia they could see through the bars. Those who couldn't get close had peeled away and were running through the channels between the prison blocks. The prisoners targeted two or three redcoats high up on the military walk, then unleashed a volley of whatever projectiles were to hand. As the soldiers raised their guns, the attackers dispersed. Occasionally, a double or triple hit would cause a guard to stumble or fall; this would be greeted with huge cheers and more abuse.

'This is bad, Joe,' said Habs. 'The English are itchin' for a fight.'

As they watched from the steps of Four, raiding parties, arms full of newly acquired weapons, ran between Two and Three, let loose a fusillade then looped round to attack again between Three and Four. The military walk hadn't been built with any kind of assault in mind. There was no protection, nothing for the British to hide behind. They had their fifteen feet of distance from the ground, but that was it, and right now it didn't amount to much more than a long way to fall. 'Shortland gotta do something!' shouted Habs.

'And King Dick,' said Joe. 'Where is he? Someone needs to calm this down.' A band of men – twenty or so – ran past, a familiar figure jogging behind the leaders.

'Hey, Will!' called Joe.

Will Roche turned and acknowledged the greeting but carried on running.

'Will!' Joe tried again, then ran after him.

Roche was heading down to the back of Four and straight for the largest platform on the walk, a wide, triangular construction of wood and iron that now held a dozen soldiers. Two of them raised their guns, but their sergeant ordered them lowered again.

Joe pushed his way through the throng, keeping low as he grabbed hold of his old friend. 'Will, are you crazy? You want to be shot?'

Around them, the sailors hopped and jumped, taunting the militia. In front of Joe, a ginger-haired man with half an ear missing had started yelling, 'English bastards!' In his hand, three small lumps of coal. Will Roche was wired. He pointed at the guards, now arranged in a 'V' that followed the

251

lines of the platform; six could see down one side of Four, six stared at the other.

'We fought these cocksuckers at sea!' he shouted. 'We sank their ships! Our armies smashed theirs. We kicked 'em out of our country, Joe – are we just gonna let 'em keep us here? Sailors' rights, remember? Or are you too busy with your show? Too busy with your new friends?' The briefest of glances towards Habs, then he let fly with what looked like a ceramic mug, which smashed against the iron palisades. More missiles were thrown, and the guns were raised again.

A shout of 'Cover!' and all the sailors ran for the partial protection provided by the wall of Four, flattening themselves against its slabs.

'And when you're done fighting them with mugs and plates,' cried Joe, 'then taken a fine English bullet in the face, how will your rights be looking then?'

Two shots in quick succession. With seven prisons and many walls, their source wasn't obvious, the sounds bouncing and rattling around the courtyard. Joe, Roche, Habs and the rest of the sailors by Four threw themselves to the ground, grit scraping their hands and faces, then scrambled round to the front.

'Where were the shots? Where were the shots?'

'Out by Six and Seven, I think!'

'One was from Three, I'm sure of it!'

Habs beckoned the sailors inside Four, only a few hesitating before entering the coloured block. 'Two separate shots!' he called, arms pointing left and right. They watched thousands of prisoners run into the block nearest them, large scrums forming at each entrance. Within seconds, hundreds of inmates flew through the door of Four, the whites choosing to stay in the hallway rather than go any deeper into the block. When there was no more firing, some chanced a sprint back to their own. Joe and Habs stood together; Will, with his raiding party, near by.

'Welcome to Four!' Joe called.

Again, an acknowledgement; nothing further.

'He really don't like me,' said Habs.

'Seems it worked out that way.'

Each new arrival brought a different story. Two men killed outside Block Two, one man injured by the back of Five, three men killed near Six.

'With two bullets?' asked Habs. 'That don't seem right.'

King Dick finally appeared, striding from the ground-floor hammocks, his club, hat and blankets all in order. But still Habs frowned. 'He's got dirt on his face,' he said. 'The King don't ever have dirt on his face.'

'He must've been in the kitchens,' said Joe. 'Near where Haywood is. There's nowhere else.'

'Well, thinkin' 'bout it, yes, there is.'

4.3

Block Four

AFTER AN hour of chaos, word reached Four that no one
had been shot. The injuries had been caused not by
English bullets, which had been aimed skywards, but by
American boots, which had trampled on fellow inmates.
However, the mood was still grim as much of the block
waited to hear from King Dick.

'All our people back inside?' The King's voice was
barely more than a growl.

'Ain't taken a count,' said Habs, 'but no one's reported
missin'.'

The King nodded but said nothing. He was sitting on
his mattress, back against the wall, unlit pipe in one hand,
club in the other. Alex and Jonathan sat together, perched,
silent, watching.

'Only reason the riot stopped,' said Sam, who had
appeared with a deep cut to his forehead, 'is the firin'. But
next time, that won't stop nothin'. If we don't get no wages,
we won't get no market.'

'And then the peace will be worse than the war,' said
Habs. His words were considered in silence until Sam said
what many were thinking.

'Well, ain't nothin' for it. We gotta 'scape.'

Now the King spoke again. 'I been in the tunnel.'

He waited for the gasps and exclamations to die away.

'That's where I was when the shootin' started. No one's
been down there for a year or more, so I figured someone

254

would want to see for themselves soon enough. Thought that person should be me.' He paused, found a bottle from the folds of a blanket and drank deeply. There was a breathless silence as everyone waited for the King's verdict.

'It weren't ever discovered 'cos Four is the worst point in the prison to start a tunnel. Why try? Block Four in the middle, farthest away from the walls – it never made no sense. But someone did try. Tunnel goes from the kitchen storeroom, jus' behind where Mr Haywood stayin', down maybe six feet, then out north-northeast for maybe fifteen feet. Still short o' the palisades.'

There were some groans at that.

'Nowhere near the military walk, and weeks o' diggin' from the outer wall. And the walls are crumblin', fallen in in places . . .'

'But it's somethin',' said Sam. 'And right now, if you asked for volunteers to get diggin' again, you'd have a long line. You know that, King Dick.'

There were murmurs of approval around the mess and Habs shifted uncomfortably.

'Where are the ships, King Dick?' he asked. ''Cos if they're close, most of us'll wait, I reckon.'

The King hit his club against the wall with an angry backhand strike. Everyone jumped.

'They are stalled, Mr Snow, they are stalled! Agent says our government and the British are arguin' over who should pay for the ships and, until that is settled, we ain't movin'. No one movin'. Now the war is over, no one wants to pay for nothin'.'

'And what if they can't stop with the arguin'?' asked Sam. 'What then?'

'Then this place will burn,' answered the King. 'So we ain't got that long.'

Joe caught his eye and the King shook his head, understanding instantly.

'Today ain't the day to put on a show, Mr Hill. I ain't filling that cockloft with men in this state.'

'Postpone the play?' Joe asked.

'Postpone the play,' the King replied.

4.4

Block Seven

Every mess was standing room only, every speaker seethed with anger. The *Eagle* crew were pressed in against those from Boston and Newport, ginger Joseph Toker Johnson leading the attack.

'We got to forget the way it's been here,' he said, glancing around him, checking faces, looking for and receiving confirmation that he was speaking for them. 'Forget the order, forget the rules. S'all changed. We don't get paid, they don't sleep. We make their lives hell. Every chance we get. Shout somethin', throw somethin', curse, spit – whatever.'

Roche pushed his way through to the front.

'And we tell the English that when we'll be goin' home – though the good Lord knows when that'll be – they'll still be fightin'. Fightin' without end. That Napoleon will battle 'em for years. And when they're gettin' shot at by the Frenchies, their wives and daughters'll be spreadin' their legs for every Tom and Dick that passes their English hovel.'

Ribald cheers greeted this, and Toker Johnson pushed himself back in, unwilling to relinquish the mess. 'If we push 'em enough, they'll break. Today was proof o' that.'

Robert Goffe and Jon Lord exchanged nervous glances.

'And then what?' called Goffe, and all heads turned to him. 'Once they've broken – then what? Are you volunteerin' to stand in front o' the English guns? 'Cos when they've shot you, how's that get the rest of us out o' here?'

'Damn right about that!' came a voice. 'These English

257

are bastards, but I'll be damned if they kill me just as the war is finished.'

Lord wiped his face with his hands then raised his hand to speak. 'How much money've we got?' He cleared his throat and spoke louder. 'If we all put all our wages and prize money together, what'd it make?'

Rose, the ex-president of Seven, still in his long brown coat, laughed. 'You proposin' we bribe our way out? All eight hundred of us? Your brain has rotted, man . . .'

Roche wasn't impressed either. 'You're a good man, Lord, and we've survived a lot together, you an' I. But I'll be damned if any o' these red-coated sons of bitches take my money. I'm not payin' no toll to walk through them gates.'

'You wanna fight instead?' asked Goffe.

'Damn right. What's the other side o' this block? A large British wall. And what's the other side o' that? A large British armoury.'

There was a silence after that. 'What you suggestin', Roche? Armed rebellion?' Lord sounded incredulous.

Roche tugged at his beard, smoothing it between his fingers. 'I call it a patriotic revolt. I dunno where you were in '76, but seems to me that the Revolutionary War ain't over just yet.'

4.5

Block Six

THE ROUGH Allies had taken over half of the messes on the ground floor, pushing out any other inmates. In recent weeks, the number of extravagantly bearded inmates had increased dramatically. Horace Cobb, leaning on a stanchion, counted his troops. 'Two twenty-six. We could man a Navy if they wasn't so agitated.'

An eve-of-battle urgency clung to the Allies' conversations, the sudden shivers of fear causing voices to rise and emotions to spike.

'And we could fight them English,' breathed Lane, next to him, a new, manic energy in his voice. 'That's two hundred twenty-six angry, starvin' Yankees against a thousand fat English who don't give a good goddamn.'

Cobb shrugged. 'Maybe. But that's a thousand fat English with guns. And that's a thousand more guns than we got.'

'Right now, that may be so,' corrected Lane. Cobb raised an eyebrow and Lane leaned in close. 'If the market comes back next week,' he whispered, 'I'm hopeful of a delivery. It'll only be a sidearm, but . . .'

Cobb's lips were pinched together to hold the cigarillo in place, but he still managed a smirk. 'Well, well,' he said, smoke shooting out of both sides of his mouth. 'Think of the . . . opportunities.' He blew smoke high into the cloud that hung from the ceiling. 'You trust your trader?'

Lane laughed again. 'Not even slightly. A Jew, jus' like the rest o' them, swindlin' every last penny out of us they can.'

'How much?'

'Two pounds ten shillings.'

Cobb whistled. 'Swindle is right.'

A cluster of Allies nearby, heads together, launched into a patriotic song while others clapped their support. 'Well, maybe when we 'scape we can pay the villagers a visit,' said Lane, louder now.

'And escaping,' said Cobb, 'is the only way we'll ever get out of this godless, infested sewer. I used to think – like that bandit Crafus – that we'd all be released in the end, that Madison'd send ships and we'd all sail home in triumph, but now it seems clear to me that the President don't want us back. He's done a deal with the mad king.'

Lane wasn't keeping up. ''Scuse me, Mr Cobb, but I ain't got that exactly. D'you mean to say America don't want us back?'

'Isn't that what it feels like, Mr Lane? Is that not obvious to you now? We're an embarrassment, that's what we are. "The war was won, but not by these men." Can't you hear them say it? Who wants to see the men who lost? No one. That's the truth of it. We're thousands of miles away. It'd be more convenient if we stayed that way. If we jus' disappeared. That's what they're saying.' He drew deeply on his cigarillo, then exhaled slowly.

'Who's sayin' that?' asked Lane. 'Pardon my ignorance, but who's sayin' that?'

'The men round Madison. Catholics. Jews. The profiteers who just made their own fortune from the war. If we just "disappeared", who'd know the truth?'

Lane stared back at Cobb. 'So today . . . it was jus' the beginning?'

Cobb nodded. He dropped his voice further and Lane leaned in to catch every word. 'And don't be surprised if that African pox makes a return, this time in all the blocks.'

Lane had heard enough. Clearly agitated, he paced

around the hammocks, ignoring the keenly offered greetings of the men he passed. At last calmer, he returned to Cobb. 'When the men hear o' this, they gonna go crazy. You think we can get out?'

'I do. We are many. We can overwhelm them, but we need firepower. With your gun, we can make a start. But it's just a start. The nigger play is just a nigger escape plan, I'm sure of it. And whatever it is, we need to be a part of it. We need to be watching. We need to be ready. We need to be *in charge*.'

'So,' said Lane, the softness of his tone exaggerating the high pitch of his voice, 'I reckon we should take up Crafus's offer. He says there ain't no 'scape plan – well, let's see 'bout that. How 'bout I go an' see what I can find out? Spend an hour or two with them blackamoors, see what tricks they're plannin'?'

Horace Cobb's eyes narrowed as he inhaled deeply. 'Good,' he said, then exhaled slowly. 'Crafus invited you personally – I reckon you'll be safe enough. But' – he pulled on the cigarillo again – 'there is of course the matter of Ned Penny . . .' He looked at Lane, who shrugged.

'What 'bout him?' A nearby card game finished amid a flurry of insults and threats.

Cobb waited for them to subside. 'Well, you killed him, Mr Lane, so if you're planning to spend some time with his shipmates, I had better feed them some names. Else they might want to keep hold of you awhile.'

'Whose names?' asked Lane. 'I told James 'n' Hitch that doin' Penny was our idea.'

'We don't need to explain nothing,' said Cobb. 'Just give them a pair of names. Anyone who's causing you trouble, maybe . . .'

Lane looked relieved. 'If they find out I had anythin' . . .' he began.

'Then you'll be prepared,' insisted Cobb.

'Always.'

Cobb nodded. 'You don't stay there any longer than you need. I'll want you back here soon enough.' He indicated the other Allies, stabbing his cigarillo as he spoke. 'Time'll come when they'll fight. They want to fight. They need to fight. Whatever's happening in Four won't do for all of us.' He flicked ash from his arm. 'First, though, we have some prison visits to make . . .'

4.6

The Hospital

THE INJURED from the morning's riot were laid wherever space could be found. Elizabeth Shortland had seen worse, but Magrath seemed anxious as he bandaged and strapped. 'None of this feels safe,' he said, glancing up and down the ward.

She wasn't immediately sure of his meaning. 'There's a desperation here, now, with these men. I haven't seen it before,' he said. 'They understood the war, knew why they were held here. But this damned peace has turned their heads.' He indicated a man with bandages wrapped tightly around his chest. 'Do you see that man, Elizabeth? I just strapped him up. He was agitating in the courtyard, attacking the troops. Broken ribs from a crush. He says as soon as he can bear the pain, he'll be back and doing it all again.' Magrath shook his head in despair.

He looked exhausted, she thought, strained; the lean on his cane heavier than usual. She resisted the temptation to assist him. She smiled instead. 'They can't just open the gates, George. Thomas wants them gone, too, but until there are ships . . . Just letting seven thousand men out on to Dartmoor would be a catastrophe.'

The returned smile was brief, reluctant. 'I know his hands are tied,' he said, sighing deeply. 'But we all need to take care now.'

Echoing bootsteps rattled along the corridor and they both turned, instinctively stepping apart from each other as they did so. Captain Shortland and two redcoats marched into the ward.

'Elizabeth. George. A minute, please!' he called out.

Magrath and Elizabeth walked through the rows of beds towards him, a few heads following them as they passed.

Shortland nodded the briefest of greetings at his physician. 'What injuries from this morning?' His eyes scanned the room, alighting on the recently arrived mattresses in front of him.

Magrath followed his gaze. 'Broken ankles, legs and ribs. Bruising, cuts. We got away with it, but only just,' he said.

'Meaning?' asked Shortland, irritated.

Magrath shrugged. 'Meaning we could easily have had fatalities out there, Thomas. The bullets missed, but—'

'The bullets didn't "miss", George, they were fired over the heads of rioting prisoners. It was strategic, and it worked. The riot is over.'

'I think what George is trying to say—' began Elizabeth.

'I know very well what he's trying to say!' snapped Shortland. 'And I don't like it one bit. Would you care to hear my opinion on your patients' health? Shall I make an inspection? Well?' The challenge was clear.

Elizabeth flushed. 'Thomas, that's not fair. We talk to these men, we know what they're saying. Surely that's helpful to you?'

Shortland's blood was up. His eyes narrowed. 'I'm not sure that it is, Elizabeth, not sure at all. Maybe you talk to them too much, eh? How did the meeting with the English boy's grandmother go? Did you recruit him, or do I have to get the recruiters back?'

With a start, she realized that she recognized his tone, that patronizing petulance she had heard so often. It was her father's voice. Her husband now spoke to her as though she were a child. Elizabeth fought to keep the contempt from

264

her voice. 'Well, first of all, he's not English,' she said. Shortland was about to interrupt, but Elizabeth persisted, talking over him. 'I know what our law says, Thomas, but that's not how he sees it. Me telling him he's English won't stop him feeling American.'

'Well, happily, he can now feel as American as he wants and still join up. We are fighting the French again, Elizabeth. This may very well be a good time for a visit from the recruiting sergeant.' He glanced at Magrath. 'I'm sending the turnkeys out, George. Locking the prisons down until it's all quietened somewhat. Make sure the hospital is secure also.' Shortland nodded at them both, turned on his heels and marched back down the corridor, the two redcoats following behind.

'Locking the prisons!' said Elizabeth, exasperation and fear in her voice. 'I think he's learned nothing, George.'

Magrath nodded slowly. 'The turnkeys won't quieten anything. Quite the reverse, I fear. Quite the reverse.'

4.7

Block Four, Cockloft

THE COCKLOFT was rammed, each of its traditional func-
tions of sanctuary, town hall, bar, casino and church now
fully engaged. The belief that their tuppence ha'penny
daily wage had been stopped triggered wild, reckless gambling in some and panicked, immediate thrift in others.
Pastor Simon had tried to call for prayer but, without support from King Dick, had got nowhere. Now, he queued for
his attention. The King was besieged by questions. He
answered as best he could.

'No, it ain't the last times. No, no one died today. Yes, I
believe the ships are on their way. Yes, I would like coffee. I
agree we need to be on our guard. No, I don't think the British King is Satan Himself.' He looked up. 'Ah, Pastor Simon,
you are, after all, a blessin'. Our very own Pontifex Maximus.
Come, let us climb the stage. Let us see what Church and
state can manage together. I'm sure Thomas Jefferson won't
be concernin' himself with us anytime soon.' The King and
the pastor pushed their way through the melee.

'I'm hopin' you gotta spiritual song for us, Pastor? Some
succour for our ravaged souls? We got some work to do right
now. Anythin' 'bout peace an' patience would be fine.'

Pastor Simon turned as they stepped on to the stage.
'We sing 'em sperichills all day, King Dick, and half the choir
are right there.' He pointed to the first few rows.

'Get 'em up here,' said the King. 'Put 'em to work.'

266

Pastor Simon waved his men up, and eight of them clambered on to the stage. Straight away, two of them began clapping and stamping, the rhythm quickly taken up by the others. Simon bowed his head then, resting a hand on the man next to him, and began to sing.

> 'I ain't gonna tarry here,
> I ain't gonna tarry here.'

The choristers responded, they, too, resting an arm on the sailor next to them.

> 'I ain't gonna tarry here,
> I ain't gonna tarry here.'

Pastor Simon led them on, his querulous baritone finding its range and passion.

> 'But my Lord, He knows the time,
> My Lord, He knows the time.
> And when He calls me home,
> And when He calls me home,
> Gonna ring that freedom chime,
> Gonna let that freedom chime.'

Many in the crowd began to sing, too, but the moment was short-lived. Cries and shouts cut across the singing. The whole cockloft could hear 'Sweet Mary, Mother of God!', then 'Get King Dick!' and a sharp, forceful slamming.

The King jumped from the stage. 'Everyone stay here!' he yelled, and was about to open the door when he was met by an anxious trio of lookouts falling over themselves to get to him. 'You have left your posts?' called the King.

'It's Cobb and Lane. Horace Cobb and Edwin Lane.'

The look-outs' words were tumbling fast. 'The Rough Allies. The leaders, from Six, they're outside, and they're just standin' there. Right by the steps!'

'You gotta do somethin', King Dick,' panted one of them. 'They could be invadin' or somethin'.' The crowd in the cockloft stirred.

The King turned back. 'Y'all stay and watch!' he shouted. 'Y'all stay and listen! I'll take the first thirty men here with me; the rest of you, stay and watch. But steady now. Two men in beards ain't even a boardin' party, never mind an invasion. So, before you go off makin' war, let's see what they want.'

The King crashed down the two floors, and a posse followed, Habs, Joe and Sam riding the wave. He stopped by the doors, held up four fingers then pointed them at the kitchens. Four men silently peeled off, doubling the protection for John Haywood.

King Dick stepped outside, bearskin strapped high, his men packed tightly around him. The sun was slipping away, the vast shadows thrown by the blocks overlapping each other in the darkening courtyard. No more than ten feet from the steps, Cobb and Lane stood waiting. No cigarillos, no pipes, arms folded and beards partially hidden by their tunics – every man present knew this was as unthreatening as the Allies could be.

'With a hatchet in one hand and a Bible in the other,' said the King. 'Gentlemen, are you sure?'

'Sure of what?' asked Cobb, taken aback.

'Comin' so close. What'll people say?'

Cobb ignored him. 'You made an offer. Extended an invitation to Mr Lane here to watch your rehearsals. If it still stands, we would like to accept.'

Lane fidgeted nervously beside him, his balance shifting from leg to leg, his thumbs running endlessly over his clenched fists. Cobb, like King Dick, was motionless. The few men remaining in the courtyard had stopped what they were doing to watch the stand-off.

Eventually, King Dick said, 'We've put the play back. Today ain't the day. Like you say, it's gotten even more serious. Reckon you think so, too, or you wouldn't be standin' there. The offer to Mr Lane still holds; watchin' a rehearsal won't hurt no one. But my question to you, Mr Cobb, holds, too.'

'And what question might that be?'

The King continued to look unblinkingly at him. 'The question is, who killed Ned Penny?' he said quietly. 'And you can tell it to his family here.' He nodded to Habs and Sam standing behind him.

It was, as Cobb had forecast, the entrance fee that needed paying. Without it, no one was going anywhere. Cobb glanced at all three men.

'Matthews and Drake,' he said. The King waited for more. When nothing came, he spread his arms, the club swinging casually from his fingers.

'Go on, Mr Cobb. I am not the keeper of your register.'

'John Matthews and Robert Drake. From Detroit.'

The King was waiting for more.

Cobb folded his arms. After a while, he said, 'I'm dealin' with it.'

The sun had gone now, the courtyard in twilight.

'Well, Mr Cobb,' said the King with the beginnings of a laugh in his throat. 'You'll forgive my stupidity. I know there are other matters to address but, jus' for now, what does you "dealin' with it" actually mean?'

'It means, if I have to, I'll hang 'em myself.'

'You told the British that?'

'I don't talk to the British.' His eyes narrowed. 'Not all of us talk to the Brits.'

'Well, not blessed with the moral purity that comes with bein' white, maybe you wouldn't mind if *I* tell the British,'

269

said the King. 'In your place, you understand. Save you the effort. Keep you *special*.'

'Like I said, Crafus,' said Cobb, 'I'll deal with it.'

The King indicated Habs and Sam next to him. 'These here is Mr Penny's closest,' he said. 'They're also in the play. They get the final say. They say you can watch, you can watch.'

Habs knew what Sam was thinking. He ducked behind the King, put his arm round his cousin and pulled his head close.

'Hey, cuz,' he said, before Sam could say a word in a half-whisper. 'It's jus' upstairs. Jus' the cockloft.'

Sam could barely speak, his eyes wide with incredulity. 'Are . . . you . . . crazy?' he spluttered. He flicked his eyes towards the open door of Four and beyond. To the hidden, protected, damaged John Haywood.

Habs understood. ''S'jus' the second floor, Sam. He ain't goin' nowhere but the second. He got us with him, always. A thousand of us against one o' him. Reckon the King thinks there's some sport to be had.'

Sam looked utterly unconvinced, his eyes darting from Cobb to Lane and back again. At last, he shook his head and shrugged, surrendering to Habs, deferring to him, as ever. Habs and Sam sprang back to their positions either side of the King.

'We're all right,' Habs said to the King. 'Let him in.'

4.8

Block Four

WHEN KING Dick stepped aside, most of the crowd on the steps of Four followed. Their reluctance was clear – glares and muttered curses followed Lane every step of the way – but they allowed him to approach their prison. A few didn't move; Abe Cook from Connecticut took a blow to the chest from the King's club before he gave way. The sailors of Four packed themselves around Lane then shuffled back into the block.

'We swallowed him whole,' hissed Habs to Sam in an attempt at reassurance.

Sam said nothing, his eyes locked on Lane. The entrance to the ground-floor beds was filled four deep with bristling, hostile inmates who stared at Lane as he was pushed upstairs.

Joe fought his way through the swarm. 'This is ridiculous,' he said. 'It just looks like we're hiding something.'

'We *are* hidin' something,' said Habs, 'but mainly it looks like we're takin' care of ourselves. It looks like we're in charge here, looks like our Rough Ally might have to show some respect.'

'Or just like we're hiding something,' repeated Joe.

In the din, no one heard him. Nor did they hear the turnkeys call: 'Tumble down and turn in! Tumble down and turn in!'

By the time the inmates of Four and the one inmate of Six realized what was happening, the huge block doors were crashing shut.

271

'Hey, you're early! That's too early!' shouted the nearest man, accompanying his protest with vigorous banging against the door's heavy panels. 'It ain't dark yet!'

'Orders of the Agent,' came the reply. 'Go fuck yourselves.'

'They do that, anyways,' said another voice, followed by laughter, which faded as the turnkeys moved away.

The door-banger turned to the waiting crowd. 'Shut for the night, he said. Orders of the Agent, he said.'

All eyes turned to Edwin Lane. 'But I got to get back. I'm in the wrong block.'

'Ain't no one gonna disagree with that one,' said Sam.

Lane, for the first time, looked unsure of himself. His eyes darted up and down the stairs. 'This is a trick. Where's Crafus? Where's . . .' In an instant, he was on the floor, knocked sideways by the three nearest inmates. The biggest of them grabbed his beard in both hands and pulled hard until Lane's head lifted off the steps. Then he let it go. The thud echoed around the stairwell.

'You called him what?' spat the man. He put a tattered boot to Lane's neck. 'This is Block Four. Look round you. You a long way from home, mister. Now you try that again.'

Lane tried to twist his neck away from the boot, straining to speak.

'Let him go!' King Dick was at the bottom of the stairs but moving fast. 'Get him up!' He pushed his way through, hauled Lane to his feet by his coat and didn't stop. The King half marched, half carried him to the cockloft, kicking open the door and pushing Lane in front of him and on to the floor. The many hundreds still in the cockloft strained to see what the commotion was. 'Ten seconds!' bellowed the King. 'Tha's all it took. Ten seconds of me not watchin' you.'

Lane scrambled to what he thought might be a safe distance, coughing and spitting as he went. 'Where were you?' he said, wiping his mouth, crouching.

'Oh, so you in charge here? You askin' the questions? I have to give an account o' my time to you? Well, well.' He heard the sound of his 'throne' being placed behind him and, without taking his eyes from Lane, eased himself down.

'Your men attacked me.'

'Did they now?'

'Turnkeys locked us in for the night.'

'Did they now?'

'Dammit to Hell, Craf—' Lane checked himself, almost wincing as he glanced around. 'Dammit to Hell, anyways. I don't wanna spend the night here.'

'Oh, trust me on this, Lane,' said the King. 'The feelin' there is quite mutual.'

He looked up and around the cockloft. On the stage, the choir still stood as though they were mid-song. Habs and Sam stood with crew and mess mates, Joe with Alex and Jonathan. Behind them, the rest of Four, on edge, were waiting to see how this was going to play out. Those watching the King saw him nod to himself, his mind seemingly made up on some matter.

'So, Mr Lane,' he said, removing his bearskin and folding it in his lap. 'So. Seein' as we none of us has any choice in the matter of who spends the night where, we might as well make the most of it.'

Lane looked nonplussed, waiting for some clarification. 'You gonna show me round, then?'

The King ignored him and, with the smallest of gestures, summoned the pastor, then Habs, then a crippled card-dealer named Hopper and, finally, Alex and Jonathan. Each received their instructions; each set off with purpose. 'Jus' watch this, Lane,' said the King, sitting back on his tea-chest throne.

Habs grabbed Joe as he ran past. 'King Dick wants the play. He wants some *Romeo and Juliet*. Now.'

'He wants what?' Joe was flabbergasted.

'A rehearsal,' said Habs. 'Or some of it, anyways. What

scenes can we do with you, me, Pastor Simon, Sam and Tommy?'

Joe thought fast. 'And King Dick? Is he in? Or is he busy with that bastard Lane?'

Habs shook his head. 'This gotta work. King Dick wants Lane to understand that this is a real play. Not some dumb-ass foolin' around. Not a "nigger play" – that means no play at all. That means poor quality. That means grinnin' like you got no brain in your head. It means embarrassin'.'

'But you said he came to *Othello* . . .'

'So he knows what we can do already, then,' said Habs. 'Maybe he jus' needs it knockin' into him. It ain't 'bout who plays what or which scene we do. It's 'bout convincin' Lane we ain't plannin' on 'scapin'.'

'We should get the scripts,' said Joe, and they ran for their mess as the choir started.

The notes began low, a drone that was, to begin with, swallowed by the noise of the room. As it rose in volume, the hubbub fell away and heads turned. This was 'Balm in Gilead', and Pastor Simon, in the middle of a circle, started the clapping. Most of his services and the rehearsals included at least a few of its verses. But this was different; everyone felt it. They had a new audience. They didn't know much about Edwin Lane, but they knew enough. They knew his gang, knew his friends, knew his type. Every ship had them, every farm, every town hall. They sang it for him, they sang it *at* him.

'There is a balm in Gilead,
To make the wounded whole;
There is a balm in Gilead,
To heal the sin-sick soul.
Sometimes I feel discouraged,
And think my work's in vain,
But then the Holy Spirit
Revives my hope again.'

'You ever feel discouraged, Mr Lane?' King Dick sat in the middle of the cockloft, Lane as close to him as he could manage. The Rough Ally shot glances around the room, seeing threats in every face. There was no reply, just a shrug of the shoulders. Now, half the cockloft was singing, Pastor Simon beaming as he conducted.

> 'Don't ever feel discouraged,
> 'Cos Jesus is your friend,
> And if you lack for knowledge,
> He'll never fail to lend.'

The King leaned over again. 'Do you ever lack for knowledge, Mr Lane?' He didn't wait for a reply. 'You see, I think you do. I believe there're maybe just a few things you don't quite understand. You might not get a whole lotta sleep tonight, but you might jus' get yourself an education.'

'I have an education,' said Lane. 'Sure don't need another damn one. Not from here, anyways.'

'What sorta education you get, Mr Lane?'

'The Bible and the Declaration of Independence,' said Lane. 'That's enough truth for anyone right there. It's what we're fightin' for.'

'Indeed it is.' The King nodded earnestly. 'Indeed it is. But I'll be charitable with you and assume that you maybe cannot read with any distinction. And that your memory got blown away with your face. Would I be right?'

Lane bridled. 'I can read, and I can remember jus' fine,' he muttered.

The King kept all his attention on Lane as the players gathered. 'That's good. So you'll remember at least, say, the first few lines of the Declaration?'

Lane stared at the King, realizing the trap that had been sprung. 'Maybe I do,' he said, then shrugged.

King Dick stifled a laugh. 'O' course. I understand. Let

me help you. "We hold these truths to be self-evident, that all men are created equal." Did your "ed-u-ca-tion" get to that part? You fightin' for *that* line, eh, Mr Lane?'

Lane retied his beard. 'I'll not argue with you,' he said.

''Course you won't,' said the King. 'When you don't understand your own language, that'd be mighty difficult.'

Alex and Jonathan brought meat, bread and ale, and the King passed them to Lane. A wave of annoyance suffused the room. Lane, expecting a projectile at any second, bent low as he bit into the pork. The choir made way for the band. A heavily bearded, crouched man in a battered top hat thrust his violin under his chin and produced a bow from inside his jacket. He stepped forward, and everyone in the room stood. Shouts of expectation and excitement came from all sides. He played a single note, adjusted his stance, and the music began, a selection of reels and shanties that sent the cockloft into a frenzy. When his bow broke, the hairs all worn through, he swapped it with another from his jacket. The inmates of Four danced as though it might be their last, danced for either death or freedom.

Joe, Habs, Sam and Pastor Simon watched the mayhem from the side of the room.

'We're goin' on after *this*?' asked Joe.

'We always go on after the band,' Sam replied, bewildered.

'We got the wrong scenes, Habs,' Joe carried on. 'They not going to sit and watch some clever words after this. We need something more . . . vigorous.'

Habs looked around. 'We had somethin' vigorous,' he said. 'We was told to take it out, remember?'

Joe winced. 'Not that kind of vigorous.'

The band finished a tune and the fiddler looked across at the King. A sideways shake of the head from the throne and, bow back in his jacket, he took the band off the stage. The crowd jeered.

'We're on,' Habs said. 'And remember, the only crowd that matters is that duck-fucker Lane. Act Two, Scene Six for Joe, me and the pastor. Then run on to Act Three, Scene One for Sam. I'll read Mercutio, too.'

There was no time for discussion. Habs, Joe, Sam and Pastor Simon climbed up on to the stage and the noise gradually abated. Habs stood downstage, his arms wide.

'My friends. My friends. And also Mr Lane there, visitin' from Six.' Habs nodded to Lane as the inmates laughed. 'We had hoped to be performin' *Romeo and Juliet* for you this very night, but what with the peace an' all we ain't quite got to it . . . so here's a couple of scenes anyways. I'm Romeo . . .' He bowed low.

'Joe here is Juliet . . .'

The room rang with catcalls and whistles, Joe took a little bow.

'Pastor Simon is Friar Lawrence, Sam is Benvolio. This is Act Two, Scene Six, where—' He was interrupted by three slow, declaratory bangs of the King's club on the floor.

'Look alive there!' called the King. 'Get on with it, Mr Snow.'

Habs bowed slightly and waved the pastor on. Pastor Simon, script in hand, started to read carefully.

'So smile the heavens upon this holy act. That after-hours with sorrow chide us not.' It was not the encore the cockloft was looking for. The crowd began to stir almost immediately. King Dick intervened before the situation deteriorated further.

'Mr Lane, you familiar with *Romeo and Juliet*?' he asked, leaning in close. 'Was that in your ed-u-ca-tion?'

Lane sat up, cleared his throat. 'I have a . . . loose understandin' of some of its . . . aspects.'

The King nodded, then rose and banged his club on the floor once more. 'Come,' he said.

Lane looked horrified. 'Come where?'

277

'You wanna know if there's a play, Mr Lane? Well, here's the best way to find out,' said the King. 'Come.'

A path opened for the King as he walked through the cockloft, but there was no disputing the looks of puzzlement and, in some cases, anger on the faces of the sailors of Four.

'We don't want him here, King Dick!'

'Don't need no Allies on our stage. Not now, not never.'

The boisterousness of the dancing had turned quickly to a jostling, truculent fury. No one questioned the King publicly, never – until now. But here he was, in front of the men of Four, taking noisy and sustained insubordination. Hat high and club held in readiness, he pushed his way through, Lane following swiftly in his wake.

'Stay here,' said the King, and climbed on to the stage. Joe, Habs, Sam and Pastor Simon watched him carefully, waiting for a cue. King Dick faced the crowd. Club over his shoulder, his eyes worked the room. In a matter of seconds, he seemed to have glanced at everyone, acknowledging a select few with a nod or a brief wave. Unhurried. Assured. In charge. He measured his words carefully. 'Men of Four,' he said, 'the turnkeys came early. The Agent has locked us away again. But even he now senses somethin' we all known for a while – that his time is over.'

Nodding heads already.

'Agent Shortland knows that we will be home with our sweethearts and children soon.'

A few shouts of 'Yes!' Alongside Joe, the pastor uttered an unusually hesitant 'Hallelujah!'

'But still the cursed gates are closed,' said the King, 'and we gotta live here for a few hours more. Maybe a few days. Maybe a week. But back home, our marsh marigolds are in bloom. Back in Maryland, the Dutchman's breeches are bustin' their white-and-yellow pantaloon flowers all over, and I intend to see 'em. *This* season, *this* spring.' Each 'this' was accompanied by a thump of the club; there was matching applause. King Dick pressed on.

'Back home, the winds are light and the winter storms are gone. Might always be winter in this forgotten part of England but, back home, the Potomac and the Rappahannock are peaceful now, flowin' strong, and them oysters are sweeter than ever.'

The King was pacing the stage now, using his club to point to sailors who caught his eye. 'John Ridge, you wanna sail into Chesapeake Bay again? Mr Jennings there, you always talk o' the Blue Ridge, the bears and the coyote. Well, let's go back there. Let's not die by a redcoat's musket. No one else is dyin', when there's peace in America. To get home, we gotta have peace in the blocks. Mr Lane here did not intend to stay with us. We did not intend to invite him. But here he is, anyways. Step this way, Mr Lane.'

Edwin Lane climbed reluctantly on to the stage. The King directed his club at him. 'Mr Lane here ain't so sure we really practisin' for a play. He thinks maybe we jus' . . . pretendin'.'

There was laughter then and a shout of 'I'll pretend to cut him, then!' More laughter.

Joe whispered to Habs, 'He thinks he's going to die – look at him.'

Lane's eyes were flicking around the room and his mouth was working silently. 'That sure looks like a man prayin', all right,' said Habs.

'So, bein' the peaceable type, we gonna give a copy of the play to Mr Lane here. Act Three, Scene One is lively enough. Romeo, Benvolio and Tybalt are needed, and you, Mr Lane, will read Tybalt's line, your skin bein' a perfect match. Mercutio is dead.' He waited until Lane was looking at him. 'That was Ned Penny's part . . .'

The words hung between them. The room held its breath.

The King walked to the centre of the stage, and hit the club into the floor. 'Sam,' he said, 'do we have a play?'

'Yes, King Dick,' he replied, handing over one of the scripts to Lane.

'Uh-huh. So let us begin.'

Habs took a few steps to the front of the stage as Sam began his speech.

> 'O Romeo, Romeo, brave Mercutio is dead!
> That gallant spirit hath aspired the clouds,
> Which too untimely here did scorn the earth.'

Joe glanced at Lane, waiting for his reaction. The man appeared stunned, transfixed, afraid.

'Here comes the furious Tybalt back again!' Sam's voice rose in anger.

Habs matched him in volume and fury: 'Alive in triumph – and Mercutio slain!'

Joe watched Habs approach Lane. There was a new passion in his words. With Lane in his sights, an urgency and threat infused his speech that hadn't been there before. Habs filled the stage. He pointed both hands at Lane.

'Fire-eyed fury be my conduct now!' he roared, then advanced until their faces were inches apart. Habs lowered his voice a little: 'For Mercutio's soul is but a little way above our heads.'

There was a sudden and profound moment of understanding between the two men. This wasn't a rehearsal, it was a trial. A white man on trial for the death of a black man. He had buried his friend from the *Bentham*, the murderers were still at large, and this man, this preening Rough Ally was, Habs was sure, at the heart of it all.

'Tybalt, you ratcatcher . . .'

The crowd sensed it, too. There was a silence, a dangerous stillness, over the room. Habs felt the King's stare; in a glance saw him nodding his approval. His blessing. Habs swallowed hard, then said Romeo's line again, forcing himself slower.

'For Mercutio's soul is but a little way above our heads.' Slower still. 'Staying for you to keep him company.' He emphasized the 'you' and Lane's eyes popped. Habs knew that if he had a sword in his hand now, he would use it. He looked around for a weapon, and the fiddler in the wrecked hat understood, threw him his bow. Habs jabbed it into Lane's chest. 'Either you or I, or both, must go with him.'

Lane may have been unprepared, unrehearsed and surrounded by his enemies, but there was no mistaking the malevolence he put into his words as he read from his script, his reedy voice managing to sound contemptuous and fearful at the same time. 'You, wretched boy,' he spat, 'that didst consort him here. Shalt with him hence.'

Habs scraped the bow up Lane's jacket until the tip was pushing into his neck.

If the audience were expecting – hoping – for an execution, they were disappointed. Lane broke the spell. He pointed at the pages.

'It says here we fight, but I ain't got no weapon.'

King Dick strode over. 'And that'd be jus' wrong,' he said. 'A one-sided fight against a defenceless man? No, that's not right either.' He turned to the audience. 'And o' course, this is where Tybalt is viciously slain by Romeo.'

Habs raised a hand, and the inmates cheered. Lane was momentarily shocked, then balled his fists.

'Says who?'

'Shakespeare,' said Habs.

Lane shrugged. 'Another slack-assed Englishman.'

'Mr Lane,' said the King, 'you might be a vile, murderin' son of a bitch but you ain't stupid. This is where Tybalt dies. I'd die now, if I were you.'

Lane shrugged. 'You want me dead? How's this?' He fell to his knees, held out his arms, 'There, you got me.'

Habs threw the bow at him. 'One day, maybe,' he said, then jumped from the stage.

The King clapped his hands to break the tension. He waved at a lopsided man leaning against the cockloft door. The rehearsals were over. Within minutes, the gambling tables were up. At the back of the room, a few members of the band had teamed up with some of the choir, and more songs of home and the sea filled the cockloft. Lane, escorted to a stool, watched in some surprise.

'I know what you're thinkin', Mr Lane,' said the King, his hand firmly on Lane's shoulder. 'You thinkin' you ain't got nothin' like this back in Six. Am I right? 'Course I'm right. Now, why might that be, d'you reckon? Why might Six be so lackin'—'

'I need the heads,' replied Lane.

'Is your cockloft like this one? Does it move like this one?'

'I need the heads,' repeated Lane.

'You can piss in a pot,' said the King. 'I'll go get you one.'

'That ain't too helpful.'

'You can shit in it, too. We don't mind.'

Lane sighed. 'Can't I do my toilet in peace?'

'Be my guest.' The King took his hands from Lane's shoulders and Lane spun where he sat.

'Jus' like that?'

'Jus' like that. I wish you good luck. Know where it is? Same as your block. First floor, jus' under here.'

Lane looked around at the many hostile faces that were watching their conversation. 'I wouldn't make it twenty yards.'

'Aye, there is that. But if you gotta go . . .'

'It can wait.'

'Till morning? You Allies must have mighty strong

282

control.' He put his hands back on Lane's shoulders and pressed as he bent to speak in his ear. 'O' course, the other conclusion is you jus' wanted to go snoopin'. Maybe to see if we got that tunnel goin' somewhere.'

'Can I see it?' said Lane.

'No, you cannot. We ain't havin' that. But you seen the play. And you got my word on the tunnel – it ain't goin' nowhere.'

Lane snorted, and King Dick squeezed, his fingers digging deep into the Ally's shoulder. 'It's the word of a king,' he said. 'And right now, tha's all you gettin'.'

Lane was watched every minute up to the time the turnkeys opened up the next morning. The cockloft gathering had become an all-nighter, with the band, the choir and the card tables running strong until the money, the alcohol and the energy ran out. As soon as Lane left, the King closed his eyes. Everyone slept where they fell. The only movement came from the diminutive, scuttling secretaries Daniels and Singer, who were busy removing plates, bottles and cups from around the King and his throne.

'I'm not asleep,' murmured King Dick. 'But I would sure like to be. Mr Daniels, Mr Singer. Would you assist in this matter?'

'Yes, King Dick,' they said in unison. They knew the routine; they had done it before. They took one arm each and the King allowed himself to be pulled upright. Alex offered him his bearskin, Jonathan the club. The King opened his eyes enough to take both.

'Knowest thou the way to Dover?'

The well-drilled reply. 'Both stile and gate, horse-way and footpath,' they said, and tugged him towards the exit. It took longer than usual to negotiate a safe passage to his bed.

'Stay with me,' said the King, his eyes closed. 'Sit with me a moment.' Alex and Jonathan glanced at the King, then at each other. Alex shrugged, and they sat at the end of his mattress and waited. King Dick's breathing became deep and rhythmic.

Sliding from the bed, the boys had started for their hammocks when the King spoke in a low, private rumble.

'And how did we do, then, m'boys? How did we do?'

Alex and Jonathan stood up straighter.

'It was one of the best nights, King Dick, everyone said so,' said Alex, almost standing to attention. When Jonathan hesitated, the King opened his eyes. It was all the prompting the boy needed.

'No one liked having the Rough Ally here, King Dick,' he blurted. 'They said it wasn't right.' The King waited for more. Jonathan swallowed and carried on. 'But then you did your speech and it was all right.'

The King sat up, propping himself against the wall. 'Tell me what else you hear from the men.'

'I don't hear much, sir, not really.'

'Tell me what you do hear.'

Now Alex piped up. 'Some talk 'bout 'scapin'. Everyone talks 'bout gettin' home.'

The King nodded. ''S'only natural,' he said. 'Any mutinous talk? You hear any o' that?' He caught the glance between Alex and Jonathan before they both shook their heads.

'No, King Dick,' they said together.

'Though a lotta folk are scared,' added Jonathan, and then bit his lip.

'And are you scared?' asked the King.

Both boys nodded and Alex shuffled his feet.

'Will we be all right, King Dick?' he asked, his voice shaking slightly.

The familiar light, running steps of the crier halted their conversation. The King held his answer as Tommy arrived at his bedside, breathless and glowing.

'Beg pardon, King Dick, sir,' he said, 'but the Agent wants to see you.'

'Tommy,' said the King, 'I was jus' 'bout to tell Mr Daniels and Mr Singer here that, in my opinion, the play will be the best we have seen, that Madison's ships will arrive and that we will indeed all be home soon.'

Tommy smiled broadly. 'That sure is good news, King Dick, sir, but I've got to take you to see Captain Shortland.'

The King rose from his bed with a deep sigh. 'How poor they are that have no patience,' he muttered. He took his bearskin from Alex's outstretched hands and strode from the room.

4.9

The Agent's Study

SHORTLAND (*his tone is brusque, urgent, almost panicky*): Mr
Crafus, good day. You should know the recruiters are
back; two of them are waiting in the barracks. They
want to make a sweep of the blocks. They say it's overdue, anyway, but they've heard of your Mr Hill and want
to see him. I have my . . . reservations. What say you?

KING DICK (*exhausted, though Shortland hasn't noticed*): Reservations? You got reservations? Ain't it jus' a little late for
that?

SHORTLAND (*waits for King Dick to say more then realizes he's
finished*): I'm concerned that the men in the blocks
would react . . . badly. Aggressively.

KING DICK (*stares at Shortland; he hasn't been offered a seat but
takes one anyway*): Why have you asked me here, Captain? What do you want? What could you possibly want
from a prisoner like me?

SHORTLAND (*taking notice now*): Why, answers to questions, of
course, Mr Crafus. I thought . . . I thought you'd have a
view on the matter . . .

KING DICK: On what would happen if your recruiters tried to
do their recruitin'? If your recruiters, with all their uniforms, their bulgin' stomachs and their fulsome lies,
went from block to block to say, 'Join the Navy! Fight for
the King!'? Sure, I got an opinion. (*The King closes his eyes
briefly; Shortland waits.*) Ever seen a lynchin', Captain?
'Cos I have. Your men'd make it far as Block One, where

286

those who can still see an' those who can still move'd get a rope round their necks and be swingin' from the kitchen rafters before they can say 'God Save the King!'. Might even cut off their balls, if they feel like it. Which, seein' as they've survived war, smallpox and your barbarous prison, they probably would. That is my view.

SHORTLAND (*visibly shocked*): Even if the recruiters have a troop with them?

KING DICK: Especially if they have a troop with 'em.

SHORTLAND (*after a long silence*): So what do I tell them? That I am no longer in control of my own prison?

KING DICK: That's for you to decide. Men are sometimes master of their own fates. You have stopped the men's wages. The war is over, but we're still prisoners. There's a price to be paid, Captain Shortland. And none of us can be certain who'll be payin' it.

SHORTLAND (*incredulous*): Are you saying your position in Four is threatened? Surely that cannot be right?

KING DICK: O' course it is threatened! Everythin' is threatened. You gotta bring back the wages, increase the bread ration, do somethin' to slow this all down.

SHORTLAND: They are orders from the Transport Office. My hands are tied.

KING DICK (*aside*): Well, that's how a lynchin' starts . . .

SHORTLAND (*has an idea*): And what of your play, Mr Crafus? How close are you to being able to perform it?

KING DICK: The play? A few days, maybe.

SHORTLAND: Soon, I have to leave on prison business to Plymouth and London. I will argue your case, believe me, and on my return, Elizabeth and I will come and watch the show. How's that?

KING DICK (*astonished*): You wanna visit the cockloft? With Mrs Shortland?

SHORTLAND: It'll hold the prison together, Mr Crafus. Invite some of the other blocks. I'm 'slowing this thing down', as you asked. I can't guarantee more bread and wages, but a Dartmoor *Romeo and Juliet* will be quite a distraction. I will not be away long. So shall we say the sixth?

KING DICK: Assumin' your prison is still standin'.

SHORTLAND: And now, Mr Crafus, I believe you are being overly dramatic. I look forward to seeing your show on the sixth. Elizabeth will be thrilled.

KING DICK (*leaving*): I jus' thought of a job for your recruiters.

SHORTLAND: You have?

KING DICK: I have. They can visit Block Seven. Find John Matthews and Robert Drake. They from Detroit.

SHORTLAND (*disbelieving*): Might they want to serve in the Royal Navy?

KING DICK: They might. Mr Cobb and Mr Lane outta Six tell me they're the men who killed Ned Penny.

SHORTLAND (*astonished*): Really? And why would they tell you that?

KING DICK (*shrugs*): Maybe their natural sense o' justice. Maybe they settlin' scores. More likely hidin' their own involvement. Either way, Matthews and Drake are in trouble. If it's a choice between a hangin' or your Navy, they might jus' be tempted.

❧ ACT FIVE ❧

5.1

Friday, 24 March
The Market Square

THE MARKET struggled on for a week. None of the stall-holders truly believed the British would stop the Americans' wages; they were expecting a reversal as soon as the implications became clear. Even when none was forth-coming, there was enough cash in circulation to keep most of the stall-holders, if not happy, then at least in attendance. But takings were down and thieving was up.

Today's market was smaller, quieter. Empty spaces appeared in the market square where, previously, stalls had jostled for the best position. The bakers of Tavistock were there still, but only just.

Betsy Wade was rearranging her baskets of bread. 'This is no good, Martha, no good at all.' She looked around the square, counting. 'Sixteen, we've got. That means we lost nineteen. Not much of a market with just sixteen stalls.'

Martha shrugged. 'You got beer an' clothes. Meat. That man selling shoes an' boots. Keep most men happy enough.'

'And how many honest men do you see, Martha? At least, men with money in their pockets to go with the tongue in their mouths?' The square was full of inmates, very few of them buying. Most of them were gathered in groups, hands deep in their pockets, their faces grey and sullen.

'Not many,' she acknowledged.

'We have two baskets of unsold bread, Martha. You know if we don't sell here we'll have to find somewhere else.

Trading with Yankee sailors is one thing, but trading with hungry, angry Yankee thieves is quite another.'

'Talk of the devil,' said Martha, nudging Betsy and nodding at the gates. Edwin Lane emerged, flanked by two other Allies.

'What's up with them, then?' said Betsy. 'They normally just march in and take what they want.' Lane was smiling, pulling at his beard and nodding greetings at fellow inmates. He examined some meat, peered at some fish, picked up a bottle then moved on.

'Not exactly stocking up on supplies, is he?' said Betsy.

'So where's he heading?' said Martha. She scanned the depleted market. 'Not many of us left. Are you sure he's not after bread?'

Betsy nodded. 'I am. Look at the cobbler.' The stooped man behind the shoes twitched as he saw Lane and the other Allies approaching. 'Cover the loaves, Martha – stow 'em. Quickly. He might need some help.'

Lane had reached the cobbler's stall and was picking up shoes at random. His two cohorts had turned their backs to Lane and were now watching the square. Betsy glanced at her fellow stall-holders but none of them seemed interested in what was going on, talking among themselves instead.

'Just me, then,' she said. 'Walk with me, Martha.'

The two women set off across the square, apparently deep in conversation, heading for the stand next to the cobbler's. 'The woman selling the clothes is Clarity,' said Betsy. 'One of us talks to her; the other listens to them.' She indicated the Allies and the cobbler, who had just ducked behind his stall and was searching for something.

'Hey, Clarity, still here then?' called Betsy, as they approached.

A mousey woman with pinched cheeks and a sullen expression greeted them with a shrug. 'For what it's worth,' she said. 'Which right this minute is precisely nothing.'

Martha picked up some folds of cloth from the stall then held them up for closer inspection, blocking Lane from her eyesight. The cobbler, however, was in plain view. He found what he was looking for and, hands trembling, passed Lane a single brown leather boot. She saw it tilted, as if for inspection, heard words exchanged, then the boot, and the Allies, disappeared.

As soon as they had gone the cobbler hurriedly scooped all his shoes into a canvas bag.

'You all right, m'love?' Martha asked him. 'They giving you trouble?'

The cobbler didn't reply, didn't even look up. As soon as his table was empty, he heaved the bag over his shoulder and ran from the square.

'Rude man,' said Clarity.

'Rude man in a hurry,' said Betsy.

Martha watched the cobbler go. 'How can one boot cost two pounds ten shillings?' she said.

5.2

Monday, 27 March
Block Four

JOHN HAYWOOD didn't like visitors. He peered at Joe and Habs from under a sheet, his sickly eyes shot wide with fear. The news from King Dick that two men from Six had been named as his attackers had pushed him further under it. There was a guard present at all times, but that seemed to give him little comfort.

'They don't notice nothin'. They're playin' cards most o' the time,' he whispered. 'Wouldn't notice if the King of England walked in to stab me. If I hear anythin' bad, I jus' head down the tunnel the King built for me.' He gestured through the precarious wooden slats at the back of the cupboard.

'You hide in the tunnel?' asked Habs, astonished. 'Is it safe?'

'No, it's dangerous,' whispered Haywood, then added, 'obviously.'

'Why are we whisperin'?' whispered Habs.

Haywood looked contemptuous. 'You know as well as I do,' he said, and disappeared under the sheet once more. Joe and Habs glanced at each other.

'Don't think we do, Mr Haywood,' said Joe.

'Well then, you're as foolish as you look,' said Haywood.

'Is it 'cos of Matthews and Drake in Six?' asked Habs.

Even though Habs was still whispering, the mere mention of the Allies' names sent a spasm through Haywood. He curled up into a ball, pulling the old sheet tightly around his thin frame.

'They can't get you here, John, and they can't hear us either.' Joe nodded to Habs to continue.

'Was it them, John? Was it them that attacked you and Ned? Did Edwin Lane have anythin' to do with it? You said you dreamed of three shadows . . .'

A yellow stain had appeared on the sheet, the pungent smell of urine filling Haywood's makeshift bedroom.

Joe flicked his head to the door. 'We should leave,' he mouthed.

Habs nodded and they stood.

'We'll be home soon, John,' said Habs. 'Don't you worry – the ships'll come.'

They walked outside, squinting in the misty haze of the morning.

'That's one scared sailor,' said Joe. 'Maybe we should've changed the sheets?'

'He wanted us to leave,' said Habs.

'Maybe the guards'll do it.'

'Once they've finished their game of Twenty-one, maybe.' Habs peered around the courtyard and to the market square beyond. 'What day is it?'

'Monday.'

Habs shook his head. 'So they actually gone an' done it. They really have shut it down.'

Joe followed his stare. The market square was empty, the gates to the courtyard locked. Hundreds of men had gathered to take turns to rattle the padlocks and jeer any soldier who came into view. The steps of Four, perfectly aligned with the entrance to the square, gave Joe and Habs all the information they required.

They stared at where the traders should have been. 'No more loaves, no more grog,' said Habs.

'And no more people. No more normal people. Now

everyone we see is either a sailor or a soldier, a Yankee or a Brit. That's all.'

'It was jus' possible,' said Habs, 'when you were hagglin' and buyin' and jostlin' in there, it was jus' possible to imagine for a second that we were free. Free and in some mad market at home, tradin' food for earrings. Or earrings for food, dependin' on what week it was. Outside of our cockloft, that was the liveliest place in the whole goddamn prison.'

In the courtyard, only the craft-sellers and the coffee-brewers were trying their luck, but, with money running out, trade was slow.

'If anyone did have a spare shilling, does old Jonah there think anyone would spend it on a ship in a bottle?' asked Joe.

'Maybe it'd make a fine weapon,' suggested Habs. 'Fill it with oil. The miniature sails would balance it jus' right. And imagine the enemy's surprise when they're brought down by a tiny USS *Constitution*.'

'Might as well stick to the courtyard coffee,' said Joe. 'Half a pint of grey, warm water?'

'I swear it's turning *me* grey.'

Joe almost smiled. 'Somehow, Mr Snow, you have retained your colour, while mine is draining away. That's the rumour, anyway.'

They sat on the ground, their backs against the block, faces once more to the sky. The air held a fragrance which Joe hadn't noticed before. 'Somewhere out there,' he said, 'there are flowers blooming. What grows on this godforsaken moor, Habs?'

Habs shrugged. 'I never noticed, Joe, and tha's the truth. All I smell in here is sweat, tobacco and sickness.'

The doors of Six opened and a group of Allies sauntered out. Joe and Habs watched as they stopped by Seven and another, similar-sized group of inmates joined them, Will Roche the last to appear. One of the sailors from Seven produced a rough leather ball and threw it against the courtyard wall. It bounced high, then dropped to the ground, whereupon everyone in the vicinity fell on it. Up against the wall, they tussled, fighting each other and yelling at the tops of their voices. The scrummage was never-ending, with men tumbling out of the brawl then piling back in again.

'Well, I'll be damned,' said Joe. 'I never saw Will play any sport before.'

More men arrived, and the wrestling for the ball spilled further out along the wall.

'Ever seen anything like this?' asked Joe.

'No.' Habs leaned forward, watching intently. 'I reckon we should take a closer look.'

They walked with as much indifference as they could muster, arcing right to take them closer to Blocks One, Two and Three. Each prison had spilled hundreds of its sailors on to the courtyard, the men gathering in groups to argue, protest, sing, smoke and – around Pastor Simon – to pray. Outside One, an inmate was reading a newspaper article to a row of the newly blind.

'We was lucky,' muttered Habs as they passed. 'So goddamn lucky.'

The wall that separated the prisons from the market square captured the afternoon sun and, even in late March, it carried enough heat to draw a crowd. Joe and Habs had to squeeze their way to a better view of whatever game the men of Six and Seven were playing. A ball appeared only occasionally; the rest of the time everyone just wrestled everyone else.

'They seem to be making the rules up as they go along!' shouted Joe over the yelling.

From deep in the melee, a flash of metal caught the sunshine. 'Sweet Mother of God!' exclaimed Habs. 'That's why we ain't seen nothin' like this before. They ain't playin' no sport.'

Joe turned to look at Habs. 'What are they doing, then?'

'Watch carefully, Joe, an' you'll see. One of 'em has a knife or somethin' like it. Or some metal, anyways. I jus' saw it flash.'

Smaller skirmishes were breaking out, but the main group stayed stuck to the wall. Joe stared at the broiling ruckus.

'They're not attackin' one another,' observed Habs, 'they're attackin' the wall.'

'They're escaping?'

'The start of it, maybe. They must be tryin' to make a hole in the wall. Must be shieldin' a man doin' the scrapin', loosenin' the rocks.'

'Won't that be obvious?' said Joe. 'Wouldn't even the most stupid English soldier notice a hole in the wall leading to the armoury?'

'It won't be a hole,' said Habs. 'Not if they're just scrapin' the cement away. But yes, if the Brits have hard-workin' troopers, nimble of mind and quick of thought, it might get spotted.'

Joe and Habs exchanged glances.

'The hole is safe, then,' said Joe.

Habs tugged at his sleeve. 'C'mon, we need to find King Dick. He'll want to know what's happenin'.'

As they climbed the stairs of Four, the unmistakeable sounds of construction drew them to the cockloft. Through the doors, and thirty men were across the stage. Painting, sawing and hammering, there was no disputing what the King had set them to do.

'So Verona comes to Dartmoor,' said Habs.

Large sections of the old French scenery were being cut up and repainted, with the King directing proceedings from the floor. Bearskin high on his head, he jabbed his club in all directions: 'Mr Johnson! A darker brown, please. Mr Cook, more to the left. And again. Thank you.'

He broke away and came to meet them. 'My favourite part,' he said. 'Watchin' a new world bein' formed. Take a brush – these are your new streets. And they're a goddamn sight safer than the ones we walk here.' He registered their expressions at last. 'You got news?'

Joe and Habs explained what they had seen.

'So they're really doin' it,' he said, once they were clear of the stage party. He swiped the bearskin from his head. 'They gonna run the English guns one more time.'

Habs thought the King sounded bewildered. He'd never heard him sound like that before.

'But they're doin' *somethin*',' he said. 'They ain't got no tunnel. They ain't got no play. They ain't got nothin'. If you think the ships ain't comin', why wouldn't you try to bust out?'

''Cos you'll get killed?' suggested Joe.

'But if the fates are against you and you think you gonna die anyways,' said Habs, 'better to go runnin' at a British gun than die wastin' to a skeleton in here.'

'You wanna escape now, Mr Snow?' The King seemed puzzled.

'No, I wanna act!' said Habs, struggling to keep his voice quiet. He pointed to the stage and the men working on it. '*This* is our escape. *This* play, *this* show. Everythin' out there is madness. To me, this makes sense. It's a love story . . .'

'It's a tragedy,' said the King.

'It's both,' said Habs. 'It's ink and paper. It's a book. It's solid. It's a chart – you can set your compass by it. It counts for somethin'. But for everyone else? If you're in Six or Seven, scrapin' a hole in a wall probably makes more sense than doin' nothin'.'

King Dick nodded. 'Well spoken, Mr Snow. Let's find Mr Goffe and Mr Lord, get ourselves informed.'

Tommy the crier found Goffe and Lord, then Pastor Simon and Sam. Within minutes, they had most of their principal cast and, with the stage still hectic, they gathered at the far corner of the cockloft.

'Gentlemen,' said the King. 'Some of you may have seen what Mr Snow and Mr Hill saw this mornin' in the courtyard. That "game" up against the wall ain't no such thing. Mr Jackson, you jus' ran past there—'

'Yes, sir, King Dick, sir!' said Tommy, his face still glowing from the exertion. 'They been scrapin' away all right, and clearin' up, too. You'd only see if you walked close by. But up close, that's a dig happenin'.'

'In full view of everybody and everythin',' said the King. 'So it's jus' the masonry they chippin' at, leavin' the rocks in place, Mr Jackson?'

'Yes, King Dick.'

The King nodded. 'And the Brits are thinkin' more 'bout fightin' Napoleon again than the upkeep o' this place,' he mused. 'It's bold, I'll give 'em that. Mr Goffe? Mr Lord?'

Jon Lord's battered face was a study in anxiety. 'We're in the wrong mess to know for sure. Ol' Will Roche has taken himself and half the *Eagle* crew to the mess with some Newport men. He's fired them all up with revolutionary talk. And them's the ones that's fightin' against the wall. Roche said it's the armoury they're after.'

'Lord have mercy on us,' muttered the pastor.

'The armoury over at the barracks?' Sam was incredulous. 'They all got jail fever or somethin'?'

Robert Goffe stepped forward, almost bowing to the King, then, embarrassed, changed his mind. He pulled nervously at his prison jacket instead. 'Yes, I do believe they have.' He stepped back again.

'You're quiet, Mr Hill,' said the King.

Joe collected his thoughts. He'd listened to the exchanges with a particular despondency. 'Will feels lost to me,' he said. 'We did everything together, but it seems the prison has taken him. I feel as though I should talk to him, but I'm not sure what good it would do. If he's taken to sport, well, his head is turned and no mistake.'

'How long till they break through?' asked Sam. 'Assumin' no Brits put their head near that hole first?'

'Tommy? You been up close,' said the King.

'Oh, they're jus' gettin' started. That's a big, thick wall. From what I saw, they've done about half an inch today, so . . . ten more days?'

'Which takes us to . . . when, exactly?' asked Sam.

'April sixth,' said Joe.

5.3

Saturday, 1 April
The Agent's House

'ARE YOU sure now is a good time?'

Breakfast had been quietly efficient, with few words spoken. Thomas had announced his imminent trip to Plymouth and London and had not been planning on discussing the matter further. But Elizabeth's question had changed things. She had thought her tone breezy enough, but the scowl on her husband's face suggested otherwise. He dropped his knife and fork with a clatter.

'Elizabeth,' he said, through a mouthful of bacon, 'I know you speak with the prisoners, I know you ... wish what is best for all of us, but just for once' – he swallowed then wiped his mouth with a napkin – 'just for once, will you trust me? I do not embark on these trips lightly.' He took a breath, controlled himself. 'All you need to know is that meetings in Plymouth and London have been called and my presence is requested. With the major still sick, my senior guard commander will be in charge here. Fortyne knows what he's doing, he's a good man.' Shortland managed a conciliatory smile as he poured more tea, seemingly happy that he had said all that needed saying.

Elizabeth braced herself. 'Thomas, I understand you are wanted at meetings, but do these people know what a powder keg this prison has become? You should tell them—'

Shortland slammed his cup into its saucer, tea slopping as far as the tablecloth.

'I should tell them what?' he snapped. 'That my wife knows how to run my prison better than I do? That she thinks I have lost control of my prison and need her educated counsel to put things right? Is that it?' She gently replaced her knife and fork either side of her plate.

'That is not what I intended to say, Thomas—'

'Well, unfortunately for you, that is *precisely* what you *did* say.' His face was crimson now. She knew she was on dangerous ground.

'Unfortunately for me?' she said. 'I wonder what you might mean by that?'

Shortland closed his eyes, as if praying for guidance or self-control. It worked. The pause checked his headlong rush to battle and he swept from the table.

'Good day, Elizabeth,' he managed, before disappearing into the hall.

'Good day, Thomas!' she called after him. 'And travelling mercies!' She listened intently to the sounds of his departure – the orders, the door slam and the carriage – then glanced at the clock. She waited five tedious, unbearable, tea-drinking minutes. Satisfied he was gone, she pulled on her pelisse coat and walked the short distance to Magrath's house. Once there, the coat, her dress, petticoat and pantaloons lasted three minutes.

'Everyone will know you're here,' said Magrath, dressing for the second time that morning.

'They will,' agreed Elizabeth from the bed. 'We work together. Remember?'

'We work very well together,' laughed Magrath. 'I know that, to my pleasure. But I think Captain Shortland's idea was probably that we work in the hospital and for the benefit of the inmates. Wouldn't that be right?'

'He never specified, George,' said Elizabeth, 'and, anyway, this *is* for the benefit of the patients. You look so much more relaxed now.'

'But I'm fifteen minutes late for my rounds . . .'

'Blame me!' she called after him. 'Just say you were fornicating with the Agent's wife. I'm sure they'll understand.'

She heard Magrath laugh quietly under his breath and pull on his boots.

'Wait, George,' she said, swivelling out of the bed. 'I should leave with you.' She dressed hurriedly, retying her hair in seconds. 'The one solitary advantage of being the only woman here,' Elizabeth declared as she walked down the stairs, 'is that no one will judge me if my linen is crumpled.'

From Magrath's house on the prison's outer wall, they passed through the three double gates needed to reach the blocks, each time receiving salutes – and sly grins – from the guards.

'My God, they all know!' said Magrath as they arrived in One. 'By the time Thomas returns, the whole of the bloody Navy will be talking about us.'

Elizabeth knew this was true, knew that, however meatheaded her husband was, eventually even he would realize his wife was sleeping with his physician. They would row, he would demand an end to it, and she knew she would say no. Beyond that, she couldn't say. The impossibly gallant, sweet-talking officer, the man who had dazzled her and her parents with his talk of adventures in New South Wales and sailing with Lord Hood's fleet in the Mediterranean, seemed to her now to be something from another century, another life. Jaded, disappointed, peripheral. Napoleon and Dartmoor had taken a heavy toll on her husband. The stomach-churning nerves that were currently coursing through her body were only partly due to her imminent arrival in Block One. The rest were due to her husband and her yearning to be free of him and his wretched prison.

Once the round duties began, all conversation returned to the medical. Lists of medicines and dressings required were compiled, patients' demands collated and symptoms checked. Elizabeth stayed tightly to Magrath's side. She was sure she was safe, but being the only woman in a seven-thousand-man prison never felt entirely comfortable.

'Thanks, Doc. I'll never forget you saved my life,' said one smallpox victim, left blind.

'And he'll never forget the ass of your girlfriend neither,' said his colleague. 'Says it's the last thing he saw 'fore he lost his sight. Thinks about it a lot, he says.'

Magrath harrumphed. 'I think you're referring to my assistant, Mrs Shortland. The Agent's wife, you'll remember.'

'Don't remember the name. Just the ass.' He smiled, pleased with himself.

Elizabeth crouched in front of the men. 'Well, just remember I bathed your wounds,' she said, 'and tied your bandages, too. Remember I helped save your life. Then you can remember my "ass".'

Both men blushed fiercely.

Block Two was rougher, the atmosphere unfriendly from the steps onwards. Three was more encouraging, the greetings civil, if not warm. By the time they reached Four, they were tired and wary.

'I wonder how we'll find John Haywood,' Magrath murmured.

'I do hope he's holding up well,' Elizabeth replied. Looking back down the steps of Four, she noticed for the first time how busy the courtyard was. But her concern was not for the healthy or the games they were well enough to play.

Inside Four, Joe and Habs were waiting for them, and Elizabeth nodded. 'Mr Hill, Mr Snow,' she said. 'Good morning.'

'Mrs Shortland, Dr Magrath,' said Joe.

'We saw you comin',' said Habs. 'When you've done your walkin', we'll be waitin' for you out back.'

Magrath and Mrs Shortland nodded a silent reply before

quickly completing their rounds of the ground floor. At the entrance to the kitchens, a row of men six across parted to allow them through. King Dick stepped forward, indicating the store cupboard into which they had squeezed Haywood and his mattress.

Magrath crouched in the entrance.

'Morning, Mr Haywood.'

Magrath lowered the blanket. Haywood stared at him; the last traces of his beating were still visible around his temples and ears, but a fresh series of cuts had appeared on his nose and forehead. Magrath glanced back at the King. 'What in God's name happened here?' he asked, his anger and astonishment whispered and piercing.

The King beckoned him over. 'I am told he was fightin' to get out – had enough of goin' nowhere. So we had to politely insist.'

'By hitting him? A man who only just survived an attempt on his life? Are you mad?' Magrath was breathless with indignation.

'He was almost outta the buildin'. It was the only way to stop him. We've doubled the guard now.'

When Magrath returned to his patient, Elizabeth was already dressing his new wounds.

'Well, you can come every time, ma'am,' drawled Haywood. 'That surgeon is so rough and ugly.'

'Hush now,' she said. 'Any more cuts and bruises and you won't be such an oil painting yourself.' Haywood winced as the astringent did its work. 'Do you understand why you can't leave?'

Haywood shrugged. 'I guess.'

'You being here has to stay secret. The man, or men, who killed Ned Penny think you're in Plymouth. If they know you're here, they'll kill you, too. Do you understand?'

'I guess.'

'And do you remember anything more about the attack? About who killed Ned?'

Haywood closed his eyes. 'I've tried to remember, I really have, ma'am. But all I see is shadows. A few lights, a few flames. But the rest is shadows.'

Habs appeared over Elizabeth's shoulder. 'Are there men in the shadows, John?'

A pause. 'Yes, I think there are,' he said quietly.

'What else, John?' said Habs, a twist of excitement in his voice. 'Can you see anythin' else? How many shadows?'

Another, longer pause. 'Maybe three. I don't rightly know, to be truthful.'

Magrath left a supply of dressings and more ointment. 'Take more care, Mr Haywood,' he said, 'and keep yourself out of sight.' He turned to King Dick. 'There is a date for the play, I hear?'

The King nodded. 'Fixed by the Agent for when he returns. April sixth.'

'He wants it to be quite something,' said Magrath. 'Bring the prison together. Invite men from the other blocks, and so on.'

The King looked intently at Magrath, then at Elizabeth. He pushed the bearskin high on his head. 'I don't hate your husband the way some men in here do, Mrs Shortland,' he said. 'I want you to know that. We talk sometimes. But, and no offence, Mrs Shortland, sometimes, he got shit for brains. First, we always sell tickets to the plays. Anyone can come. Your husband, he should know that. But second, we ain't gonna do that this time. This play requires two warrin' families, so we got that quite easy – some men from Seven, friends of Mr Hill here – are playin' the parts of the Capulets. But we ain't invitin' the other blocks, not this time. Not with Mr Haywood here to protect.' He glanced between Magrath and Elizabeth; both looked too stunned to reply. The King pressed on. 'The captain wants the blocks

307

"brought together", he says. Does he think this is some kinda church congregation? These are the men who asked for the Negroes to be put away. And he's the man who agreed to it.' The King folded his arms, managing to make it look like a threatening gesture. 'The only way we bein' brought together is on the ships outta here.'

Elizabeth cleared her throat. 'Very well,' she said, 'I will make sure my husband knows of this. And what of your Romeo and your Juliet?'

The King pointed to Joe and Habs. 'Well, they both here – why don't you ask 'em?'

Under scrutiny, Joe was suddenly awkward. 'Why, yes, it's happening just as King Dick says it is,' he said. 'And we have the men from Seven in the cast, too, so . . .'

'And you are Juliet?' asked Magrath. When Joe nodded, he said, 'And the kiss?'

'Obviously, there are some things that are intolerable,' said Joe. 'Not stopping our wages, not losing the market, not keeping us here when the war is over, no none of them. But Romeo kissing Juliet . . . well, we had to put a stop to that. Of course we did.'

Magrath nodded, smiling. He turned to Elizabeth. 'I think this play might be rather good, don't you?'

'Yes,' she said, looking between Habs and Joe. 'I'm sure you'll negotiate the . . . challenges with style.'

Just before they reached the steps, the King called after them. 'You visitin' all the blocks?'

'We are,' said Magrath. 'Why do you ask?'

'When you get to Seven, could you ask after a John Matthews and a Robert Drake? From Detroit. Ain't seen 'em in a while. Tell 'em to watch out for themselves. Tha's all.'

As they were walking down the steps of Four, Elizabeth hesitated, tugging at Magrath's arm.

308

'What was that?' she asked. 'Who were those men he was asking after?'

'John Matthews and Robert Drake. Maybe they killed Ned Penny,' said Magrath, climbing the steps to Five. 'I heard from the guard that Thomas had had a tip-off about the murder. That he'd sent some men to investigate but nothing had happened.'

Enthusiastic singing was coming from deep within the block.

'You know, King Dick is certainly right about one thing, George,' said Elizabeth, peering through the doors. 'They have to protect John Haywood. We have to persuade Thomas to accept that it wouldn't be safe to invite the other blocks to the play.'

'He'll see that,' said Magrath, 'I'm sure of it. Now let's get this done swiftly. They're usually an orderly crew in Five.'

A prison representative greeted them with a list of the sick who had asked for attention. To the accompaniment of non-stop patriotic singing, Magrath dispensed what he could, advised where he could. Everywhere, men were involved in crafts of some kind; on closer examination, it turned out to be flags and banners that were being stitched, most of them bearing slogans. An American Stars and Stripes bore the words 'Death to King George'. Elizabeth looked on, mouth agape. Until now, she had only seen Yankee slogans. This felt like an escalation, a deliberate provocation. A strip of cloth proclaiming 'We are slaves too' was hung from a hammock, and a hangman's noose had been added to a crude Union flag. She showed it to Magrath, but he'd seen enough.

'I won't be back until there's a civil spirit in this place!' he yelled at the block representative, slapping the list he'd been given back into his hand.

Still angry, he stormed towards Six, Elizabeth close behind. Tommy, the crier, ran past, nodding a greeting to them both, but they missed it. They found Block Six deserted and pulled up short. While Magrath inspected the rows of empty hammocks, Elizabeth spotted Cobb's obscene flags strung high on a stanchion.

'Oh my!' she said. She mouthed the rhyme, glanced again at the crude drawings. 'Oh my!' she repeated.

Magrath followed her gaze then shouted his disgust. 'Brutes! Brutes is what they are!' He swiped his stick in the air, missing the flags by many feet. 'If I could climb, Elizabeth . . .'

'Come,' she said. 'Let's not stay where we're not wanted. Where are they all, anyway?'

A huge cheer came from the courtyard, and they hurried outside.

'How did we miss that?' asked Magrath, staring at a particularly anarchic ball game being played hard against the market square wall.

A man with a face full of scars sat on the steps of Seven watching the game and nursing a bloody nose. Magrath handed him a gauze and he took it gratefully.

'Everyone playing?' asked Magrath.

'Pretty much,' said the man.

'Looks rough.'

'Yup.' The man noticed the Agent's wife for the first time. He made a point of allowing his eyes to wander slowly over Elizabeth's body, his hand slipping inside his breeches. 'But not as rough as your Limey whore,' he said.

In an instant, Magrath had swiped at the man with his walking stick, its steel point catching him on the ear.

The man's howls managed what hadn't seemed possible – it stopped the game. In seconds, they were surrounded by a crowd of angry, dusty men. Magrath brandished his stick like a sword to fend them off.

'Stand back now!' he cried.

Elizabeth glanced up to the military walk. Everywhere,

redcoats were readying their rifles. Horace Cobb pushed his way to the front of the scrum, his face streaked with sweat.

'Mr Magrath,' he said, spitting dirt. 'You may be our respected physician. You also may be screwing the Agent's wife here. But you have attacked one of my men.' Shouts from the walkway, keys rattled in the market square gate. 'And that we cannot accept.'

'You cannot accept?' echoed Elizabeth in a fury, letting go of Magrath's arm and pushing forwards. 'You, sir, are a prisoner-of-war. And we are tending the sick. We have no guns, no weapons. You will allow us free passage.'

Bellowed commands from the walkway:

'Back away!'

'Stand down!'

'Go back to your blocks!'

Elizabeth saw the raised rifles and froze. Some of the inmates peeled away, running low and away from the firing line. The market square gates burst open, twelve militiamen running through, guns held high in readiness. As most of the inmates scrambled away, Elizabeth felt rough hands around her mouth, felt her head pulled back by the hair and a sharp serrated object pressing into her throat. She heard a shout from just behind her right ear. Cobb.

'Drop your weapons, you redcoat bastards! Now!' he yelled. And then, as an aside, 'Get Lane. And his new toy.'

Somewhere in the distance, Elizabeth heard the alarm bell being rung. She wondered what Thomas would do if he were there, and where his guard commanders might be. Magrath was pinioned by both arms, an Ally on either side of him, his stick broken in two on the ground. The militiamen had pulled up, uncertain how to continue. The rifles on the military walk had been lowered, the men unwilling to aim, however inadvertently, at the Agent's wife.

Cobb's mouth was against her ear, his body pressed hard

against hers. Her skin prickled with fear. She could feel his words as he spat them out.

'I'm taking you to our prison, whore,' he growled. 'You're gonna be our ticket out o' here. And maybe a bit of entertainment while we're waitin'.'

5.4

Block Four

H E RAN soundlessly around the back of Blocks Five and
Six, a vast, dark figure suddenly right-turning into the
channel between Six and Seven. The straight line it took to
the courtyard meant that, by the time he hit the open ground,
King Dick had reached maximum velocity. He burst into
Cobb like a cannonball into ship's timber: relentless, unstoppable, explosive. Elizabeth, the knife and six of Cobb's teeth
went flying into the dirt – mere splinters from the explosion.
A dozen men were sent sprawling in his wake, crying out in
fear and alarm at the speed and malevolence of the attack.
Beneath the King, whether dead, unconscious or merely
stunned, Cobb lay motionless.

Joe, Habs, Sam, Tommy and a hundred others from
Four arrived in time to see Magrath and Elizabeth gather
themselves and make for the protection of the militia, saw
them hurried through the market square, a guard commander at their heels, saw the King pick up the still,
seemingly lifeless form of Cobb then offer him to his men
like some broken sacrifice.

But the Rough Allies were back on their feet and bristling with fury. Edwin Lane appeared, adjusting his belt and
buttoning his jacket. He pushed through the crowd and the
Allies jostled around him, a noisy phalanx pressing forward,
edging closer to the King. This humiliation was not going to
pass.

The men of Four instinctively fell in behind King Dick,

but he waved them out again. 'Man the yards!' he called, and they hurried to form straight lines across the courtyard. The Allies, briefly bewildered, had little choice but to line up against them. High on the walk, the redcoats played their rifles over the prisoners, as if hoping for some target practice. They saw the arc of the seven prisons cut in half by two ribbons of men, one black, one white.

Habs and Sam blocked Joe from joining their line.

'Not helpful,' Habs muttered. 'Not this time.'

For once, Joe was happy to hold back, unwilling to confront his old shipmates. He stood away from the line, pacing anxiously.

'Mannin' the yards s'posed to be peaceful, ain't it?' said Sam, linking arms with Habs.

'Never done it before,' said Habs, eyeballing the long beard in front of him. 'But yeah, all men aloft. Shows the cannons ain't ready. Somethin' like that.'

'Not feelin' too peaceful this time, cuz,' muttered Sam. 'More like we're topside, eyein' each other from closin' ships.'

Some of the men began pushing up against each other, locking heads. Where the line tailed to the steps of Block Six, Joe saw Will Roche getting in the face of one of King Dick's old shipmates from the *Requin*. He was about to run over, warn him off, when the King himself interrupted.

'The job is done!' he called to his men. 'Mrs Shortland is safe, the doctor, too. We should stand down.'

A voice from the end of their line: 'Only when they do! We ain't runnin' from no one.' Another small rebellion.

Joe hid his surprise and stepped behind Habs. 'Who said that?' he said in his ear.

'Sounded like Abe Cook,' said Habs. 'Headin' for a busted head later.'

From the distance came the low, sustained rumble of troops running. The alarm bell had triggered a full emergency, and now all available soldiers in the barracks were heading their way.

Habs eyed the two hostile lines, neither wanting to move first. 'Looks like we're waitin' to board each other's ships.'

'Except it's us about to be boarded,' said Joe. 'By the Brits.'

Tommy pushed his way between Joe and Habs, pulling at their jackets. 'Watch Lane,' he hissed, and was gone again. They looked across to see Edwin Lane standing behind the first row of Allies. Unusually silent, his right hand was constantly inside his coat, touching, feeling, adjusting. His left hand rested on his hip, occasionally feeling the fabric of his jacket, absent-mindedly tracing an outline.

'Sweet Jesus and Mary,' muttered Joe.

'Could be a knife?' suggested Habs, knowing otherwise.

'It could be, but it isn't. We've all seen that before, many times. If a man has a new pistol about him, he stands different. He stands awkward. He stands just the way Lane there is standing.'

Lane realized he was being watched and instinctively pulled his hand out of his jacket.

Without speaking, Habs peeled away from the line. He reached the King just as a squadron of redcoats arrived in the market square.

'Lane has a gun,' he breathed in his ear, staying just long enough to feel the King's reaction, then striding away from the lines. Within seconds, he'd been joined by Joe, Sam and the handful of men they'd been able to scare. As the gates from the square were unlocked, the King called the retreat. With the line broken, most of the men of Four withdrew. By the time the redcoats were in the courtyard, the only sailors left to confront were from Six.

Those who knew nothing of Lane's gun were the ones doing the talking; constant excited, nervous chatter accompanied the walk back to Four. Those who knew that the game had just changed were silent and sombre. King Dick's only words were to Sam.

'Get Tommy. Find the others.'

Sam peeled away to find the crier, and everyone else returned to their mess. Alex and Jonathan were waiting with the King's club and bearskin; he took the club, spun and caught it, rammed his hat down hard.

'Get them doors shut. Ten men on sentry. At all times. Mr Goffe and Mr Lord will soon be here with the crier. Then, no one comes in.'

One of the King's messmates, a nervous-looking man with scar tissue where his hair had been, nodded, accepting the order. 'Yes, sir, King Dick, sir.' And he set about rounding up the first shift.

Like a ship readying itself for departure, Four was instantly full and clamorous, everyone wanting to shout their opinions. Joe and Habs remained with the King as he heaved his way towards the stairs. They began to climb. The King's voice was heavy with exhaustion.

'Gonna try to talk to everyone. Mr Hill, you downstairs. Mr Snow, you upstairs. See if you can get some silence in this bellowin' chamber. Meantime, I'll stay here.' The King walked to a step midway between the floors, then sat, spent from his exertions outside. Like small, administering birds, Alex and Jonathan brought him bread and coffee and then hovered, unsure what he would want next.

While Joe pushed his way back towards the hammocks, Habs sprinted away upstairs. The first-floor messes were in the same tumult. There was no way he could shout above the men. Instead, he went from hammock to hammock, waiting for breaths to be taken, for brief lulls in the storm.

'King Dick has news,' he said, as each opportunity arrived, his urgent delivery compelling the end of each argument. 'King Dick has news' was repeated across the floor and triggered a drift to the stairs.

A flurry of activity at the doors turned heads. 'Doors open! Visitors!' called the sentry, as Sam and the crier, now with Goffe and Lord in tow, were hurriedly ushered inside.

'Doors shut!'

Not knowing where else to take them, Sam headed towards his mess.

'Thank God you're here!' Joe couldn't keep the relief from his voice. He nodded at the stairs, flustered. 'King Dick wants to speak, but I can't get anyone's attention. Habs is upstairs. They'll listen to him and they'll listen to you.'

Sam understood. 'You too pale, Joe,' he said, almost smiling. 'Maybe they can't see you – you like some kinda ghost.'

'Something like that,' said Joe.

He watched as Sam flitted from mess to mess, speaking a few words to each, arguing with a few. As the noise dropped, the message spread faster. Within minutes, most of Four had gathered to where they could see, or at least hear, the King, pressing in on each other as they waited for him to speak. The staircase was nothing but a solid mass of men.

King Dick pushed himself up with his club. It swung from his wrist as he placed his hands on his hips. For the first time since Joe had known him, he looked weary. Gathering himself, the King looked up and down the stairs, to the landing and then to the hall. Every man whose eye he caught would swear he was talking straight to him.

'Men of Four. Today we saw Mr Cobb try to kidnap the Agent's wife, and we took the necessary steps to prevent that happenin'.'

'Shame!' called a voice. It came from somewhere above the King, somewhere in the gloom of the first-floor hammocks. The King's voice had been controlled but powerful, his words filling the prison. Now, he flooded it.

'A shame? Really, a shame? You have prison madness, too?'

The men closest to the King – the ones who could smell

317

his boot polish and the sweat on his body – began to edge away from him, shuffling to the next step. When the King needed a platform, half a step just wasn't enough. He swung the club, pointing it high.

'I'm surprised I got to be sayin' this, but let me make it clear.' This was loud now, even for the King. 'Takin' the Agent's wife as a hostage is in-tol-er-ab-le. Doin' it, and believin' for one minute that the redcoats wouldn't come in shootin', is the thinkin' of a lunatic.'

His gaze scoured the crowd, looking for and receiving approval. 'Today is April first, the fools' holy day. Horace Cobb, if he still thinkin' at all, will remember it. It was the day King Dick took his senses. And some of his teeth.' Some of the men laughed, but he cut them off. 'Hear this now. The British guns are loaded. They are primed. And they are pointin' at *us*. If we shout, "Fire!", they will fire. They will fire, I tell you. And now, a new danger.'

King Dick folded his arms, the club resting over his shoulder. Each man leaned in closer to hear this unexpected news. His voice dropped only slightly. 'Y'all need to know that the Rough Allies have gotten themselves a gun.'

The whole prison took a breath, then, on the exhale, started to shout.

He held up his hands to calm the uproar. 'Hear me now! Hear me now!' he bellowed. 'You ask what should we do? I say this. We stay in here. We wait. We take courage. This is our stickin' place. We know it. We close the doors. In here, we understand how it is. And so we will watch. We will listen. We will be ready. Ready for the Allies if they come, ready for the ships *when* they come.' He paused for a moment. 'Who is our head cook now?'

There was a moment of surprised silence at the unexpected question, before a chorus of voices called back.

'Portland Byrne, King Dick!'

A small, round-shouldered man was pushed to the front

318

of the first-floor railings. He raised a shaking hand. 'That's me,' he said, though most missed it; his voice didn't carry beyond the railings.

'Mr Byrne,' said the King, pointing his club at him. 'What supplies do you have in store? And speak truly. And as loud as you ever have.'

Byrne shrugged. 'Not much, King Dick.' Now, at least the landing and stairs could hear him. 'Two days' worth, maybe. With the market closed an' all, everyone's eatin' more. I'm havin' to watch my store cupboards, if I'm honest with you.'

'Thievin'?'

'Thievin'.'

The King cracked his club on the stairs. 'Goddammit, this will stop! There will be no thievin' here. Am I clear?'

This, Habs thought, is his battle voice, the voice that could cut right through enemy fire.

'Anyone caught stealin' in this place will find himself cast out. And with a broken face for their sins. We need all those who have been cooks, all those who have money spare, all those who have food spare, to work together.' He produced two pockets' worth of coins and notes, thrusting them at the nearest men. 'Buy what you can from any sailors' stalls still standin', then bring it to Mr Byrne there in the kitchens.'

Byrne raised a hand in acknowledgement.

'The Agent returns on Wednesday. I will talk to him before we perform *Romeo and Juliet* on Thursday. Until then, we *choose* to be separate. Back in '13, we had it forced on us, but now, with them Rough Allies roamin' round, armed, this is *our* decision. We choose to be in control, choose to close the door. We *choose* to be apart.'

319

5.5

Block Four, Cockloft

THE DARTMOOR Theatre Company's cast of *Romeo and Juliet* sat in a circle on the cockloft stage. The painted backdrop showed the roughly drawn brick walls of Verona. King Dick, Joe, Habs, Tommy, Sam, Pastor Simon, Goffe and Lord all sat facing each other. A few extra faces had turned up. To a man, they were the King's old crew mates. They all drank coffee, they all smoked pipes; even Tommy, who hated tobacco, felt he had to try what was offered. Alex and Jonathan did what Alex and Jonathan did best – they stood where no one noticed, eyes only on the King.

'Welcome to the men of the *Requin*,' said the King. 'I have found that, in times of need, the men of the *Requin* will not fail me. They will not let me down.'

Joe sensed Habs shift uncomfortably next to him and shared his evident apprehension. This was not how King Dick talked – 'fail' and 'let me down' were not his words; they had been disguised by a nod to his men, and their salute back, but to Joe's and Habs's ears, they were still stark and shocking. 'Same as when we performed *Othello* here, if we need more voices, more hands for the fight scenes,' the King continued, 'my old shipmates will be there. We fought the real battles, we can fight these, too.'

The pastor leaned forward. 'The choir could also lend a hand, King Dick. Good men, stout hearts.'

Sam blew an elegant stream of smoke from his lips. 'I was wonderin', King Dick, if you could use more men to build scenery, make costumes, that kinda thing? Now that we all stayin' inside for a while . . .'

The King nodded. 'Thank you, Mr Snow, yes, that would help focus minds. And I know you will organize that well. Mr Goffe, Mr Lord, you got somethin' to say?'

It had been obvious for a while that the most agitated men in the company were Jon Lord and Robert Goffe. They had fidgeted and sighed since their arrival in the cockloft. Goffe had sucked his pipe so hard his tobacco was all burnt up; he waved his pipe as he spoke.

'I mentioned this to Joe here on the way up, but he said to tell you straight, sir,' said Goffe. 'We came here to rehearse, but then we got to go. We're not stayin' here till the sixth, no goddamn way.'

'You got to let us say our words then let us go back to Seven.' Lord spoke more slowly than Goffe. 'And in Seven, you gotta know, no one thinks any ships are comin'. Not now, not never. That's why 's'all gone desperate.'

'They really think that?' asked Joe.

'Yup,' said Goffe. 'So no wonder they're tunnellin' fast.'

'You tunnellin', too?' asked Habs.

'Not so far,' said Goffe. 'We're here, ain't we? But if we stay here, if we stay in Four, then we can't never go back. They won't take us. Not even when the ships come.'

'*If* the ships come,' said Lord.

The King raised both hands. 'Gentlemen. You're right, o' course, you gotta come and go as you need. Your mess is in Seven; they'll not be wanting to lose any more fine seamen from the *Eagle*.' All eyes flicked momentarily to Joe, but his reaction was lost beneath his tricorn.

Goffe and Lord nodded their thanks, and the King tapped his club twice on the floor.

'So. Unless there're other matters to attend to, we gotta get to rehearsin'. We're doublin' up some roles, o' course – Pastor, you got Montague and the Apothecary – and if you need to have them words in front of you, you jus' go right ahead. I don't reckon I'll know all of Mercutio's and Friar Lawrence's words by Thursday, so don't no one worry about that. Mr Snow and Mr Hill?'

Joe was leafing through one of the scripts. 'When Act Two, Scene Three ends and becomes Scene Four,' he said, 'you leave as Friar Lawrence, then straight away enter as Mercutio.' He looked up at the King.

'Why, it's theatre, Mr Hill. We are in the business of illusion, are we not? I will hope that my priestly robes fit over my kinsman costume. A swift change, and all will be well.'

'And by then,' said Habs, 'the magic of the story will have worked its way into their hearts.'

'You mean everyone will be drunk,' said Joe.

'That is true,' said the King. 'For *Othello*, we had to break a few heads 'fore some scenes, jus' to get some quiet.'

Those who had been there laughed and nodded.

'And did that work?' asked Joe.

'What do you think, Mr Hill?'

'My guess is it did, King Dick.'

'And your words? Do you know your Juliet? Habs, how goes your Romeo?'

Habs and Joe looked at each other.

'Well, we got most of it,' said Habs. 'My speech before I take the poison in Act Five is fiendish long. Tha's the one I'm forgettin' the most.'

'Eyes look your last!' said the King, 'That one?'

'There. You got it already.' Habs bowed his head towards the King.

'Arms, take your last embrace!' the King bellowed, a titan now. 'And lips, O you the doors of breath, seal with a righteous kiss, a dateless bargain to engrossing death!'

There was applause from the company.

'And so you have it,' said the King, easing his way down again. 'What's so hard there?'

'I'll try harder,' said Habs.

'You rehearse well together?' asked the King. 'Seem like you practisin' a lot.'

'We speak of little else,' said Joe. 'The bunk whispering you hear is usually Act Two. Sometimes Act One, but mainly Two.'

'What light through yonder window breaks?' said the King.

'Yes,' said Habs. 'Then Joe says, "The barracks are on fire." And that's the end of it.'

'And the kiss?' asked the pastor.

'Not happenin',' said the King.

Pastor Simon persisted. 'So what *is* happenin', then? We don't want to upset no one.'

'Show them.' The King waved Joe and Habs into the circle.

Joe scrambled to the middle, sitting, leaning back on his hands. Habs stooped over him until their heads touched, then stood up again, shrugged, went back to his place. The pastor nodded approvingly. Goffe snorted.

'What was that?'

'That was nothing,' said Joe. 'Nothing at all.'

'But a "nothin' at all" that means, gentlemen, that we can still do the play. As we all know,' said the King, a gimlet gaze fixing them all in the circle. 'Mr Sam Snow. Your Benvolio is failin' in one regard.'

'I know it,' said Sam.

'You are kind an' gentle.'

'I know it.'

'You are a fine peacemaker.'

'I know it.'

'But you are weak. When Mercutio has been slain by Tybalt, you drag him offstage. Tha's what Benvolio does.'

'I know that, too, King Dick, but the thing is . . .' He paused briefly then sighed. 'When Ned was Mercutio, I could do it. Now . . . it's you and I jus' worried I can't.' The distress in Sam's face was real.

'Well then, I will make it easier for you, and fall by the edge of the stage.' Sam looked unconvinced, but the King had moved on. 'And young master crier, how do you like the Count Paris?'

Tommy grinned widely. 'I like him very much, King Dick, and 'specially the way he fights Romeo.'

'And gets killed,' commented Habs.

Tommy's smile became even broader. 'I never been killed before. I reckon I could do it right, King Dick. I been practising, look.' He ran to Habs, who shouted, 'Have at thee, boy!' then mimed a few sword thrusts. Tommy's legs buckled, and he fell, clutching his heart. 'Oh, I am slain! Lay me with Juliet!' he cried.

Joe led the applause, and Tommy risked a brief bow.

'Bravo!' said the King, tapping his club on the floor. 'Now, Mr Lord, Mr Goffe. While we have you . . .' He gestured for them to speak.

'Nurse is funny,' said Goffe. 'She got some good lines, but I don't reckon she'd wear a dress. I could play her in trousers, I was thinkin', and see—'

This time the King hit the club hard on the floor, a staccato rap which stopped Goffe dead. 'Romeo will dress as Romeo. Juliet will dress as Juliet. Nurse will dress as Nurse. And in a dress, please, Mr Goffe. It is the way of things, even in here, and it'll make her funnier. Mr Hill, is there somethin' we might have for Mr Goffe? I asked for the *Othello* costumes to be kept; I recall Desdemona and Bianca had a pretty fine line in frocks.'

Joe put his arm round Goffe, then patted his stomach. 'If we have some dressmakers, King Dick, we could set them to sewing two dresses together. Maybe even Desdemona's gown with a big slice out of Iago's shirt would fit.'

324

'A sailmaker could do it,' said Habs. 'I only got six months' trainin', but I reckon I could fix it.'

Goffe looked unimpressed. 'I don't want to wear no sail. Jus' trousers.'

Habs tried to be encouraging. 'You'll look ... extraordinary, Mr Goffe. Everyone loves Nurse.'

Goffe harrumphed. 'Romeo don't love Nurse,' he said, 'and Nurse disapproves of Romeo. So let's hear no more of your bluster, Mr Snow.'

'No more bluster? Bluster's all I got, Mr Goffe. C'mon, Mr Lord, this is your cue. Let's show what we can do.'

Lord sprang to his feet, his enthusiasm for the role plain for all to see. The King threw them their swords – painted chair legs with cloth-wrapped handles – and they set about each other with a fearful intensity. The 'blades' cracked and thudded against each other until the King called a halt.

'Remember to lose, Mr Lord – that, we cannot change,' he called, whereupon Lord collapsed in a heap. The cast applauded until the King stood up, looking unimpressed. 'Fight was good, but the dyin' needs work. And there's a whole lot a dyin' to be done in this play, gentlemen, so it gotta be right. Mercutio, Tybalt and Paris by the sword, Romeo by poison, Juliet by her own dagger. Tha's a lot of us. We all know how a man dies, we all seen it. In battle, in prison. With guns, bayonets, cannonball, smallpox, pneumonia. The audience know all this, too. We don't have no blood, no amputations, no guts on the floor, but if we can't die right, it won't feel right. So, while we have Mr Goffe and Mr Lord here with us, we should practise dyin'.'

Sam leaned in towards Joe and Habs. 'Ain't that what we do most days anyways?'

As King Dick had ordained, for the next four days the doors of Block Four stayed shut. When the turnkeys came to

325

unlock each morning, there was always a sentry on hand to close the doors again once they had gone. Sam enlisted as many hands as he could to finish the scenery and make the costumes; the one hundred and thirteen men who had been sailmakers or tailors before the war had never been busier. All the *Othello* outfits were altered, cut up or restitched; any old cloth, however thin and worn, was brought into service. Byrne, the head cook, found himself with a legion of helpers; anyone who had taken their turn in the kitchen now volunteered. With barely enough food to go round, the work was slight. Alex and Jonathan, their pockets full of the King's cash supplies, hovered around the ground-floor windows. If an inmate started setting up a stall within hollering distance, the boys swooped and bought him out. As word got out that Four were still buying, more stall-holders turned up and prices climbed. On Sunday, they had purchased portions of hot freco stew for threepence; by Monday, it was a shilling. No one knew how deep King Dick's pockets were, but without the proceeds from the gambling tables, there was a danger that even his money could run out any day.

Outside, the withdrawal of Four's inmates from prison life was greeted with bafflement, then indifference. With the exception of the few sellers taking advantage of the King's largesse, most inmates were simply grateful for the extra space.

In Block Six, the flintlock pistol was handled like a holy relic. Every man present had fired better weapons, but that had been in a previous life, a life of liberty, a life at sea, a life of colour. Now, they spoke in hushed tones of the miracles this single firearm would perform for them.

'One shot to Shortland's head and we'd be straight out o' here.'

'We could blast the armoury door right off its hinges.'

Its walnut stock, worn-grey lock-firing mechanism and brass barrel were examined in minute detail. Cobb, still groggy from his clash with King Dick, lay on his hammock, an unlit cigarillo stuck to his dry lips. Lane handed him the shooter, then leaned against the nearest stanchion. Their invited guests from Seven, Joseph Toker Johnson and former president Rose, stood with him, shielding the weapon from onlookers. The Rough Allies had discussed inviting Will Roche – he had been the most vocal advocate of rebellion – but his closeness to Joe Hill had ruled him untrustworthy.

Cobb turned the pistol in his hands, feeling the weight, smelling the acrid gunpowder residue. He closed his eyes with pleasure. 'How sweet this moment is. Not since the *Antelope*, not since then have I held such power in my hand.' He studied the woodwork again. 'French, I'd say. It's got 1805 stamped right here, so this here pistol has had some work to do. Hopefully killed a few English already.' He ran his fingers along the length of the six-inch barrel. 'An over-coat pistol wouldn't be my choice of weapon, but up close . . .' He closed one eye and sighted an imaginary shot, causing the others to move swiftly out of his way, shuffling around his bedside. 'Up close, I could blow Crafus's brains into his lap with one shot.'

Toker Johnson rolled two small tubes in his trembling hand. 'You could,' he said, nodding fast, keen to agree. 'We got jus' the six cartridges, though. We got to pick our targets well.'

'Did you know there'd be just the six?' asked Cobb.

'Asked for twelve,' said Lane. 'Paid for twelve. Hard to complain right now. I'll get the swindlin' bastard when I'm out o' here.'

'Do we know it works?' asked Rose.

Toker Johnson sighed, embarrassed by his colleague. He had pushed for Roche to be invited instead of Rose, but had been overruled. 'You wanna use up one of them cartridges to

327

find out?' He shook his head. 'We clean it, load it and pray. Same as always.'

'Back on the *Siroc* one time,' said Lane, reclaiming his weapon, 'I had a gun wouldn't fire 'cos o' the rain. Got myself into some trouble, as you see right here.' He drew the barrel along the scar tissue on his face. 'Can't let that happen here. The pistol and the cartridges feel dry, but as this whole goddamn country is drenched in rain or snow all year round and this whole goddamn prison runs with piss and spit, we got to make sure everythin' *stays* dry.'

'And secret,' added Cobb. "Specially in Seven. How many from the *Eagle* you got in there?'

'Don't quite recall.' Rose shrugged. 'But around twelve, somethin' like that.'

'And two of them in the play, too?'

Rose nodded. 'Jon Goffe and Robert Lord. They come and go a lot.'

'Do they?' said Cobb. 'Well, it's your job to make sure they mainly go. Keep them well away from us. That clear?' Rose and Toker Johnson nodded. 'And if they ask about the wall, you say you got no idea how long it will take to get through it.'

'Won't take long now and we'll be through the wall, and the weather looks set fair, so . . .' began Toker Johnson.

Cobb pushed himself up on the hammock. 'No, it doesn't help. We go on Thursday.'

'But we can go sooner,' said Toker Johnson. 'Why wait and risk bein' found out? We got boys in Seven want to push through now.'

Cobb lit his cigarillo from the nearest candle, and Lane pocketed the cartridges for safety.

"Cos the nigger play runs on Thursday, that's why. The Agent has said he is going to see it. Everyone will be worrying about whether he'll be safe in that den of depravity. They won't be worrying about the little game we're playing against the wall now, will they?' He put the cigarillo between his lips and inhaled deeply. No one said a word, everyone waiting for the exhale, knowing he would answer his own question. Cobb blew the cloud lazily. 'If we stand a chance of makin' it to the armoury, we got to wait till their curtain goes up. Or down. Or however they do it in blackjack land. We leave just enough wall to break through, and then . . .' He held both arms out wide and smiled his pinched-lipped cigarillo smile. 'Then, gentlemen, the stage will be ours.'

5.6

Wednesday, 5 April
The Agent's House

ELIZABETH HEARD his carriage arrive, gathered her wits and her shawl, then descended the stairs to greet him. She had much to report. In her husband's absence, she had been attacked and Block Four had shut its doors; this much she would explain. She had also slept at the doctor's house every night since he had been gone; this, she hoped to keep secret a while longer.

But she knew there was gossip. Inevitably, the prison talked. As the only woman within its walls, she was endlessly studied, observed, noticed. She was the entertainment.

And even under such scrutiny, she knew how Magrath looked at her. Even with his resolute discipline, she often felt his gaze: loving, curious, hungry. And knew that others saw it, too. Elizabeth knew that if Thomas hadn't yet been told of their affair, it was only a matter of time.

She had barely arrived in the hallway when he bustled through the door, followed by one of the guard commanders. 'Thomas. Welcome home,' she said, smiling.

'Thank you, Elizabeth,' he replied, his tone brisk.

'Lieutenant Fortyne, good morning.' She nodded at his extravagantly moustachioed second-in-command and he bowed.

'Mrs Shortland.'

'Fortyne has a report of everything that has happened in my absence,' said Shortland and, with a pointed look, he handed her his hat and cape and walked into his study. Fortyne followed, managing to look both embarrassed and censorious at the same time. The study door clicked shut.

'He knows,' she said to the empty hallway.

Their evening meal would arrive from the guards' mess in half an hour, at precisely seven o'clock; by her calculation, neatly coinciding with the end of their marriage. She waited for her husband at the kitchen table, her heart racing, her stomach heaving. Somehow, she had resisted the urge to tell Magrath what was about to happen. Instead, she reached for her snuffbox. Two small, pinched mounds. Two sniffs. She blinked and dabbed with her handkerchief.

'Ready when you are, Captain,' she muttered.

There were voices in the hallway, then the sound of the front door opening and closing. She sensed a pause, a momentary hesitation followed by a gathering of nerve. Five strides, and he stood in the kitchen doorway. The blue frock coat was still on, the white waistcoat unbuttoned.

'Elizabeth.'

'Thomas.'

He took a few paces towards her. 'Lieutenant Fortyne tells me you were assaulted by one of the prisoners.' His voice was tight, controlled.

'I'd have told you myself if you had let me.'

He frowned at the rebuke. 'Are you hurt?'

'I was shaken, of course, but no, I am not hurt.' She spun the box around her left hand, then her right.

'How did it happen? How is it possible that my wife, the Agent's wife, had a knife held at her throat?'

'There was an altercation.'

'But you were tending to the sick?'

She fumbled the box and it spun away across the table. She watched it until it stopped rolling and tipped over. 'An inmate from Six called me a whore.'

331

'I see.' Thomas Shortland folded his arms. 'And are you?'

She gave a short, stabbing laugh. 'Am I a whore? Really? That is what you want to say to me?'

He pulled up a chair, whisky fumes enveloping her from across the table. As he spoke, one hand tapped the table.

'There is much I want to say, Elizabeth. I could talk about the embarrassment of realizing that naval colleagues and brother officers have been laughing at me. I could mention the barely suppressed sniggering from the ranks in the barracks. And yes, an old friend did eventually take me to one side to tell me that you were fucking Magrath!' He shouted his obscenity, its violence filling the room. 'But do you know the words that have really stayed with me? That shout from an inmate. When we were having our vaccinations. Do you remember, Elizabeth?'

She held his gaze, determined not to look away. Of course she remembered.

'"Prickin' 'er, like most nights, then," I believe was the phrase employed. And it's true, isn't it? That is precisely what has been going on. And now I realize that that American prisoner-of-war knew more about what you are up to than I.'

Shocked by his vulgarity and the brutality of his assault, Elizabeth could not find the words to answer.

'Thomas,' she said eventually. 'There was a time . . .' But she got no further.

'And my shame will be as nothing to Willoughby's,' he said. The tapping hand was tapping harder now. 'At sea, fighting for his country, while his mother has taken to *fornication*.' He smacked the table hard. 'For shame, Elizabeth!' His cheeks were flushed and his eyes glassy. 'For shame.'

'I am sorry, Thomas, for the embarrassment, truly I am.' Elizabeth's hands were trembling but her mind was clear. 'Much as I am sure, in time, you will be sorry for your neglect of me. It is the men here that are your family, not me. You speak to them, understand them, spend time with them. It is they that satisfy you, not me. And as for Willoughby, I believe he will be fine. He understands more than you know. And hates this place as much as I do.'

'That is as may be,' said Shortland, his chin raised. 'But this war with America is finished, and the men will return home soon. There will be no need of a physician here. Your' – he searched for the word – 'your *paramour* will be disgraced. We have the play tomorrow in Four. You and I will attend, applaud politely, and after that we will address the issue of your adultery. But be clear on this. When the Americans leave, so do the Irish.'

He stood to leave, wobbled slightly, then marched out. Elizabeth recovered her snuffbox and measured out two generous piles of tobacco. She sniffed them both, then dabbed her eyes.

'Then so do I,' she said.

5.7

Thursday, 6 April
Block Four, Cockloft

4.40 a.m.

BEFORE THE turnkeys, before the sunrise, before the nerves, it was the gulls that woke Joe. Lying in his hammock, he listened, transfixed. In the still-shuttered and locked prison block, it was hard to judge direction and distance, but he imagined he saw six birds, maybe more, as they screeched and wheeled. He remembered red bills, pale grey upper wings and black-tipped feathers. Always hungry, always scavenging, always fierce. He lay still, not wanting to miss a single call.

For Joe, it was the sound of home, of America, and of sitting astride the *Eagle*'s bowsprit, of hauling in and repairing the mainsail. Gulls were the soundtrack to everything he could remember, everything he had ever done.

Except here. He hadn't heard them in Dartmoor, not once, he was sure of it. Now, their calling moved him deeply.

'Can you hear that?' he whispered, his voice thick with sleep.

Habs's upside-down head appeared in an instant, his corkscrew hair swinging as he spoke. 'I been awake for hours, speakin' my lines into this dead air. But you never said nothin' back. If I say, "That I might touch that cheek!" and you don't say . . .'

334

'Ay me!' said Joe eventually, finding his place in the new conversation.

'Correct,' said Habs. 'And if you don't say that, me sayin', "She speaks. O, speak again" just sounds plain dumb.'

'Did you hear the gulls?' said Joe, reluctant to leave his reverie.

'I been tryin' not to but o' course I heard 'em,' said Habs, with a frown. 'Wind must be blowin' from the Atlantic. But I'd rather listen to Sam snorin'.'

'Really?'

'I hate them birds, Joe. They're mockin' us, can't you hear it?'

Joe swung his legs out and pushed his stockinged feet into his boots. 'No, can't say I can, Habs.'

'It's that haw-haw-haw sound. They look down at us in this pitiful place, and they laugh. They work with the sea, so should we; they move with the wind, so should we. They're free, and we ain't. I always think that.'

'You've heard them here before?'

'Sure. But not since before the winter set in. Not since before you came.'

'Well, if they're blowing in from the Atlantic, maybe our ships will be blowing in just behind them. Maybe today's the day.'

'You want them to come today?'

Joe sighed, ran his hands through his hair. 'The gulls have got me thinking of home, Habs, is all. But sure, I can wait one more day. We have a show to do.' He tied his hair back with a strip of cloth.

Habs disappeared for a moment before slithering from his hammock and easing himself alongside Joe. In the near-dark of the predawn, the ground floor of Block Four hummed with a cacophony of rattly, phlegmy breathing. As far as they could see – and hear – they were the first awake, the first to rise.

'Nervous?' asked Habs.

'I need a piss, then I'll be nervous,' said Joe.

'Why don't we go up and rehearse before the others get there?' said Habs. 'Before they even up.'

Joe nodded his agreement and placed a finger to his lips. 'Before the turnkeys, too,' he whispered.

The cockloft's height gave it the day's earliest light, and their first view of the finished streets of Verona took their breath away. Two of the upper room's four windows had been left open, their shutters unfastened, and two beams of dusty, weak sunshine were cutting the air. They hit the stage high on the backdrop, where hundreds of brown and grey bricks had been painted to form the city walls. The effect was magical.

Joe and Habs climbed on to the stage. Two wooden crates had been placed at the centre, costumes and fabrics spilling out of both.

'What does Romeo wear?' asked Joe, lifting a torn and moulding cotton sheet from one.

'Not that,' said Habs, sifting through a selection of shoes, capes and hats.

'Well, when you wear a French officer's jacket all the time, I guess you don't need no fancy costume anyway. You can just dress like you always do.' A velvet cap hit him in the face.

'A son of Montague does not wear French,' said Habs. 'He wears somethin' like this.' Habs held up a deep red satin shirt with oversized buttons and a high collar. 'What d'you think? I wore it for Iago, so these sweat stains are all mine.'

'Well, you don't need me to tell you, Mr Snow. Can we think of it as your lucky shirt?'

'We can, Mr Hill.' Habs removed his blue jacket, placing it over the side of the crate. 'Unless I got too skinny in here. Don't want it billowin' like a topsail that's lost its wind.'

He pulled the two shirts he was wearing over his head and placed them on top of his jacket. 'Still like you to like it, though. You'll be marrying me in this, after all.'

'Yes, but then killing myself, so my opinions don't count for too much here.' He watched Habs as he pulled on the satin shirt, arm and stomach muscles tightening and relaxing in turn. Each of his ribs was visible and his trousers had slipped below protruding hip bones. Joe hooked his fingers into the tops of Habs's trousers and hoisted them higher.

'I don't know how you looked for *Othello*,' he said, 'but my guess is I wouldn't've needed to do this. Wouldn't've needed to hold your trousers up. But you still look good to me, Habs, and once you get some New York food inside you, all this will fill up fine.' Joe patted Habs's stomach and, suddenly, his hand was covered, held fast by Habs's own. Heart racing, Joe tried, weakly, to pull his hand away, but Habs held him firm. There was a smile coming, but it wasn't quite there yet.

'We're on stage!' Joe whispered, glancing to the four corners. Their close proximity alone would have been cause for comment and rebuke; this new, public intimacy an outrage.

'That is true,' said Habs. 'An empty stage with no audience. And we'll hear if the stairs creak.' Still Habs held Joe's hand tight to his abdomen. Joe tried to speak, but nothing would come. He felt his hand being pushed lower. He let it slide briefly but, as his fingers dipped under the waistline of Habs's breeches, he pulled it back, horror, shock and a thrilling arousal coursing through him.

Habs's face was a mirror, a steadier reflection of the pyrotechnics going on inside his own head.

Joe cleared his throat as quietly as he could manage. 'Rehearsal, you said, Mr Snow?' His words were calm but his head was on fire. He avoided Habs's gaze by fastening the buttons of the red shirt. The lower four were wooden discs – replacements, Joe guessed – and the top two were shell. Joe's fingers twisted and pushed until they were all home. He brushed the shirt down with the back of his hands, straightening the fabric over the top of Habs's trousers. Now he looked in his eyes. 'There's too much at stake today. You know that. We can't afford to make this place any crazier.'

'It don't make it crazier, it make everything simpler.'

'What does?' asked Joe, but Habs was back at the costume crate.

'I made you this.' From the crate, Habs pulled a black dress. 'It isn't much – more of a nightshirt, I s'pose – but I figured you might prefer it that way. Nothin' too fancy.' He handed it to Joe.

'You made this?'

'I had a bit of help, but mostly . . . It was part of the drapes but I figured there was jus' enough cotton to fashion somethin' for Juliet. My stitchin' is better suited to a foresail, as you'll see, but at least you won't look like a Regency madam or a whore.'

Joe held the dress up. It was long and round-necked, and some high-waisted stitching had indeed given it enough shape to pass as a dress rather than a curtain.

'I wondered what this moment would be like,' he said, still in a half-whisper. 'Hoping folk wouldn't laugh for too long.' He handed it back to Habs, unbuttoned the thick jerkin he had traded for in his first, freezing month, then his regulation prison jacket and shirts. He shivered. 'Half-naked on stage is not a good place to be. So let's try it.'

Habs gathered the dress in his hands and eased it over Joe's upstretched arms. The sleeves were wide and he wriggled his arms through easily. Habs dropped the remaining folds – it fell to just below Joe's knees – and he stepped back to inspect.

'Well?' said Joe, feeling his colour rise again. 'It feels as rough as timber, but please tell me it looks all right.' He picked at it a few times, moved around to see how it felt, grateful it was just Habs at the first viewing.

'It's all right,' said Habs. 'You're all right. With more work, it could look like less of a drape. Some embroidery, maybe, but I don't think anyone'll notice after their first ale.' He walked around Joe. 'And your hair is grown. You must feel safer.'

Joe nodded. 'Of course. Dartmoor is bad, but it's not the worst.' The words 'not yet' formed in his head, but he bit them back.

'I have one more suggestion,' said Habs. He put his hands on Joe's hips and walked him backwards until they were behind one of the flats. Habs began to gather the dress fabric in his fingers. Joe closed his eyes. He knew what the suggestion was going to be, knew from the moment the dress had come out of the crate. He felt Habs's fingers at the fly front of his breeches. Two buttons on the waistline, thirteen on the fly, but Habs worked swiftly. As they came loose, he felt his breeches fall to the floor, and Joe forced himself to step out of them. On the edge of a precipice, he reached for Habs, but held him at arm's length. One hand held Habs's shoulder, the other reached for a curl of his hair then twisted it around his fingers.

'No,' said Joe, the tightness in his voice giving it a rasp. 'Maybe. You can't . . .'

Habs put two fingers on Joe's lips. 'I know,' he whispered. 'I know all that, know they'd hang us for certain.'

Joe removed his fingers, held Habs's gaze. 'If they do see thee they will murder thee. I would not for the world they saw thee here.'

Habs dropped his head on to Joe's shoulder and started to laugh.

'Juliet speaks! So we are rehearsin' after all.' He closed

339

his eyes. 'So, let me think.' He slapped his own face, agitated. 'Right, same scene.' He put his arms round Joe's waist and pulled him close. 'Wilt thou leave me so unsatisfied?'

Joe's eyes crinkled. 'What satisfaction canst thou have tonight?' he said, and felt Habs's cheek move against his. There was a pause, a hesitation, and for a moment Joe thought Habs had forgotten the words. Then he felt Habs inhale and a rapid pounding against his chest.

'The exchange of thy love's faithful vow for mine,' muttered Habs.

There was movement in the stairwell: the turnkeys were at the door below. In a matter of moments, the block would be alive again. Joe wrapped his arms tightly around Habs. He knew he should break apart, knew they would have company soon, but knew also what he had to say.

'I gave thee mine before thou didst request it.'

The applause made them start, then spring apart. Just one pair of hands, but they made a big noise.

'Bravo!' said King Dick, walking from the shadows. 'Best I seen. No need to jump away like that . . .' He leaned against the stage, beckoned them closer. They exchanged the briefest of glances. Joe pulled his breeches back on, then they both sat on the edge of the stage, Joe still rebuttoning. The King, freshly shaved, with a full complement of rings and a green shirt which appeared to be clean as well as pressed, rapped his fingers on the stage. 'But that was . . . that was *too* good.' He fixed Joe, then Habs, with the most solemn of stares, every muscle in his face tight, every scar pronounced. 'We lost the kiss but, you act like that, might as well put it straight back in. You can fight like you mean it, drink like you mean it and, God knows, you gotta die like you mean it. But you gotta embrace like you don't. Like you are brothers'll be fine. Embrace like it's the only goddamn sign of affection between you, not jus' the first of many. Am I clear on this?'

'So it was too good?' Habs immediately regretted the defiant tone of his voice.

'Good enough to stop the play, Mr Snow,' said the King, his anger rising to the surface. He seemed to grow taller still as he pulled the bearskin forward on his head. 'Good enough to get you in the cachot, and good enough for a lynchin'. This play is what we got. This is it. Our company is good. You two are good. We got one more performance here, and the god-damn Agent is comin', and *Mrs* goddamn Shortland is comin', and comin' *here*. To Four. Not to Three, not to Seven, but here, where the Negroes are. To see their English Shake-speare performed by coloured American sailors. 'Fore the Agent leaves tonight, he will know that, he loses us – if he loses the men o' Four – the whole goddamn prison is lost. But if the men o' Four are busy bein' outraged 'bout what you two doin' on stage, we lost everythin'. Everythin' is gone.'

Habs couldn't get his words out quickly enough. 'Sorry, King Dick,' he said. 'I never meant . . .'

'I know what you meant. I'm jus' tellin' you to be care-ful.' The King gave the weariest of sighs.

'We will,' said Habs.

'And John Haywood should see all this,' said the King, waving at the scenery. 'Both Shortlands know what's hap-penin' here; would do him good.'

'We'll tell him,' said Joe.

The King nodded. 'And the dress is a good fit, Mr Snow. You like it, Mr Hill? It'll do the job, I reckon.'

'I do, sir, yes. We came up to rehearse Act Five and our dying lines, but then . . .' He pulled at the dress fabric.

'You got distracted.' He looked at them closely for a moment. 'It happens. How do you die, Mr Hill?'

Joe looked upstage. 'You want us to show you?'

'Jus' where you are'll be fine.'

Joe closed his eyes, miming a short knife held between his hands. 'O happy dagger. This is thy sheath. There rust and let me die.' He made two short stabbing moves to his stomach, then fell sideways, away from Habs. The King nodded.

'O' course. And you, Mr Snow? Remind me.'

Habs held up an imaginary cup, the King raising his arms as if to conduct the moment. 'Here's to my love,' said Habs, then drank and clutched at his stomach. 'O true apothecary, thy drugs are quick,' he said, swaying. 'Thus with a kiss I die.' Slowly, he lay back on the stage.

'Good,' said the King. 'Very good. And there's the warnin' – it's right there in the play. You kiss, you die.'

5.8

Block Six

12.05 p.m.

THEY NOW had three functioning scraping tools. Small enough to be hidden in a palm, strong enough to carve cement, they had been constructed from floorboard wood, threads of hammock rope and discarded, sharpened keys. During the game, they had been passed from hand to hand; now, they were all in Horace Cobb's jacket pocket, his left fist enclosing them. He eyed the militia on the military walk.

'Shock of their lives,' he growled to Lane, who followed his eyes and guessed the rest. His hands, too, were thrust deep in pockets, one closed around the cartridges, the other around the pistol.

'It'll be quite a sight,' he said. 'Yankee men against English boys. And boys that most probably never seen a battle. Barely even fired a rifle.'

'The most dangerous kind of soldier,' said Cobb. 'They won't have a clue.'

The courtyard was teeming with men. A gentle westerly had allowed the temperature to rise and, when the sun eased through the clouds, a few corners of the yard enjoyed what, in Dartmoor, passed as warmth. From one of these, by the back of Seven, the Rough Allies observed both the British and their own handiwork.

'I'm tryin' not to stare at the hole we're makin',' Lane muttered, looking skywards. Cobb inspected the unlit

343

cigarillo between his fingers – his last – and laughed. 'The whole place's crumbling. They're not stonemasons. Why'd they want to inspect a wall?'

'But can't they see?' whispered Lane, incredulous, his eyes dragged again to the smudge on the brickwork that marked their weakening of the radius wall. Beneath it, the ground was scuffed and, despite the clear-up, peppered with crumbled cement. He shook his head in disbelief. 'We got to get the game up soon, cover our work.'

'If it was a hole, even the English would spot it,' said Cobb. 'But for now it's just a scallop, a mere scraping. By the time it's a hole and the bricks are pushed through, it'll be too late.'

'And we can do that anytime,' said Lane.

'You're sure it's that close?' said Cobb.

'Could've gone through yesterday. But we held back, like you said.'

'The play's at three o'clock,' said Cobb. 'We give them twenty minutes to settle, give Shortland time to realize what a godawful mess the blackjacks are making of everything, then we go. You go through first – you got the gun. By the time the alarm bell's ringing, we should all be armed.'

Lane glanced over the radius wall, the central tower of the barracks clearly visible, and swallowed hard. 'We shoot our way out?'

'We take hostages. Just like I tried with Madame Shortland. Grab the nearest redcoat we can find and walk out behind him. And with that bloodsucker Crafus busy and all made up like the fancy woman he is, this time, we might make it.'

The shout of orders, a flash of red at the market square gates and Cobb was on his feet.

'Get some players out!' he snapped. 'Go now. Cover what you can – they're coming in.' A company of militia, fully eighty or ninety men, were entering the courtyard.

'What's happenin' here, then?' said Lane, hesitating. The gates swung open, and around twenty soldiers took up positions around the market square entrance, the rest marching straight ahead in the direction of Four.

'Maybe they found the tunnel?' Cobb slipped one of the shanks to Lane. 'I'll get the men together. You get to the wall.'

Lane called out to the inmates as he ran past and, by the time they reached their 'scraping', as Cobb had labelled it, he had at least forty players, with onlookers providing raucous support. Six men threw themselves against the wall, and the scrummaging began. Twenty yards from the gates, they were close – and noisy – enough for the militia to view them warily. A few swung nervous rifles their way, triggering first panic, then anger. Some of the men edged away from the game, towards the troops. Three Allies, arms outstretched, taunted the British.

'You wanna shoot Yankees? Jus' for goin' 'bout their business? S'that why you're here?'

More of the troops now swung their guns to cover the advancing Americans.

Cobb, running fast and now flanked with Allies, called the men back. 'Just the game, m'boys! Just the game!' The vanguard sloped back to the wall, leaving Cobb to watch the soldiers watching him. Three redcoats standing together were the last to lower their rifles. Their faces partially obscured, the only man he recognized was the sergeant; the three stripes on his arm and the striped scar on his forehead gave him away. He stood with his feet firmly planted, like a Devon farmer. 'Ol' Fat Bastard,' muttered Cobb. 'Of course. It'll be a pleasure.' He saluted the man until his fellow soldiers lowered their aim. 'You got to keep your bullets for Napoleon. You don't want to be losing two wars in a row, now, do you?'

Cobb saw the men bridle, the sergeant's two colleagues raising their guns again.

'You need to read the treaty!' shouted the sergeant, pushing their guns down. 'Though maybe the words are too long for you. You lost Canada and you lost your White House. Burned pretty easy, they say.'

Cobb bit down on an instant retort, in danger of making the same error he had come to prevent. He shoved his hands in his pockets and gripped the shanks again. Reassured, he studied the three men. Ol' Fat Bastard was making his stand with two of the youngest, skinniest soldiers he had ever seen in uniform. One gripped his rifle like a shovel, eyes squinting with fierce concentration; the other, his face reddening with excitement, hopped from one foot to the other, ready to let loose. 'Farmhands,' he said to himself. 'Know-nothing farmhands.'

Lane appeared at his shoulder. 'You got to see the wall.'

'Is it good?' asked Cobb, turning away from the soldiers.

'It's beautiful.'

They joined a rolling maul, hooking arms with a row of other Allies. Pushed through flailing legs and tumbling bodies, Cobb quickly found himself lying against the retaining wall. As the 'game' heaved and sprawled around him, a phalanx of players provided a temporary shield behind which Cobb could run his fingers across the masonry. Over an area of around two square feet, the cement which had bound the irregular lumps of granite together since its construction had been worked loose. Some lay in small clumps on the ground; the rest had been roughly pushed back, filling in the deepest cracks in an attempt to camouflage their work. He pushed gently with both hands and felt one of the smaller stones shift under the pressure. He pulled back, fearing imminent collapse and exposure, but the wall held its shape. Cobb crouched, replaced some more broken cement, then patted it flush with the brick. Forcing his way back through the melee, he rejoined Lane. A crowd of many hundred were throwing insults at the British, the troop hunkering down nervously behind their rifles.

'Well?' said Lane.

Cobb brushed cement fragments from his beard, his face flushed. 'Just as you said. The wall will go when we need it to go.' He stared at the soldiers massed outside the steps of Four. 'If they've discovered the Negro tunnel, we can forget about everything.' He wiped dust from his face and beard. 'But if they're just checking plans before Shortland gets here, well then . . .' He looked back to Lane. 'With their play, your gun and our Yankee hearts, God willing, we'll be free men by sundown.'

5.9

Block Four

KING DICK pulled deeply on his pipe and studied the guard commander standing nervously by the steps of Block Four. He looked barely older than the men he led, and his oversized shako cap sat awkwardly over his ears. The officer's hands rested briefly on his sword grip, before anchoring themselves behind his back.

'I demand entrance to your cockloft!' he said, his pale eyes wandering along the lines of inmates that had clustered around the King.

'You mighty early, the play ain't for a few hours yet,' said the King. Laughs from the inmates, more discomfort from the officer. 'You got tickets?' continued the King. 'S'jus', you got so many men with you, and it's sixpence each.'

Four lines of redcoats had assembled briskly behind their commander, many of them wide-eyed at the King's air of authority and command; he was actually making fun of them.

'We might be able to let *you* in, Lieutenant . . .'

'Lieutenant Aveline,' said the commander, now even more irritated.

'But not your friends, Lieutenant A-ve-line.'

Aveline stepped forward, provoking the inmates to close tightly around the King. Foot on the step to Four, Aveline's face was flushed.

'Captain Shortland and Mrs Shortland will be in attendance for your . . . performance this afternoon,' he said. 'He has

348

ordered me to ensure his safety, and I am ordering you to step aside.'

The King swung the club from the ground to his shoulder, pushed the bearskin to his forehead. 'Maybe you're new here, Lieutenant. Maybe you missed the last few months. Maybe the Agent never told you. But King Dick has guaranteed the safety of the captain. When Mrs Shortland was taken by that savage Cobb, who rescued her, Lieutenant? Was it you? Was it anyone in a fine red jacket? No, it was King Dick. In this block, if the King says the captain will be safe, then you take it that it will be so.'

The lieutenant took a breath. 'I have my orders.'

'You have my reassurance.'

The tightness of the lieutenant's voice betrayed his anxiety. 'You will step aside and allow my men to enter.'

'I will not.' The King blew another cloud of tobacco smoke towards the soldiers. The lieutenant pursed his lips. Behind him, redcoats bristled at the insubordination. 'But I can offer you coffee.' The officer looked astonished, but the King continued. 'It's made from peas, y'know. Quite a flavour, really – maybe different to what you're used to – but there's some in the cockloft right now.'

'You are really in no position . . .' blustered Aveline.

'Oh, but I am,' said the King. 'I really am. O' course, you could shoot us, I realize that. You have the guns. Though' – and here he gestured to the large and growing crowd of inmates watching their altercation – 'you might need quite a few bullets for all of us. But if you wanna report back to Captain Shortland without causin' a riot, I'm offerin' the solution. *And* you get coffee.'

'I don't want your bloody coffee!' snapped Aveline. 'I am instructed to ensure the safety of the Agent. If I cannot do that, the Agent will not come.'

'Very well,' said the King. 'He can stay away. He ain't needed. We perform for our own pleasure, not yours. Or the

Agent's. D'you get that? We ain't sittin' here waitin' for your blessin', or even your attention. If the Shortlands come, there'll be chairs so their plump and tender asses don't touch the cold ground. And if they don't, two lucky American sailors will rest their bony asses there instead. Romeo will still marry Juliet, he'll still take poison, she'll still stab herself, life an' death will go on, like it always do.'

Applause from the men around the King.

'Now, you sure 'bout that coffee?'

There was a nervous energy to the assembled players of the Dartmoor Amateur Dramatic Company as they stood on the stage and waited for the curtain to be completed. Joe and Habs had kept their costumes on. Lord wore a striped necktie and the pastor was sporting a crown made from parchment; 'Montague's,' he said. 'Gives him authority.' The rest were yet to change, prison yellow mingling with old coats and dirty blankets. They could all hear the singing below and knew their shipmates would soon be on their way up. The King had posted some more of his *Requin* men on the door to keep the cockloft empty, but everyone wanted the curtain in place as soon as possible.

'It is the start o' things,' the King had said. 'Without it, this is just a room with a stage. But when the curtain is in, the magic begins its work.' His voice softened, adopting the cadence of a priest uttering holy words. 'It becomes a theatre.'

Surrounded by large pieces of cloth and rope, Sam, in his pale green Benvolio shirt, called, 'Final stitches!'

Joe and Habs jumped from the stage and stood poised to help hoist his handiwork.

'Done.' Sam jumped to his feet, rolled the finished cloth into a long roll. With Joe at one end and Habs at the other, Sam directed the curtain's placing between the two stage flats. The King, at full stretch, hooked the curtain's two roughly cut eyelets over nails in each flat then let the fabric drop.

Sam had taken six of the sailors' banners and flags, stitching them together with old blankets. Tommy had begged one from his colleagues in Three; Goffe and Lord had found two in Seven. Together with three from their own, Sam had created a patchworked curtain of sailors' protest. 'Don't Give up the Ship', 'Free Trade and Sailors' Rights' and 'All of Canada or War Forever!' were written or stitched on to the huge rectangles of cloth. Between them were American flags and images of large, aggressive eagles. The whole stretched across the stage, and Verona had all but disappeared.

'Bravo!' called Goffe. 'You're quite the artist.'

'Wonder what Shortland will make of it, cuz?' said Habs.

Sam shrugged. 'He's a Navy man, ain't he? He can admire my stitchin' if he don't like anythin' else.'

The King clapped his hands. 'On stage, behind that curtain. Everyone in costume, now.'

Tommy Jackson, a fistful of shirts in one hand and his sword in the other, ran to the King's side as they climbed back on the stage. 'Which costume, King Dick?'

'I'm Mercutio before I'm the apothecary,' he replied, pushing past the curtain, 'so something a kinsman to the Prince of Verona might wear. A military jacket, I reckon.'

'Oh, right, sir,' said Tommy, looking confused. 'Sorry, but I meant which of these shirts for me, for Paris.' He held up the shirts in his hand. 'They're all too big, but I can't find anythin' else in them baskets.'

The King sifted through the worn and torn shirts Tommy had been given and shook his head. 'Paris is a young count, not a street urchin. None of these will do.' He flung them back in one of the costume baskets. 'Mr Daniels! Mr Singer!' he bellowed, and the boys appeared in seconds. 'Mr Jackson needs to look like a suitor of Juliet might look. Give him one o' your shirts and see what he looks like. Dress 'im, boys, and be back in two minutes.'

The three boys sprinted from the stage, the cockloft doors crashing open like a musket shot. The *Requin* men playing soldiers, servants and torchbearers rummaged for anything to mask the yellow of their prison uniform.

'Crowd'll be in shortly!' shouted the King. 'If you need the heads, go now. If you *think* you might need the heads, go now. Even if you *don't* need the heads, go now.'

'And what'll I do?' asked Goffe, emerging from behind the scenery. Over his prison jacket and stockings he had pulled a grey, low-cut ballgown with a lace collar. An extra seam had been added, as promised, to accommodate his girth, a slice of stained, green blanket stitched in to take the strain. His weathered features were set, his hands held in tight fists.

'You and Juliet had better piss in a bucket.' The King laughed.

The sounds of raucous singing came more loudly now. Some messes had decided they'd had enough of waiting below and begun the climb to the cockloft. Shanties, hymns and patriot songs ran into each other in a cacophony of expectation.

Joe looked at Habs and grimaced. 'When you're sober, all these songs sound threatening.'

'Same as happened for *Othello*,' said Habs. 'Wait till they're out there.' He pointed through the curtain. '*Then* it's noisy. They'll be drunk and bored till we start. Then they'll be drunk but enchanted.'

'Hopefully. What if they're drunk, then fight?'

'Then King Dick's mighty club will swing,' said the King, handing Habs his wooden sword. Quietly, he passed Joe a small, silver-coloured knife. 'It's one o' mine. Everyone assumes it's wood an' paint, but it's for real. I keep it for the big shows – it looks better'n the fake ones. Can't have Juliet stabbin' herself with a bit of blunt wood.'

The cockloft's doors burst open and Alex and Jonathan ran in, followed by the smartest-looking crier anyone could remember. Tommy jumped to the stage with a white dress shirt tucked into his trousers. 'Alex found it,' he said, smiling at everyone. 'He says I can keep it, too.'

'That is a fine improvement,' said the King. 'Now you are Paris. Now you can rival Romeo for Juliet's hand.'

'Thank you, King Dick.' Tommy glanced again at his finery. 'Oh, and I got a message from John Haywood for you.'

'You do?' said the King. 'Underneath that fancy linen, you're still the crier?'

'O' course. Always. His guard called us over. Says he won't be ready for the start of the show, but to start without him. He might be sleeping.'

'He's not ready?' said the King, incredulous. 'How long does he need to get ready? How much sleep can a man take?' He shrugged. 'Time is up. Come, gentlemen, we burn daylight.'

5.10

Block Six

2 p.m.

'WHO'S GOIN'?' said Lane. 'Who's runnin'?' He fluttered about the mess like a bird pecking at seed before settling on the hammock across from Cobb.

'Everyone,' said Cobb, playing with a pipe and missing his cigarillos. 'Eventually. Once we're through the wall and into the armoury, we'll need every damn Yankee we can find.'

'But Allies first.'

'Of course Allies first,' affirmed Cobb. 'D'you see any other leaders here?'

'I do not, sir.'

Cobb leaned forward. 'D'you see anyone else armed?'

'I do not, sir.'

'Well, then.' Cobb sucked on the unlit pipe. 'Shut the doors.'

Lane checked that he'd heard right. 'Completely? Like in Four?'

'Shut the doors,' repeated Cobb, his voice barely more than a growl. 'Yes, completely. Yes, like in Four. Have you gone simple, Mr Lane? Do I need to do it myself?'

Lane shook his head then scuttled to the large double doors. He pushed each shut with both hands, the clicking of its lock cylinder and the loss of light causing heads to turn and shouts of alarm.

'Hey, what's with the dark already?'

'Are the turnkeys mad?'

'Is there a riot? Are we locked in?'

Lane scurried back to Cobb. 'You need to speak up,' he hissed, and started to flutter again.

'Sit down, Mr Lane, I know what I have to do.' He stood, then stooped close to Lane's ear. 'Check the cartridges. Check everythin's dry.'

He turned quickly and, before he could witness Lane's scowl, he had walked to the nearest stanchion. Using each hammock rope, he climbed it like a ladder. At the top hammock – the fifth – he tightrope-walked his way to its centre. He stood with his arms, and legs, wide.

He'd had silence from the moment he stepped out. 'They can take many things from us,' he said, his voice bouncing from the roof now not far from his head, 'but they can't take an ol' sailor's balance.'

Cheers rang from every mess.

'And the sea is still! Look – no waves at all. We are becalmed here and have been for too long. But that finishes today. We have a storm brewing, and it's an American storm.'

A loud knocking on the doors caused heads to turn and sparked startled, worried faces. Cobb faltered. 'Check who it is,' he ordered, and Lane grabbed the handles.

'It's men from Seven!' he called after the briefest of checks. 'Dozens of 'em.'

'Let 'em in!' called one.

'Yeah, let 'em in!' shouted many others. 'They been attackin' that wall, too.'

Cobb thought for a moment then called down to Lane. 'If they come in, they're staying in. No leaving from now on. When the door opens again, it'll be 'cos we're getting out of here. Tell them that. If they can't stay, they ain't coming in.'

They all came in. Forty or fifty of them shuffling into Six, each glancing in turn at Cobb's lofty, precarious position and realizing they had interrupted a speech of some sort.

They settled quickly. Cobb saw them all: Will Roche just behind the ginger-headed Joseph Toker Johnson.

'No one leaves till we all do!' Cobb's eyes rested on Roche. 'I hope that's clear.'

Roche, and all of the Sevens, nodded, and cries of ''S'clear!' and 'We got it!' rang through the block.

'All right,' said Cobb. 'The nigger play starts in one hour. Maybe they're acting, maybe they're escaping. Maybe both. But, anyways, it don't matter to us. We got our own plan. We got a wall that's about ready to crumble and we got stout hearts. And we got a gun.'

It was like a lightning bolt. Some jumped up; some sat down; everyone exclaimed. It was too good to be true. What type of gun? A rifle? A musket? How many bullets? Had anyone fired it? Cobb realized he had released a whirlwind and held up his hands in an effort to quieten the storm.

'It's nothing grand. An overcoat pistol with only a precious few cartridges. But it is ours and, with it, we can secure others. Once the play has begun, we go back to our wall game, spill through to the armoury. Lane goes first with his gun, in case we encounter any redcoats. We get in, arm ourselves and attack. We take control, gentlemen. Everyone thinks this war is over, but we know there is one battle left to fight. Share what food and drink you got left. Your enslavement is at an end.'

To an explosion of cheering, Cobb walked back to the stanchion and shimmied down.

As he walked back to his mess, back-slapped and applauded all the way, Lane greeted him with a small bow.

'Looks like you jus' got yourself an army,' he said.

5.11

Block Four, Cockloft

Backstage, lines were repeated, cues checked and sword fights rehearsed. No one cared how much noise they made – the audience was in. To start with, they sat in groups, filling up from the stage outwards, but within minutes it became clear that sitting was not an option. Thirty minutes before curtain, everyone stood. Twenty minutes before curtain, the front rows were so crushed they spilled on to the stage. Viewed from the other side of the curtain, Sam and Lord, now in their opening positions, watched the scores of shadows milling around a few feet in front of them.

'King Dick's gonna hate this,' said Lord.

'King Dick is already hatin' it,' said Sam. 'Look.' A giant silhouette had appeared on the curtain, its size exaggerated by the King's closeness. Viewed from their position upstage, the black and almost-white images looked like more of a puppet show than the opening of a Shakespeare play – an ogre swiping at dwarves.

'Step back!' he bellowed. 'Everyone step back off our stage!'

Habs, Joe and most of the cast found the temptation to peer at the audience overwhelming, and they jockeyed for position at the edges of the curtain. As some of the crowd tried to follow the King's command, tiny gaps began to appear in front of him. 'Fill the hole, sailors,' he said, inviting, then pushing, men off the stage.

'It's like it's Washington's birthday all over again,' said the pastor. 'Everyone got a bottle.'

'At least one,' said Habs. 'And a few in their pockets for later, too.'

Joe felt a tug on his shirt. An awkward, hand-wringing crier looked desperate to speak to him.

'Is there a problem, Tommy?' asked Joe. 'You really look the part now, you know.'

Tommy ignored the compliment. 'I think we got trouble,' he said. 'I think we got trouble.'

'We?'

'You and me.' He waved his finger between the two of them. 'You and me, and Mr Goffe and Mr Lord.'

'Agreed,' said Habs. 'You all too white.' He laughed, but Tommy nodded in agreement.

'Yes, that's exactly what it is. Outside. By the steps. I jus' seen 'em.'

'Seen who, Tommy?' asked Joe, alarmed.

'When I was gettin' the shirt. I heard 'em. Recognized the voices, y'see.'

'Who, Tommy?' tried Habs.

'Our shipmates.' Tommy said it as though it had been obvious all along. 'Mine from the *Orontes*.' He turned to Joe. 'Yours from the *Eagle*. They're outside, and they want to see the show.'

'Really?' Joe was flabbergasted. 'I assumed they'd rather burn in Hell. Is Mr Roche there, too?'

'No, Mr Hill, he ain't.'

'No, o' course not. Foolish question. How many in line?'

''Bout twelve, I s'pose. And . . .' Tommy flushed with embarrassment once more. 'They seem quite keen to see how I do. Some has been doin' the lines with me, y'see. I might've said they could see the play.' He stared at the floor.

Joe and Habs exchanged glances, Habs shaking his head. 'You know it's Four only now, Tommy. It's not safe to

358

start letting outsiders in. And there ain't no room – where'd they go?'

'I know!' said Tommy. 'I know. I know. I didn't know how to tell 'em. But what can I do now? I can't send 'em away.' He was on the brink of tears.

Habs produced a scrap of cloth from his pocket. 'Take this,' he said. 'Paris can't go on with snot down his shirt.'

Tommy smiled his thanks, dabbed and wiped, then pocketed the cloth.

'Wait,' said Joe, wiping a tear from Tommy's eye. 'First, you only have to deal with your mates from Block Three. I'll deal with the men from the *Eagle*. And that's only if we have to. Because, second, this is for King Dick to decide, no one else. Agreed?'

'But it's so late—'

'Agreed?'

The crier nodded his thanks, and the three of them waited for the King.

'What is it?' he said, as soon as he stepped through the curtain. He noticed the crier's red eyes. 'Mr Jackson?'

Tommy's breaths were coming in ever shorter bursts and, as he tried to tell his story, he started to cough and splutter. The King had seen enough. 'Mr Hill, Mr Snow, will you explain what has upset my Count Paris? We ain't got much time.'

Joe told the King how the men of the *Eagle* and the *Orontes* came to be waiting for admission. The King's eyes never left Tommy. As Joe talked, Tommy squeezed his eyes shut, releasing a river of tears down his face. The King crouched and took both of Tommy's hands in his.

'Mr Jackson. We can't do this play without you. No one can perform *Romeo and Juliet* without Paris. We got to have you here. How many men from Three have come to see you?'

'Just four, sir.'

'And do you know them all? Can you vouch for their good character?'

'I can, sir.'

'And would these tears leave us if we allow your friends in?'

'Yes, sir.' Tommy was smiling now.

'Then it is done. Your first line, Mr Jackson?'

Tommy wiped his nose again. 'Er, it's "Of honourable reckoning are you both, and pity 'tis you lived at odds so long—"'

'Exactly,' said the King. 'Ain't that the truth. Get ready, please, Mr Jackson. Mr Snow, Mr Hill, a word?'

As the crier ran off, Habs could wait no longer. 'Sir, you said only men of Four could attend. How can we protect John Haywood if we don't know who's here? How—'

The King held up his hand. 'Enough. There ain't time. It's a risk, yes, but we need our Paris actin', not sobbin'. Mr Hill, take the crier and some of the *Requin*. Go to this line. Only let in the men of the *Orontes* and the *Eagle*. Men you can vouch for. And make sure they're escorted straight here. Mr Haywood still has his guard.'

There was no time to discuss it further. Habs, clearly unhappy, held on to Joe's arm, his grip firm. 'Just the men you're certain about, Joe, for Chrissake. Of all the crazy—'

Joe cut across him. 'I get it. I agree. Only the *nice* white men.'

Habs did what he could to clear some space. He shouted into the bedlam that some latecomers were on their way and that it was King Dick's idea that they should stand along the wall. Some moved; some didn't; most couldn't.

'This is such a terrible idea,' he said into the thick, smoky air. Some choir members proved malleable, a few even helping in the herding, and one mess out of Charleston

360

took pity on him and forced their way into the crowd. Everyone else just cursed and stayed put.

'Wait till you see who's comin' in,' he muttered to himself.

Two minutes later, Joe, a coat over his dress, led his shipmates from the *Eagle* into the cockloft. Right behind him, a beaming crier walked at the head of his small *Orontes* crew. From the looks of trepidation and wide-eyed astonishment on the men's faces, it was quite clear that most of them had never attended an event here before. They shuffled their way into the space Habs had tried to create and, slowly, the room fell silent.

Joe and Tommy were almost back on stage when the shoving started. It was innocent enough to begin with, fuelled only by a desire to see what was happening in the room, but when the word went round that 'a hundred or more' white sailors had just forced their way in, it became organized and violent. Waves of men staggered towards the new arrivals, pinning them against the wall. The wave then melted away, only to roll back again with even greater force seconds later. Joe and Tommy shot through the curtain to find the King, but the shouts and howls had been loud enough to bring him back to the stage anyway. It took the strongest pounding of his club and the loudest, most piercing tones of his stage voice to quell the storm.

'Enough! Come to order! We must have order!' The King's neck bulged with the force of his projection. 'These men are shipmates of Mr Hill, and Mr Jackson, our crier. There are jus' twelve of them. They are guests in this place and they will be made to feel welcome.'

The swirl of the crowd calmed.

The smallest of gaps appeared, a fault line between the black and white inmates that ran along the side of the cockloft. The *Orontes* and *Eagle* men called out to each other and drew in tighter, unsure of what was coming next. Some men of Four, still suspicious and resentful, glowered at the new-comers; others held out helping hands and murmured apologies.

'Is there peace?' called the King. The muttered and muted affirmations spoke more of a truce than a peace, but it was enough. He had what he needed to work with. 'Is there peace? Do you want a show?' The cry this time was more full-blooded. The King spread his arms wide. 'We have peace, we'll bring you a show!' he called, and by the side of the curtain, Habs, along with everyone else, applauded. King Dick waved his arms for quiet.

'As you know, the Agent and his wife will be here shortly.' Whistles and boos accompanied this announcement, but the King held his hands up again. 'As you can see from our cur-tain, we have prepared a warm American welcome.' He acknowledged the cheers, then peered into the crowd. A few feet from the stage, two high-backed chairs had been placed for the Shortlands, but they had disappeared from view ages ago. The King now waved four *Requin* guards in to evict the occupants, two of whom drunkenly decided to fight.

'Will Shortland really sit there?' wondered Habs out loud. He sounded doubtful.

'The King says he wants to come,' said Joe, shrugging. 'He must've known what it was going to be like.'

From the doors, men started to wave at the King, calling him over.

'Well, we'll find out,' said Habs. 'This'll be him now.'

'My money says the Agent'll take one look at all this and run for his life,' said Joe.

'You ain't had any money since you got here,' said Habs.

5.12

Block Four

2.45 p.m.

KING DICK emerged on to the steps of Four to find Captain and Mrs Shortland waiting for him. They both looked strained and nervous but managed courteous smiles.

'Mr Crafus,' said Shortland, nodding.

'Captain Shortland. Mrs Shortland,' said the King. 'You came. I was wonderin' if you might go and change your mind.' Behind them, Lieutenant Aveline and a score of redcoats bristled at the indignity of it all. 'Lieutenant,' said the King. 'You missed the coffee and the spaces, I'm 'fraid. There ain't no room for you now. The house is full, but we got your seats reserved, Captain and Mrs Shortland.'

The Agent looked briefly at Aveline, then back to the King. 'You guaranteed our safety here but, after what happened to my wife, I will need more than that. My guard commander will be in charge.'

'Your guard commander was nowhere when your wife needed rescuin',' said the King. 'None of your troops were. King Dick, on the other hand . . .'

'I am aware that I owe you my thanks,' said Shortland. 'Elizabeth has told me what happened. But even so, you cannot expect me to enter one of my prisons without a guard.'

Before the King could answer, Elizabeth stepped forward. 'I never had the chance to thank you myself, Mr Crafus,' she said, offering her hand.

'We don't like Cobb here,' said the King, taking it. 'We don't like the Rough Allies, and we don't behave like 'em neither. You'll be safe in Four.'

'And how many weapons would you say are in the cockloft right now,' asked Elizabeth, 'knowing sailors like you do? Many hundreds would be my guess.' She cocked an ear to the riotous singing from the cockloft and pressed on, sensing he was off guard. 'And how much ale and grog is being drunk right now? Many gallons, I'd assume. So you see why my husband and I wish to seek further protection, beyond your word.'

'You may walk away, if you wish, Mrs Shortland,' said the King. 'You have not come to our other productions, there is no reason for you or your husband to attend this one.'

Shortland looked exasperated. 'Damn you, Crafus, is there no compromise you will accept? I could have marched the whole bloody barracks in here to see the show, if I'd wanted. We just want to be safe – is that really too much to ask?'

The King held up his hand. 'If I let you in, it gotta be on my terms or I lose the block. If I lose the block, you lose the prison. So. Your lieutenant can join you, if you wish, but tha's all.'

'I want a crew of men by the cockloft door.'

'You can have your *lieutenant* by the door,' said the King, 'if tha's where you choose to deploy him. The rest can wait here. If you need 'em, they'll be jus' seconds away.' He could see Aveline was about to protest, so he added, 'And the curtain goes up in a matter of minutes. Please, let me escort you.'

The Shortlands hesitated, then it was Elizabeth who moved first. 'I have heard about your play from young Mr Hill,' she said, walking through the door. 'And I declare I have never in all my life seen *Romeo and Juliet*. How very strange that I should see it here.'

The King allowed Captain Shortland and his guard

commander to follow on, then overtook them all on the stairs. As he led the way up the final flight, the noise of singing barrelled down to meet them. Elizabeth shrank back a little, Shortland walked taller, Aveline kept his hand on his sword. They all stared ahead to the doors of the cockloft.

At the top landing, the King waited for his moment, biding his time until there was a lull in the singing. He gave his club a few more practice swings, then kicked at the door. The King walked in, shouting.

'Make way, brothers! Make way! Clear a path!' He swung the club, catching a slow-moving cook from Baltimore full in the face. On the swing back, he caught one of the block's barbers in the neck. The singing had fallen away swiftly, so many heard the nose break and the yelps of pain. In the line between the King and the chairs, men scrambled away as far as the crowd permitted.

Behind the King, the Shortlands and Aveline scurried to keep up. When they reached the chairs, they found an inebriated inmate lying face down across the arms of both. The King hailed him. 'So, Benjamin Scarisbrick, you in need o' sleep?' He grabbed one ankle and suspended the man in front of him. The startled sailor woke with a jump and began wriggling like a fish on the end of a line. Laughing bystanders – including the Shortlands – watched him trying to work out why King Dick was suddenly upside down. 'Mr Scarisbrick, it's showtime.' The King was now swinging the unfortunate sailor like a pendulum. 'We are about to perform one of Shakespeare's greatest plays, *Romeo and Juliet*. The Agent and his wife are in attendance, the whole block's here, even some men from the other blocks here.' The man vomited into his own hair. 'Today,' continued the King, 'will be remembered by all who witness our tragedy. But not by you.' The King marched him back through the crowd to the cockloft doors, and tossed him out, his howls and yelps as he fell down the stairs audible to all.

'Bravo!' muttered Shortland in admiration.

The King strode back, inviting the Shortlands to take their seats. 'They were stage thrones left by the French. We used 'em in *Othello*, but we don't need 'em for *Romeo and Juliet*. Please . . . and, Lieutenant, you can stand behind the chairs. You won't see the play, but you'll be close enough.'

Aveline stepped behind the thrones, and the Shortlands sat tentatively, glancing at the many hundreds who were standing around them. Captain Shortland tried nodding politely at a few of the closest but received only glares in return. Elizabeth fared slightly better, a few of her patients acknowledging her but then looking away. She heard her husband snort and, following his eyeline, noticed the curtain for the first time.

'This is an outrage!' he blustered. She could see him twitch in anger. 'Crafus! What is the meaning of this propaganda? You expect me, a captain in the King's Navy, to sit here, looking at all your ballyhoo?' His obvious discomfort was met with laughter by the nearest inmates.

''S'jus' a curtain,' said the King. 'A curtain made o' flags . . .'

'A curtain made of insults, more like,' huffed Shortland.

'Though more courteous than some I have seen,' said Elizabeth, smiling. 'If I were you, Mr Crafus, I'd start the show as soon as possible.'

She watched him walk to the stage and just caught the sight of Magrath slipping through the doors. He walked without trouble to the rear of the cockloft, the men parting to allow him passage. As he disappeared from her view, she turned her gaze back to the stage. Thunderous applause greeted the removal of the curtain. The streets of Verona were running through Dartmoor.

The play was on.

Habs was suddenly terrified. Awash with nerves, he rested a sweaty hand on Joe's shoulder. Joe glanced round, tried to smile, but he, too, was struggling; Habs felt his body trembling. Sam and Lord, wide-eyed and poised like runners, glanced over as Habs mouthed a 'good luck'. All the cast watched as four of the *Requin* men – two black Montagues and two with painted white Capulet faces – began insulting each other. The crowd took to it immediately.

'Sam's next,' he whispered.

As the quarrel between the men of Capulet and Montague escalated, Sam made his entrance. Many in the crowd cheered him, his *Bentham* crew leading the way. His first line – 'Part, fools! Put up your swords!' – brought Jon Lord to the stage. Now the *Eagle* crew noisily cheered their man and, when Benvolio and Tybalt started their sword fight, the shoving began again. Up and down the fault line, small scuffles broke out. As the wooden stage swords were drawn, angry, intoxicated men started to flail at each other. From the stage, they heard the words, 'Strike! Beat them down!' and decided to do just that.

The actors hesitated, unsure of whether to continue. In front of them, the Shortlands were still seated but craning their necks to see what was happening. Aveline, hand still resting on his sword, looked ready for a duel. Captain Shortland attempted to stand, but his lieutenant held him back. The King, now in Mercutio's uniform, burst from the stage. His club made short work of the first fighting group he came to, four men receiving blows to the head and chest. Blood streaming through their hair, they staggered for the cockloft door. One of the men from Three remonstrated with the King; lifted by his sideburns until he was at eye level, he swiftly and painfully apologized for his poor judgement.

The skirmish dealt with, King Dick stayed in the crowd.

'Proceed!' he called. 'Montague, Pastor. Your line, I believe.'

5.13

Block Six

3 p.m.

Horace Cobb's new army, now many hundred strong, was having to be very patient. They had rolled from Six a few minutes before three o'clock, jostling, play-fighting, singing. Balls were hurled and kicked between the men, most of them sailing over the retaining wall and into the market square. They watched from afar as the Agent, his redcoats and King Dick seemed to be involved in a stand-off on the steps of Four. When that seemed to have been resolved and the Agent had gone inside, his troop marched back to the market square gates. There, they waited.

Frustrated lines of inmates buzzed around. Escape was now in their blood and the inactivity was driving them crazy.

'Sweet Mary and Jesus,' said Cobb, sitting on the steps. 'We can hardly break out if half the British army are watching.'

'What are they waitin' for?' said Lane. 'The play's two hours long, at least. They can't be waitin' there all that time.'

'We could start the game, but there don't seem much point if we can't . . . finish it.' Cobb stroked and separated his beard as he watched the British soldiers. 'I'd thought about getting caught, thought about getting shot, too, but I never thought of this – this . . . waiting.' He kicked at the ground in frustration. 'We're all greased up, Mr Lane, ready for battle, but we got nowhere to run.'

A roar of laughter and applause erupted from Block Four and both men glanced along the courtyard.

'An idea, Mr Cobb,' said Lane, still staring at Four.

'Go on.'

'The play sounds like it's goin' well.'

'It does,' conceded Cobb.

'Must be quite a pull if you're inside Four.'

'What's your point, Mr Lane?'

'You see a guard outside their block? Or in the doorway? Anywhere?'

'No.' Cobb drew the word out as he began to realize what Lane was thinking.

'If they got a tunnel, now might be a good time to find out. My bet is, ain't no blackjacks downstairs at all.'

'Unless they're escapin'.'

'And if they are, shouldn't we know 'bout it?'

They sat in silence. The would-be escapers from Six and Seven were still play-fighting, singing shanties or insulting the British. Across the yard, the men of One were cooking on an old stove; others were throwing balls off the roof and catching them.

'We should know,' decided Cobb. 'Of course we should know.'

369

5.14

Block Four

ROMEO'S FIRST appearance was applauded; his first line – 'Is the day so young?' – cheered. His discussion with Benvolio about love was greeted with much hilarity; when he reached the line, 'In sadness, cousin, I do love a woman,' many voices called back, 'No, you don't!' and 'Liar!' Juliet's first appearance received the expected whistles but, along-side the rotund and embarrassed Goffe making his debut as Nurse, Joe was all poise and delicate grace.

When Nurse said, 'Go, girl, seek happy nights to happy days,' they left the stage to rapturous applause. By the time King Dick entered the stage as Mercutio, the mood in the cockloft had changed – the play was working. The fights of the opening scene had calmed, a truce engineered by comedy, intrigue and the promise of doomed love.

Backstage, Joe and Habs drank swiftly from a water jug.

'They're lovin' it!' said Habs.

'I was watching the Shortlands when you were on with the King,' whispered Joe. 'Slightly less miserable, I thought.'

'Kiss next, then.'

'Imagine. The whole place'd go crazy.' He knew Habs was joking but made his point anyway. 'Nothing stupid, Habs. You know it's not worth it.'

'Ain't it?'

'Not if I kick you in the balls, it isn't.'

*

Joe felt sure that Habs would never disobey the King, especially now, especially here. He walked on stage with Lord and Goffe and some of the *Requin* extras. Two fiddlers stood at the side of the stage and began playing a reel, 'The Female Cabin Boy'. Some of the crowd recognized the tune, laughing and clapping in delight at the joke. On stage, Joe stepped and weaved with the others, everyone making it up as they went along.

The dance over, Romeo spotted Juliet and the crowd started to buzz. When he asked, 'What lady's that?' a few even applauded. A shiver of dangerous expectation ran through the cockloft. The players felt it, too, all eyes switching between Habs and Joe then back again. When Romeo finally approached Juliet's bench, there was a shout of, 'Aye-aye! Here we go!' before the man was roundly shushed. Joe saw that Habs was enjoying himself; his nerves had gone, the audience was his and there was a swagger to his performance that Joe hadn't seen before. He sensed danger. He knew that when Habs's blood was up, anything was possible. He noticed Elizabeth Shortland staring at him, eyebrow raised. Joe thought he understood. If the play was to get to its end, Juliet would need to be in charge of their imminent first encounter.

Habs finally sat next to Joe, and the cockloft held its breath. Fixing him with a glare, Joe swung his legs to form a barrier between them. He wanted to scream, 'This is a statement, not a challenge!' but hoped his body language would do that for him. Habs grinned, flattened some out-of-control curls behind his ear and took Joe's hand in his. An audible gasp from some in the crowd lit the fuse.

Romeo spoke. 'If I profane with my unworthiest hand, this holy shrine, the gentle sin is this. My lips, my two blushing pilgrims, ready stand, to smooth that rough touch with a tender kiss.'

Joe, eyes on Habs, slowly and deliberately shook his head. Then Juliet spoke.

'Good pilgrim, you do wrong your hand too much, which mannerly devotion shows in this. For saints have hands that pilgrims' hands do touch, and palm to palm is holy palmers' kiss.'

The cockloft fell silent. They all knew – they had all heard the stories – that in rehearsal a black Romeo had kissed a white Juliet. That it wasn't a prim little peck on the cheek but a full-blooded, open-mouthed embrace, and that the Agent had banned it. They knew all that, yet here were the two men, one black, one white, speaking of nothing else. Lips, hands, holy oil, touching. It was manifest to all that the fuse was still burning.

Joe noticed Captain Shortland shift awkwardly in his seat, saw the King strain for a better view; he cast his eyes to the floor.

Juliet again. 'Saints do not move, though grant for prayers' sake.' Joe tensed. Every nerve, every fibre, was alive to the dangers of the moment. Unwanted, the memory of that first, thrilling kiss returned and Joe dug his nails into his palms to clear it.

Romeo again. 'Then move not while my prayer's effect I take.'

The men in the cockloft held their breath. Joe and Habs stared at each other, their faces frozen. As Habs began to lean closer, Joe pushed their still-held hands in front of Habs's mouth. A flicker of a smile, and Habs kissed Joe's hand. The collective release of breath was so loud it generated its own embarrassed laughter, drowning out Romeo's 'Thus from my lips, by thine my sin is purged.' When the second kiss was due, Joe again blocked with his hand and the fuse was out. The applause to mark the end of Act One was deafening. In the brief respite, Habs waited for Joe, his eyes dancing with delight.

'You really thought I'd do it, didn't you? And in front of Shortland!'

'Tell me you weren't tempted,' said Joe, unconvinced. 'I saw it in your eyes, Habakkuk Snow.'

'A trespass sweetly urged,' said Habs.

'And sweetly denied,' said Joe.

The King strode over, his expression sombre. Habs raised his hands in mock surrender. 'I know what it looked like, King Dick, but, really, I was just teasin'. I would never go against—'

'That ain't what I saw, Mr Snow,' said the King, cutting across him. 'I saw Mr Hill here rescue a dangerous situation with great cunning – thank you, Mr Hill.' The King looked around. 'John Haywood here yet? He's missin' a fine show. I'm tempted to go down there myself, persuade him to attend.'

'I think maybe you're needed here,' said Joe. 'I'm sure he'll be up shortly.'

5.15

Block Six

3.40 p.m.

Back in the darkness and quiet of his own block, Lane forced himself to be still. Reckless speed now would be catastrophic. He placed the pistol and the cartridges on his hammock. He'd kept everything as dry as he could, folding the cartridges into a small piece of cloth and placing them in a metal tin. He'd kept the gun with him, kept it warm, kept it shielded from the prison damp. The cartridges felt dry, the gun felt dry, but there was no proof without firing. With a quick glance around, he picked up the pistol, unclipped its ramrod from under the barrel and pulled the cock to the half-cock position. The loading mechanism was sound. He ran his finger over the flint, the frizzen and the flash pan, then pulled the trigger. It snapped into action, the cock hitting the frizzen and then the pan. There would be two puffs of smoke – one from the pan, one from the barrel – then the deafening crack of the gunpowder igniting and the sharp recoil from the blast.

The cartridges looked the same. Maybe one was slightly discoloured, the paper surrounding the bullet and powder beginning to yellow, but it was nothing serious. He had six good shots. He reached for the nearest and, placing it in his teeth, tore off the top. With the gun again at half-cock, he poured some of the cartridge's powder into the pan then closed it. Holding the pistol vertically, he poured the rest of the powder down the barrel, spilling a few grains on his trousers in the process. Cursing quietly, he shoved the cartridge into the barrel, then used the ramrod to force it and the powder all the way down to the breech. His gun was loaded. He felt the weight of it in his hand and unwound a slow smile. There was a smell to a loaded pistol, and he breathed it deeply. Charcoal from the powder, oils, wood and steamy sulphur from the gun; gooseflesh ran over his arms and neck. He was ready to play.

The English were still encamped by the gates, so he resumed studying the entrance of Four. Both doors appeared closed, but a deep shadow running down the middle suggested a partial opening. Though hundreds walked around and between the blocks, Lane saw no one arrive or leave Block Four. Many turned their heads as another wave of applause or shouting leaked from the cockloft, but still no one tried to enter.

'You want some freco, mister?' asked one of the boys from Five, appearing over Lane's shoulder. 'Cheapest in the yard.'

'I doubt that,' said Lane, and walked from the steps. He crossed the thirty yards to Four and, with only the briefest of hesitations, slipped inside. In the darkness of the hallway, Lane palmed the shank from his boot then slid it into his sleeve. He listened hard. Upstairs, the noise from the play was overwhelming but, in time, he caught other sounds: movement and conversation on the stairs and upper landing, singing in some hammocks above him, vomiting from the heads nearby. The sick man left, then re-entered the toilet, vomited some more, before walking unsteadily back up the stairs.

Lane edged his way into the dormitory. Its layout was the same as in Six. Four rows of hammocks tied as high as the stanchions and human nerves would permit. Great heaps of clothes, bottles, plates and cups lay in each of the aisles; playing cards and backgammon sets had been left deserted on the mess tables. It was the kitchens at the far end that Lane needed to reach. If any tunnel existed, that was where it would be disguised. The tunnels Shortland had discovered in

Five and Six had both started in the store cupboards between the enormous stoves and sinks. It would be the work of seconds to determine if the Negroes had done the same.

Mess by deserted mess, Lane crept towards the kitchens. Not all the hammocks were empty: he saw – and heard – many sleeping sailors too intoxicated to get to the play; none of them stirred. Then, conversation. Two, maybe three, voices. Lane froze, stepping instinctively behind the nearest stanchion. He was close enough to know they were coming from the kitchen, but all the words were lost in the architecture and echo of the room. He tightened his grip on the shank; felt, too, for the pistol. Still there, still armed. He walked closer. It didn't sound like the breathless, exhausted talk of diggers, of frantic men seizing their last opportunity to escape. On the contrary, the words – still unclear – were lazy, the to-and-fro more like the work of men reminiscing over a bottle of brandy. One voice was becoming clearer – he seemed to be the main conversationalist – another seemed as indistinct as ever. One more mess before the kitchen. He stepped behind what had once been the block's end wall and strained to catch the exchanges.

'It'd drive me crazy,' said the clearer voice. 'Seems like such a waste.' This produced another smothered reply. Lane frowned. Maybe there were other men, deeper in the tunnel, and these were just the sentries.

Silence. Then footsteps moved towards him. A cough, a swig from a bottle and a belch. 'I'll get it, then,' said the clear voice. The man sidled from the kitchen and walked straight into Lane. He was stocky, shorter than Lane and bald. When he recoiled from his collision he dropped a bottle, which smashed, spraying their feet with beer and broken glass. Lane reacted first, slamming him against the wall, one hand pressed firmly against his mouth, the other holding the shank to his neck.

'You got a tunnel, nigger?'

5.16

Block Four, Cockloft

4.10 p.m.

KING DICK tapped his feet impatiently. He had, in rehearsal, urged Habs to slow down, to take more care with his lines, but now that very precision was driving him to distraction. On stage, Romeo was taking his leave of Juliet, banished after his killing of Tybalt.

'Farewell! I will omit no opportunity that may convey my greetings, love, to thee.'

'Yes, yes,' muttered the King. 'Now hurry up and get banished.' He caught Habs's eye and gestured that he should move things on.

'Dry sorrow drinks our blood,' said Romeo, conspicuously faster. 'Adieu, adieu!' he cried, and ran from the stage. 'What is it, King Dick? What's happened?'

'Nothin', probably,' said the King, 'but John Haywood ain't here yet. He said he'd miss the beginnin', not the whole show. You're not on again in Act Three or the whole of Act Four, and he trusts you, Mr Snow. He likes you.'

Habs didn't like where this was heading. With a head full of lines and stage directions, the only place he needed to be was precisely where he was. But the King hadn't finished.

'Mr Haywood talks to everyone, but he listens to you. I want you to run down to the kitchens and instruct him.' Habs's eyes betrayed him. He would never question a direct

377

instruction, but the King saw his annoyance anyway. His large black eyes narrowed. 'It is two minutes' work, Mr Snow, and you are not on for twenty. Swiftly, please.'

Habs snatched a glance at Joe and Goffe on stage, nodded at the King, then ran.

Habs moved without thought, ran without sight. His body might have been descending the stairs, but his head was already back on the stage. Act Five began with him and him alone. The words had already begun to run in his head when he heard a bottle smash. He stopped abruptly, pulled from his daydream. To begin with, he wasn't sure why he had pulled up. It wasn't the glass breaking – God knows, there had been plenty of that in the cockloft. It was another sound, one that had followed the dropped bottle – a sound that had alerted him to danger. After the smash there'd been an extra beat, Habs was sure of it now, and it had been enough to stop him in his tracks. He squeezed his eyes shut, trying to recall the last few seconds. Gooseflesh crawled over his neck and arms. What sound, buried deep in a sailor's soul, could trigger this? The slow unsheathing of a blade, the cocking of a rifle. At sea, the sudden, whipped tightening of the bolt rope usually meant trouble, but it couldn't be that. Eager to be on his way but unwilling to ignore what his body was telling him, Habs hesitated. And then he had it.

Skull on brick. It was a sound he'd been familiar with all his life.

5.17

Block Four, Kitchens

JOHN HAYWOOD'S guard, a young seaman out of Concord, New Hampshire, named Cole, recognized Lane the instant he walked into him. The scarred skin, the high voice, the forked beard was some of it. The reputation for casual violence and hatred of blacks was the rest. Lane's mouth tightened as he watched the fear bloom in the man under his knife.

He had dragged him around the wall, into the kitchen and away from any casual passers-by. 'You know me, slave?' he whispered.

Cole nodded. Lane held the shank in front of the man's terrified eyes.

'You know what I do with this? I kill people like you if they give me a reason. An excuse. So listen carefully. You gonna get a question once – I ain't got much time. You make a mistake you end up like ol' Ned Penny. Am I clear?' The mention of Ned's name made the guard whimper. Lane leered. 'Oh, you knew him, then? Such a small world in here. So you'll know the answer to my question. You ready?' More nodding.

'Is there a tunnel?'

The guard swallowed twice. 'Yes.'

Lane was triumphant, his face contorting with pleasure. With difficulty, he controlled his excitement. 'It's bein' used now, ain't it? While the play is runnin', you got men 'scapin'. Well, we gonna join your party, boy.'

But Cole was shaking his head. 'No one 'scapin',' he said, his hands gripping the sides of his jacket. 'There's no one, really, in there now.'

Lane's eyes closed as the tip of his shank cut into Cole's neck. 'Tell me that again, slave,' he whispered. 'I jus' need to be clear. You're sayin' there ain't no one in the tunnel? That right?'

Cole said nothing. He tried to pull his head away from the blade, but Lane kept it close to his flesh. 'Y'see, I heard two voices,' said Lane. 'Two voices from right in here. So, unless it was the Devil Himself I heard you talking to, your nigger tunnel is in use.' He placed one hand against Cole's mouth and, with the other, pulled the shank sideways, opening a one-inch cut in Cole's neck, blood running along the blade and on to the handle. The guard's smothered howl delighted Lane. 'For every lie you tell me, slave, I cut you. So. Is your tunnel in use, yes or no?' Lane removed his hand from Cole's mouth.

'Yes, but not—' began Cole, but then Lane's hand slapped back again.

'Spare me the detail,' he spat. 'It's in use – that's it. How many men have escaped?' The hand came away again and Cole swallowed hard.

'None,' he said.

'How many are in there tryin' to 'scape?' Lane tried.

Cole looked conflicted. 'Honest answer is none, Mr Lane. Truly there ain't. No one's 'scapin' here.' He squeezed his eyes shut, waiting for the knife. He felt its edge pressed hard against the cut.

'Where is it? Where's the tunnel?'

'Store cupboard. Behind the boards, but like I was sayin'—'

'Tell me what I'll find there, slave. If you lie to me, I'll slice you open like a pig. Tell me now.'

Cole fixed Lane with an impassioned stare. He spoke as

380

clearly as his fear allowed. 'You'll find jus' one man in fifteen feet o' tunnel.'

Lane frowned. 'One? One man?'

Cole nodded.

'And fifteen feet? Just fifteen feet o' tunnel?'

Cole nodded again.

'Well, that ain't goin' nowhere,' said Lane, considering Cole's words. 'So what in God's name are you doin' here?'

'He's sick.'

'Sick and in a tunnel? Why's he not at the hospital?'

Cole stared at the floor, and Lane suddenly knew the answer.

''Cos he's hidin',' he said softly. Cole stared at his feet. 'And if you got someone hidin' . . .' Lane grabbed him by the collar, the knife still hard against Cole's neck. 'Show me!' he ordered.

Cole peeled himself from the wall and staggered the few steps to the second storage cupboard.

'Open it.'

Cole pulled at the double doors and they swung towards him. Shelves and produce lay discarded on the floor. Six of the wooden back panels had been removed, the dark opening of a tunnel dug into its centre. The smell of damp earth seeped into the kitchen. Lane whistled. Crouching down, he picked up a handful of potatoes. 'I'm imaginin',' he said, 'that I'm at the fair, and all I have to do to win the prize is get one of these into that hole there.' He turned to Cole. 'Whaddya think, slave, reckon I'll win a prize?'

'Mr Lane—' began Cole.

'Shut up, I'm tryin' to listen.'

'Mr Lane,' persisted Cole, and Lane slashed out, catching the guard across the stomach. The shank cut through his prison jacket and vest, slicing into his stomach. Cole gasped as he fell against the doors, hands held over his wound.

'I told you I was listenin'.' Lane spoke as though nothing

had happened. 'You hear that? Maybe you got mice and rats down there. You need to do somethin' 'bout that. We don't have this problem back in Six, y'see. This seems to be jus' a Negro problem. Listen.'

From below ground there was a cough, then the sound of hawking and spitting. Slowly, a figure appeared in the tunnel. A high forehead, receding black hair, hollow, terrified eyes.

'Now,' said Lane, pointing with his shank, 'I reckon I seen this vermin before.' His voice grew softer, his lips now barely moving. 'I was told you'd gone to hospital, but it seems you been right here all along. Now you stay right there.' Lane reached for his jacket pocket. 'I always known there's only one way to deal with vermin.'

5.18

Block Four, Ground-floor Hallway

Habs stood motionless, his Act Five lines slipping fast from his mind. He heard the sounds from the cockloft, but he was straining for sounds from the kitchen. He knew it was John – it could only be John. He ran into the dormitory, then made himself check and pull back. A four-high stack of hammocks by the door provided him with immediate cover, and he peered between the hemp and canvas. There was nothing to see, but there was plenty to hear. The voices were quiet, but one was carrying just fine – Habs would recognize Edwin Lane's shrill, girl-high voice anywhere.

He had no time to run for help. Skin crawling, heart thumping, he walked with as much speed as he dared towards the kitchen. He bent to pick up a discarded grog bottle, holding it tight in his fist. Every step clarified Lane's voice. The game was up. John Haywood had been found, recognized and was now in grave danger.

Twenty yards away, partially obscured by the cupboard doors, Lane was crouching on the ground, looking into the tunnel. Habs glanced around the kitchen, knowing there would be better weapons than his bottle not far away. But any detour could well bring discovery, and there wasn't the time to risk failure. He stepped closer, then froze as the guard, hands against his stomach, collapsed against the open doors. Blood seeped between his fingers. 'Sweet Christ alive,' muttered Habs. He recognized the man now – John Cole was in the mess across the way from him – and he fought back the urge to charge at Lane. He has a gun, I got an empty bottle, he thought. Habs wiped the sweat from his palms, adjusted his grip on the bottle and resumed his approach.

He could still hear Lane talking, but his voice had gone much quieter now and all the words were lost. So when Lane's right hand pulled the pistol from his pocket, Habs knew that the battle had started.

He covered the remaining ground in four arcing steps. As Lane raised his gun, Habs brought the bottle down on to his head with every ounce of force he possessed. He felt the glass shatter and its hilt catch on Lane's skull. Before Lane fell, Habs hit him with the jagged shards again, this time slashing a deep groove into his scarred cheek. Lane howled with pain, surprise and pure fury. His blood ran fast. By the time Lane realized he had dropped the gun, he could barely see. Frantically wiping his eyes with his sleeve, he could just make out John Haywood reaching from the tunnel and grabbing the barrel. Lane launched himself at Haywood, landing on top of him. He struck out wildly, landing blow after blow on the lamplighter. It was only the click of the pistol going to full cock that made him stop.

Haywood had managed to throw the gun free before Lane descended; by a miracle, Habs had caught it. He knew the rules, knew you didn't throw pistols around without serious risk of killing yourself. He had almost fumbled it, trying to avoid the firing mechanism, but his two hands gave the gun a gentle landing. Now it was aimed at Lane's head. Habs's eyes flicked between the gun in his hands and the man in his sights and Lane saw his uncertainty.

'Nothin' in it,' he said. 'Ain't even loaded.'

'I'll take that chance,' said Habs, feeling the weight of the gun in his hands. 'I'll take the chance that, when you got hold o' this gun in the market, you traded for cartridges also. And that when you came huntin' for coloured men, you came

384

armed and ready to fight.' He raised the gun, and Lane fell back. 'My point exactly.'

He had fired a pistol in the action that saw the *Bentham* taken two years ago, but that had been into the melee of battle. He wasn't even sure he'd hit anyone. He had never fired one at close quarters, and Lane seemed very close indeed.

He glanced at Cole, who had his eyes closed, bloodied hands still held against his stomach. 'You bad?' he asked.

'I'll be fine,' he whispered. 'I'm jus' sorry I didn't see—'

'Hush,' said Habs. 'We'll get you bandaged up. Jus' hold on.' He focused on Lane, holding the gun steady. 'You won't make it to the hospital. The cachot, then the hangman's noose, will suit you fine.'

He called into the tunnel. 'You recognize this man, John?' Haywood had ducked back into the tunnel but now he slowly emerged, hands over his face. He opened his fingers enough to stare at Lane and nodded. 'That the third shadow?' asked Habs. Haywood nodded again. 'Guilty,' said Habs. *'Murderer.'*

Lane wiped more blood from his face. 'You ain't the judge. And your friend here is sick and ranting like a madman. Wretched boy, can you not hear that? No one'll listen to him.'

Habs swallowed hard. He wanted to run for help, to get the doctor for Cole and to have Lane arrested, but all that would have to wait. He felt a cold fury take him.

'You call me boy?' he said, his hands tightening around the pistol.

Lane shrugged.

'Did you call me boy?'

'Wretched boy,' corrected Lane. 'It's in the play you made me read. And that is what you are. 'S'jus' a statement of fact.'

'Your facts, Lane, not mine.'

'God's facts, Mr Snow. God's natural order. No judge will hang me. It's niggers that swing. My story will out.'

Habs lined Lane up in the gun's sights.

Then footsteps. A tapping stick. They all heard it, all knew who was coming.

'In here, Dr Magrath!' Habs turned his head to angle his voice better, and Lane's fingers found the knife again, wrapping themselves around the hilt. Habs called a second time, but his sentence was hardly formed before Lane, shank high, flew at him.

5.19

Outside Block Seven

4.35 p.m.

THE REDCOATS had finally moved from the gates. Under a barrage of further insults, they had retired to the safety of the market square. With the gates locked and the Allies out of view, some propped their guns against the wall, kicking the lost balls between them. Stifling their cheers, the would-be escapers had at last been able to resume their game against the wall. But without Lane, and without Lane's gun, they were just going through the motions. It was the gun that redressed the odds, only the gun that gave them any chance of reaching the armoury.

Pent up since dawn, the men of Six and Seven took to the wall – and each other – with ferocity. Two deputations of Allies had approached Cobb, wanting to begin their excavation. Both had been sent away.

'Come on, Lane, where are you?' he muttered, staring at the doors of Four. 'The Brits are gone, we want to be going.' Running feet behind him, another delegation. He turned briskly.

Joseph Toker Johnson from Seven, and four Allies this time, all new recruits. Toker Johnson was agitated but held eye contact.

'What is it?' asked Cobb.

'Beggin' your pardon, sir, but can we go knifin' the wall

yet? It looks like it's maybe goin' to be thirty minutes before we're through, so we could start now?'

'You could start now, yes,' said Cobb, his tone studiously neutral. 'But is Mr Lane back? D'you see him anywhere?'

'No, sir,' said Toker, 'but the play might be done soon.'

'Well, Mr Toker Johnson, when the order comes to break through the wall, I'll make sure you get your turn with the knife. Until then, you wait for my word.'

Toker Johnson, unperturbed, had another question. 'How long will you give him, sir, 'cos if we don't start—'

Cobb hit him so hard he fell cold, three feet from his friends.

'When he comes round,' said Cobb, 'tell him – and anyone else who might need to know – that we go when I say and not a moment before.' Cobb turned back to look at the steps of Four.

He found his empty, cold pipe and placed it between his teeth. More applause from the cockloft of Four rolled across the courtyard. 'Need you now, Lane. Need you right now.'

5.20

Block Four, Cockloft

KING DICK had always been clear about it: Act Four is Juliet's. With Romeo in exile, the stage is hers. The Friar has given her the mixture she needs; now, she needs to 'die'. This was Joe's moment. In the thirty seconds he had before Juliet was back on stage, the King explained to Joe why Habs had run off. Joe nodded his understanding. He didn't have time to worry. Juliet had to mourn Tybalt's death, agree to marry Paris, then drink the mixture to fake her death.

On stage, Joe said his lines, moved, reacted and responded, but as the act played out he was aware of the King's ever more agitated demeanour. From most places on the stage, Joe could see him: he'd watch for a few lines then turn and look at the backstage door. He would then watch for a few more lines, the worry etching deeper on to his brow. On more than one occasion Joe came close to missing his cue. Tommy, as Paris, was starting to look concerned.

Ignore the King. Just act. Habs is fine.

It was Tommy's favourite scene. Paris gets to say he loves Juliet, announce their wedding, then leave with a 'holy kiss'. Tommy, blushing deeply, kissed Joe on his cheek then ran from the stage. Alone now, Joe found he was delivering his words to the places where Habs might appear. These were his big scenes, Juliet's tumultuous decisions, but his heart was elsewhere.

One final speech, Juliet's longest. 'Farewell! God knows when we shall meet again.' Now Joe turned to the crowd and spoke of hidden love. He felt nothing but panic and dread, but he knew the speech and did it well. When he reached for the Friar's potion, the crowd fell silent.

> 'Oh, look! Methinks I see my cousin's ghost
> Seeking out Romeo, thou did spit his body
> Upon a rapier's point. Stay, Tybalt! Stay!
> Romeo, Romeo, Romeo.
> Here's drink. I drink to thee.'

Joe drank its contents – water, after all – and collapsed. There was an intake of breath from some, applause from others. Joe had fallen, sprawled across a bed. The audience saw Juliet in a drug-induced sleep; the actors backstage saw Joe – eyes wide open – anxiously watching for Habs.

5.21

Block Four, Kitchens

LANE'S BLADE buried itself in Habs's shoulder. The force of the lunge toppled them both and, as they hit the floor, Habs pulled the trigger. At point-blank range, the bullet tore through Lane's body, blowing half his stomach on to the floor. Habs felt Lane bounce on his stomach then lie still, his blood drenching him in seconds. Grey, sooty smoke filled his vision; a fierce ringing filled his ears.

'Sweet Jesus. Sweet Jesus. Sweet Holy Jesus.' Habs pushed Lane's body away. It rolled once and lay face down.

Habs's breathing was coming in short, rasping gulps. 'Christ, what have I done?' he breathed. He scrambled to his feet, then walked to Lane's body and back again; back and forth, a hand over his mouth.

'I saw everything!' said Cole, trying and failing to get up.

'But you're black, you won't count!'

'Haywood saw it all, too.' They both glanced at the tunnel. Haywood had disappeared again.

'He's black *and* crazy,' said Habs, panic settling deep in the pit of his stomach.

The shuffling figure of George Magrath appeared in the kitchen, his stick working hard to move him as swiftly as he desired. Greeted by the horror show of a bloodied Habs, a still-bleeding Cole and the wrecked body of Lane, he staggered to a stop.

'Dear God, what has happened here?'

Habs, now shaking from head to toe and bleeding from

his shoulder wound, started to approach Magrath. It was only when the doctor retreated, horrified, that Habs realized he was still holding the pistol.

'No, Doctor!' he cried. 'He attacked me, I was . . .' He dropped the gun and felt his head spinning. The pain from his shoulder pulsed strongly through his body. He could barely think, never mind speak. He had killed a man. He was a murderer. Worse. He was a black man who had killed a white man. The worst kind of murderer, the most guilty kind of murderer. What had Lane said? 'It's niggers that swing.'

Magrath was crouched over Lane's body, his fingers holding the dead man's wrist briefly, as much instinct as professionalism. There was a hole in the man's back the size of a grapefruit. He moved on to Cole, pulling gently at his bloodied shirt.

'Lane killed Ned Penny,' said Habs. 'He came lookin' for a tunnel, but he found John Haywood. He was about to kill him, too.'

'You had a gun?' Magrath was incredulous.

'No, *he* had a gun. He was 'bout to shoot John. I hit him with a bottle, then we fought and—'

'You blew his stomach away.'

Habs stood with his eyes screwed tight and his hands balled into fists. How was it possible to feel numb and on fire at the same time? He needed to run; he needed to stay. He needed to say nothing; he needed to explain everything. He needed to see Joe; he would never see him again.

'Yes, I – I did. We fell and—'

'You blew his stomach away.'

'I fired, yes.'

In the kitchens, there was silence as the doctor knelt by the stricken Cole. In Habs's head there was a riot of noise. He missed the distant cockloft applause and Magrath's soft words of comfort to his patient. It was pain that brought him round.

'Show me,' said Magrath. Habs knelt down and eased his shirt from his shoulder, wincing as the fabric snagged on the open wound. Magrath leaned in close, his fingers pressing gently around the cut. From his medical bag he produced a roll of lint, cutting off a large square.

'Hold this to it. The knife went deep, but you've had worse.' He looked into Habs's agonized eyes. 'You're a good man, Mr Snow, but you are in trouble here, I cannot pretend otherwise. You have killed a man in one of His Majesty's prisons. Whether it is English law or Navy law, they will see you swing for it – if you are taken.'

Through the swirl of pain and anguish, the hard facts hit Habs clearly enough, and he fought the tears. He had dreamed of home, of New York, of a sweet return to peace. He had dreamed, too, of a cockloft curtain call, a bow with Joe as the men of Four roared their appreciation. All gone.

'*If* I am taken?' said Habs.

'If you are taken,' repeated Magrath, now returned to tending Cole. Habs waited for more, but the doctor remained silent.

'I cannot hide here.'

'Then hide somewhere else.'

Habs shook his head. 'I'm sorry, Doctor, I'm not thinkin' straight—'

'Well, try harder, man. You have a few moments before I have to raise the alarm.'

As Magrath finished with Cole, he turned to the tunnel and called for Haywood. Hiding somewhere else meant escape. And then he had it. The Allies' wall game. Was that happening now? Would they let a black man run with them? Did Magrath know about it? He didn't know the answers to any of these questions, but he did realize that Magrath was telling him to go.

He stood and winced again as his shoulder muscles tightened.

'Take something for the pain!' called Magrath by the tunnel entrance. 'Brown bottle, green stopper. Take it. Now, be gone. Away!' Habs found the bottle in the doctor's bag, shoved it deep into his jacket and ran.

Past the hammocks, through the hall and out of the doors, he forced his leaden legs to move. The late-afternoon sun made Habs squint and he hesitated on the steps, wiping his eyes. He felt utterly overwhelmed, lost in a whirlpool of pity. Just minutes ago, he had left the stage as Romeo, now he was leaving the block as a murderer. And a murderer who was on the run; he wasn't sure how long it would be before Magrath raised the alarm, but it could only be a few minutes. Maybe seconds. He couldn't stop now.

Habs stared up the crowded courtyard. To the left of the market square gates, hundreds of men – watched and cheered by hundreds more – rolled and fought. It looked as chaotic as it was intended to, and it answered his first question. Yes, the escape was on. He jumped from the steps, pushing through the throng of sailors, his bloodied appearance causing many inmates to stop. Some shouted questions. He felt no need to explain anything to anybody.

By the time he was alongside Five, a clear passage was opening up ahead of him. Bored with their courtyard routine, the sailors saw a bloodied, beaten-up, crazed-looking black man running towards them and got out of his way. Habs slowed his approach as soon as he realized that the man watching him at the end of the makeshift alley was Horace Cobb – the man whose deputy was lying face down in his own blood back in the kitchens. The Rough Allies' leader ran a few steps towards him, then pulled up. The two men stared at each other. Cobb took in Habs's blood-soaked shirt and jacket; Habs saw him recoil in horror.

He knows. He was expecting Lane and he got me. He knows.

Cobb turned on his heels and ran back towards the wall

394

game, the crowd filling in behind him. So that answered his second question: no, he wasn't welcome to join the escape. There was a chance, of course, that, if the wall was breached, it would become a free-for-all, but Habs knew he didn't have the time to wait and find out.

Out of options and in excruciating pain, he turned and ran back into Four. In the darkest corner of the ground-floor dormitory, he flung himself unseen under a pile of broken hammocks. He would hang for certain, he knew that. There wasn't a judge in England would save him from the gallows. Magrath would report the murder, the guard would be called and he'd be in the cachot before the day was done.

His shoulder sent a spasm of pain down his side and he remembered the bottle he'd taken from Magrath's bag. He lifted it from his pocket then pulled back a few hammocks to examine it. He held a green bottle with a brown stopper. Habs frowned. 'Brown bottle, green stopper' was what Magrath had said, he was sure of it; he could hear the words still. 'Wrong bottle,' he said to himself. 'I got the wrong fuckin' bottle.' He flipped it over. 'Strychnine,' he read. 'Stimulant. Tonic. Poison.'

From the cockloft, the sound of stamping feet and rousing applause. Habs's first thought was that the play had finished, then he managed a laugh. Not without Romeo it wouldn't. He realized with a start that it was just the end of Act Four – he hadn't even been missed yet. It seemed like a whole lifetime had swept past him since he took King Dick's errand, yet it had been just one act. He looked again at the bottle, weighing it in his hand. He felt its contents slop around.

Stimulant. Tonic. Poison.

5.22

Outside Block Seven

COBB HANDED out the knives. No Lane, no gun, but they were going anyway. As he walked to the wall, his lieutenants surrounded him. The Allies were leading this, but the men from Seven were right behind, pushing and jostling for position. Will Roche slid through the throng.

'Are we goin'? We must be goin'. S'time, surely?'

Cobb nodded. 'We go now. Dig till you're through. The English ain't far away, so we move fast. Take hostages if you got to – that should get us into the armoury. Go!' He watched as the tools were distributed, passing their way through the scrummaging and up to the wall. On the military walk, the redcoats took no notice; their watch was over, their replacements overdue.

At the wall, under the ruckus, a bloodied Joseph Toker Johnson attacked the cement in a series of stabbing actions. The stones were loosening, he could feel that, but men needed to crawl through this hole. His guess was that they needed to move five. Six stones would be ideal – anyone could crawl through that – but five might suffice. He slashed again across the wall, a large slice of crumbling cement falling on his boots. He pushed the largest stone with his shoulder and it dropped a quarter of an inch. Next to him, a grim-faced Ally, dust and powder settled deep in his beard, felt the change. He nodded confidently.

'Felt that,' he said. 'Can y'see much?'

Toker Johnson squinted through the crack in the

retaining wall. 'Nope. But I can see the armoury door, true 'nough. Twenty yards, I reckon. Pass the word back. When the wall goes, we all go with it. We're clear for action.'

In the thrill and bedlam of the moment, Toker Johnson and the would-be escapers missed the shuffle of boots above them, high up on the military walk. The new shift had, at last, arrived.

5.23

Block Four

As HABS climbed the stairs to the cockloft, the crowd had begun to slow-handclap and shout abuse. Habs pushed open the doors and elbowed his way through. Shouts of protest were silenced as they saw their Romeo return.

'He's back! Here he is! Bravo!'

Backstage, his reappearance triggered a convulsion of relief, then, when his fellow players saw the blood, cries of alarm. Habs ignored them all; he knew he didn't have long. He caught sight of King Dick approaching, Tommy jumping to his feet and then Joe running; he ignored them, too. Pushing past Sam and the pastor, he walked straight out into the middle of the stage.

The crowd applauded wildly, many assuming the blood was part of the show. Romeo had returned from exile – why wouldn't he have been fighting? Captain Shortland and Elizabeth Shortland clapped, too, then Elizabeth, leaning forward, stopped abruptly.

She could see something was different. Something was wrong.

The entire cast had gathered in the wings, Joe frantically calling him back in, his voice lost among the crowd's noise.

Habs began his speech but, instead of beginning where he should, he skipped two whole scenes. His mind was clear. In fact, he realized with grim certainty, it had never been clearer.

'Death, that hath sucked the honey of thy breath, hath had no power yet upon thy beauty.'

He was supposed to be talking to Juliet.

Joe walked out on stage, visibly uncertain as to what to do next. The crowd began to sense that all was not well.

'Ain't Juliet asleep?'

Joe made a tentative step towards Habs, his horrified face trying to comprehend the mess Habs was in. 'What happened?' he mouthed, even now unwilling to interrupt Romeo's big speech. He edged closer, and Habs grabbed his hand, pulling him to his side. Shoulder to shoulder, Joe smelled blood and sweat, but the true horror was the sulphur. When you have fired cannon, you never forget the assault it makes on your senses. And there was no doubt that Habs smelled of burnt gunpowder. Joe looked again at his jacket and shirt and choked. He had missed it at first, distracted by the blood, but now he saw it clearly – Habs's shirt and jacket were burnt, the black-and-brown discharge spread across his stomach.

'I will stay with thee, and never from this palace of dim night depart again.'

Habs could see Joe piecing everything together and squeezed his hand. He knew he had just a few seconds left. The pain in his shoulder was gone. His head was clear. He saw everyone with stunning clarity. He reached for the bottle in his pocket.

> 'Eyes, look your last!
> Arms, take your last embrace! And lips! O you
> The doors of breath, seal with a righteous kiss
> A dateless bargain to engrossing death.'

Habs took the strychnine in one hand and Joe in the other. Face to face now, Habs could see Joe's pale blue eyes illuminated with fear. He kissed him. He pressed his lips against

Joe's and held him fast. The roaring he heard could have been his shell-shocked ears, the outraged audience, or a force nine out of Nantucket. He didn't care. This was their kiss, the one they should have tried in Act One, and if it was to be his last, he wanted it to count. If it was the end of the play, then so be it.

Joe pulled away. Breathless, stunned, afraid. Now Habs heard the crowd. The howls of outrage crashed on to the stage like a tidal wave. Fists were shaking, bottles thrown. Captain Shortland was on his feet. Behind him, Lieutenant Aveline had drawn a pistol. Even Dr Magrath was pushing his way to the stage, red-faced and shouting.

But Habs was unstoppable. Romeo had four final lines and a drink to wash them down. He uncorked the bottle, his eyes swimming with tears.

'A dateless bargain to engrossing death!' Habs's voice was losing strength.

'Come, bitter conduct, come, unsavoury guide!'

Magrath, clearly distraught, was shouting at the King but his words were lost in the noise. Somewhere, a bell started ringing.

'Thou desperate pilot . . .' Habs was faltering.

Magrath was pointing now, stabbing his arm at Habs and shouting one word over and over. Now Joe had seen him and he leaned to catch it. From the whirlpool of slurred profanity and outrage, he finally caught it.

Poison. The word was 'poison'. And he wasn't pointing at Habs, he was pointing at the bottle he held. The bell kept ringing.

Habs held the bottle high, his arm shaking, his grip uncertain. 'Here's to my love!' he cried, and tipped the clear liquid into his mouth.

5.24

Block Seven, Retaining Wall

5.25 p.m.

It was Will Roche who tipped the first stone. When Toker Johnson was spent, he passed the knife to the next in line, and Roche made sure it was him. He crouched low as the wall-gamers huffed and puffed above and around him. A patchwork of rocks roughly the size of a barrel had dropped, the stones no longer supported by anything but each other. A hole the size of an apple had appeared between them, and Roche's view of the armoury and the barracks was clear.

'The Yankees are comin',' he said as he peered through. 'The Yankees are finally comin'. And with a fair wind, we ain't stoppin' till we get to Boston.' He turned his head to call to the others – 'Well, m'boys. We're in!' – and put his shoulder to the biggest stone. Others around him dipped and leaned their weight, too, and suddenly, the granite slid six inches. Now, they needed speed and surprise. The very closeness of escape, the proximity of guns and freedom, was a powerful drug. With a series of powerful lunges, four of the stones began to move. Inch by crunching inch, the centre of the granite wall was moving.

Around the back of Seven, at the end of the military walk, the new watch of the Somerset militia were completing their first patrol. The six men stopped briefly. The view to the left was Dartmoor; the view to the right took in Seven then ran along the retaining wall, the market square gates and One. They were about to march back around the arc when their lieutenant ordered them to halt. He turned to study the prisoners by the wall.

'What is it, sir?' asked one of his men.

'This tedious game the Americans are playing,' he said, 'seems to have become more frantic.'

They saw men dip, disappear, then reappear at the back of the scrum. There was no disguising an increase in their speed and rigour.

'What if it isn't a game at all?' said the lieutenant.

'Sir?' His men leaned, disbelieving, against the walk.

A sudden shift in the patterns of the players, and a beam of light appeared in their midst. The lieutenant frowned. 'That's not possible,' he said.

One of his men leaned in closer, as far as the military walk would allow. 'It is if there's a hole in the wall.'

When the beam of light doubled in size, the lieutenant gripped his rifle. 'Dear God in Heaven,' he said. 'Sound the alarm.'

5.25

Block Four, Cockloft

JOE SMASHED the bottle from Habs's hand just as King Dick tackled him to the ground. The strychnine spun away, spilling its poison in circular patterns. Habs crashed to the stage, the air from his lungs squashed out of him. Magrath arrived seconds later. 'Did he drink? Did he drink?' he yelled.

'Yes, yes, I think so,' said Joe, his words clear but his tone manic. 'What was it? Why was he even—'

Magrath had rammed his handkerchief into Habs's mouth, dabbing and wiping. He felt for a pulse.

'Is he breathing, Doctor?' Joe rasped. 'Is he dead?'

The cry was taken up around the cockloft. 'Habs is dead!'

In the pandemonium that followed, only Joe heard what Magrath replied. 'He's not dead. Not yet, anyway. It depends how much of the strychnine he swallowed. We'll know soon enough – the spasms will start in about fifteen minutes. Maybe sooner. It's possible he'll vomit it all back up again. Time will tell, Joe, time will tell.' To Joe's blank face, he added, 'He killed Edwin Lane. Shot him with a pistol. Self-defence, he said.' Magrath ignored Joe's bloodless face, carried on wiping moisture from Habs's mouth. Joe watched the physician's frantic work on Habs's limp body, momentarily stunned by the horror of what he had seen. Then came the fear and the battle-induced instinct to do something.

'What can I do? What should I do?'

'Try to wake him up,' said Magrath. 'Or pray. Whatever you're better at.'

Joe fell to his knees, then leaned forward so his head touched the ground alongside Habs. 'You don't leave like that!' he shouted into his ear, his voice tight. 'You don't leave me like that! Habs, wake up!' Then a whispered, 'And I need you. You know I do.'

A fearful-looking Sam stood at Habs's feet, his arm around a red-eyed Tommy. The pastor was praying; the rest of the cast stood motionless, too shocked to know how to react.

King Dick had disappeared. A quick scan of the room was all it took to know that he wasn't there and, with the King absent, the fighting and the panic returned.

Joe helped Magrath push Habs on to his side, then pulled some damp strands of hair from his face. 'Is he safe here, Doctor? Should we move him?' Habs made a deep groaning sound, then his body arched, his head and neck snapping back sharply.

'Spasms have started,' warned Magrath. As Habs's muscles contracted, he vomited copiously. Magrath wiped his mouth. 'He's not going anywhere just now,' he said.

Magrath glanced at the crowd just as Elizabeth Shortland clambered on to the stage. She had just opened her mouth to speak when a gunshot ripped through the cockloft. The crowd dived to the floor; Magrath dived to cover Elizabeth. The gunman was six feet away. Lieutenant Aveline, standing over Captain Shortland, held his pistol high above his head, a hole blasted in the cockloft roof. The hubbub slowly faded but, in its place, came the sound of an entire prison tipping over the edge. The alarm bell was being rung and then, from the barracks, the drums. The call-to-arms.

The Agent and Aveline were first to the doors. The Agent shot the briefest of glances at the stage, where Magrath was still lying on Elizabeth Shortland, and they were gone. It

404

was the start of a stampede. From the stage, Joe watched them go. Eroded by alcohol, panic and fear, any remaining vestiges of ship discipline disappeared and the men fought, screamed, scratched and kicked their way to the exit.

On the stage, the play clearly over, the cast still seemed separate, adrift from the proceedings that had overtaken them. As their shipmates pushed and heaved for the door, they stood watching, the last strands of the play's camaraderie holding them back.

'Do we go, too?' asked Tommy.

'I guess so,' said Sam.

'Go where?' asked Magrath, helping Elizabeth to her feet. 'A riot? If you have any sense left in your bones, you'll be keeping well clear.'

'A riot or an escape?' said Elizabeth. 'I've never heard the drums before.'

Magrath shrugged. 'Maybe both. We're going to be busy. We need to go.'

'Doctor!' Joe called Magrath back. Habs was spasming again, and Magrath hustled over.

'Nothing we can do,' he said. 'Pray God he didn't swallow much.' He watched as the convulsion faded. 'That was milder, less violent. I am encouraged. But if he survives, he'll be arrested for murder. I did try to help him, but I must report what I saw. And Mr Snow here admitted to killing Mr Lane. Shot him in the stomach. We'd have heard the shot here, but Lane fell on the gun. Muffled it.'

The cast, open-mouthed, looked at each other in shock. Sam spluttered to life first.

'No way! No way would Habs do that.'

'That will be for a court to decide,' said Magrath.

'Where is King Dick?' asked Elizabeth. 'I didn't see him go.'

'No one did,' said Joe. 'He dived for Habs, then just disappeared.'

'He does that sometimes,' said Sam.

'Well, let us pray he is making himself useful,' said Elizabeth. 'I think you'll be needing him. I think we'll all be needing him.'

Habs coughed, retched, then opened his eyes. 'Drink,' he whispered. Joe clambered for one of the backstage jugs, relief powering his every move.

'It's good to see you again,' he said, holding it to Habs's lips and smiling.

Habs closed his eyes.

'What were you thinking, Habs?' whispered Joe. 'What in Christ's name were you thinking?'

Habs opened his eyes again. 'I was thinkin' it was a better way to go than hangin' on the end of an English rope.'

Joe pushed the image from his mind. 'Did you swallow much?'

Habs shook his head then winced. 'No idea. Don't remember.'

'The King flattened you.'

Habs grimaced. 'That'll be why, then.'

As the cockloft emptied, Magrath and Elizabeth Shortland left the stage. 'Stay clear when he spasms,' Magrath called to Joe. 'I pray he'll pull through. We need to get to the hospital.'

Goffe looked around him. 'Well, that's it, then,' he said, and, followed by Lord and the *Requin* men, he made for the doors, too. Their running footsteps echoed around the now quiet cockloft.

'Last men on the ship,' said Sam. 'We should go, too.'

The alarm bell still rang, the call-to-arms still beat, and now a new sound emerged, swelling, rolling, enveloping everything. Tommy took a few steps towards the door. It was voices. Thousands of voices.

'It sounds like . . . like everyone.'

406

Tommy, then Sam, ran to the single cockloft window that overlooked the courtyard. They stood, transfixed, for a long time. It was as though the seething, broiling uproar of the cockloft had transferred itself to the entire prison.

'It *is* everyone,' said Tommy, his voice awed by the spectacle. 'All the blocks are out. Every one.'

'And I've found King Dick,' said Sam.

5.26

The Market Square

5.50 p.m.

THEY EMERGED on to the steps of Four, Sam and Joe helping a recovering Habs, Tommy running ahead to hold the doors open, and gasped.

'All hands,' muttered Joe.

It seemed as though all seven prison blocks had emptied, and each one of the seven thousand prisoners was yelling, pushing, scuffling. Every inch of the courtyard was taken, the sea of sailors now lapping at the edges of the prison's steps. The focus of their attention was, as ever, the market square gates, and there, holding up both hands and swinging his club, was King Dick.

'He must have heard the alarm bell before anyone,' said Sam. 'Must've known what it meant.'

'What does it mean?' said Joe.

'Escape,' said Sam. 'It means someone's tryin' to escape.'

'And gettin' shot,' said Habs, his words still hoarse with the poison. 'It usually ends with 'em gettin' shot. Or hanged.'

Tommy was torn. 'I'll stay to help Habs, but—'

Joe waved him away. 'Go, Tommy. Get back to your crew mates. Stay safe.' The crier nodded his thanks, squeezed his way into the crowd and disappeared.

'Listen,' said Habs, still holding tightly to his cousin. 'This is bad for me. Once this riot is done, Magrath will make his report and the redcoats will come. I took Lane's

408

gun and, when he attacked me, I shot him. They're the facts. Plus, he's white.'

'What are you sayin'?' asked Sam.

'I'm sayin', if there's a breakout, I wanna be a part of it, whatever happens.'

'Cuz, you'll get shot.'

'Yeah, maybe. But maybe not, maybe I get lucky and I 'scape the redcoats and their press gangs and make it to Boston. Or Philly. Or anywhere that ain't England.'

'Habs—' began Joe, but Habs put a hand out.

'I know,' said Habs, 'I know. But I'm right an' you're wrong. And that's all there is, Mr Hill. And you're still in your dress.'

'I got 'em,' said Sam, and threw Joe his trousers.

'I'd forgotten,' said Joe, pulling them on and dropping the dress. 'I'd actually forgotten.'

'Let's go.'

'Go where?' asked Sam. The throng of inmates in front of them hadn't moved; from the market square gates, down through the courtyard and across to the palisades, this crowd was stuck fast.

'To find a hole in the wall,' said Habs. 'This way.'

5.27

The Barracks

THE AGENT, sweating hard and a commandeered pistol in his hand, listened impatiently as a sergeant explained what had happened. Around them, red-jacketed militia sprinted in all directions, many still buttoning up as they ran. Shortland struggled to hear his man over the cacophony of an out-of-control prison.

'By the time the alarm was raised, sir, lots of prisoners had climbed through the wall. They headed for the armoury and when they found it was locked, they tried to kick the doors in. They nearly succeeded, too, but—'

'How many?' snapped Shortland. 'How many got though the wall?'

'I would estimate thirty or forty, sir, with lots more ready to go through.'

'Dear God . . .' said Shortland.

'But as soon as the guard deployed, many of them ran straight back again. Back through the wall.'

'You didn't stop them?' spluttered Shortland.

'The men were safeguarding the armoury first, sir, I considered that the priority.'

Shortland nodded. 'Quite so,' he said.

The seven captured escapers, now surrounded by at least twenty militia, were kneeling on the ground, heads bowed. Some cast rueful glances at their hole in the wall, now with an arc of guns aiming straight through it.

'Mostly Rough Allies, by the looks of it,' said Shortland.

'Yes, sir.'

'Throw them in the cachot when it's safe.'

'Yes, sir.'

'And Captain,' said Shortland, 'thank your men for the panic ladders. Good work.'

'Yes, sir.'

The swift throwing of the emergency ladders had enabled Shortland and Aveline to climb from the courtyard then run between the palisades and the military walk to the guards' gate. They arrived as the last of the fleeing prisoners was disappearing back through the hole.

'Is Mrs Shortland safe, sir?' asked the captain, looking around.

'She's fine. The physician is with her.' Shortland glanced briefly at the ground.

'Right you are, sir.'

Rocks and bottles flew over the wall, striking a number of soldiers.

'Your men will need to be steely, Captain,' said Shortland. 'Protect this hole. God knows if anyone else will try to use it, but my order is to shoot anyone who does.' He listened to the sounds of pandemonium coming from the other side of the wall. 'There is much work to do today, I fear.'

5.28

The Back of Block Six

WITH NO way forward from the steps of Four, Joe, Habs and Sam had retreated. Flat up against the iron palisades that arced around the prisons, they inched their way to the alley that ran between Six and Seven; funnel-like, it was at least thirty men wide at the top, tapering to a space barely large enough for three at the bottom. Joe shook his head.

'No way we're getting to the gates from here,' he called to Habs and Sam. 'And if the hole in the wall is where the Allies were playing that game, we can't get there either.'

Habs squeezed himself past Joe. 'Watch me,' he said. 'You'll be surprised what you can do if you don't want to hang.' And, like a man possessed, Habs began to fight his way through. Sometimes he span, sometimes he twisted, sometimes he scrapped; yard by yard, Habs headed for the steps of Seven. He took the punches, the kicks and the curses; he seemed unstoppable. Then, as he was climbing over some men's shoulders, the strychnine came again. Joe saw his body spasm, his legs and head jerk backwards, and he fell, disappearing into the crowd.

'Habs!' shouted Joe, then, to Sam, 'He's fallen.' Now it was their turn to scrap their way through. Joe and Sam followed Habs's rulebook. It cost them split lips, ripped clothes and scratched faces and, by the time they found him propped up against an old-timer from Five, they were nearly spent.

'He don't appear too well, your friend here,' said the man. 'We had a sailor on board the *Perseus*. Used to fit like that. We learned to leave him be, mostly. He'll get better.'

'Oh, thanks,' said Joe. 'We'll take him from here.'

'I'm all right,' said Habs eventually, croaking again and wiping bile from his cheek. 'Really. They're gettin' smaller.'

By the steps of Seven – sometimes on them, sometimes off, depending on how the crowd shifted – they studied the market square gates, the King still perched on the top and flashes of red in the square beyond.

'The call-to-arms has stopped,' called Sam. 'So I guess that's half the British Army lined up for us.'

'And the other half by the hole,' said Habs. 'Unless someone busts those gates, ain't no one gettin' out now.'

Fights were breaking out all over, each one causing waves of stumbling, angry inmates. Other movements appeared like eddies, currents in a turbulent river. Thirty yards from the gates, a band of men, arms wrapped around each other, swayed sideways and back, then forwards and back, each movement triggering another wave. Joe realized they were singing.

'I know this,' he said. 'It's "The Hornet and the Peacock". If it catches, those gates are going down.' The first verse got lost in the whirlpool of shouts and insults that was flowing around the courtyard, but by the time they reached the chorus, everyone could hear.

'Sing hubber, O bubber, cried Old Granny Wale,
The Hornet can tickle the British bird's tail
Her stings are all sharp and they'll pierce without fail.
"Success to our Navy!" cried Old Granny Wale.'

Riotous, patriotic and anti-British, the song was a perfect fit.

No one was sure of the verses, so they quickly gave way to a constant repetition of the chorus, each one more

413

boisterous than the last. At every 'Success to our Navy!' the crowd surged.

'We need to be in this!' cried Habs. 'I need to be in this,' he corrected himself.

'Right first time!' shouted Joe.

'Wait – what?' said Sam, but they had jumped.

Habs turned briefly to wave, encouraging Sam to join them, but then they were gone. Arm tightly in arm, Joe and Habs fought their way into the heart of the melee.

'Better step back from that fence, King Dick!' cried Habs. 'This crowd is coming through.'

'Her stings are all sharp and they'll pierce without fail.
"Success to our Navy!" cried Old Granny Wale.'

The fifth chorus was the one that crashed against the gates, the sixth the one that burst the locks. With a triumphant roar, the sailors of Dartmoor swarmed into the market square. Joe and Habs were lifted off their feet. They had surrendered all control – it was the crowd which now determined where they went and how they got there. All they could see were the heads of the men around them; all they could feel was a terrifying, breath-crushing pressure against their ribs. They held on to each other with a fierce determination, knowing that to fall now was certain death. Sometimes their feet touched the ground, sometimes it felt like they touched flesh and bone, some poor wretch who had lost their footing and gone under.

'I just trod on someone!' gasped Habs, twisting to see more, but they had already been carried past the fallen man. He levered himself away from the man in front of him, to ease the pressure on his chest. He glanced at Joe, whose face was turning crimson. 'Do it!' he shouted to Joe. 'Do it!' Feet alighting briefly, they both fought for an inch of space that might relieve the pressure on their lungs. Joe scratched,

Habs elbowed, and when the crowd surged again they could see more and breathe easier.

They were carried past the hole in the wall, the five removed blocks revealing the glow of many redcoats and muskets on the other side. Habs ran despairing hands through his hair.

'Sweet Heaven, that was my best way out!' he yelled, watching it go. 'I was gonna join 'em, y'know,' he said. 'Came down here, just after I killed Lane. Thought it might work.'

'You wanted to join the Allies?' Joe was astonished.

'Joe, I'm goin' to hang. You got that?' Habs's eyes were wide. 'This is the end for me. I either get out or I'm taken away. I can't stay here no more.'

The crowd surge ebbed away, depositing them, breathless, at the gates. The last time they had been here was to trade with the stall-holders; now, as they looked beyond the hundreds of sailors in front of them, they faced line after line of British soldiers, muskets level and bayonets fixed.

'Shit,' said Habs. 'We're trapped.'

5.29

The Courtyard

Tommy Jackson's route to the gates had been straightforward. Skinny, small and nimble, he had twisted and squeezed himself into any gap he found in the tightly packed wall of angry prisoners. If he pushed too hard, if anyone took offence, their anger lasted only until they recognized him. Running errands for seven prisons wins you friends and a prisoner's patience. 'Crier comin' through!' was the shout, and the sailors moved if they could.

Tacking right, he was twenty yards from the gates when he felt powerful hands around his mouth and waist, a full beard pushing against his neck. He knew who it was from the smell. Only one of the Rough Allies smoked cigarillos.

'And you are just who I wanted to see,' growled Cobb. 'It was good of the crowd to point you out.' He pushed him out towards Block Two, the nearest of the prisons, Cobb's face the only weapon needed to clear the way.

Clear of the crowd, Cobb threw Tommy against the wall of Two. The scraping tool appeared in Cobb's hand and he held it tightly to Tommy's throat.

'You saw. You knew. You told,' he breathed. Tommy, panic in his eyes, knew exactly what Cobb was talking about. 'You need me to explain?' Tommy shook his head.

'No, that's 'cos you're smart. Traitorous little bastard, but smart all the same. You saw Lane with the gun, didn't you? You guessed what he had and then you told that cockroach Crafus.'

Tommy hadn't seen Cobb in a rage like this before. He gave the smallest of nods, as if to move any more would enrage Cobb further. Cobb pushed the blade until its tip pierced Tommy's skin. ''Cos the truth, Mr Jackson, is that you love it with the niggers, don't you? If you had to choose between them and your own, you'd pick the niggers every time.'

Tommy shook his head now, eyes swimming with tears. 'They been good to me is all,' he managed, his mouth hardly moving.

'I bet they have,' spat Cobb. 'You know our escape failed, yes? While you were in that damn fool play, brave Americans were being attacked.' His spittle ran down Tommy's face. 'So now you're comin' to a show with me. You're goin' to climb on my shoulders and we're goin' to a show.' Cobb held the bloody scraping tool blade in front of Tommy's eyes. 'And if you shout and scream like a girl, I'll cut your cock off. I hope I'm makin' it quite clear?'

Tommy nodded. 'Yes, sir, Mr Cobb, sir.'

5.30

The Market Square

THE GATES had been blasted open and pushed flat against the market square walls. King Dick had climbed to the top of one and was staring into the throng.

'What's he doing?' asked Joe.

As they approached the gate, the King suddenly stabbed his club at someone below.

'Hail, Mr Boyce from Indiana!' he yelled, 'And hail, Mr Gilmour from Illinois. Turn back now! Turn away from the guns!' The men from Four, startled to be addressed by the King from atop the market square gates, looked all around. They indicated the thousands of inmates pressing in behind them and shrugged.

'Can't move neither way!' they shouted back.

Habs put one hand to his mouth.

'Hey, King Dick! Down here!'

The King twisted back and forth until he found them in the crowd. 'You!' he bellowed. 'You, Mr Snow, and you, Mr Hill!' The King was now standing on top of the gate, balancing precariously, one foot either side of the bar. 'Have you seen' – he hesitated just briefly – 'have you seen our friend John? He's missin', y'see.'

In spite of the shooting, or maybe because of it, the King obviously still felt the need to speak obliquely. Habs followed his lead.

'Not in his hole, then?' he called.

418

The King shook his head. 'Spoke to Mr Cole in attendance there. Like I said, he's missin'.'

'Sorry, King Dick, we'll look out for him,' Habs said. He and Joe wedged themselves into a breathing space behind the gates.

'You got to go back.' The King had started pointing the club again, down to the prisons. 'Everyone got to go back! Away from here. Away from the guns. You need to tell all our men.'

Habs was unsure what to say. King Dick astride the gates was a magnificent sight: his bearskin, club, rings, earrings, sloped shoulders, the extraordinary height, the unrivalled strength. Even from the ground, Habs could follow those fierce eyes, like black opals, scanning the crowd for his men: watchful, protective, possessive. This was the King as the prison knew him, as Habs knew him, and yet all around, men continued their pressing, their singing, their confrontation. King Dick was being ignored. The men of Four who had made it this far couldn't turn back if they wanted to, but Habs could see they didn't want to and they wouldn't anyway.

A great hollowness fell on him. 'They told me I was everythin',' muttered Habs. ''Tis a lie.' He tugged at Joe's jacket. 'And where in all the world will I find another Joe Hill?'

'You don't need to,' said Joe. 'I'm coming with you.'

Habs shook his head. 'No, sir, Mr Hill, you are not. You have not killed a man, you will not swing. You stay here for the peace. You live a good life. Visit your grandmother, go home to Boston, sing for money, write books.' He spoke softly, with a quiet melancholy. He looked at Joe and managed an exhausted smile. 'Stay beautiful.'

'Shut up, Habs,' said Joe. 'You're being dramatic. I'll do all those things, and I'll do them with you. If you escape, I can escape with you. Anyway, you probably need me to get you out.'

'Is that right?'

'Probably, yes.'

'And how do we do that?'

'Bribery,' said Joe. 'It's the only way.'

'With what?' said Habs. 'If you'd kept your dress on, maybe . . .'

'Where's the gun?'

'Back in Four.'

Joe reconsidered. 'Are your earrings precious? They look tradeable.'

Habs fingered the black-and-ivory hoops. 'A few dollars, maybe, a few shillings . . .'

A cry from above them: the King was on his feet, the club pointing again. 'Mr Jackson!' he shouted. 'No, sir! Turn back!'

Joe and Habs turned to catch sight of the crier, carried on shoulders, moving through the gates and up towards the front line.

'Tommy!' they shouted together. He swivelled around the neck that supported him, his worried face searching eagerly for the King, for Joe and Habs, for voices he would recognize anywhere. 'Turn back, Tommy!' yelled Joe. 'It's just the army that way!' Tommy shook his head, pointing to the head of the man who was carrying him, drawing a finger across his throat. Habs noticed two white hands tighten their grip around his thighs and then the crier swivelled back.

'Whose shoulders are they?' said Joe. 'Who's got him?'

'Can't see,' said Habs, 'but someone who don't mean him no good.' Tommy Jackson's head continued to bob as he was carried further into the square. They could see the top gates open again and more troops rushing to take up position. There were now four lines of soldiers, each fifty men strong, and Tommy was being taken closer to them by the second.

'A Rough Ally, then,' said Joe. They didn't need to say

420

anything else. Joe and Habs both stepped out from behind the gates and launched themselves back into the crowd.

The market square, enclosed by four walls, had produced an even tighter squeeze.

'Side wall,' said Habs. 'Safer that way.'

They threw themselves against the brickwork, then, using the wall as a backstop, began their fight to get Tommy. More fists, more scratches, more cursing, but they just about kept track with the crier's head. They saw him twist again, urgently, frantically, looking for his friends. The crowd seemed to be parting for him. Despite the abuse they were hurling at the British, the men stepped aside if they could.

'Do you see that, Joe?' said Habs, pushing away an incensed inmate they recognized from One. 'When they see who's comin', who's doin' the carryin', everyone tries to move. Jus' like that.'

'Which means it has to be Cobb.'

5.31

Magrath's Office

ELIZABETH SHORTLAND bustled in ahead of Magrath. He slammed the door, then, from drawers and shelves, began to restock their medical bags. 'Splints, gauzes, bandages, ligatures, tongs, a knife. That's it,' he said. 'That's all we take. And hurry.' He handed her an armful of supplies.

'George.'

'Elizabeth, there'll be time for this later. I know what I saw. I have to be a reliable witness.'

'You know what Lane was like,' she said. 'He was an animal. Snow did what anyone would have done.' She realized it sounded as though she was pleading. Maybe she was. 'You'd have done the same, George,' she said. 'I'd have done the same.'

'I can't say I'm not conflicted, Elizabeth,' he said. 'I had hoped he might join the escape, but he did not. So there is still a man in Four with his stomach blown away by a pistol fired by Mr Snow, and I am a witness to that fact. However . . .' He looked across to Elizabeth and swallowed hard. She knew his words would be forbidding, recognized his grim, businesslike countenance. 'Elizabeth, I know an eve of battle when it comes along. I recognize it, I've seen so many. It was the same on the ships. The grievances, the posturing, the manoeuvres. Both sides *want* to fight. Shots have been fired already, and they are a harbinger, I believe, of what's to come. We need to be ready for the whirlwind that is surely coming our way.'

'I must talk to Thomas,' she said, snapping her bag shut. 'He won't want a fight.'

'Elizabeth, you are the last person he'll talk to. Closely followed by me. You say he knows about us – very well, then. We'll do what we can here, then there'll be a reckoning for certain. But, for now, we have work to do.'

She stood against the door and closed her eyes. She saw Habakkuk Snow kissing Joe Hill then drinking the poison. She saw Aveline firing his pistol then running from the cock-loft with her husband. She saw Willoughby, dressed in his Royal Navy finery, waving her farewell.

'I must write to Willoughby, tell him what has happened.'

'In due course . . .'

'But before Thomas does.'

'Elizabeth . . .'

A roar from the market square. Elizabeth pulled the door open. 'I know, George. First, we survive today.'

'And you go nowhere without an armed troop. Cobb has made his intentions clear. He'll snatch you again if he can.' Magrath made a last-minute check of his supplies. Satisfied, he took his new stick in one hand and his bag in the other. When he reached the door, he kicked it shut again. He leaned his forehead against hers.

'The first time I saw battle injuries I vomited for two days,' he said. 'In the end, I sang to drown the frenzy and pain. Clean what you can, dress what you can. It's all you can do.'

She kissed him, both hands cradling his face. 'Then may God grant us strength,' she said.

5.32

The Market Square

JOE AND Habs had fought their way to the mid-point of the square, and, eyes on the crier, hadn't registered how close they were to the loaded muskets.

'Steady,' said Joe, pulling Habs back to the wall. 'Tommy might be fine. You, on the other hand, are not. We're twenty yards away from the British Army, and British guns. A couple of hundred British guns. Then there are gates, then more gates, then that foul arch we all arrived under.'

'*Parcere subjectis*,' said Habs. '"Spare the vanquished," you said.' Habs ran his eyes along the four lines of troops, muskets held in readiness, the late sunshine catching on buttons and bayonets. 'It don't look like they're 'bout to do much sparin', if you ask me.'

'Agreed.' Joe could see some of the soldiers lining their guns up, taking aim, fingers already curled around the trigger. 'They can't wait,' he muttered. Many were the same age as him, younger maybe. He recognized Ol' Fat Bastard and his skinny farmhand friends, hopping from foot to foot with nervous excitement. As stones and more abuse rained down on them, Joe could see they'd had enough. He could almost smell their rage.

The top gates opened again and in marched three men they knew. Captain Shortland and his lieutenant, Fortyne, marched towards their soldiers, behind them Dr Magrath, keeping pace as best he could. The Americans sensed a slight lowering of tension – and guns – as the Agent took control. He saluted his troops, then walked straight towards the inmates, hands held high.

'You must retreat!' he shouted, waving them back. 'This is a forbidden area. Retreat, I say! Go back to your blocks!' The inmates in front of him laughed. Retreat was impossible.

'There's too many men pushin' to get in,' said Habs. 'Can he not see that?' Magrath was now in earnest conversation with some inmates, pleading with them to push back. He wasn't laughed at – he had gained too much respect for that – but he wasn't listened to either. Foot by foot, the inmates advanced. A few tried to double back into the crowd, but there was no room for them now and they turned, out of options, to face the bayonets. Behind them, Rough Allies taunted the soldiers, inviting them to open fire.

'C'mon! Shoot! See what happens!'

Joe and Habs pressed themselves against the wall, shrinking behind the inmates in front of them. 'What madness this is,' said Habs, his breath coming in short bursts. 'The Brits are desperate for a fight, an' we're askin' them to go ahead?'

'Where's Tommy gone?' asked Joe. The mop of red hair had disappeared from the crowd, the crier nowhere to be seen. They both stood tall again, straining to catch sight of the boy.

'Well, he won't have gone far,' said Habs. 'Not even Tommy could thread himself through this crowd.'

'Can't see that bastard Cobb either.'

Shortland and Magrath fell back behind the first line of militia, the Agent snapping a command to his lieutenant. Fortyne called it for his men and, so there was no mistaking their intention, for the benefit of the inmates, too.

'To the charge!' he yelled, and two hundred members of the Somerset and Derbyshire militias levelled their guns and advanced. Within three steps, the first bayonets were

425

pressed against sailors' chests. The inmates pleaded, incredulous. 'We can't go back! We can't move!' was shouted over and over, as men with tears rolling down their faces pleaded with individual soldiers for mercy. More bottles and stones crashed over the soldiers' heads, followed by American cheers. A half-dozen sailors grabbed the guns in front of them, wrestling the soldiers for control.

'Steady, men!' called Fortyne. The bayonets were biting. Some men screamed.

'We're outta time,' said Habs. He cupped his hands to his mouth.

'Tommy! By the wall!' he yelled.

'Get to the wall!' yelled Joe.

There was a brief moment when Joe thought he heard a reply, a cry of 'Joe! Habs!' before his stomach lurched and the blood drained from his face. It could have been Fortyne, it could have been Shortland, it could even have been Ol' Fat Bastard who gave the command. In the cauldron of the market square, it wasn't clear and it didn't matter.

The word was clear, the order given.

'Fire!'

5.33

The Market Square

6.25 p.m.

THE FRONT line of the militia disengaged their bayonets and tried to aim their guns, but the crowd surged forward and the guns all went high. An erratic volley of musket fire rang out, the bullets whistling over the heads of the inmates. If they had room to cower or duck, they did so, some falling in the process. The British advanced a few steps, reloading as they went. As men at the rear fled the market square, the pressure at the front eased and the sailors were able to retreat at last, the bayonets following them all the way.

'They got a taste for it now,' cried Habs, pulling Joe back. 'They ain't gonna stop there.'

'Don't even look at them, don't give them a reason,' said Joe, turning away. He recognized the sounds behind him; the clatter of muskets' ramrods pushing another cartridge to the breech, the snap of the ramrods being replaced under the barrel and then the death rattle – a hundred guns going to full-cock.

'Fire!'

Another volley – louder, longer this time – and the square crackled with gunshot. The four walls bounced the sound around between them – many inmates assumed they were surrounded. White smoke billowed from the British soldiers' guns, the cloud rolling high over the square.

'Can't see nothin'!' shouted Habs. 'Who's down? Anyone down?' They started walking sideways, backs to the wall.

Joe shook his head. 'No one! Can't see anyone down – they're firing in the air!'

Others, too, had noticed that the guns were shooting high. A different cry now began to fill the square.

'Blank cartridges! They firin' blank cartridges!'

A new resolve filled some of the sailors. They turned around, they stopped retreating, the old Yankee defiance flooding back.

'They're bluffin'! They're fakin'!'

It took Habs one look at the closest militiaman to know there was no deception. The man was ten yards away, puce with excitement and grinning like a shot fox.

'This is no fake!' yelled Habs. 'Christ alive! Can't no one else see that?'

The clatter of loading.

Habs held on to Joe, pulled him to his knees.

The snap of ramrods.

The muskets were low. Chest high.

'Make yourself small, Joe!' Habs yelled. He looked at the twisted faces around him, then folded himself into the ground.

'Fire!'

The loudest volley. The longest volley. Now, the bodies fell.

One second. Two seconds. Three seconds. Four, and the shooting was over. Five, and Habs hauled Joe back to his feet. He was yelling, 'Move!' over and over, but Joe heard nothing save the shrill, furious ringing that was splitting his head. Spaces had appeared in the crowd, and they ran into them. Joe chanced a head turn. Ten feet away, another reload had started. Four feet away, a man sprawled with half his head missing. The militia front line was again within bayonet range of the inmates and, while some loaded new cartridges, the others stabbed. It was a murderous advance. Legs, groins, stomachs, faces, arms – whichever part of an American was within reach, a British bayonet impaled it.

Through his clanging head, Joe now heard the screams.

Habs had Joe by his jacket, the fabric screwed tight in his fist. They were on the front line now. They backed away from the guns as fast as they could, pressing hard against the men behind them, but it wasn't fast enough. If the next volley fired straight, it would cut them down. The ramrods were in the barrels, the grim smiles were back on the British faces. Every sailor recognized the expression; they'd seen it before in battle. It was payback. This was a British recrimination, a military-sanctioned revenge for the taunts, the abuse and the stone-throwing. A retribution for the daily indignity of their prison life. There were scores to settle, bones to break and pride to restore. Joe and Habs knew this was the end.

There was a slackening in the tension of the men at their backs, a few hurriedly taken steps to avoid falling. Cries from the market square entrance and the pounding of running feet told Joe and Habs all they needed to know. The square was, finally, emptying fast. In front of them, the ramrods were being re-clipped to the barrels.

As the guns were raised, Joe and Habs turned. Hundreds of men were running for their lives. Some were stooped, expecting the bullets; others flailed as they fled. Joe and Habs, heads low, bodies braced, sprinted for the broken gates. They heard raised, angry voices behind them. They heard two running men close behind them, one fast and easy, the other laboured and painful. They saw that the gates, now thirty yards away, were suddenly rammed, too narrow for the volume of men trying to escape. Habs swerved.

'Corner!' he yelled. They ran five more steps.

The death rattle again: two hundred muskets to full cock. Three more steps.

No one shouted 'Fire!'.

The shooting went on for ever.

Habs hit the ground first, Joe following, then other bodies – three, maybe four – landed on top of them. One convulsed, another fell silently, a third rasped and rattled, gripping hold of Habs's shoulders before lying still. Eventually, this mound of bloodied and broken bodies fell silent. Joe and Habs knew they had both survived because they could feel, then hear, the other's staccato breathing. No words were attempted – not even whispered – the sound of boots was all around. One pair ran past, then their owner doubled back and spat. 'Fucking Yankee bastard!'

Habs felt the body above him jerk hard, then the blinding pain of a bayonet piercing his arm. He fought the scream, biting hard into the dirt. He started to shake as he felt his legs and torso run with the other man's blood.

Joe left it as long as he dared. He, too, was aware of a wetness that was spreading across his head and knew he had to move. 'Hold fast,' he whispered, in the tiniest of voices. Habs said nothing; his mouth was better kept shut. 'Hold fast,' Joe repeated. 'He's gone, but wait.'

Joe opened his eyes and his vision swam with blood. He worked a hand free and wiped his eyes with his fingers.

They had landed a few yards short of the corner, sliding the last few feet as they fell. One man now lay across Joe's head, the weight pressing his face to the ground; another was across his legs. The third, bayoneted, man must have come down on top of Habs.

Joe strained to listen to every sound. He could hear the injured and the dying, cries for help and prayers for mercy, but no troops. For the moment, no troops. The gunfire was now coming from the prison yards themselves. Dear God, it was a massacre. The battle was everywhere but, just now, it was everywhere else. Joe lifted his head as far as he could, but the man on top of him was heavy, and he lowered it again. He tried to roll sideways but, drained of all strength,

430

he quickly gave up. It was only the thought of the spitting man returning that made him try one more manoeuvre. Joe gritted his teeth, breathed deep then arched his back.

It worked. He felt the heavier body roll from him, the lighter one on his legs shift, too. He froze, listening again for troops. Hearing nothing nearby, he eased himself up on to his elbows. The heavier man lay face down, his skull broken open above his right ear. Joe thought he may have been from One, possibly one of the men who had volunteered for the farm work. 'Poor bastard,' he said, then wiped his face.

'Can I move?' whispered Habs. 'I got to move. My arm . . .' He moved, anyway, the body rolling sideways. Habs knew the man was dead, could feel his blood congealing around his legs, but when he saw a black arm twisted across the man's back he shuddered.

'Holy Jesus and Mary . . .' Oblivious to his own pain, Habs leaned over and rolled the man back again. It was John Haywood.

Habs froze, looked away, then looked back again. 'Please God, no. Oh, that ain't right. No, no, that ain't right at all.' He crawled to where Haywood lay, saw the bullet's exit wound in his neck, saw the bayonet wound in his ribs, and bowed his head. 'What were you doin' here, anyways? The King was lookin' for you.' Lost briefly in a haze of grief, Habs became aware of two white arms enveloping him, then steering him gently away. 'Joe? What are you . . . look, it's John, after all, that's . . .'

He realized Joe was sobbing and let himself be man-oeuvred. As he tore his eyes away from Haywood, then took in the heavy man with his head blown in, Habs realized he knew already what it was that had broken Joe's heart. Now he saw it, too. The shock of red hair, the muddied, freckled face, the eager green eyes – still open – and the jagged hole in the body that had felled the unstoppable Tommy Jackson.

'He was following us, Habs.' Joe choked the words as

431

much as spoke them. 'We called him, and he came. John Haywood, too. And when the bullets flew, they took them for us. Cobb may have put Tommy Jackson in the firing line, but we got him killed.'

'No,' spat Habs, 'the English got 'em killed. English guns, English bullets.' He waved his uninjured arm across the body-strewn square; some men were still moving, others had succumbed to their injuries. 'Same as what did for all of these.' From the prison yards, more firing; from the top gates, more troops.

Joe didn't argue. There didn't seem much point. They lay down next to the crier. 'So that's it. This is how it ends.' Habs's voice was tight. 'We join the turkey-shoot out there, or I get arrested for murder here.' They stared at the darkening, bullfinch sky. They heard a small patrol moving around the square, moving between the fallen, but they weren't listening. Joe reached for his jacket pocket.

'There is another option.' He sat up and held out a small knife. 'King Dick gave it to me for Act Five. Warned me it was sharp, too sharp for a prop, but that it would look better.' His voice tailed away. Habs stared at the roughly made shank in Joe's hand.

'Are you sayin' . . . you think I should . . .'

'No, I'm saying I think *we* should.'

Habs shook his head in disbelief. 'This fightin' has lost you your senses, Joe Hill. This ain't no play now, this is war here, but you can wait for the peace. I can't. You can go back to your pretty, white Norfolk home and marry a pretty, white Norfolk girl and have pretty, white Norfolk children. I really hope you do, Joe, but I can't.'

Joe shook his head. 'I thought so, too. Once. But not any more.' He wiped the tears from his friend's face, took his bloodied hand. 'Why would I go back to America when you are buried here on the moor? That'd be no life at all. Why would I read more books when each turn of a page would remind me of you? Why would I go to another play, knowing that every line would be better performed by you? Why grow old and mad pretending in a Norfolk town when I could die now, my sight clear and my heart true? Answer me that, Habakkuk Snow.'

Now it was Habs who wiped Joe's tears. 'I can't answer that one,' he said. 'I can't answer that at all.' He shook his head. 'I remember that day you arrived, sang that song, told us the war was over. From that moment, my heart was lighter. Sam told me I started whistlin' right 'bout that time. I think he guessed.'

'Guessed what, Habs? Tell me.'

'Guessed I'd fallen for the most handsome, most right-eous, most blackest white boy in the land.' Habs winced at a spasm of pain. 'I'm sorry we ain't catchin' the ships, Joe. We woulda been good.' He glanced at the patrol which was closer, one of the men winding a long bandage on to a propped-up inmate. 'They'll be with us soon and the moment gone.'

They knelt facing each other, Joe with the knife to his wrist. 'I've heard it doesn't hurt much,' he said, his voice trembling now.

'I should go first,' whispered Habs. 'I'm the one they'll want to hang.'

'Is it one cut or two?' asked Joe, suddenly uncertain. 'Both wrists, or one?'

'An' I'm sorry I missed your Act Four. I bet you were dazzlin'.'

'Do you believe in heaven?'

'Says the sailor with a knife to his vein.'

'Do you, Habs?' Joe's tone was urgent now, the patrol closer.

'Does it make a difference? Heaven is here where Juliet is. That's what Romeo says.'

'And if I'm not here?'

433

'I'll follow you. I'll go wherever you go. But hurry, Joe, they're mighty close.'

Habs leaned forward and they embraced. With strong arms, they held each other, a lifetime of love in the briefest caress. He felt Joe take a mighty breath and pull away, watched Joe push the knife's serrated edge into his skin, a bulb of blood pooling around the indentation then running down his arm. Habs winced, and the tears ran, too.

'Give me my Romeo,' said Joe, his voice exhausted, weak. 'And when I shall die, take him and cut him out in little stars, and he will make the face of heaven so fine that all the world will be in love with night.'

He drew the knife long and deep, his blood running freely to the ground.

5.34

The Market Square

7.08 p.m.

SPRINTING FOOTSTEPS and a cry. A shout so unexpected Habs turned. Elizabeth Shortland flew at Joe, smacking his knife-hand high, sending the shank arcing from his hand and spinning across the macadam. One of the orderlies recovered it, swiftly placing it inside his jacket.

'No more dying!' she shouted. 'Enough life has been lost today.' She spoke fast, her eyes wild. Hair loose around her shoulders, dress drenched in blood, she knelt, grabbing Joe's slashed wrist. 'No more death, boys.'

'Then I shall hang,' said Habs, slumped, broken.

She wrapped a bandage tightly around Joe's wrist and held it hard. Joe grimaced, but she kept the pressure as tight as she could manage.

'No, you shall not,' she said. Three attendants and two soldiers approached, but she waved them away. 'Deal with the dying,' she said to her staff, then to the guards: 'Watch the square. Get to the gates.'

'Begging your pardon, miss,' said one, 'but Captain Shortland insisted we stay with you . . .'

'Did he?' said Elizabeth, still with her eyes on Joe. 'How very resolute and brave of him. The thing you need to know about Captain Shortland,' she told the squirming redcoats, 'is that he might command you, but he does not command me. And that, after this butchery, he won't be commanding

435

here much longer.' She glanced around the square. 'So. To the gates. You can protect me from there.'

Joe, head in Elizabeth's lap, whispered, 'He killed a man—'

'I know what happened,' Elizabeth cut across him. 'Dr Magrath told me.'

'So you know I will hang, then.' Habs, scornful now, stared at her. 'You save us only to condemn us.'

'No, I don't.' She cut the bandage with scissors, then resumed the pressure on Joe's arm. 'You are not condemned.'

Habs leaned in so close their noses almost touched. 'You think a coloured American prisoner who has killed a white man won't swing for it? Are you mad? You think the spirit of the peace will extend to men like me?'

Elizabeth tied the bandage off. 'Of course it won't,' she said.

Joe squinted in confusion. 'So a court would condemn Habs, even though he was the one being attacked?'

'They would, yes. Undoubtedly.' She wiped some of the blood from Joe's face.

'You playin' with us,' said Habs, disgusted.

Elizabeth looked around her. 'There *is* a game you can play, if you wish,' she said.

'Go away,' said Habs, lying back on the ground, 'but you can leave the scissors.'

She turned to Joe and, as she tied his arm in a sling, words came tumbling from her mouth.

'Listen. I shall go and attend, briefly, the wounded up near the top of the square. There's two men with bullets in their legs, and one bayonetting. You see them?' Habs sat up again. 'I will leave the gates open. Walk past the storehouses, under the alarm bell and turn right towards the physician's house. You understand?' She moved without pause to dress Habs's bayoneted arm.

'Wait—' he said.

'There is a moment here, Mr Snow,' she said, 'but it is just a moment. Mr Hill will live. His injury is bad, but I got to the wound in time, I think. This arm will heal, too. Considering what carnage has been done here . . .'

She called her attendants and, weaving her way around the fallen, strode to the top of the square. Habs sat, stunned. Had he understood her right? Another volley of fire from the prison yards and he was on his feet.

'Joe, get up.' He tugged at Joe's good hand, then pulled hard. 'Joe, we're leavin'.'

'But—'

'Get up.'

Their exhausted, traumatized bodies resisted, but they hurried as fast as they could across the square, following her zigzagging path. Some of the injured called out, but they had no time. 'The attendants will come for you!' called Habs as he passed.

'*Eagle* man, ho!' replied one, the voice pained and thin, but Joe knew him in an instant.

'Will!' He doubled back, searching.

'Joe, we—'

'One second.' Joe found Will Roche with a messy bandage around his thigh. The old man managed a half-smile, the familiar lines in his face creasing again. 'Missed the bone, she said. Jus' bleedin' is all now.' He took in Joe's bandaged hand. 'You, too, huh?' Joe knew he had no time to explain. He dropped to his knees, kissing Will on the forehead. 'Will, I . . . I'm sorry.'

'Joe . . .' urged Habs.

'I have to go.'

Roche nodded his understanding. 'Listen, I'm sorry 'bout them words we had 'bout you and your friend back there. What do I know?'

Joe found a smile for his oldest friend. 'Bless you, Will. Stay safe, won't you?'

'And down with the English,' added Roche, closing his eyes.

'And down with the English,' echoed Joe, clambering to his feet again.

At the top of the square, a man with blood-soaked bandages around his knee raised a hand in acknowledgement but pointed back the way they had come. 'Your friend . . .' he said.

They stopped and looked back. In the far corner, King Dick was stooping low over the bodies of Tommy Jackson and John Haywood, Alex and Jonathan – hands over their mouths – lurking just behind. Habs and Joe raised simultaneous arms in salute, and Alex alerted the King, tugging on his sleeve. King Dick wheeled round. Across the charnel house between them, Joe and Habs saw the King's stricken face brighten with unexpected relief. He clasped his huge hands together as if in prayer, beating them against his chest. Habs pointed at the open gates. The King nodded, then raised his bearskin in salute. It was a farewell. A haunted, devastated farewell. When Joe could look no more, he bowed slightly and found Habs doing the same. The King then knelt and lifted the crier over one shoulder, the lamplighter over the other. Standing again, he staggered, and Habs noticed his bloody shirt. 'He's hurt . . .' Steadier now, the King seemed to gather himself for one last walk. Jonathan carried the club; the bearskin, he handed to Alex. The King carried the dead away, the two boys following mournfully behind.

Now, they knew they had lost time. At the top of the square, they hesitated. The heavy wood-panelled gates were ajar, as Elizabeth Shortland had said they would be, the gap just large enough to see the alarm bell beyond and the arch it sat on.

'The bell is dead ahead,' said Habs. 'Thirty yards.'

'Habs, what are we doing?' asked Joe, tucked in tight behind him. 'What is this?'

'This is probably better than my strychnine or your knife,' said Habs, and sprinted for the alarm bell. Joe followed and, under its arch, they paused again, eyes everywhere, the crushing tiredness of the day forgotten.

'One soldier now and we're dead,' said Joe.

'Jus' like the rest o' the prison, then,' said Habs. 'She said to turn right.'

They looked across the gravelled courtyard. The *Parcere subjectis* arch, gates firmly bolted, was ahead of them; the Agent's house to the left, lights ablaze; Magrath's to the right, in darkness. Two plain slate buildings faced the physician's house, and from one of them came raised voices. Joe held tightly to Habs's arm.

'It's her! She's shouting at someone,' he said.

'She's keepin' 'em busy,' whispered Habs. 'Look, the courtyard is empty. If they're not out here killin' Americans, they're in there bein' shouted at by Mrs Shortland. She's quite somethin' . . .'

Magrath's house had five first-floor windows and four on the ground, all with curtains drawn. A small porch marked a back door.

'Do we jus' let ourselves in?' Habs's heart was thumping in his ribs. There was a sudden quiet – the haranguing had stopped. 'Too late.'

The slate house door opened, and five workmen trudged out. They walked in a diagonal towards the Agent's house. In fifty yards, they would be in Joe and Habs's eyeline; another eighty, and they would be inside.

'Soon as they shut that door, we go,' muttered Joe.

The first of the workmen came into view, a cook maybe, then two in heavy aprons, a man in a dark suit and, heart-stoppingly, a soldier, his musket held in front of him. Joe and Habs barely breathed. They prayed. They listened.

'I reckon her 'ead's been turned by all that shooting,' said a voice.

'She sounded bloody terrified, if you ask me,' said another.

'Don't see why she takes it out on us, though.'

Joe had a sudden recollection of his words to Roche, many months ago: 'That's Devonshire talk, that is.'

The first workman pulled the Agent's back door open, and the yard brightened.

'Ready?' whispered Habs.

'Ready,' confirmed Joe.

Four of the men were inside. Joe and Habs readied themselves for the final sprint. The Agent's door closed. The yard darkened.

'Shit.'

The soldier had become a sentry. He stood with his back to the door, staring out into the gloom, the silhouette of his readied musket clear to all.

'Shit. Shit. Shit.'

A voice from across the courtyard, from the steps of the slate house. Elizabeth Shortland: imperious, commanding, brooking no argument. 'At ease, Soldier. No need for a sentry, I'm sure. Thank you, we'll be fine now.'

Joe and Habs saw the soldier glance around, adjust the angle of his gun. 'With respect, ma'am—' he called back.

'With respect,' Elizabeth bellowed, 'you'll go inside, lock the doors and protect the Agent's affairs. Now!'

The soldier shrugged, disappeared inside.

Joe reached the door handle first and the door flew open. They both tumbled inside, Habs kicking the door shut behind them.

Crouched low on the physician's floor, they froze, keening for sounds from the courtyard. Joe and Habs were still hunkered down when Elizabeth entered. She clicked the door shut, turned the lock and lit the nearest lamp. 'Quick, up,' she said.

Joe and Habs scrambled to their feet.

'We have only seconds,' she said. 'Where will you go? Your grandmother's?'

Joe, dumbfounded, spluttered, trying to find a reply. He didn't know what to say, hadn't thought that far. She was already moving them to the front of the house.

'Put as many miles between you and this place as you can. After today, they might not notice you're missing for a while. Here, take these.' She threw two of Magrath's coats at them; hats, too. 'Wait,' she said, disappearing briefly, before returning with bread, cheeses and some coins. 'In your pockets. And you'll need bandages to dress your wounds.' She handed him a roll from her bag.

They were in the hall now, the huge front door at their backs.

'The other side of this door is Dartmoor. It is a hateful, godforsaken place, as you well know, but it's better than being hunted like rats in here. Today was a scandal, a disgrace. If I hadn't seen it with my own eyes, I wouldn't have thought my countrymen capable of such barbarism. I am only sorry so many of your comrades have suffered. Go now.' She moved to open the door, but Joe put up his hand.

'Wait one second. Do you know how many have died? If we're leaving, then we should know at least what happened to our friends.'

'But I cannot tell you,' said Elizabeth. 'I only saw the square, I never went beyond. Mr Haywood and Mr Jackson, you know about; others have passed also. Mainly, I tended the wounded . . .' She broke off.

'Why are you doin' all this?' asked Habs. 'We're grateful, o' course, but why you helpin' us?'

'I tolerated it for too long, Mr Snow.' She pointed right, to her house. 'I tolerated him for too long. I know it's just a gesture – what good is helping two prisoners when there are seven thousand desperate for home? But.' She smiled now.

'But when I took your knife away, all this, it seemed obvious to me.' She tucked some of Joe's loose hair behind his ear, then wiped some blood from Habs's face with her thumb. 'And I saw your show. I will never forget it.'

There was a moment of silence between the three prisoners.

'And besides, in the morning, I'll be gone, too. Let me deal with the guards at the front. Give me thirty seconds. God speed.'

She unbolted Magrath's door and slipped away without another glance. The smell of the moor rolled into the hall, moist, peaty and sweet with gorse. Both men inhaled deeply.

'I declare my head is spinnin' and my arm is throbbin',' whispered Habs.

'Mine, too,' said Joe. 'I can't quite believe any of it. What if they see us run?'

'I think you know what happens.'

They listened to Mrs Shortland's footsteps: steady, confident.

'Here's to the men of Four and all the good men of Dartmoor,' whispered Joe. 'The crews of the *Eagle* and the *Bentham*. To Sam. All our cast. I wish we could all go.'

'Amen to that. And long live the King.'

They heard the guards salute the Agent's wife.

'So where'll we go?' asked Habs. 'Now we're all dressed like gentlemen? London? Dublin? They can't be far.'

'Sure,' said Joe. 'They're just over the moor. We could be there before sunrise.' He moved closer to the door.

'And Suffolk's close too, right?'

'Yes. And you'll blend in just fine.'

'So there's more coloured men like me there?'

'Everywhere you look.'

'Thought as much.'

They could hear the gate guards talking now.

'Ready?' said Habs.

'Ready,' said Joe.

Elizabeth's voice, as fast and loud as a force nine, came at them hard, and they slipped from the house, on to the moor.

5.35

The Agent's Study

Shortland is slumped at his desk. King Dick is sitting painfully in an upright chair, staring off into the distance. Neither has spoken; they have sat in silence for many minutes. Eventually, Shortland moves some papers.

SHORTLAND: Well, then. I hope you don't mind coming back here, it's been a . . . (*clears his throat*) it's been a bad time. (*The King looks at Shortland but says nothing.*) You have probably heard there is to be an inquiry. Rear Admiral Sir Josias Rowley and Captain Schomberg from HMS *York* are on their way to, er, investigate the matter. I am sure they will wish to speak to you.

KING DICK: Really. And what would be the point of that?

SHORTLAND: The truth, Mr Crafus, the truth. We all need the facts.

KING DICK: You mean *your* facts. You mean *white* facts. *British* facts. And in this tale of woe, they most likely ain't gonna be the same as *black* facts, or even *American* facts.

SHORTLAND (*flabbergasted*): No, sir, they are the same. Facts are facts. We must agree on this, or all is lost.

KING DICK: All is already lost, Captain Shortland. If you don't see that, you don't see nothin'. But tell me your facts, anyways. I'll see how you do.

SHORTLAND (*unnerved*): Well, let me see now. (*Finds the right papers.*) Nine men died as a result of the . . . melancholy occurrence of April sixth, and thirty-seven were injured. I have the names here, if you wish—

KING DICK (*waving his hand*): I know these names. And the men you buried secretly to keep them figures low?

SHORTLAND: That didn't happen.

KING DICK: Sixty-three dead, Captain Shortland.

SHORTLAND: That isn't true.

KING DICK: And the wounded men who hid in their own prisons, too scared to come out? How many o' them never made it out again?

SHORTLAND: I don't know the answer to that, I'm afraid. That is why there will be an inquiry. They will look at the facts, then deliver their verdict.

KING DICK: Justifiable homicide.

SHORTLAND: I'm sorry?

KING DICK: S'already the verdict. Your coroner and his jury of farmers have said so. 'Justifiable homicide,' they said.

SHORTLAND (*shaking his head*): No, that was the inquest. So that the burials could take place.

KING DICK (*his eyes closed, his voice quieter*): The burials. The burials of our friends, our shipmates, our comrades. The burials you conducted without us.

SHORTLAND: It is the way of things. It is the custom.

KING DICK (*eyes open, angry*): Yes, it is. It is 'the way of things' that killed my people! It is 'the way of things' that put us in Four in the first place! It is 'the way of things' that makes you think you can keep prisoners-of-war, when there is no war.

SHORTLAND: As you know, your government's ships will be here in the next few days . . .

KING DICK: And when I get home, it will be 'the way of things' that keeps people like me separate. The way you liked it here. The way they like it there. We might be free, we might be enslaved, but we'll still be separate. It seems neater that way.

There is another silence between them, Shortland lost in thought, the King waiting for him.

445

SHORTLAND: Your *Romeo and Juliet* was first class, I thought. (*He waits for a reaction but, when there is none, continues.*) I have had cause to think deeply on it these last days. We never saw the last few scenes, of course. So I have read the last pages myself. I found it . . . uncomfortable reading, Mr Crafus, I don't mind telling you.

KING DICK: Because?

SHORTLAND: You know full well. The family heads, Montague and Capulet, they mourn their loss. They realize what they had amongst them but, by then, it is too late. Proud men, both of them, but blind. And it is their neglect that allows the tragedy to unfold as it does.

KING DICK: That is one reading of it . . .

SHORTLAND: That is my reading of it. (*Another pause.*)

KING DICK: Has Mrs Shortland returned?

SHORTLAND (*sadly*): I'll not speak of it.

KING DICK (*nods*): And the search for Mr Snow and Mr Hill?

SHORTLAND: I called it off. God knows where they got to and, frankly, they are someone else's problem now. I have enough of my own. (*He gathers his papers.*) Where will you go, Mr Crafus? When you're back in America, what will you do?

KING DICK (*standing slowly from the chair*): Are you a Christian man, Captain Shortland?

SHORTLAND (*taken aback*): I used to think so. Church of England, but . . . Why . . .

KING DICK: Do you believe in heaven?

SHORTLAND: Now I think of it, between us, no, I don't think I do.

KING DICK: We built your village church to a god you don't believe in?

SHORTLAND (*shrugs*): It would appear so.

KING DICK: So you don't think I'll see Mr Jackson and Mr Haywood again?

SHORTLAND (*reluctantly*): No, I don't think you will. I'm sorry . . .

KING DICK: I jus' been singin'. We had our own service, seein' as you didn't let us bury our own. So we sang. It was a comfort.

SHORTLAND: I'm sure it was.

KING DICK (*eyes shut, sings softly*):

> Farewell, dear friends, again farewell;
> Soon we shall rise to thee,
> On wings of love our stars will cross,
> Through all eternity.

The King nods at Shortland, then walks from the room.

'Did the world ever hear of an act like this before? In the houses of America belonging to any of the friends, acquaintances or relations of these men and innumerable other houses, their names and their story are pasted on the walls, written in blood; and in the American almanacks is recorded the anniversary of the massacre of Dartmoor.'

William Cobbett, *History of the Regency and Reign of King George the Fourth*, 1830–34

The Dartmoor Massacre

6 April 1815
Details of casualties from the report by Dr G. Magrath

The Nine Deaths

John Haywood, a black man from Virginia. Prison number 3154. Musket ball, neck injury.

Thomas Jackson, from New York. A boy aged fourteen. Prison number 6520. Musket ball, left side of belly.

John Washington, from Maryland. Prison number 3936. Musket ball, left temple.

James Mann, Boston. Prison number 970. Musket ball, right pectoral muscle, passed through right and left lobes of lungs.

Joseph Toker Johnson, from Connecticut. Prison number 1347. Musket ball to the heart and lungs.

William Laverage, from New York. Prison number 4884. Musket ball to second and third ribs, left lobe of lungs.

James Campbell, from New York. Prison number 2647. Musket ball to the right eye.

John Roberts. Prison number 486. Musket ball to thigh.

John Grey. Prison number 94. Musket ball to left arm, amputated.

Author's note

'Inspired by true events' needs a little explanation. As a phrase stuck to the front of books and films, it can often arouse suspicion, even mistrust. And when the story concerns what for many (particularly in Britain) is such an unknown war, there are precious few recognizable landmarks to navigate by. You should be reassured that 'not knowing about the War of 1812' is quite normal, in fact it has a long pedigree. The nineteenth-century Canadian historian William Kingsford said, 'The events of the War of 1812 have not been forgotten in England for they have never been known there.'

Even blunter was another Canadian, C. P. Stacey, who wrote that this was 'an episode in history that makes everybody happy, because everybody interprets it differently . . . the English are happiest of all, because they don't even know it happened.'

You see what I mean.

Only for Canadians has it retained much significance. The defence of their borders from invading Americans led the way, so the story has it, for the founding of their great nation. Even for Americans, despite both the burning of the White House by British troops and the writing of 'The Star-Spangled Banner' in 1814, it has become what Donald R. Hickey called 'the forgotten conflict', sitting as it does between the War of Independence and the convulsion of the Civil War.

Maybe this goes some way to explaining why the story of Dartmoor Prison has remained tucked away as one of history's footnotes. And yet it represents the only occasion that a prison in Great Britain has been segregated by race, the first (as far as I can see) all-black production of a Shakespeare play, and the first performances of black gospel music on British shores (many sailors later recorded their admiration for Block Four's choir).

Perhaps we just weren't looking; even though a thousand black sailors were living in Devon in 1814, perhaps we weren't interested in their story. But now – thankfully – we see matters differently. As British–Nigerian historian David Olusoga says, black history is everyone's history.

A word on King Dick. This is far from his dramatic debut. He has featured in five novels, one play and a film, the 1952 production *Lydia Bailey*, based on the best-selling book of the same name by Kenneth Roberts. Here Dick is played by William Marshall (in his first screen role) as a Plato-quoting, elegant Haitian revolutionary, confidant of Toussaint L'Ouverture, the husband of eight wives and father to a backyard full of children.

In *The Legend of Gentle Morgan* by Paul Wheeler, Dick is at least in Dartmoor but this time in cahoots with the British. After escaping, he is convicted as a runaway slave and returned to a plantation. Senator John McCain in *Thirteen Soldiers* calls him 'a natural autocrat' and 'an absolute monarch'. Some have even suggested that Dick was the inspiration behind James Clavell's 1962 bestseller *King Rat*. However, the truth is that we know nothing about his life for certain until he is captured by the British from the US privateer *Requin* and arrives in Dartmoor in 1814. Other stories suggest he was on the USS *Chesapeake* or maybe a prisoner of conscience from the Royal Navy (like Tommy Jackson here). But his productions of *Othello* and *Romeo and Juliet* are fact, as are the reports of his casual violence and 'business activities'. So, part-gangster,

454

part-theatrical impresario, I wanted Richard Crafus to dominate the book as he dominated Block Four, even if he has, by its conclusion, become more King Lear than King Dick.

As well as Dick, Captain Thomas Shortland, Elizabeth Shortland, Dr Magrath and Tommy Jackson were all real people. The attempted escape through a hole in the retaining wall is true. The Rough Allies were real and the smallpox outbreak was all too real. Dr Magrath's list of casualties at the end of the book is taken from the official records (quoted in *Prisoners of War at Dartmoor* by Trevor James). My licence has been to run the production of *Romeo and Juliet* up to and alongside the massacre, when in reality it was performed a few months earlier.

Astute Shakespeare scholars may have noticed a few echoes of *Romeo and Juliet* throughout *Mad Blood Stirring*; some Dartmoor characters shadow their Veronese predecessors and a few of their words may have seemed familiar as well. You'll have spotted Romeo and Juliet, of course, but Nurse, Benvolio, Mercutio and Tybalt are all here too.

Finally, a word on the racial language used extensively throughout the story. Its power to offend is undimmed, indeed it has been magnified with the passage of time, but it is included here as honest dialogue, using words in common usage among nineteenth-century sailors and soldiers.

Acknowledgements

So that History and Politics degree came in useful after all. I was researching where to conclude my last book *Blame* and I fancied Dartmoor as the setting. My heroes were heading south-west out of London and it seemed the obvious choice. Then I came across the nine hundred and ninety-five black prisoners-of-war from the War of 1812. Then the segregation. Then King Dick. By the time I found his production of *Romeo and Juliet*, I knew I was hooked and that my *Blame* cast would have to go elsewhere. My astute wife Hilary, followed by my astute agent (and now writer, damn him) Sam Copeland at RCW, spotted the possibilities and we were off.

I am thrilled that *Mad Blood Stirring* became a Transworld book; as a reader, their name has always seemed a hallmark of quality. My editors Bill Scott-Kerr and Darcy Nicholson were everything a writer could ask for – patient, wise and (usually) gentle. Thank you.

I have had help and encouragement from Shakespeare scholars Vicky Perrin and Crispin Letts in the UK, firearms advice from Matt Plass in New York, smallpox knowledge from Dr Christopher Smith, Consultant Virologist and Public Understanding of Science Fellow at Cambridge University, and gospel choir wisdom from Bazil Meade MBE. Ben, Natasha and Joe, as ever, thank you for your enthusiasm and forbearance. Early readers Grace Wroe, Martin Wroe, Steve Taylor, Jonathan Mayo, Anna Beasley and Travis

McCready, thank you. Harriet Cross, the UK's Consul-General in Boston, was a fountain of knowledge and enthusiasm. Malorie Blackman, Sir Ken Branagh and Sir Lenny Henry were early encouragers. Bob Digby and Mick Byrne run the most educational and dynamic taxi service across the moor.

Any mistakes are, of course, entirely mine.

Bibliography

'Self-Help in Dartmoor: Black and White Prisoners in the War of 1812', Robin F. A. Fabel, *Journal of the Early Republic*

The Yarn of a Yankee Privateer, edited by Nathaniel Hawthorne

Black Jacks, W. Jeffrey Bolster

Prisoners of War at Dartmoor, Trevor James

Staying Power, Peter Fryer

The Interesting Narrative of the Life of Olaudah Equiano, Or Gustavus Vassa, The African, Written by Himself, Olaudah Equiano

'The Strange Life and Stranger Afterlife of King Dick Including His Adventures In Haiti and Hollywood with Observations on the Construction of Race, Class, Nationality, Gender, Slang Etymology and Religion' (a thesis), Alan Lipke, University of South Florida

The Diary of Benjamin F. Palmer, Benjamin Franklin Palmer

Daughters of Britannia: The Lives and Times of Diplomatic Wives, Katie Hickman

The War of 1812 and the Rise of the U.S. Navy, Mark Collins Jenkins and David Taylor

1812: A Nation Emerges, Sidney Hart and Rachael L. Penman

Jack Tar's Story: The Autobiographies and Memoirs of Sailors in Antebellum America, Myra C. Glenn

A Sea of Words, Dean King

The New Penguin Book of English Folk Songs, edited by Julia Bishop and Steve Roud

Black and British: A Forgotten History, David Olusoga

Thirteen Soldiers, John McCain and Mark Salter

The Underground Railroad, Colson Whitehead

Tin Man, Sarah Winman

Runaway Slaves: Rebels on the Plantation, John Hope Franklin

Army Life in a Black Regiment, Thomas Wentworth Higginson

The Colored Patriots of the American Revolution, William Cooper Nell

And finally . . .

Romeo and Juliet, William Shakespeare

Q&A with the author

You've written books for children and young adults before, what was it like sitting down to write an adult novel for the first time?

Writing *Mad Blood Stirring* was really no different to the 'Itch' books and *Blame*. You might argue that with Joe and Habs both being teenagers, the book has one foot in YA anyway but I felt it was 'adult' because in 1814 there were no teenagers. Boys or men, girls or women. These are characters who had been killing, or trying to kill, British sailors for two years. It felt like a grown up story so I wrote it as one, beyond that I didn't think about it.

Mad Blood Stirring is about a little known period in history, how did you come to write about Dartmoor Prison in 1815?

I stumbled into it! My last book *Blame* needed a prison in the south west of England so I started to research Dartmoor and quickly came across the segregation story that went on to provide the framework for *Mad Blood Stirring*. It seemed such an astonishing, untold tale that I couldn't let it go. The fact that it's a little known period in our history only added to the glamour! So few people seemed to know anything about the War of 1812, the canvas appeared empty, full of opportunity; and once King Dick appeared on the scene, hat, club, Shakespeare and all, I knew the story was irresistible.

So, what in the novel is 'fact' and what is 'fiction'?

There's a lot of fact and a lot of fiction. King Dick, the Short-lands, Dr Magrath were all real people on record. The daily market was real. The massacre was real. The smallpox, seg-regation and the Rough Allies, are equally all very real. And crucially it was King Dick's production of *Romeo and Juliet* that gave me my starting point for the book; we know it hap-pened but barely any details survive. So into this already complex and explosive real-life drama, I've added Joe Hill, the crew of the Eagle, Habs Snow, Ned, Sam and our other friends in Block Four. I've also shifted the play's production date by a few months to coincide with the April massacre.

Oh and I don't know that Elizabeth was having an affair with the physician. But, why wouldn't she?

How does it differ writing about people who you know to have been real as opposed to characters you have made up? Did you prefer one over the other?

They all have to be real! Any character you write – whether once real or not – has to be drawn in such a way that all your readers believe in them and their existence, so that the cast mix and weave and all the real/made-up divisions are forgotten.

I hope the reader cares as much about King Dick as Joe and Habs. I hope the reader is cheering Elizabeth on as she fights back against her husband just as much as they do for Ned as he tells his escape story.

However, having said all that, this white Londoner certainly felt a special responsibility for King Dick. He could easily have slipped into caricature (the height, the club, the hat have all been documented) but equally he needed to dominate the book as he dominated Block Four. Whether

I succeeded in getting that balance right will be down to the reader.

Mad Blood Stirring is due to be made into a film, is there one particular scene that you're excited to see on the big screen?

Aside from the big set-pieces full of action and drama, I'm looking forward to seeing the scene where Joe, Habs and the singers of Block Four try to comfort the smallpox victims in Block One with their song. The broadside of benediction. That'll work a treat.

Finally, are you able to give us a hint at what you're writing next?

No.
Oh all right then.
It's a contemporary thriller, absolutely not set in a prison. Not yet anyway. And lots of Mozart. *So* much Mozart.